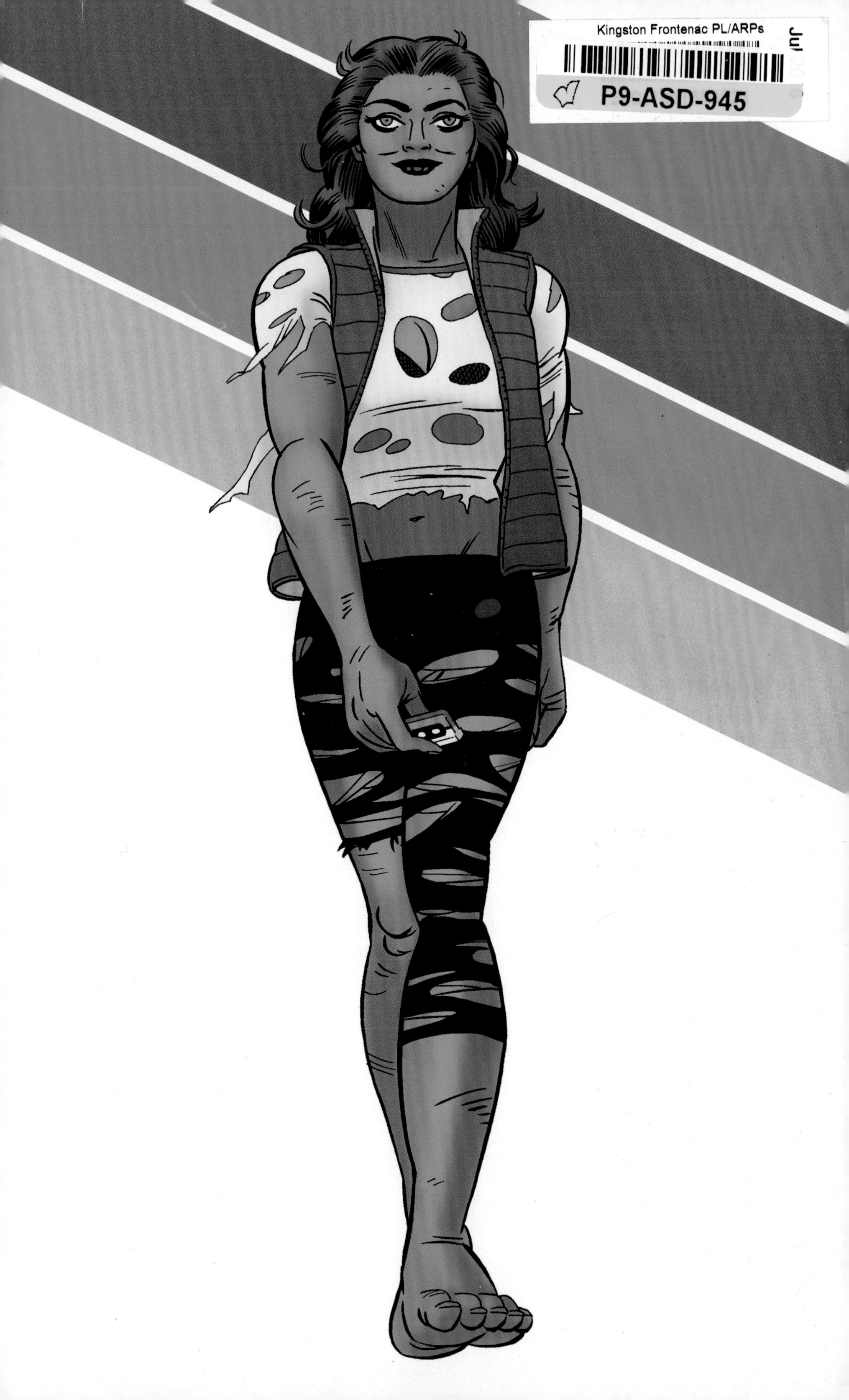

A-FORCE PRESENTS

BLACK WIDOW (2014) #3

writer **NATHAN EDMONDSON**
artist **PHIL NOTO**
letterer **VC's CLAYTON COWLES**
cover art **PHIL NOTO**
editor **ELLIE PYLE**

SHE-HULK (2014) #3

writer **CHARLES SOULE**
artist **JAVIER PULIDO**
color artist **MUNTSA VICENTE**
letterer **VC's CLAYTON COWLES**
cover art **KEVIN WADA**
assistant editor **FRANKIE JOHNSON**
editors **TOM BRENNAN**
consulting editor **JEANINE SCHAEFER**

CAPTAIN MARVEL (2014) #3

writer **KELLY SUE DeCONNICK**
artist **DAVID LOPEZ**
color artist **LEE LOUGHRIDGE**
letterer **VC's JOE CARAMAGNA**
cover art **DAVID LOPEZ**
assistant editor **DEVIN LEWIS**
editor **SANA AMANAT**
senior editor **NICK LOWE**

MS. MARVEL (2014) #3

writer **G. WILLOW WILSON**
artist **ADRIAN ALPHONA**
color artist **IAN HERRING**
letterer **VC's JOE CARAMAGNA**
cover art **JAMIE McKELVIE** & **MATTHEW WILSON**
assistant editor **DEVIN LEWIS**
editor **SANA AMANAT**
senior editor **NICK LOWE**

THOR (2014) #3

writer **JASON AARON**
artist **RUSSELL DAUTERMAN**
color artist **MATTHEW WILSON**
letterer **VC's JOE SABINO**
cover art **RUSSELL DAUTERMAN** & **MATTHEW WILSON**
assistant editor **JON MOISAN**
editor **WIL MOSS**

THE UNBEATABLE SQUIRREL GIRL (2015) #3

writer **RYAN NORTH**
artist **ERICA HENDERSON**
color artist **RICO RENZI**
letterer **VC's CLAYTON COWLES**
cover art **ERICA HENDERSON**
assistant editor **JON MOISAN**
editor **WIL MOSS**
executive editor **TOM BREVOORT**

collection editor **JENNIFER GRÜNWALD**
assistant editor **SARAH BRUNSTAD**
associate managing editor **ALEX STARBUCK**
editor, special projects **MARK D. BEAZLEY**
senior editor, special projects **JEFF YOUNGQUIST**
svp print, sales & marketing **DAVID GABRIEL**
book designer **ADAM DEL RE**

editor in chief **AXEL ALONSO**
chief creative officer **JOE QUESADA**
publisher **DAN BUCKLEY**
executive producer **ALAN FINE**

A-FORCE PRESENTS VOL. 3. Contains material originally published in magazine form as BLACK WIDOW #3, CAPTAIN MARVEL #3, MS. MARVEL #3, SHE-HULK #3, THOR #3 and THE UNBEATABLE SQUIRREL GIRL #3. First printing 2016. ISBN# 978-0-7851-9900-7. Published by MARVEL WORLDWIDE, INC., a subsidiary of MARVEL ENTERTAINMENT, LLC. OFFICE OF PUBLICATION: 135 West 50th Street, New York, NY 10020. Copyright © 2016 MARVEL No similarity between any of the names, characters, persons, and/or institutions in this magazine with those of any living or dead person or institution is intended, and any such similarity which may exist is purely coincidental. **Printed in Canada.** ALAN FINE, President, Marvel Entertainment; DAN BUCKLEY, President, TV, Publishing and Brand Management; JOE QUESADA, Chief Creative Officer; TOM BREVOORT, SVP of Publishing; DAVID BOGART, SVP of Operations & Procurement, Publishing; C.B. CEBULSKI, VP of International Development & Brand Management; DAVID GABRIEL, SVP Print, Sales & Marketing; JIM O'KEEFE, VP of Operations & Logistics; DAN CARR, Executive Director of Publishing Technology; SUSAN CRESPI, Editorial Operations Manager; ALEX MORALES, Publishing Operations Manager; STAN LEE, Chairman Emeritus. For information regarding advertising in Marvel Comics or on Marvel.com, please contact Jonathan Rheingold, VP of Custom Solutions & Ad Sales, at jrheingold@marvel.com. For Marvel subscription inquiries, please call 800-217-9158. **Manufactured between 12/4/2015 and 1/11/2016 by SOLISCO PRINTERS, SCOTT, QC, CANADA.**

10 9 8 7 6 5 4 3 2 1

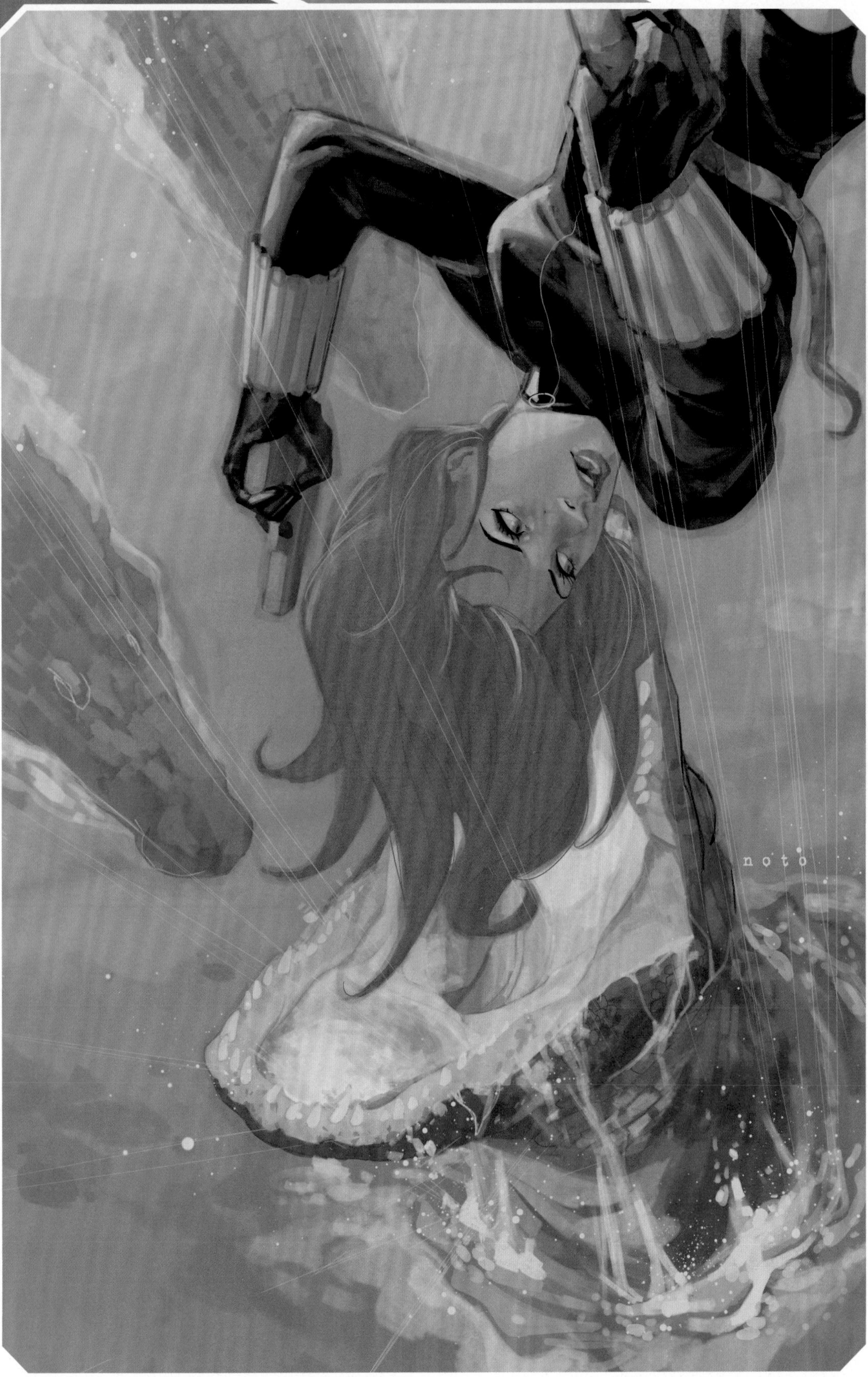
noto

BLACK WIDOW #3

NATASHA ROMANOV IS AN AVENGER, AN AGENT OF S.H.I.E.L.D. AND AN EX-KGB ASSASSIN, BUT ON HER OWN TIME, SHE USES HER UNIQUE SKILL SET TO ATONE FOR HER PAST. SHE IS:

BLACK WIDOW

"FOLIAGE"

NATHAN EDMONDSON
WRITER

PHIL NOTO
ARTIST

VC's CLAYTON COWLES
LETTERER & PRODUCTION

ELLIE PYLE
EDITOR

J.G.
JONES
VARIANT COVER ARTIST

AXEL
ALONSO
EDITOR IN CHIEF

JOE
QUESADA
CHIEF CREATIVE OFFICER

DAN
BUCKLEY
PUBLISHER

ALAN
FINE
EXEC. PRODUCER

I DON'T HAVE A HOME.

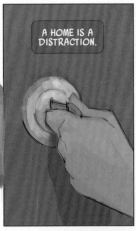

A HOME IS A DISTRACTION.

TRAVELING AGAIN? MORE OVERSEAS CONSULTS?

IN MY WORK ONE CANNOT HAVE DISTRACTIONS.

CONSULTING, YES, OFF TO CATCH THE REDEYE, ANA.

WHAT ARE YOU DOING OUT SO LATE?

I WOULDN'T NECESSARILY KNOW A HOME IF I HAD ONE, THOUGH.

I HEAR YOUR CAT LIHO. SHE WHINES AT DOOR FOR YOU.

SHE'S NOT MY--

ANA. HOW MANY TIMES HAVE I TOLD YOU TO LEAVE HIM?

EH, LEAVE TO GO WHERE?

THIS IS HOME.

GOOD NIGHT, NATASHA. I HOPE YOU HAVE GOOD FLIGHT.

SOUTH OF RESISTENCIA, ARGENTINA.

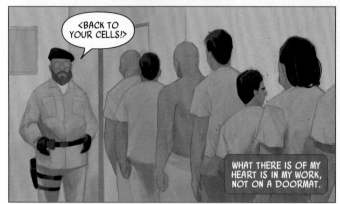
<BACK TO YOUR CELLS!>

WHAT THERE IS OF MY HEART IS IN MY WORK, NOT ON A DOORMAT.

!VAMOS!

I HAVE MET OPERATIVES WHO HAVE FAMILIES AND LIVES BEYOND THE FIELD. (THESE OPERATIVES DO NOT LIVE LONG.)

HEY!

WHAT YOU CARRY WITH YOU, IT WEIGHS YOU DOWN, DOWN, DOWN.

WHAT ARE YOU DOING? THIS IS MY--

QUIET.

YOU MIGHT THINK I'M COLD-HEARTED.

I AM.

YOU'LL DO WHAT I SAY, ANGELO. I'M GETTING YOU OUT OF HERE.

I CAN'T AFFORD DISTRACTIONS.

I'VE GOT WORK TO DO.

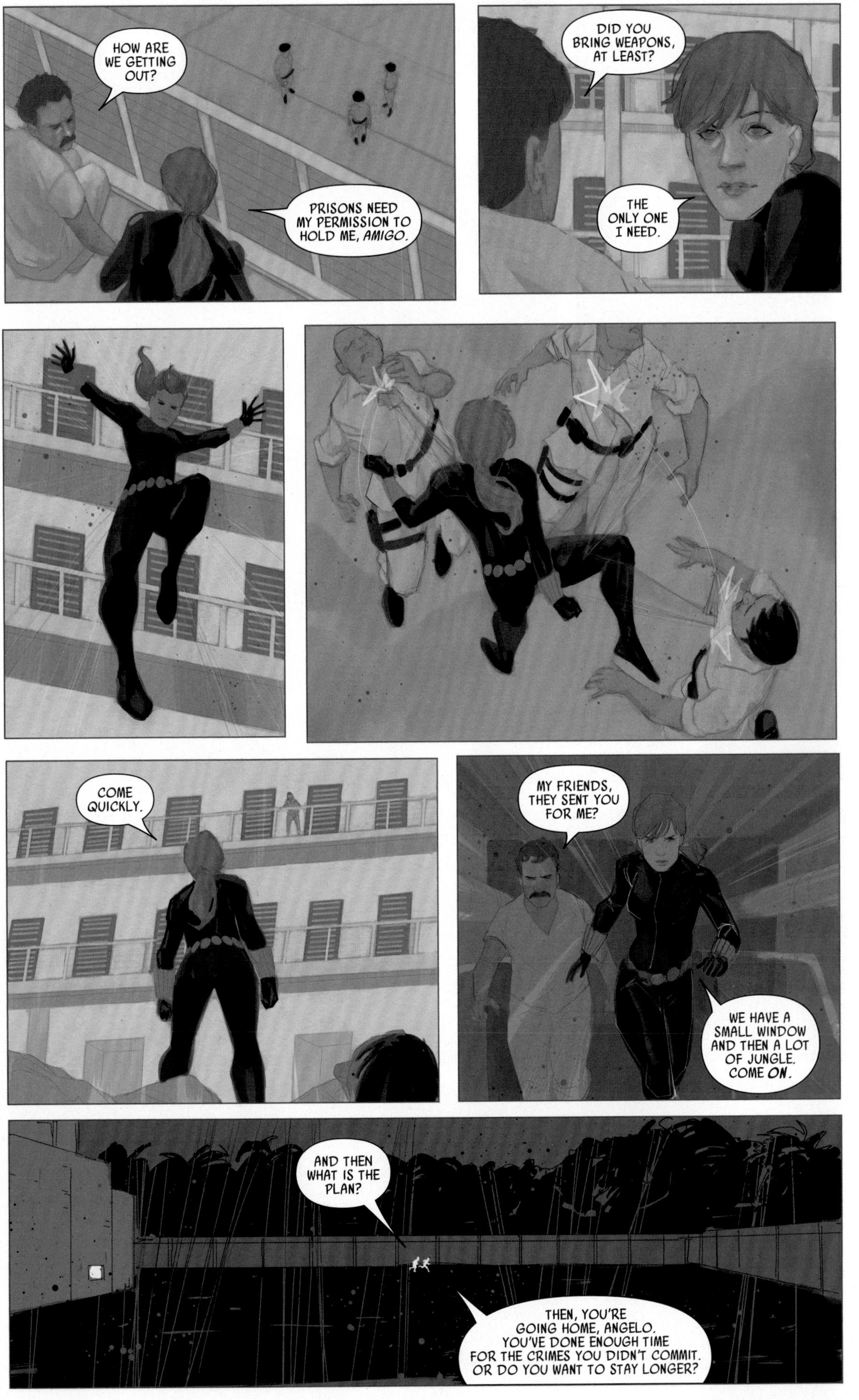
HOW ARE WE GETTING OUT?
PRISONS NEED MY PERMISSION TO HOLD ME, *AMIGO*.
DID YOU BRING WEAPONS, AT LEAST?
THE ONLY ONE I NEED.
COME QUICKLY.
MY FRIENDS, THEY SENT YOU FOR ME?
WE HAVE A SMALL WINDOW AND THEN A LOT OF JUNGLE. COME ***ON***.
AND THEN WHAT IS THE PLAN?
THEN, YOU'RE GOING HOME, ANGELO. YOU'VE DONE ENOUGH TIME FOR THE CRIMES YOU DIDN'T COMMIT. OR DO YOU WANT TO STAY LONGER?

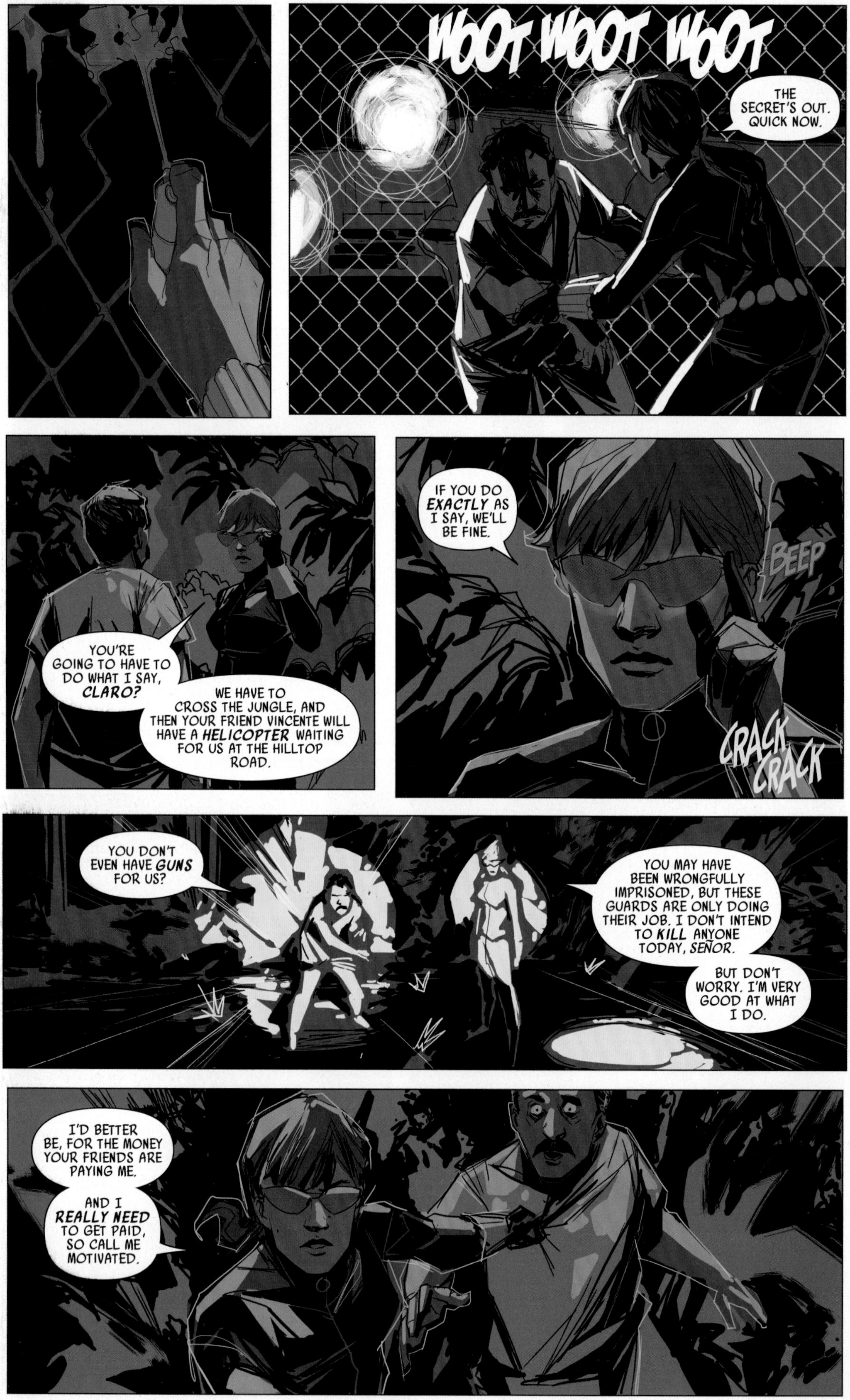
WOOT WOOT WOOT
THE SECRET'S OUT. QUICK NOW.
YOU'RE GOING TO HAVE TO DO WHAT I SAY, CLARO?
WE HAVE TO CROSS THE JUNGLE, AND THEN YOUR FRIEND VINCENTE WILL HAVE A HELICOPTER WAITING FOR US AT THE HILLTOP ROAD.
IF YOU DO EXACTLY AS I SAY, WE'LL BE FINE.
BEEP
CRACK CRACK
YOU DON'T EVEN HAVE GUNS FOR US?
YOU MAY HAVE BEEN WRONGFULLY IMPRISONED, BUT THESE GUARDS ARE ONLY DOING THEIR JOB. I DON'T INTEND TO KILL ANYONE TODAY, SEÑOR.
BUT DON'T WORRY. I'M VERY GOOD AT WHAT I DO.
I'D BETTER BE, FOR THE MONEY YOUR FRIENDS ARE PAYING ME.
AND I REALLY NEED TO GET PAID, SO CALL ME MOTIVATED.

...WHEREVER I GO, THAT IS MY HOME.

SO MY THOUGHTS CAN BE IN THIS JUNGLE AND NONE OTHER.

AND LIKE IT IS MY HOME, I *KNOW* THIS PLACE. LIKE THE CREAKING OF AN OLD APARTMENT--

--I KNOW WHICH SOUNDS DO NOT BELONG.

SNAP

HEAD NORTH. RUN TO THE CREEK.

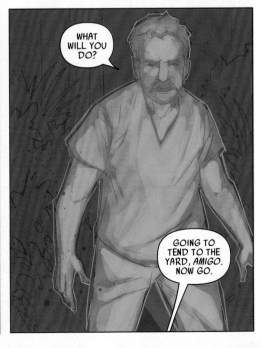

WHAT WILL YOU DO?

GOING TO TEND TO THE YARD, AMIGO. NOW GO.

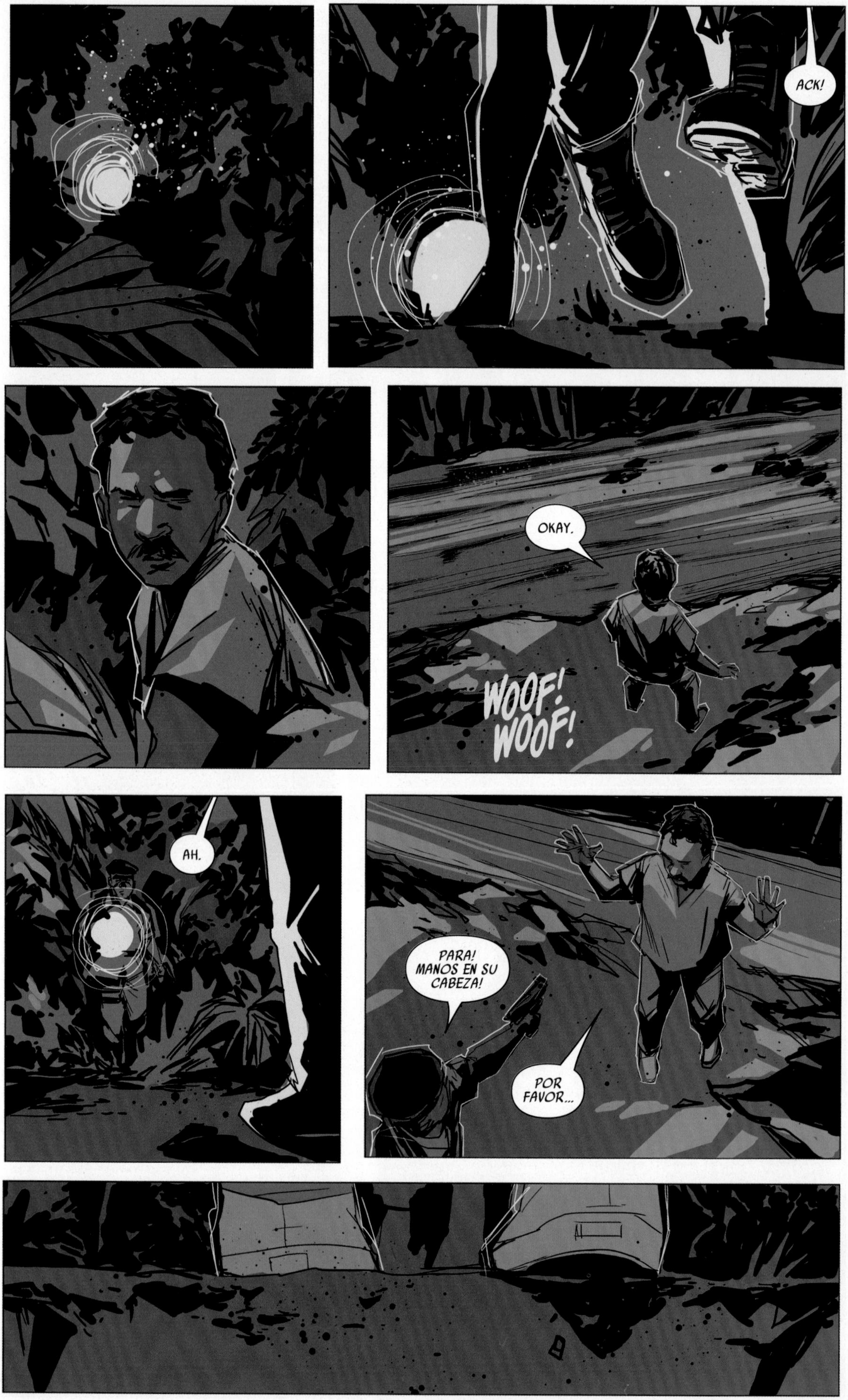
ACK!
OKAY.
WOOF! WOOF!
AH.
PARA! MANOS EN SU CABEZA!
POR FAVOR...

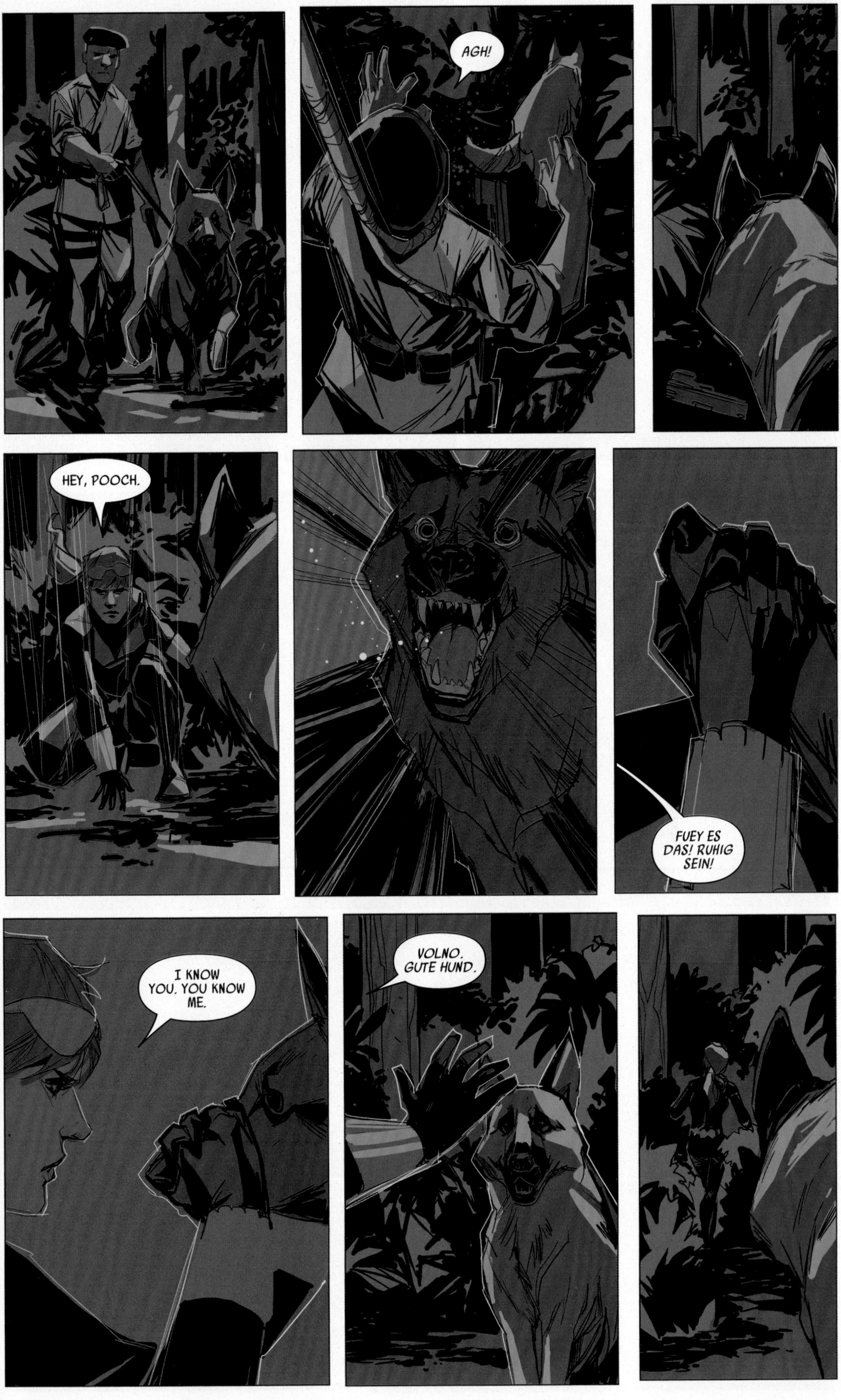
AGH!
HEY, POOCH.
FUEY ES DAS! RUHIG SEIN!
I KNOW YOU. YOU KNOW ME.
VOLNO. GUTE HUND.

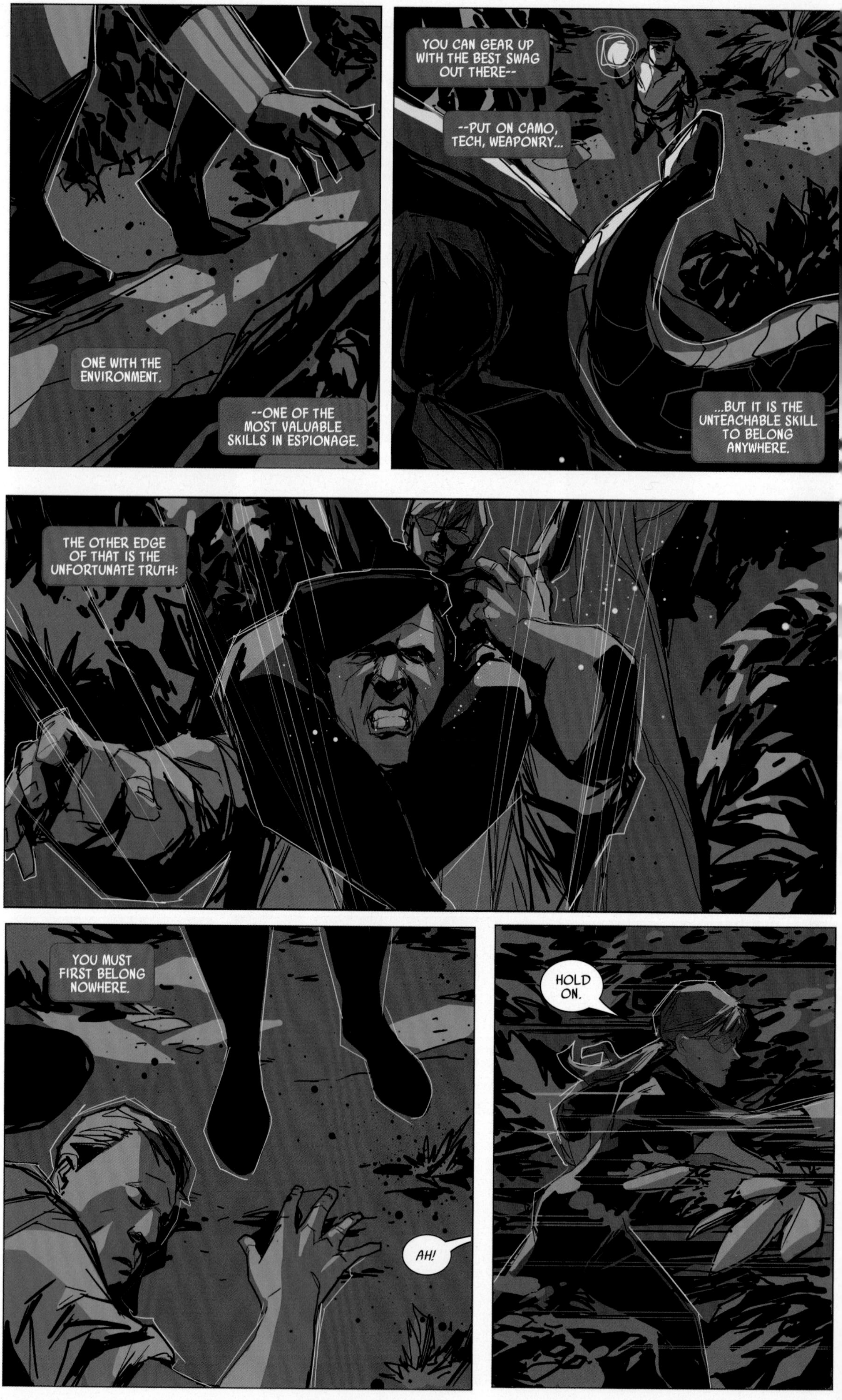
ONE WITH THE ENVIRONMENT.
--ONE OF THE MOST VALUABLE SKILLS IN ESPIONAGE.
YOU CAN GEAR UP WITH THE BEST SWAG OUT THERE--
--PUT ON CAMO, TECH, WEAPONRY...
...BUT IT IS THE UNTEACHABLE SKILL TO BELONG ANYWHERE.
THE OTHER EDGE OF THAT IS THE UNFORTUNATE TRUTH:
YOU MUST FIRST BELONG NOWHERE.
AH!
HOLD ON.

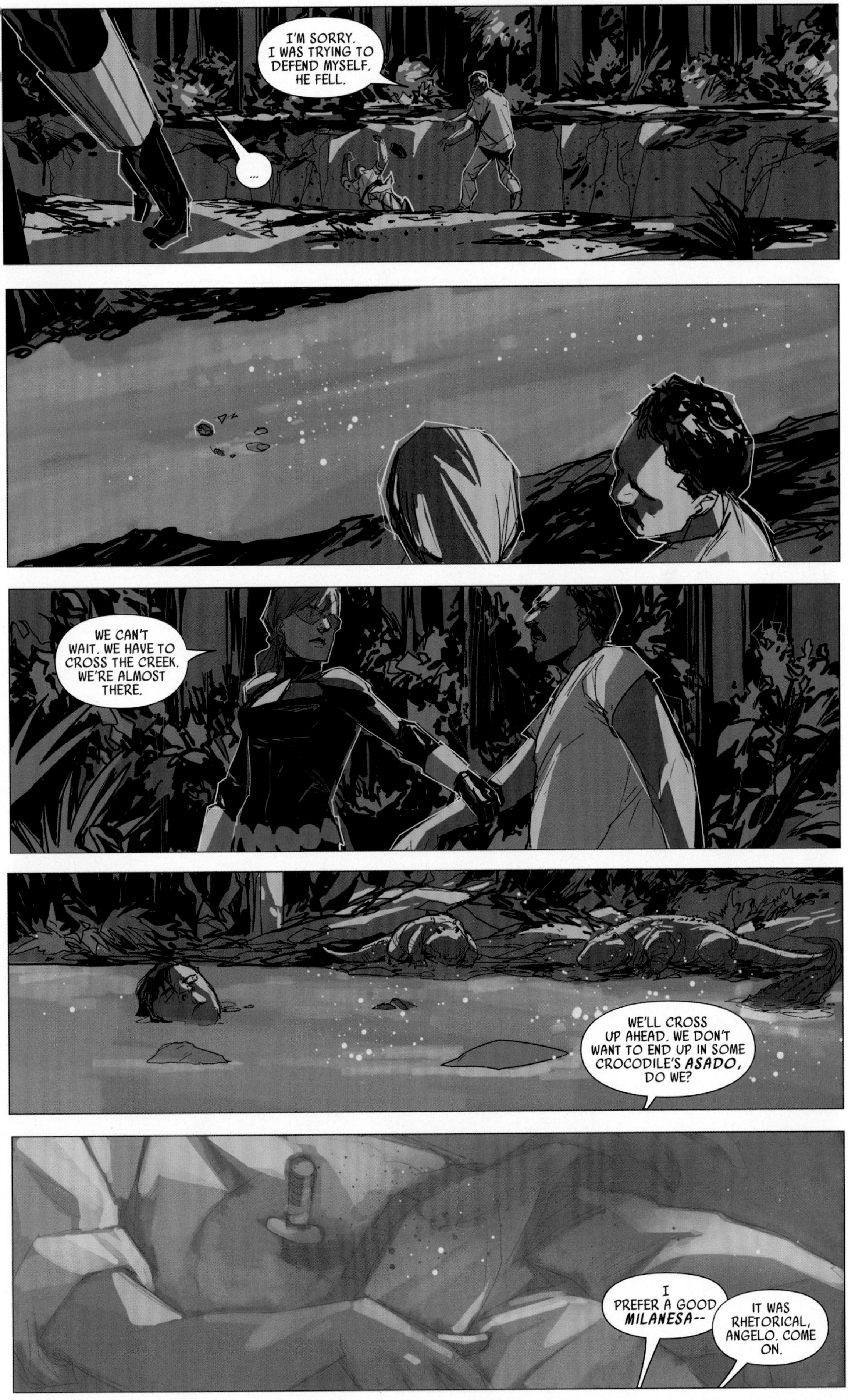
I'M SORRY. I WAS TRYING TO DEFEND MYSELF. HE FELL.
...
WE CAN'T WAIT. WE HAVE TO CROSS THE CREEK. WE'RE ALMOST THERE.
WE'LL CROSS UP AHEAD. WE DON'T WANT TO END UP IN SOME CROCODILE'S ASADO, DO WE?
I PREFER A GOOD MILANESA--
IT WAS RHETORICAL, ANGELO. COME ON.

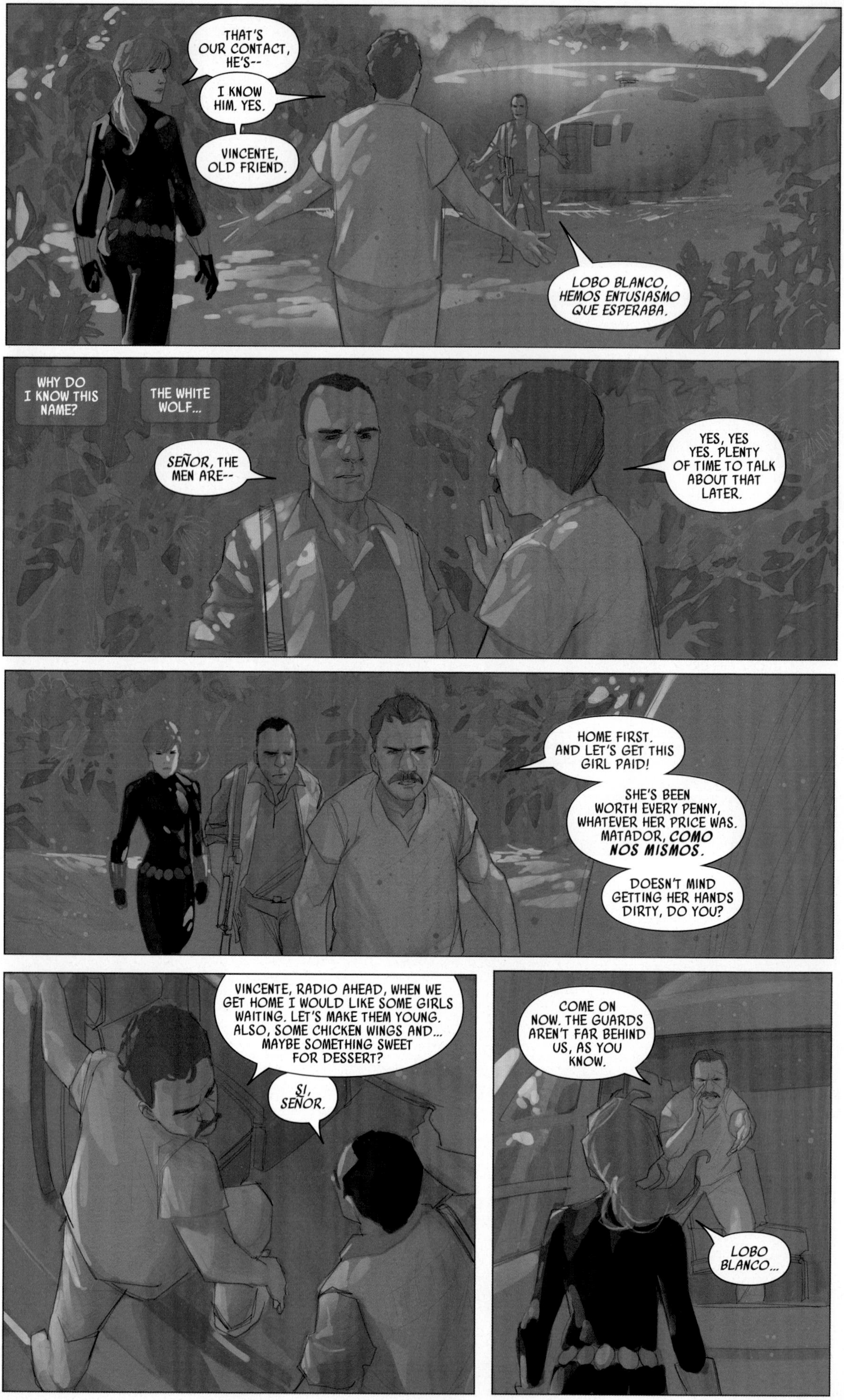
THAT'S OUR CONTACT, HE'S--
I KNOW HIM. YES.
VINCENTE, OLD FRIEND.
LOBO BLANCO, HEMOS ENTUSIASMO QUE ESPERABA.
WHY DO I KNOW THIS NAME?
THE WHITE WOLF...
SEÑOR, THE MEN ARE--
YES, YES YES. PLENTY OF TIME TO TALK ABOUT THAT LATER.
HOME FIRST. AND LET'S GET THIS GIRL PAID!
SHE'S BEEN WORTH EVERY PENNY, WHATEVER HER PRICE WAS. MATADOR, COMO NOS MISMOS.
DOESN'T MIND GETTING HER HANDS DIRTY, DO YOU?
VINCENTE, RADIO AHEAD, WHEN WE GET HOME I WOULD LIKE SOME GIRLS WAITING. LET'S MAKE THEM YOUNG. ALSO, SOME CHICKEN WINGS AND... MAYBE SOMETHING SWEET FOR DESSERT?
SI, SEÑOR.
COME ON NOW. THE GUARDS AREN'T FAR BEHIND US, AS YOU KNOW.
LOBO BLANCO...

HOW DID I MISS IT?

THE SIGNS WERE THERE.

A DESK OF TRIBUTES FROM OTHER INMATES... PROTECTION PAY.

A DISREGARD FOR LIFE... A DISINTEREST IN DANGER...

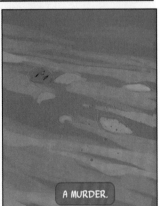

A MURDER.

I MAY NOT HAVE KNOWN WHO HE WAS, BUT I WOULD HAVE KNOWN HE IS NOT WHO THE CLIENT CLAIMED.

AT LEAST, THAT IS NOT ALL HE IS.

YES, HE WAS IMPRISONED ILLEGALLY FOR A CRIME HE DID NOT COMMIT...

BUT BEFORE THAT, LOBO BLANCO, THE BUTCHER OF ARGENTINA...

...I MISSED IT. DISTRACTED.

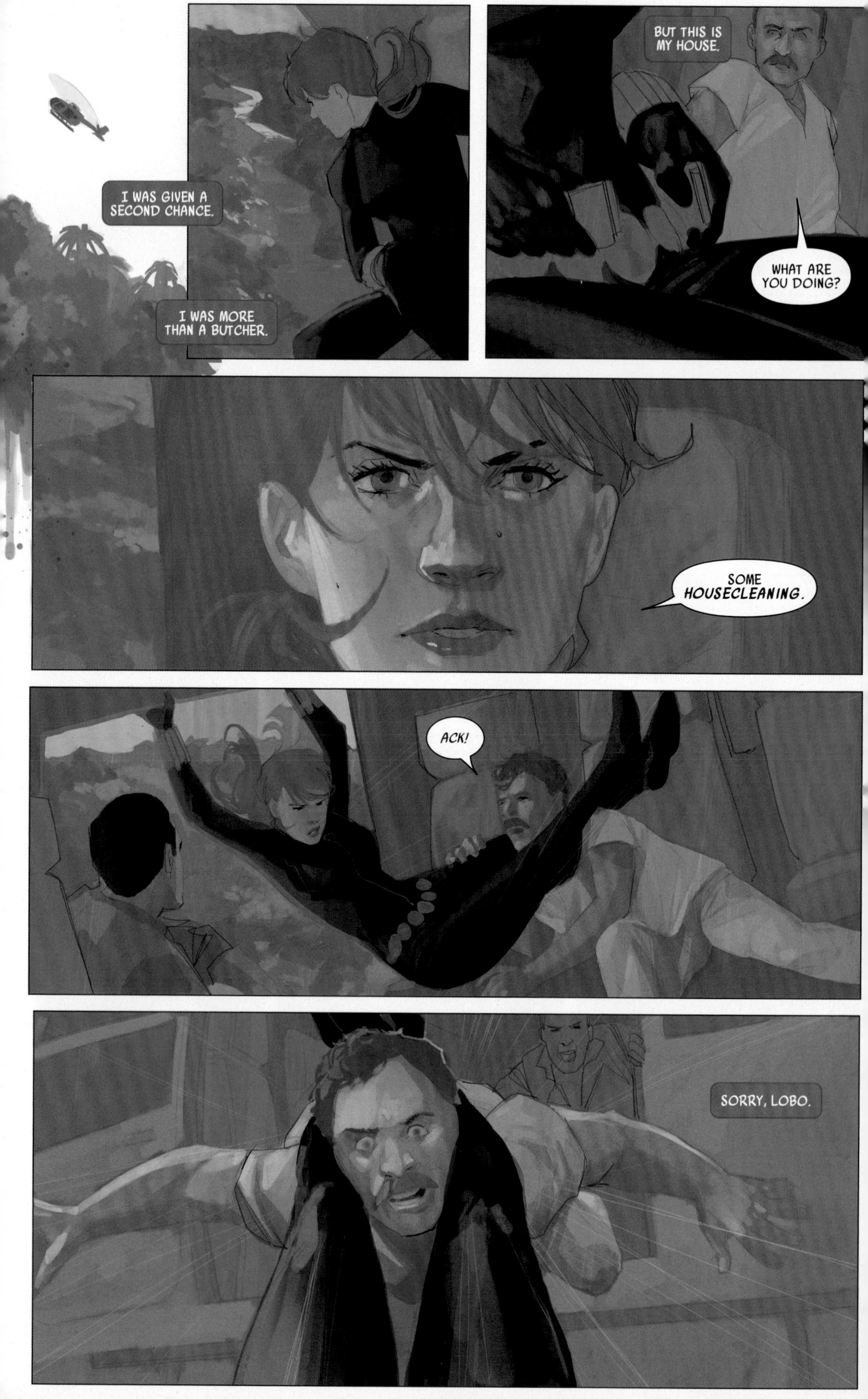
I WAS GIVEN A SECOND CHANCE.
I WAS MORE THAN A BUTCHER.
BUT THIS IS MY HOUSE.
WHAT ARE YOU DOING?
SOME HOUSECLEANING.
ACK!
SORRY, LOBO.

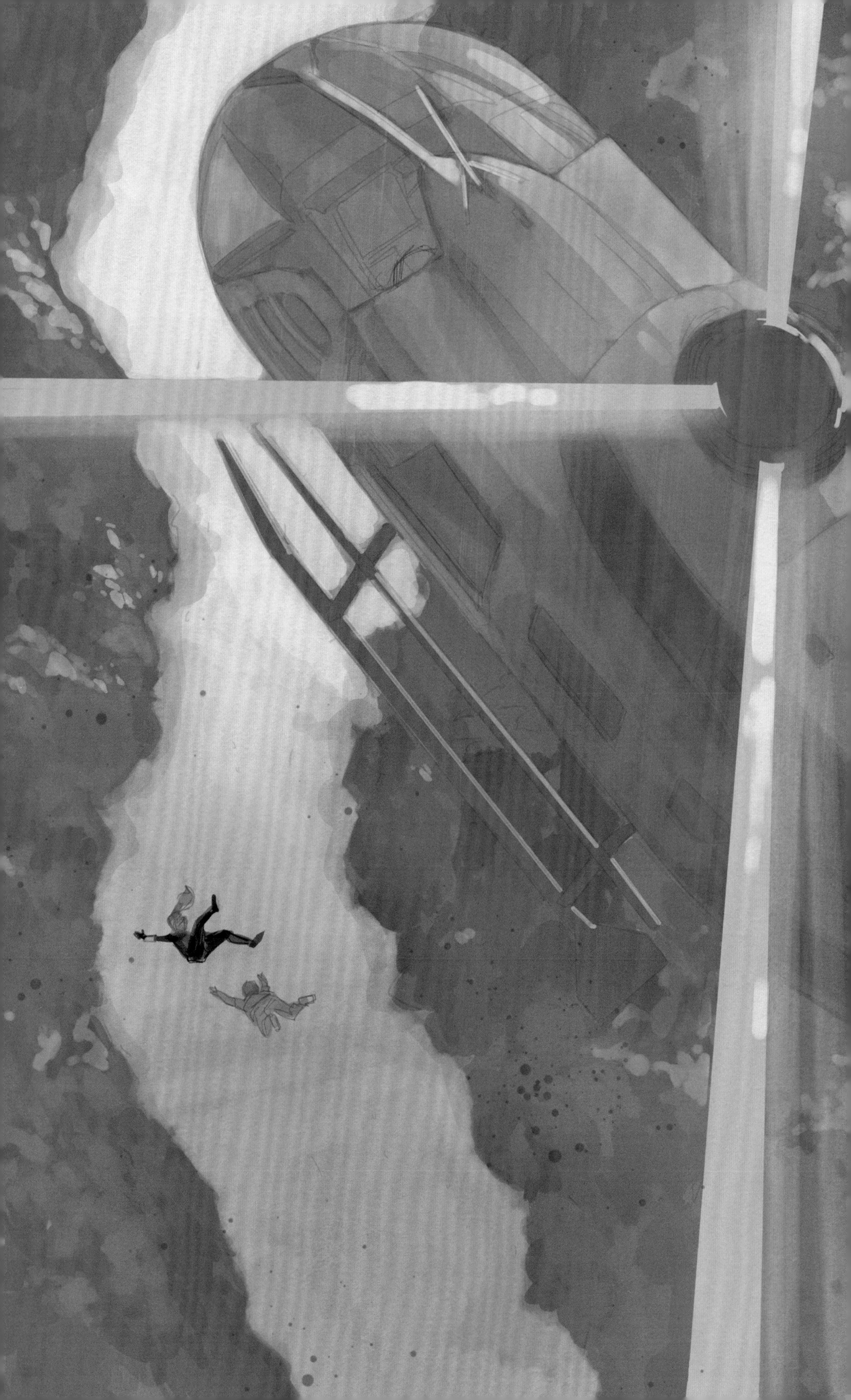

A GOOD OPERATIVE KNOWS HIS ENVIRONMENT-- HIS *HOME.*

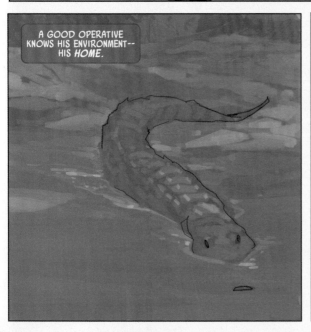

HE KNOWS WHICH CREATURES ARE DOCILE--

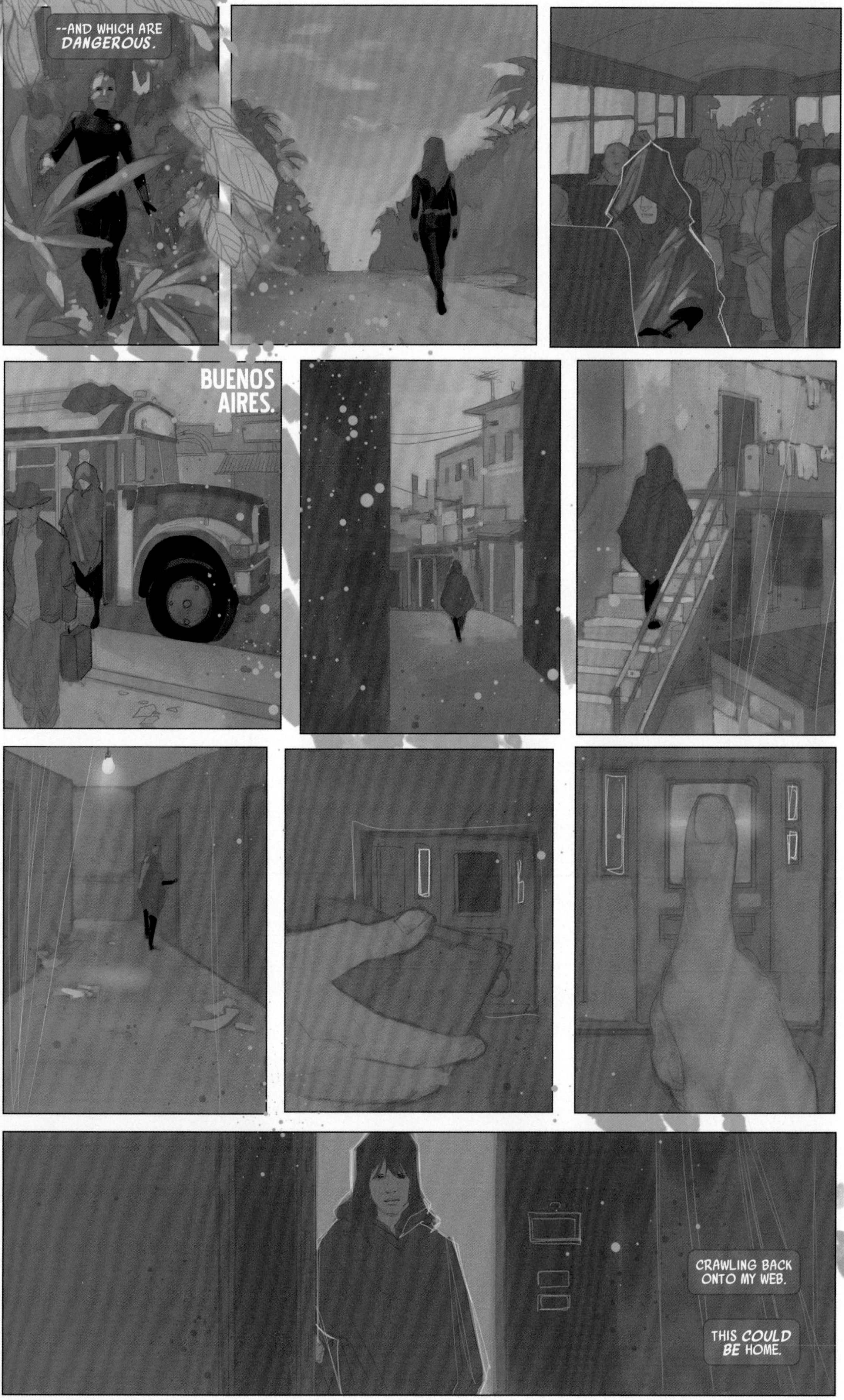
--AND WHICH ARE DANGEROUS.
BUENOS AIRES.
CRAWLING BACK ONTO MY WEB.
THIS COULD BE HOME.

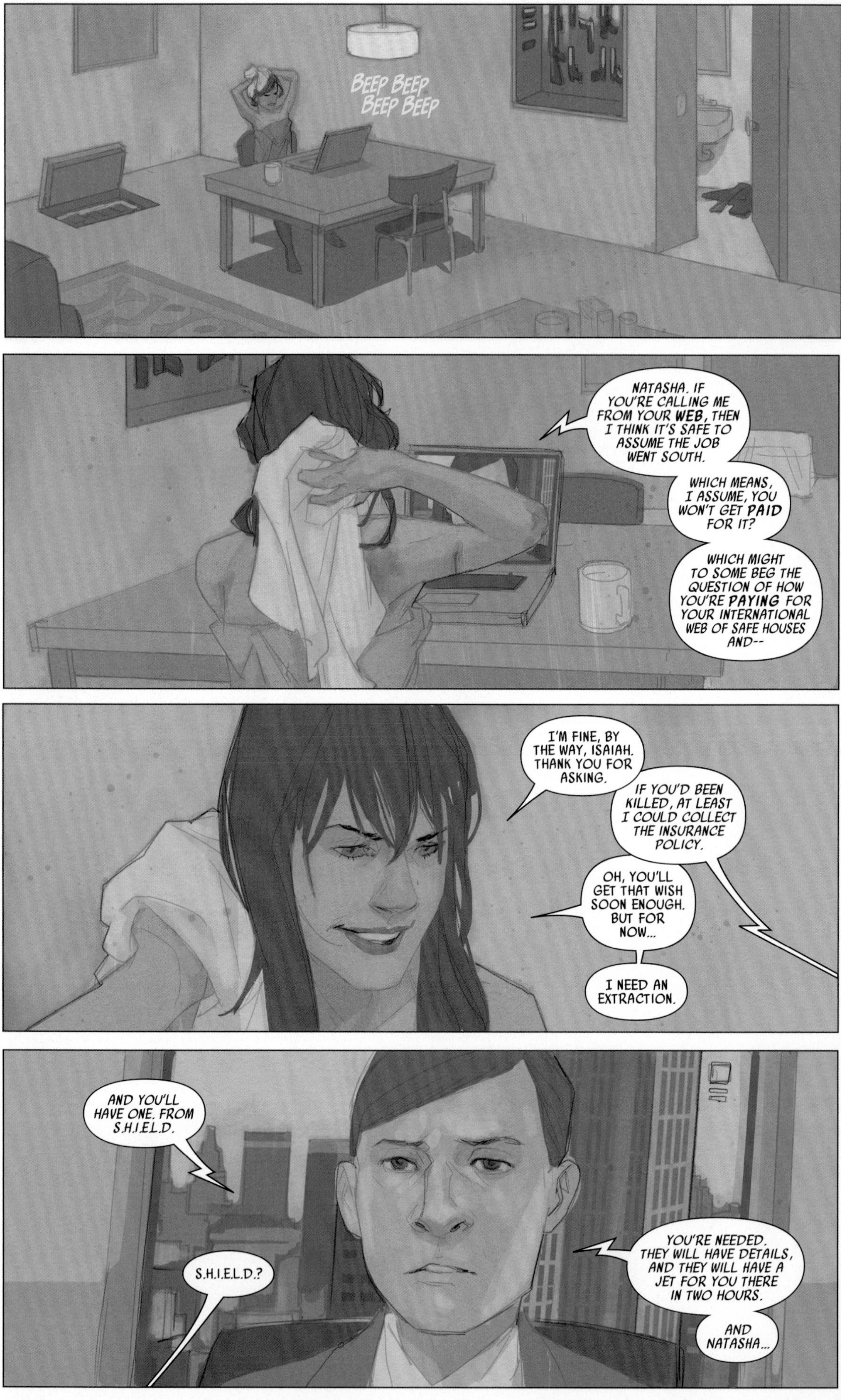
BEEP BEEP BEEP BEEP
NATASHA. IF YOU'RE CALLING ME FROM YOUR WEB, THEN I THINK IT'S SAFE TO ASSUME THE JOB WENT SOUTH.
WHICH MEANS, I ASSUME, YOU WON'T GET PAID FOR IT?
WHICH MIGHT TO SOME BEG THE QUESTION OF HOW YOU'RE PAYING FOR YOUR INTERNATIONAL WEB OF SAFE HOUSES AND--
I'M FINE, BY THE WAY, ISAIAH. THANK YOU FOR ASKING.
IF YOU'D BEEN KILLED, AT LEAST I COULD COLLECT THE INSURANCE POLICY.
OH, YOU'LL GET THAT WISH SOON ENOUGH. BUT FOR NOW...
I NEED AN EXTRACTION.
AND YOU'LL HAVE ONE. FROM S.H.I.E.L.D.
S.H.I.E.L.D.?
YOU'RE NEEDED. THEY WILL HAVE DETAILS, AND THEY WILL HAVE A JET FOR YOU THERE IN TWO HOURS.
AND NATASHA...

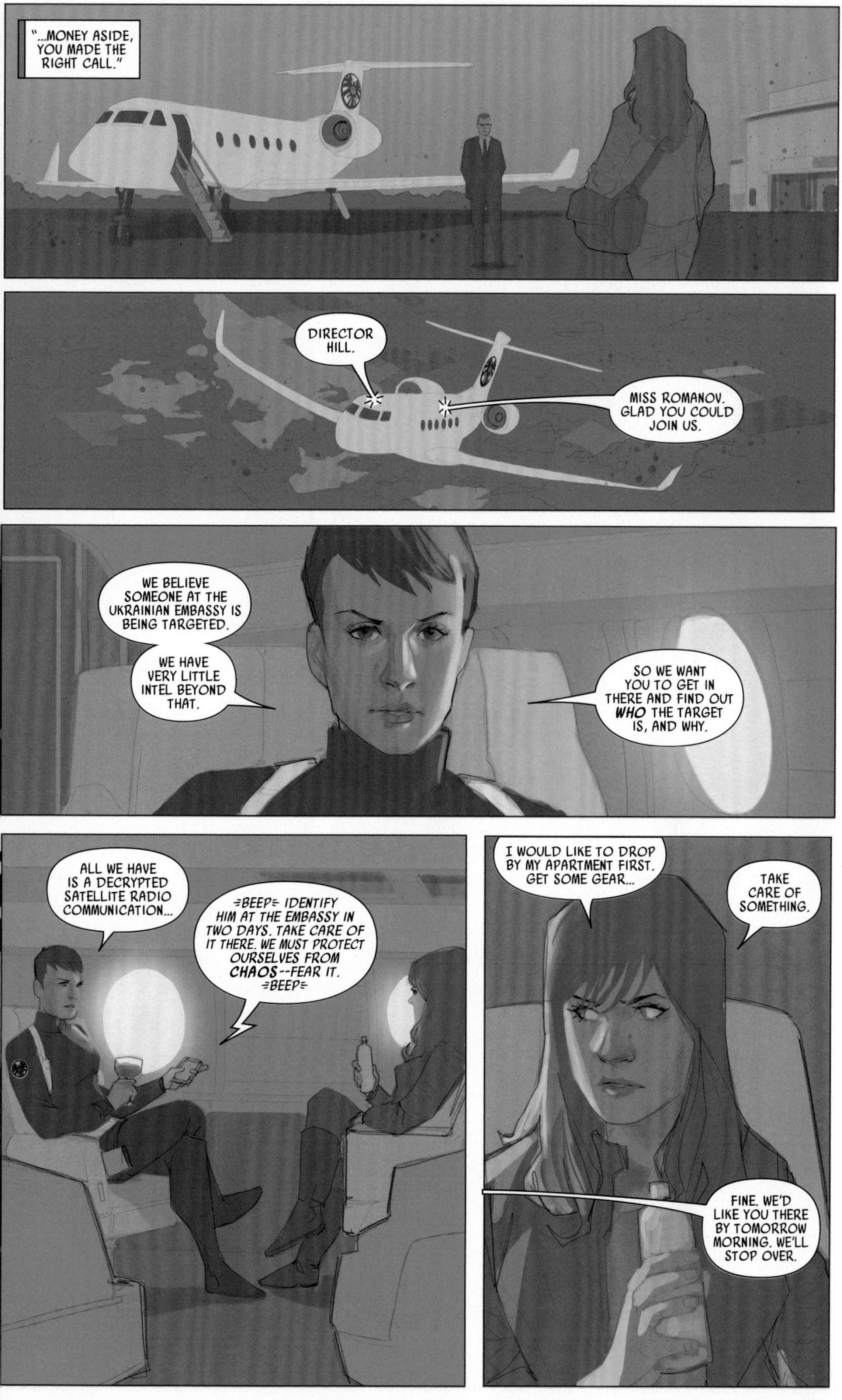
"...MONEY ASIDE, YOU MADE THE RIGHT CALL."
DIRECTOR HILL.
MISS ROMANOV. GLAD YOU COULD JOIN US.
WE BELIEVE SOMEONE AT THE UKRAINIAN EMBASSY IS BEING TARGETED.
WE HAVE VERY LITTLE INTEL BEYOND THAT.
SO WE WANT YOU TO GET IN THERE AND FIND OUT **WHO** THE TARGET IS, AND WHY.
ALL WE HAVE IS A DECRYPTED SATELLITE RADIO COMMUNICATION...
=BEEP= IDENTIFY HIM AT THE EMBASSY IN TWO DAYS. TAKE CARE OF IT THERE. WE MUST PROTECT OURSELVES FROM **CHAOS**--FEAR IT. =BEEP=
I WOULD LIKE TO DROP BY MY APARTMENT FIRST. GET SOME GEAR...
TAKE CARE OF SOMETHING.
FINE. WE'D LIKE YOU THERE BY TOMORROW MORNING. WE'LL STOP OVER.

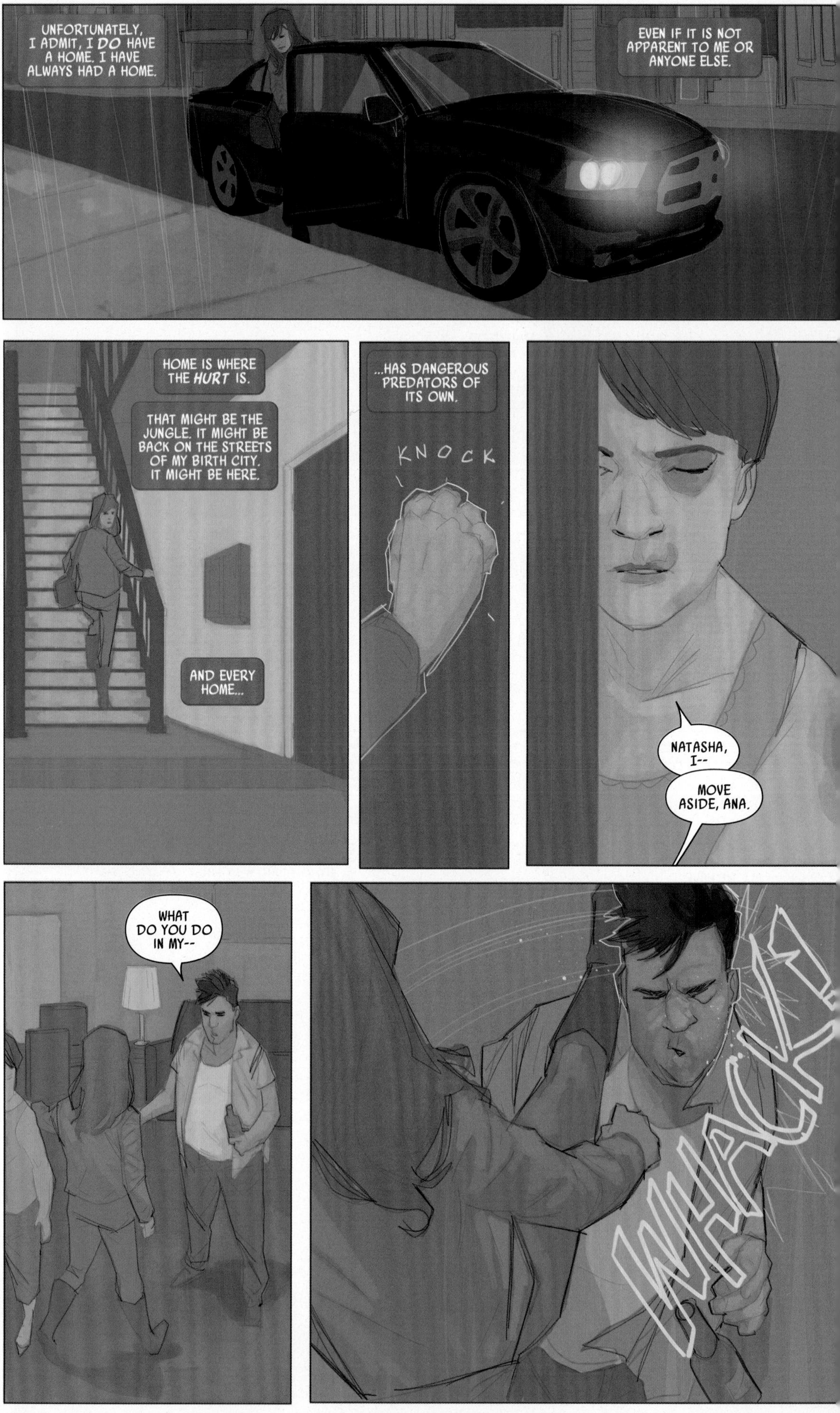
UNFORTUNATELY, I ADMIT, I DO HAVE A HOME. I HAVE ALWAYS HAD A HOME.
EVEN IF IT IS NOT APPARENT TO ME OR ANYONE ELSE.
HOME IS WHERE THE HURT IS.
THAT MIGHT BE THE JUNGLE. IT MIGHT BE BACK ON THE STREETS OF MY BIRTH CITY. IT MIGHT BE HERE.
AND EVERY HOME...
...HAS DANGEROUS PREDATORS OF ITS OWN.
KNOCK
NATASHA, I--
MOVE ASIDE, ANA.
WHAT DO YOU DO IN MY--
WHACK!

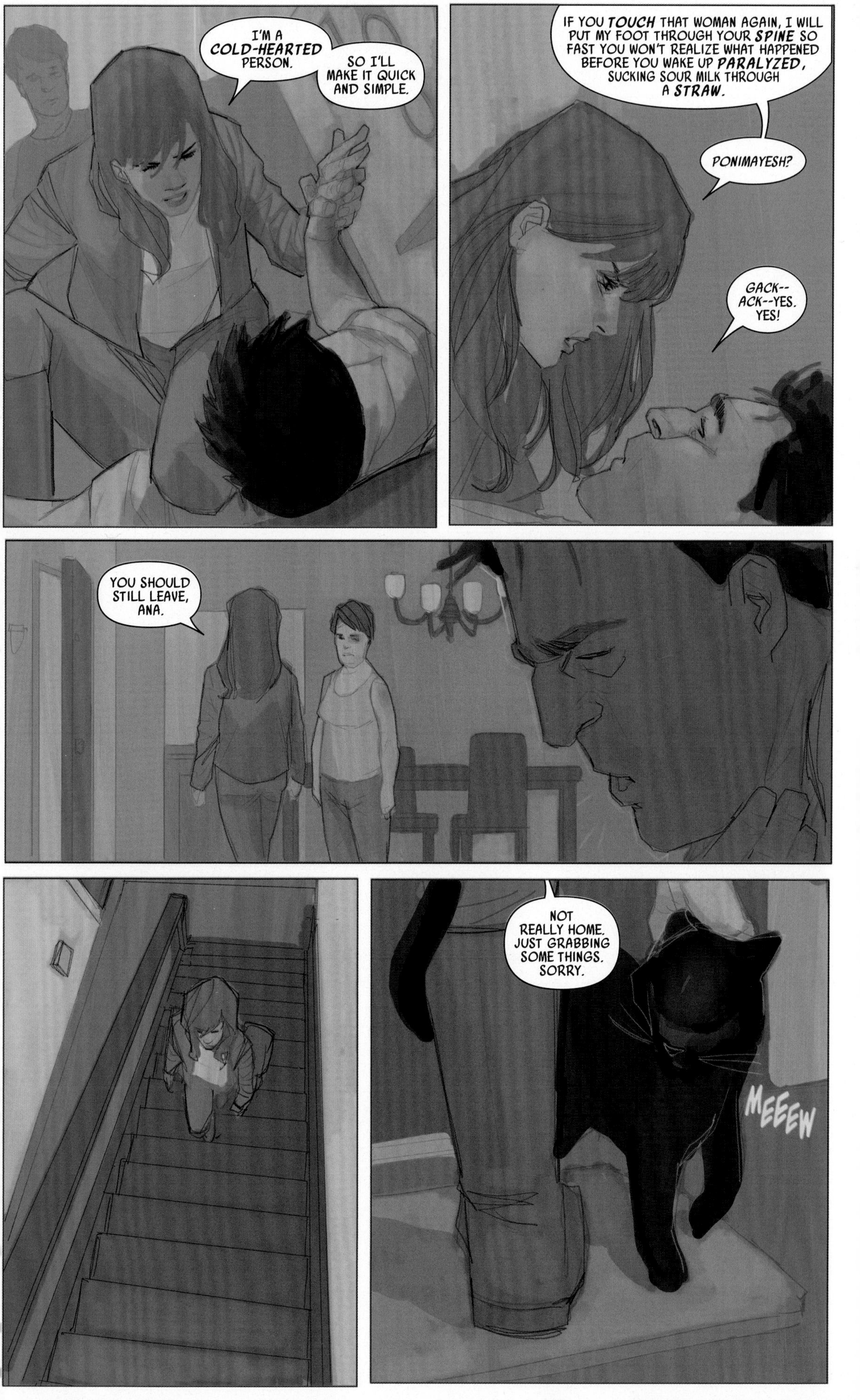
I'M A COLD-HEARTED PERSON.
SO I'LL MAKE IT QUICK AND SIMPLE.
IF YOU TOUCH THAT WOMAN AGAIN, I WILL PUT MY FOOT THROUGH YOUR SPINE SO FAST YOU WON'T REALIZE WHAT HAPPENED BEFORE YOU WAKE UP PARALYZED, SUCKING SOUR MILK THROUGH A STRAW.
PONIMAYESH?
GACK-- ACK--YES. YES!
YOU SHOULD STILL LEAVE, ANA.
NOT REALLY HOME. JUST GRABBING SOME THINGS. SORRY.
MEEEW

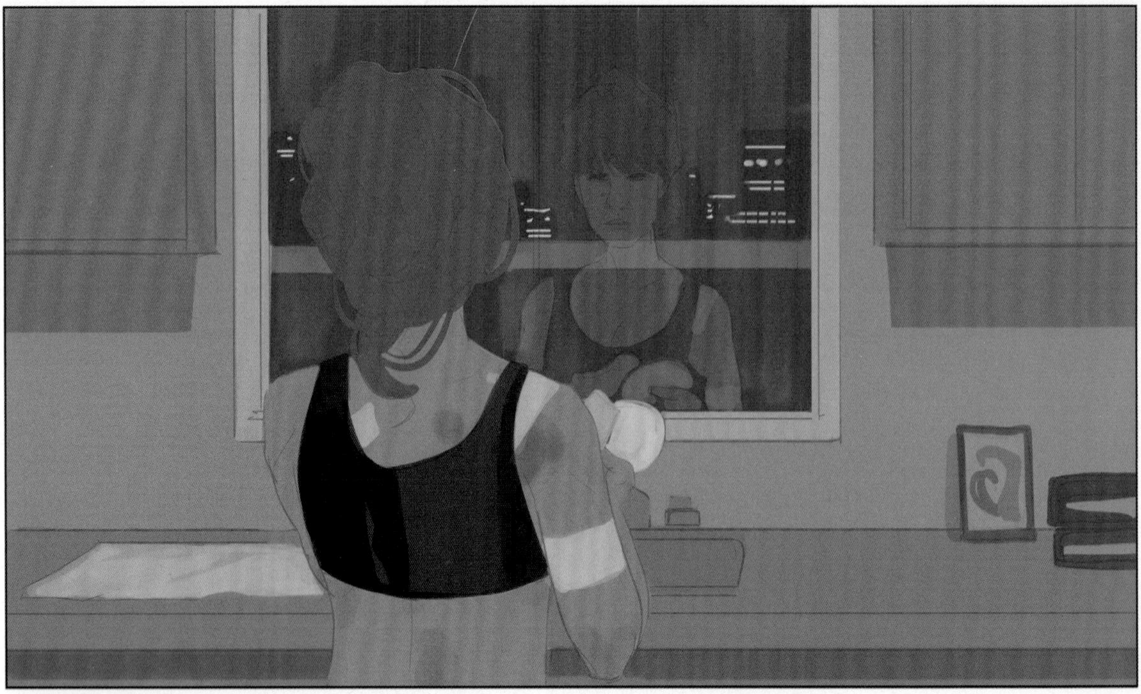

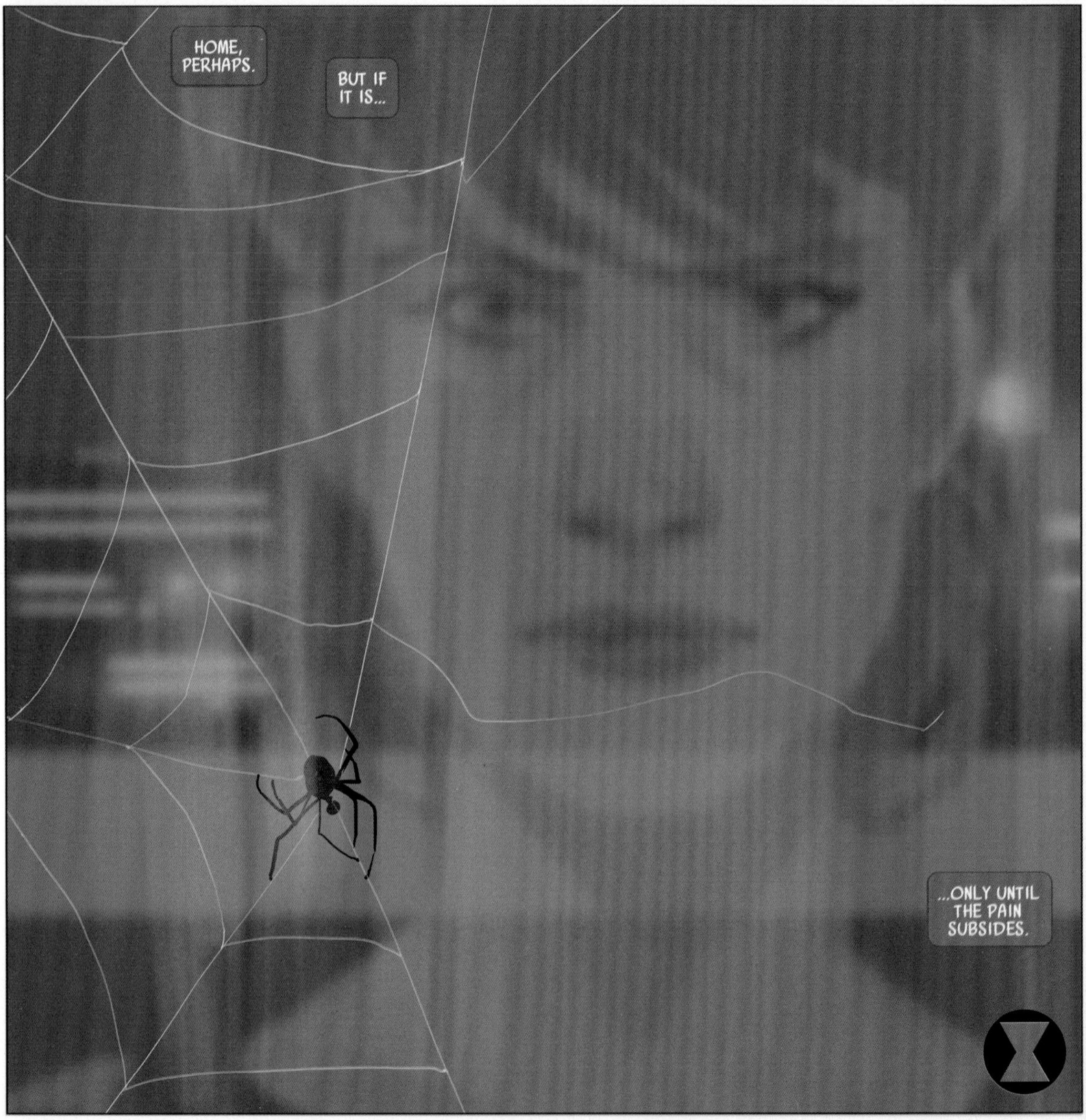

HOME, PERHAPS.
BUT IF IT IS...
...ONLY UNTIL THE PAIN SUBSIDES.

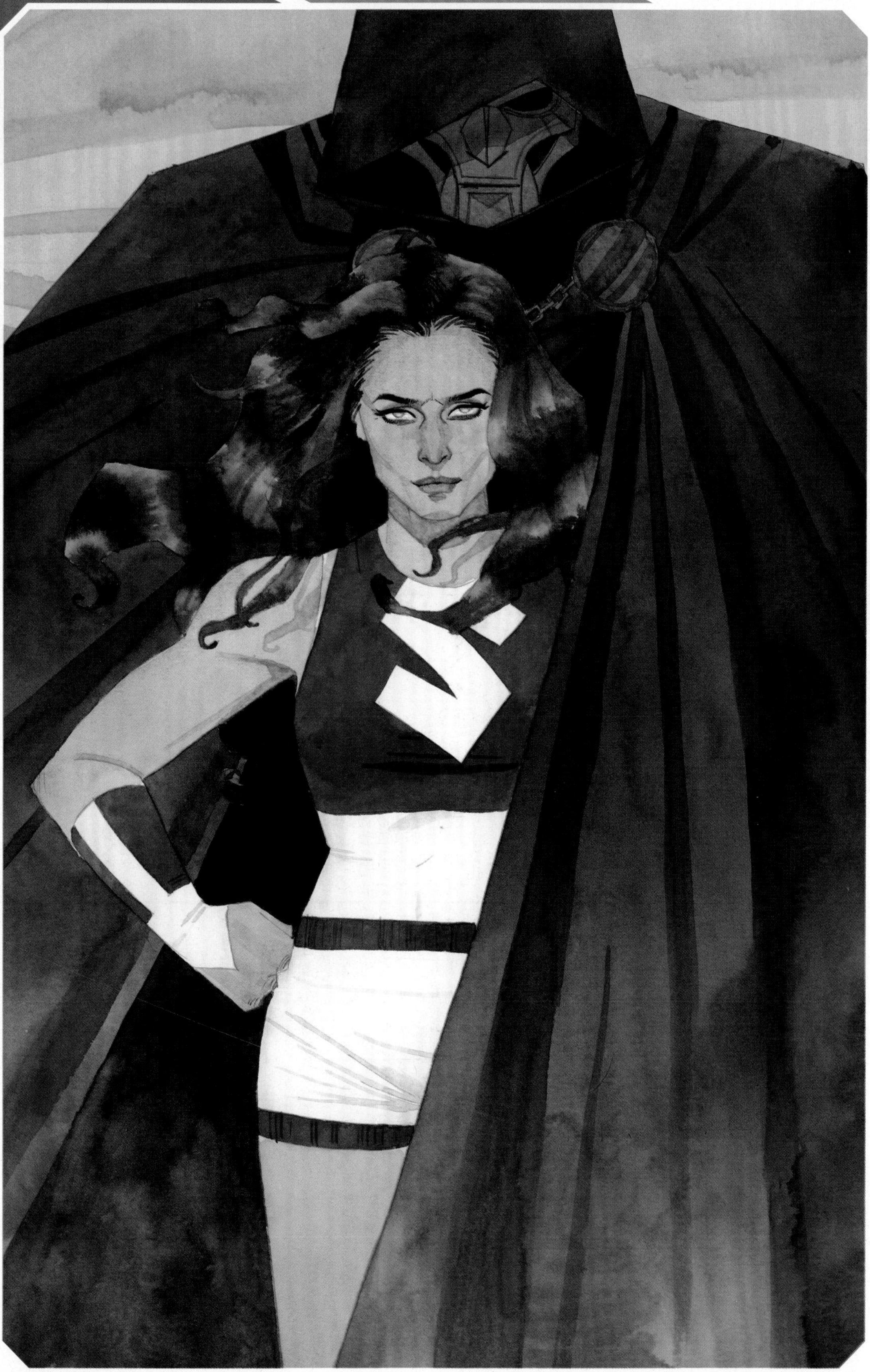

SHE-HULK #3

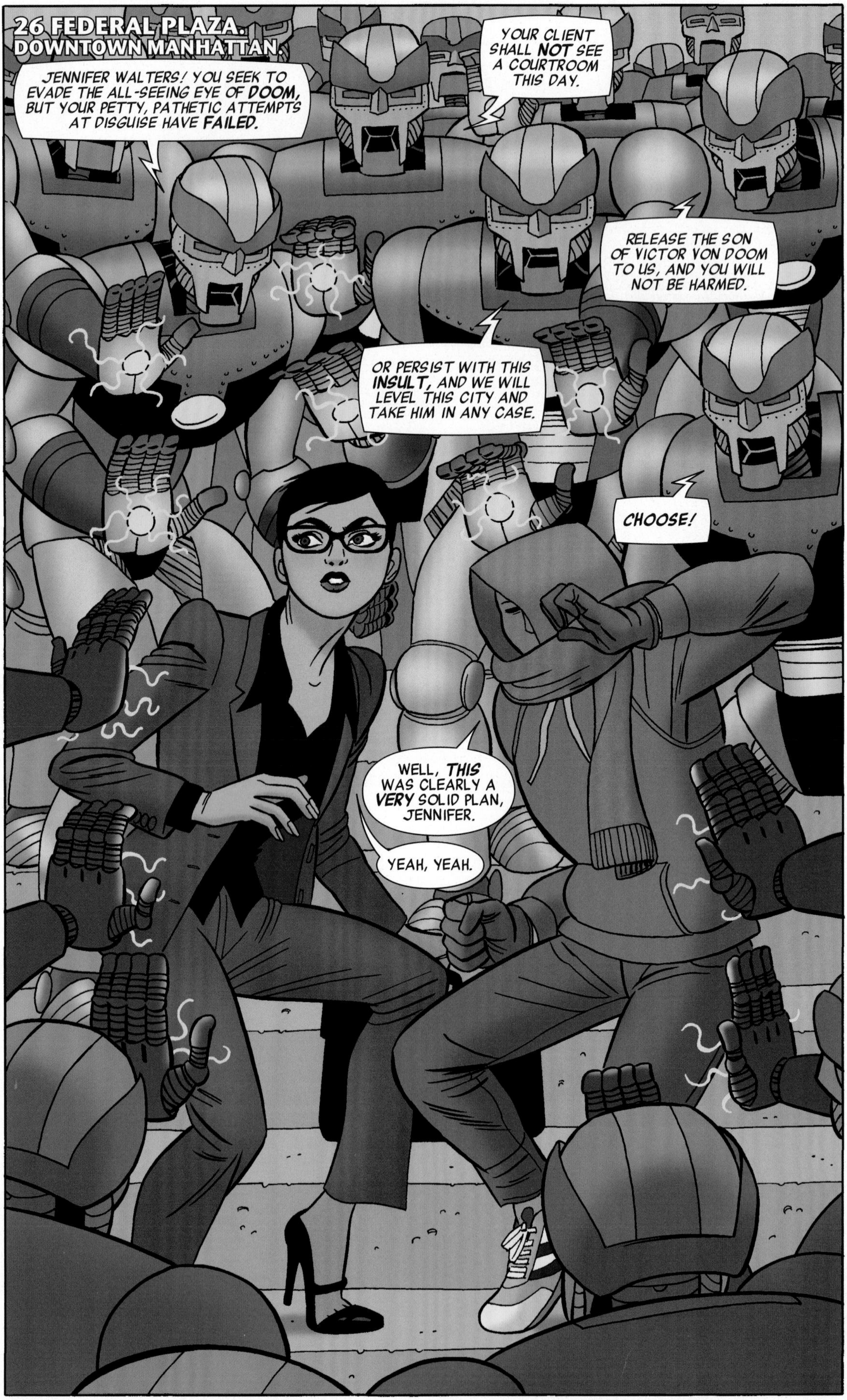
26 FEDERAL PLAZA. DOWNTOWN MANHATTAN.
JENNIFER WALTERS! YOU SEEK TO EVADE THE ALL-SEEING EYE OF DOOM, BUT YOUR PETTY, PATHETIC ATTEMPTS AT DISGUISE HAVE FAILED.
YOUR CLIENT SHALL NOT SEE A COURTROOM THIS DAY.
RELEASE THE SON OF VICTOR VON DOOM TO US, AND YOU WILL NOT BE HARMED.
OR PERSIST WITH THIS INSULT, AND WE WILL LEVEL THIS CITY AND TAKE HIM IN ANY CASE.
CHOOSE!
WELL, THIS WAS CLEARLY A VERY SOLID PLAN, JENNIFER.
YEAH, YEAH.

Jennifer Walters was a shy attorney, good at her job and quiet in her life, when she found herself gunned down by criminals. A gamma-irradiated blood transfusion from her cousin, Dr. Bruce Banner, a.k.a. the Incredible Hulk, didn't just give her a second chance at life, it gave her super strength and bulletproof green skin. Wherever justice is threatened, you'll find the Sensational...

SHE-HULK

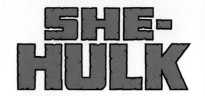

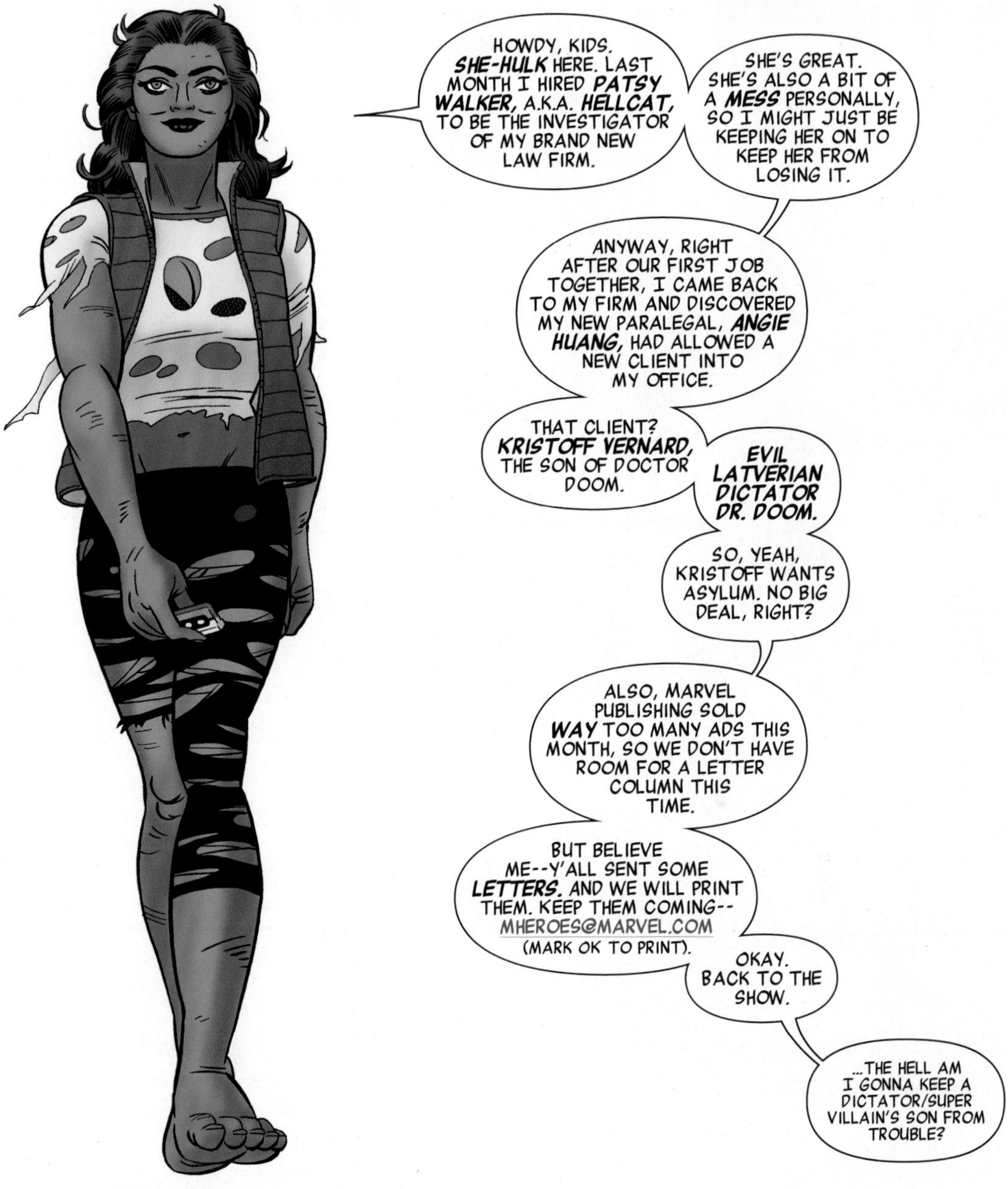
HOWDY, KIDS. SHE-HULK HERE. LAST MONTH I HIRED PATSY WALKER, A.K.A. HELLCAT, TO BE THE INVESTIGATOR OF MY BRAND NEW LAW FIRM.
SHE'S GREAT. SHE'S ALSO A BIT OF A MESS PERSONALLY, SO I MIGHT JUST BE KEEPING HER ON TO KEEP HER FROM LOSING IT.
ANYWAY, RIGHT AFTER OUR FIRST JOB TOGETHER, I CAME BACK TO MY FIRM AND DISCOVERED MY NEW PARALEGAL, ANGIE HUANG, HAD ALLOWED A NEW CLIENT INTO MY OFFICE.
THAT CLIENT? KRISTOFF VERNARD, THE SON OF DOCTOR DOOM.
EVIL LATVERIAN DICTATOR DR. DOOM.
SO, YEAH, KRISTOFF WANTS ASYLUM. NO BIG DEAL, RIGHT?
ALSO, MARVEL PUBLISHING SOLD WAY TOO MANY ADS THIS MONTH, SO WE DON'T HAVE ROOM FOR A LETTER COLUMN THIS TIME.
BUT BELIEVE ME--Y'ALL SENT SOME LETTERS. AND WE WILL PRINT THEM. KEEP THEM COMING-- MHEROES@MARVEL.COM (MARK OK TO PRINT).
OKAY. BACK TO THE SHOW.
...THE HELL AM I GONNA KEEP A DICTATOR/SUPER VILLAIN'S SON FROM TROUBLE?

CHARLES SOULE writer | **JAVIER PULIDO** artist | **MUNTSA VICENTE** color artist | **VC's CLAYTON COWLES** letterer

KEVIN WADA cover artist | **KRIS ANKA** variant cover artist | **FRANKIE JOHNSON** assistant editor | **JEANINE SCHAEFER** consulting editor

TOM BRENNAN editor | **AXEL ALONSO** editor in chief | **JOE QUESADA** chief creative officer | **DAN BUCKLEY** publisher | **ALAN FINE** exec. producer

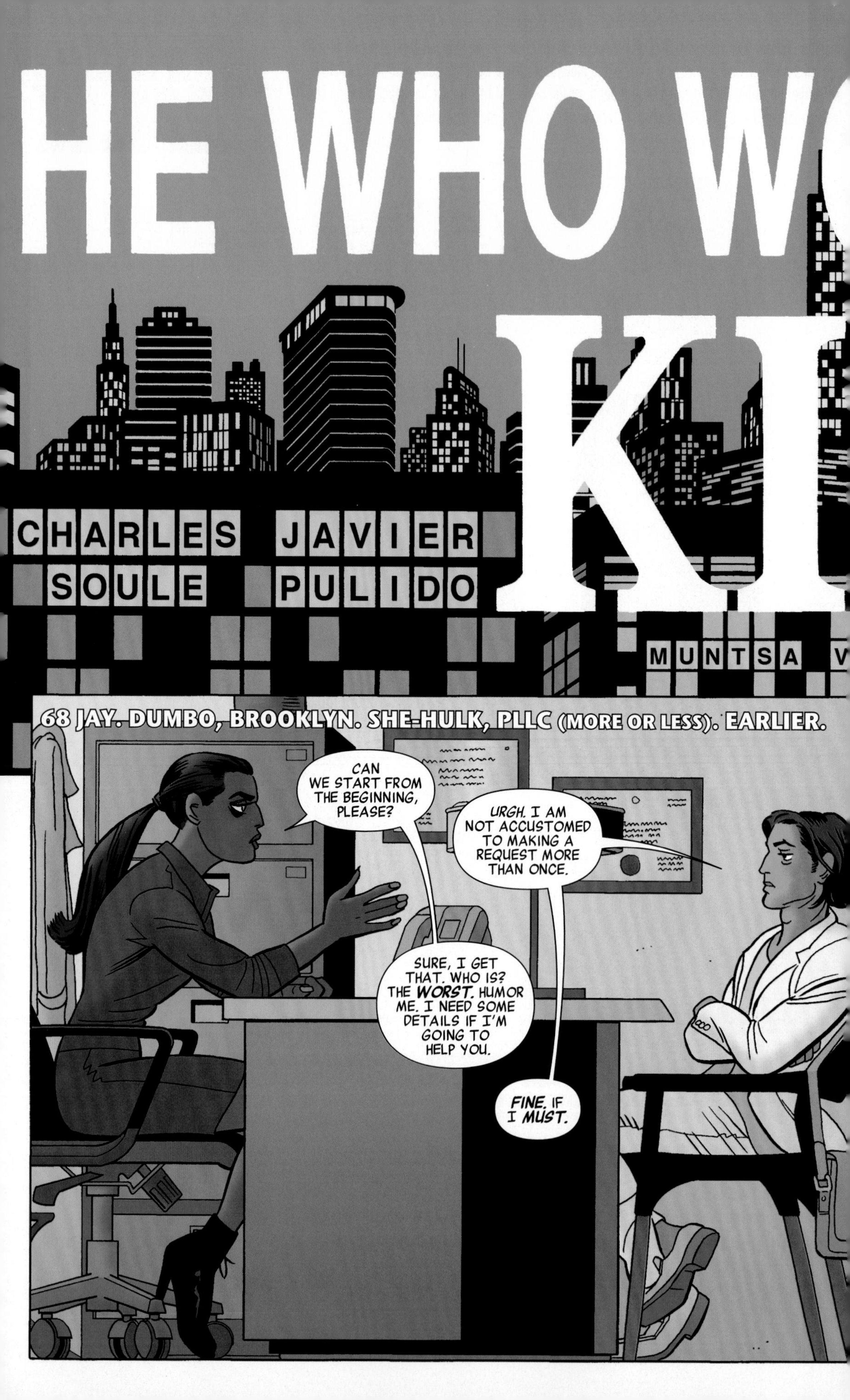
HE WHO WO
KI
CHARLES SOULE
JAVIER PULIDO
MUNTSA V
68 JAY. DUMBO, BROOKLYN. SHE-HULK, PLLC (MORE OR LESS). EARLIER.
CAN WE START FROM THE BEGINNING, PLEASE?
URGH. I AM NOT ACCUSTOMED TO MAKING A REQUEST MORE THAN ONCE.
SURE, I GET THAT. WHO IS? THE WORST. HUMOR ME. I NEED SOME DETAILS IF I'M GOING TO HELP YOU.
FINE. IF I MUST.

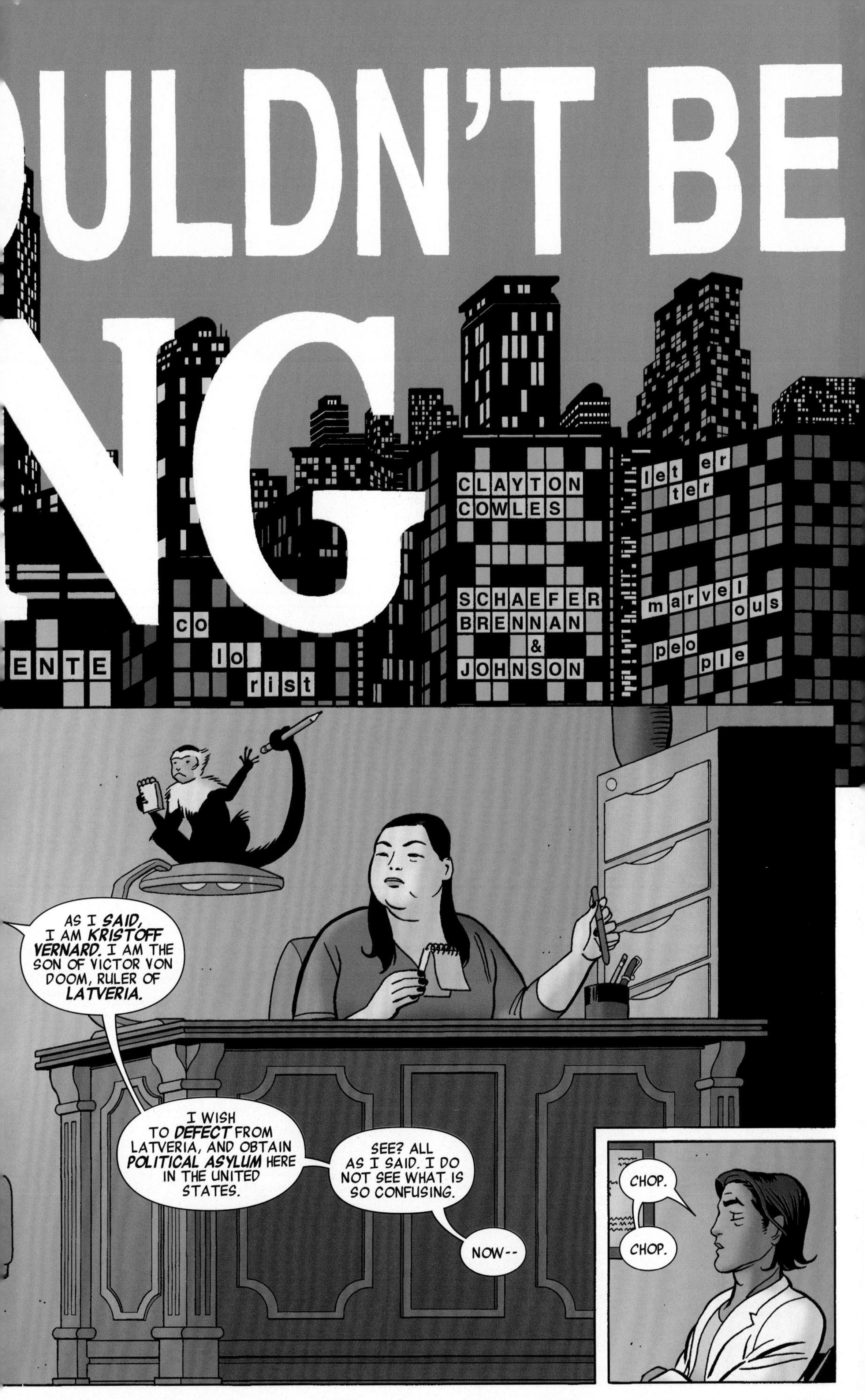

OULDN'T BE
NG
CLAYTON COWLES
let ter er
SCHAEFER BRENNAN & JOHNSON
marvel ous
peo ple
co lo rist
ENTE
AS I SAID, I AM KRISTOFF VERNARD. I AM THE SON OF VICTOR VON DOOM, RULER OF LATVERIA.
I WISH TO DEFECT FROM LATVERIA, AND OBTAIN POLITICAL ASYLUM HERE IN THE UNITED STATES.
SEE? ALL AS I SAID. I DO NOT SEE WHAT IS SO CONFUSING.
NOW--
CHOP.
CHOP.

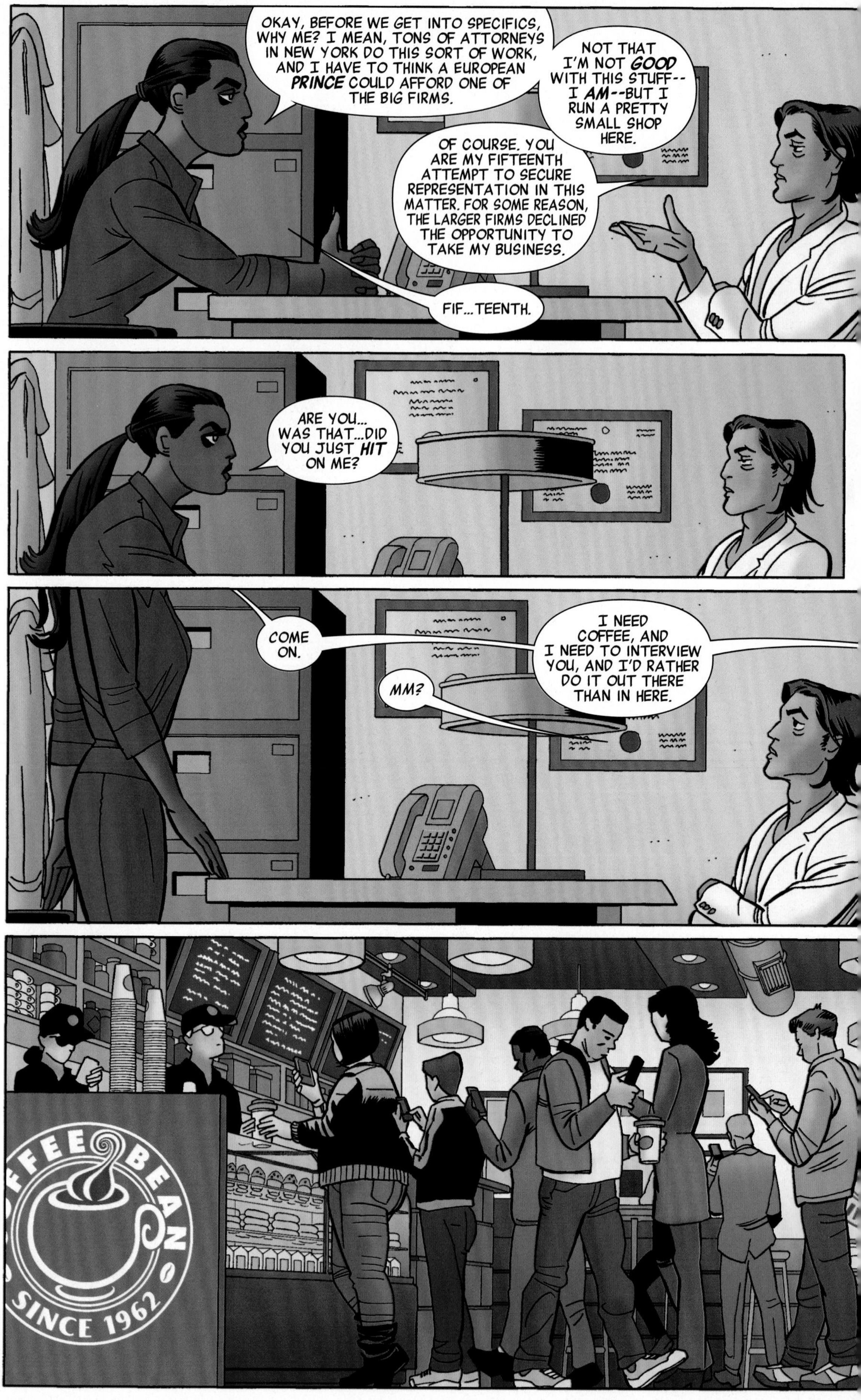
OKAY, BEFORE WE GET INTO SPECIFICS, WHY ME? I MEAN, TONS OF ATTORNEYS IN NEW YORK DO THIS SORT OF WORK, AND I HAVE TO THINK A EUROPEAN PRINCE COULD AFFORD ONE OF THE BIG FIRMS.
NOT THAT I'M NOT GOOD WITH THIS STUFF-- I AM--BUT I RUN A PRETTY SMALL SHOP HERE.
OF COURSE. YOU ARE MY FIFTEENTH ATTEMPT TO SECURE REPRESENTATION IN THIS MATTER. FOR SOME REASON, THE LARGER FIRMS DECLINED THE OPPORTUNITY TO TAKE MY BUSINESS.
FIF...TEENTH.
ARE YOU... WAS THAT...DID YOU JUST HIT ON ME?
COME ON.
I NEED COFFEE, AND I NEED TO INTERVIEW YOU, AND I'D RATHER DO IT OUT THERE THAN IN HERE.
MM?
FFEE BEAN
SINCE 1962

INDEED. ONE FELLOW ACTUALLY VOMITED UPON HEARING MY FATHER'S NAME.

EVENTUALLY, HOWEVER, I WAS GIVEN YOUR NAME. I BELIEVE THE IDEA WAS THAT YOU MIGHT POSSESS MORE FORTITUDE THAN THE *AVERAGE* MEMBER OF YOUR PROFESSION.

AND NOW THAT I HAVE MET YOU, I SEE THAT THERE IS NOTHING *AVERAGE* ABOUT YOU AT ALL.

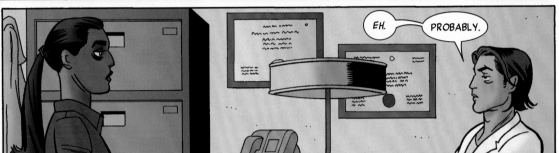

EH. PROBABLY.

HOLD DOWN THE FORT, ANGIE?

AYE, AYE, CAP'N.

SOLID WORK, HEI HEI.

EEP.

HERE'S THE FIRST QUESTION. THE BIGGEST ONE. IN ORDER TO SUCCESSFULLY OBTAIN ASYLUM IN THE U.S., YOU HAVE TO BE ABLE TO CONVINCE A JUDGE THAT YOU REALLY *CAN'T* GO BACK TO YOUR HOME COUNTRY.

THAT YOU HAVE WHAT THEY CALL A "WELL-FOUNDED FEAR OF PERSECUTION" BACK IN LATVERIA, AND LIVING IN THE STATES IS THE ONLY WAY YOU CAN GET AWAY FROM IT.

THAT SHOULD BE SIMPLE ENOUGH. LISTEN.

WHEN YOU LOOK AT ME, WHAT DO YOU SEE?

ERRR...

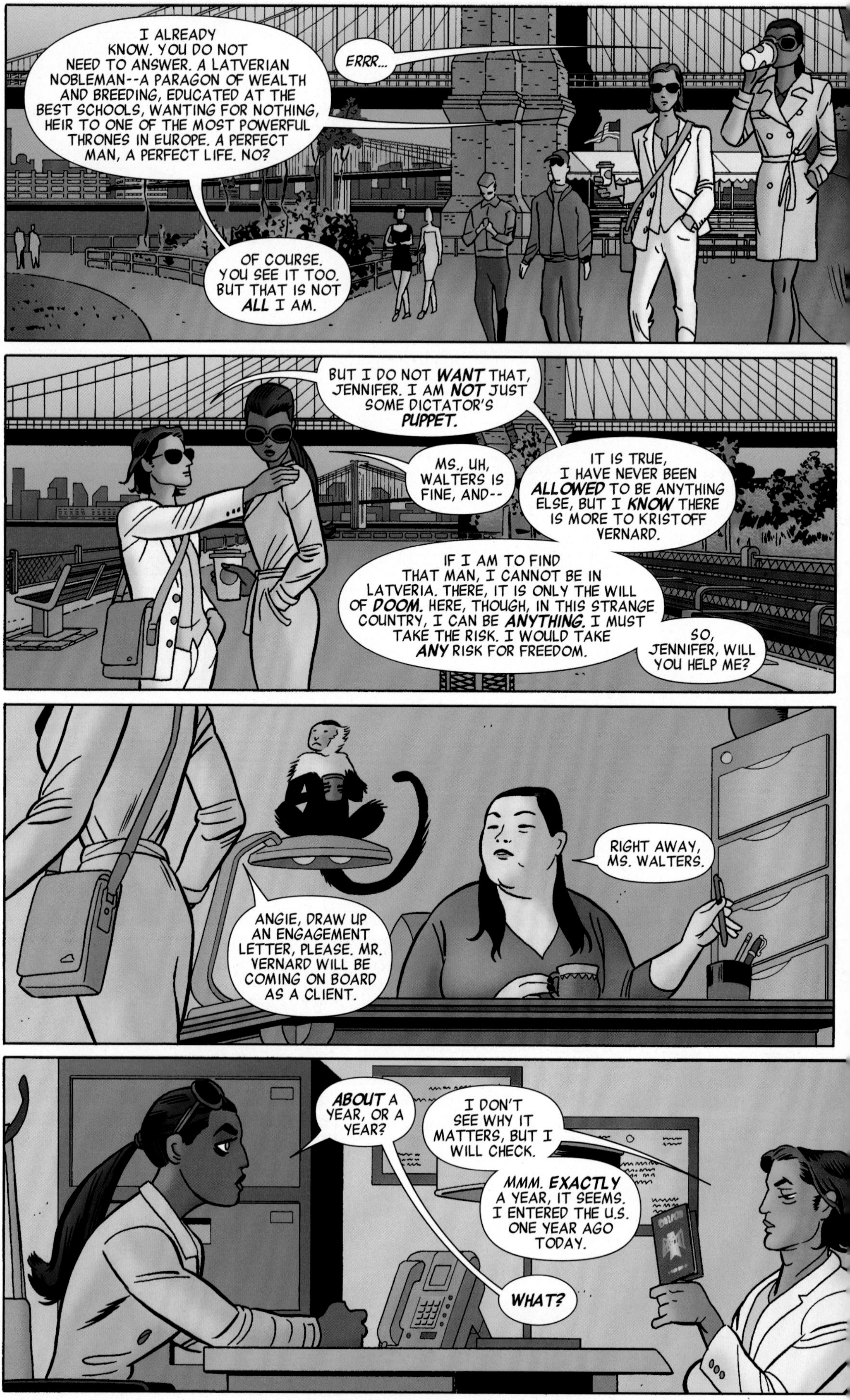
I ALREADY KNOW. YOU DO NOT NEED TO ANSWER. A LATVERIAN NOBLEMAN--A PARAGON OF WEALTH AND BREEDING, EDUCATED AT THE BEST SCHOOLS, WANTING FOR NOTHING, HEIR TO ONE OF THE MOST POWERFUL THRONES IN EUROPE. A PERFECT MAN, A PERFECT LIFE. NO?
ERRR...
OF COURSE. YOU SEE IT TOO. BUT THAT IS NOT ALL I AM.
BUT I DO NOT WANT THAT, JENNIFER. I AM NOT JUST SOME DICTATOR'S PUPPET.
MS., UH, WALTERS IS FINE, AND--
IT IS TRUE, I HAVE NEVER BEEN ALLOWED TO BE ANYTHING ELSE, BUT I KNOW THERE IS MORE TO KRISTOFF VERNARD.
IF I AM TO FIND THAT MAN, I CANNOT BE IN LATVERIA. THERE, IT IS ONLY THE WILL OF DOOM. HERE, THOUGH, IN THIS STRANGE COUNTRY, I CAN BE ANYTHING. I MUST TAKE THE RISK. I WOULD TAKE ANY RISK FOR FREEDOM.
SO, JENNIFER, WILL YOU HELP ME?
ANGIE, DRAW UP AN ENGAGEMENT LETTER, PLEASE. MR. VERNARD WILL BE COMING ON BOARD AS A CLIENT.
RIGHT AWAY, MS. WALTERS.
ABOUT A YEAR, OR A YEAR?
I DON'T SEE WHY IT MATTERS, BUT I WILL CHECK.
MMM. EXACTLY A YEAR, IT SEEMS. I ENTERED THE U.S. ONE YEAR AGO TODAY.
WHAT?

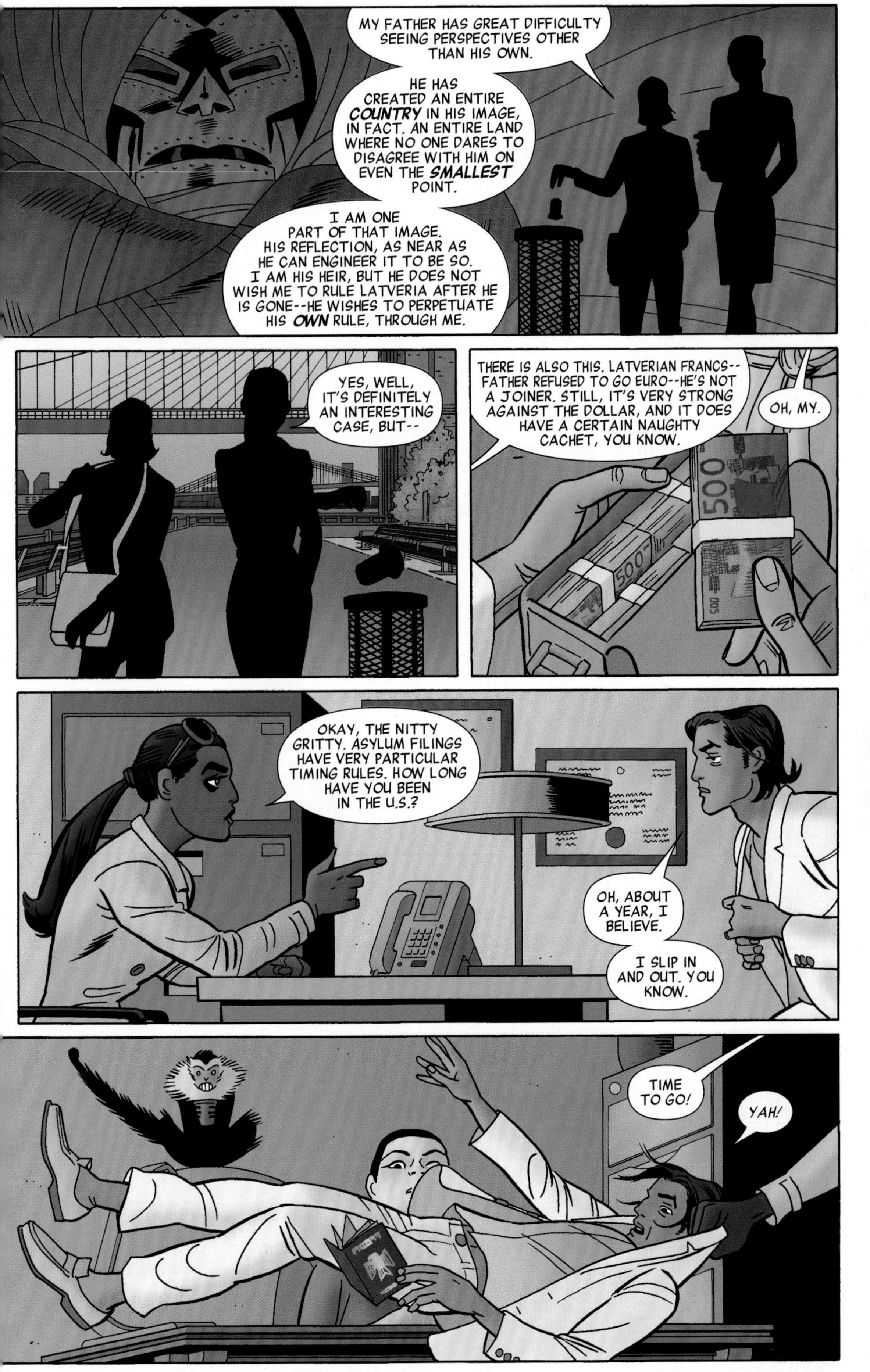
MY FATHER HAS GREAT DIFFICULTY SEEING PERSPECTIVES OTHER THAN HIS OWN.
HE HAS CREATED AN ENTIRE COUNTRY IN HIS IMAGE, IN FACT. AN ENTIRE LAND WHERE NO ONE DARES TO DISAGREE WITH HIM ON EVEN THE SMALLEST POINT.
I AM ONE PART OF THAT IMAGE. HIS REFLECTION, AS NEAR AS HE CAN ENGINEER IT TO BE SO. I AM HIS HEIR, BUT HE DOES NOT WISH ME TO RULE LATVERIA AFTER HE IS GONE--HE WISHES TO PERPETUATE HIS OWN RULE, THROUGH ME.
YES, WELL, IT'S DEFINITELY AN INTERESTING CASE, BUT--
THERE IS ALSO THIS. LATVERIAN FRANCS--FATHER REFUSED TO GO EURO--HE'S NOT A JOINER. STILL, IT'S VERY STRONG AGAINST THE DOLLAR, AND IT DOES HAVE A CERTAIN NAUGHTY CACHET, YOU KNOW.
OH, MY.
500
OKAY, THE NITTY GRITTY. ASYLUM FILINGS HAVE VERY PARTICULAR TIMING RULES. HOW LONG HAVE YOU BEEN IN THE U.S.?
OH, ABOUT A YEAR, I BELIEVE.
I SLIP IN AND OUT. YOU KNOW.
TIME TO GO!
YAH!

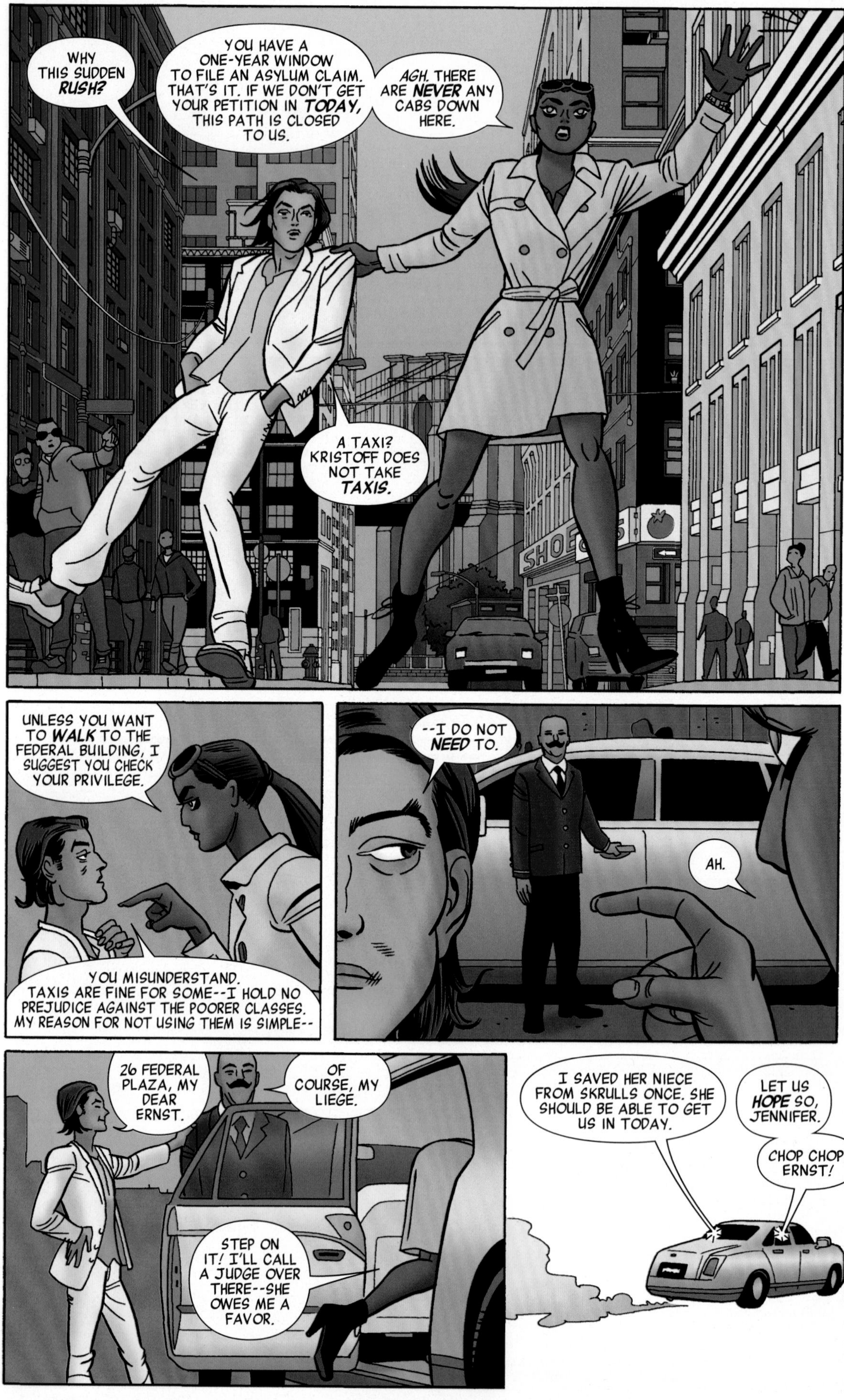
WHY THIS SUDDEN RUSH?
YOU HAVE A ONE-YEAR WINDOW TO FILE AN ASYLUM CLAIM. THAT'S IT. IF WE DON'T GET YOUR PETITION IN TODAY, THIS PATH IS CLOSED TO US.
AGH. THERE ARE NEVER ANY CABS DOWN HERE.
A TAXI? KRISTOFF DOES NOT TAKE TAXIS.
SHOE
UNLESS YOU WANT TO WALK TO THE FEDERAL BUILDING, I SUGGEST YOU CHECK YOUR PRIVILEGE.
YOU MISUNDERSTAND. TAXIS ARE FINE FOR SOME--I HOLD NO PREJUDICE AGAINST THE POORER CLASSES. MY REASON FOR NOT USING THEM IS SIMPLE--
--I DO NOT NEED TO.
AH.
26 FEDERAL PLAZA, MY DEAR ERNST.
OF COURSE, MY LIEGE.
STEP ON IT! I'LL CALL A JUDGE OVER THERE--SHE OWES ME A FAVOR.
I SAVED HER NIECE FROM SKRULLS ONCE. SHE SHOULD BE ABLE TO GET US IN TODAY.
LET US HOPE SO, JENNIFER.
CHOP CHOP, ERNST!

THANK YOU, JUDGE. WE SHOULD BE THERE IN ABOUT TEN MINUTES. I CAN'T TELL YOU HOW MUCH I APPRECIATE THIS.

OH YES, DARLING. I JUST HAVE A BIT OF BUSINESS TO ATTEND TO, AND THEN PERHAPS LE BAIN TO START? I COULD DO WITH A TOUCH OF THROB THIS EVENING.

YES. ASYLUM APPLICATION. APPLICANT'S NAME IS KRISTOFF VERNARD.

IT IS A BIT TIRED, BUT I DO LOVE THE VIEW, AND JUST BECAUSE WE START THERE DOESN'T MEAN WE HAVE TO END THERE.

WAIT A MINUTE.

WHAT THE HELL ARE WE DOING AT THE AIRPORT?

DO NOT ATTEMPT TO RESIST.

IT WOULD MEAN YOUR DOOM.

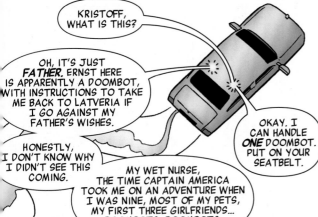

KRISTOFF, WHAT IS THIS?

OH, IT'S JUST FATHER. ERNST HERE IS APPARENTLY A DOOMBOT, WITH INSTRUCTIONS TO TAKE ME BACK TO LATVERIA IF I GO AGAINST MY FATHER'S WISHES.

HONESTLY, I DON'T KNOW WHY I DIDN'T SEE THIS COMING.

OKAY. I CAN HANDLE ONE DOOMBOT. PUT ON YOUR SEATBELT.

MY WET NURSE, THE TIME CAPTAIN AMERICA TOOK ME ON AN ADVENTURE WHEN I WAS NINE, MOST OF MY PETS, MY FIRST THREE GIRLFRIENDS... DOOMBOTS, DOOMBOTS, DOOMBOTS.

YOU CANNOT THWART THE WILL OF DOOM!

KLIK

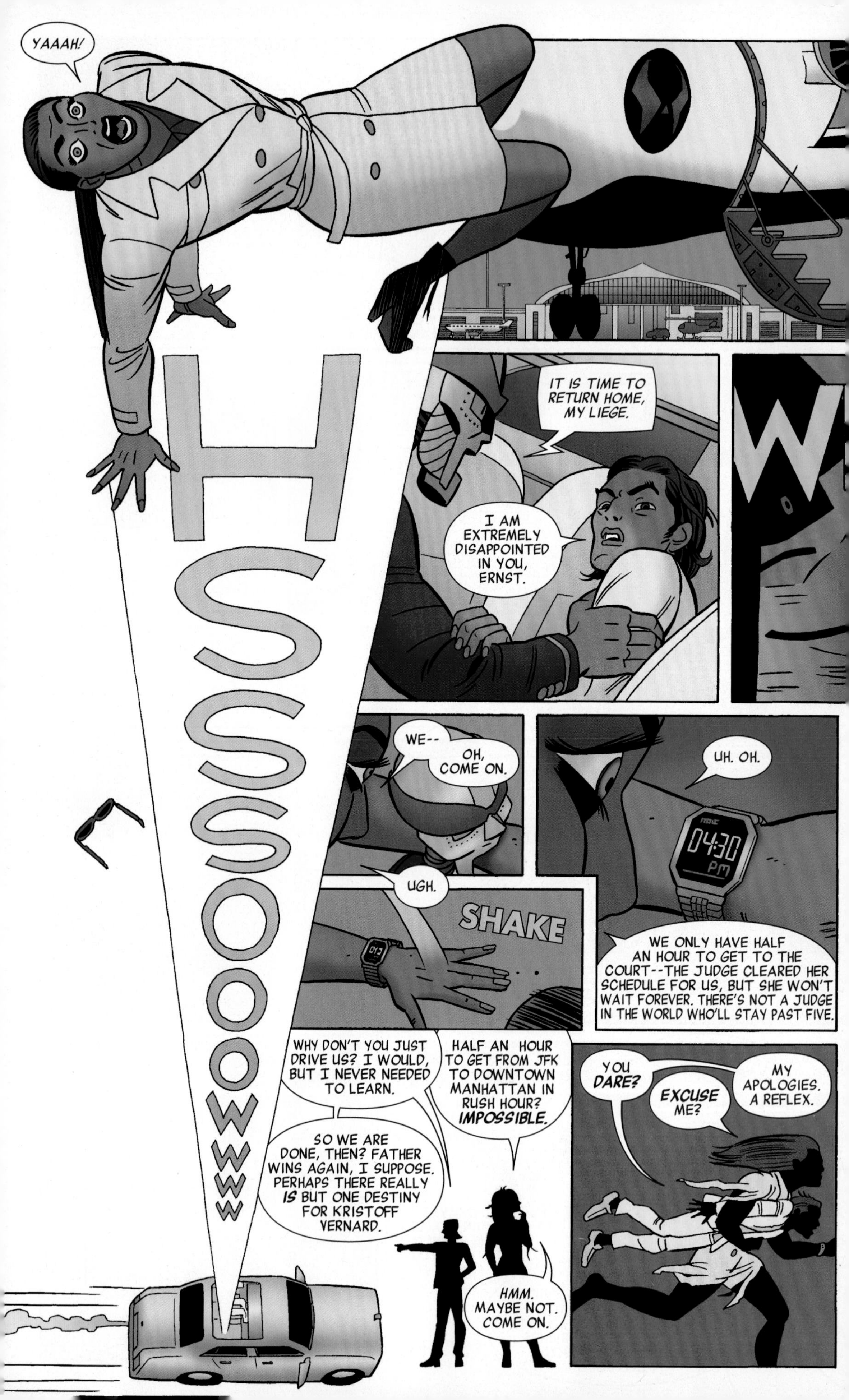
YAAAH!
HSSSSOOOOOWWWW
IT IS TIME TO RETURN HOME, MY LIEGE.
I AM EXTREMELY DISAPPOINTED IN YOU, ERNST.
WE-- OH, COME ON.
UH. OH.
UGH.
SHAKE
WE ONLY HAVE HALF AN HOUR TO GET TO THE COURT--THE JUDGE CLEARED HER SCHEDULE FOR US, BUT SHE WON'T WAIT FOREVER. THERE'S NOT A JUDGE IN THE WORLD WHO'LL STAY PAST FIVE.
WHY DON'T YOU JUST DRIVE US? I WOULD, BUT I NEVER NEEDED TO LEARN.
HALF AN HOUR TO GET FROM JFK TO DOWNTOWN MANHATTAN IN RUSH HOUR? IMPOSSIBLE.
SO WE ARE DONE, THEN? FATHER WINS AGAIN, I SUPPOSE. PERHAPS THERE REALLY IS BUT ONE DESTINY FOR KRISTOFF VERNARD.
HMM. MAYBE NOT. COME ON.
YOU DARE?
EXCUSE ME?
MY APOLOGIES. A REFLEX.

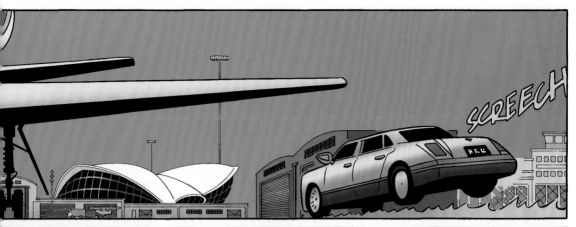

YOU OKAY?

OF COURSE. NO DOOMBOT WOULD *DARE* HARM ME.

SNAP

RRGH!

I *KNEW* THIS WAS OUT HERE!

GOODNESS.

WHOOO!

YAAAAH!

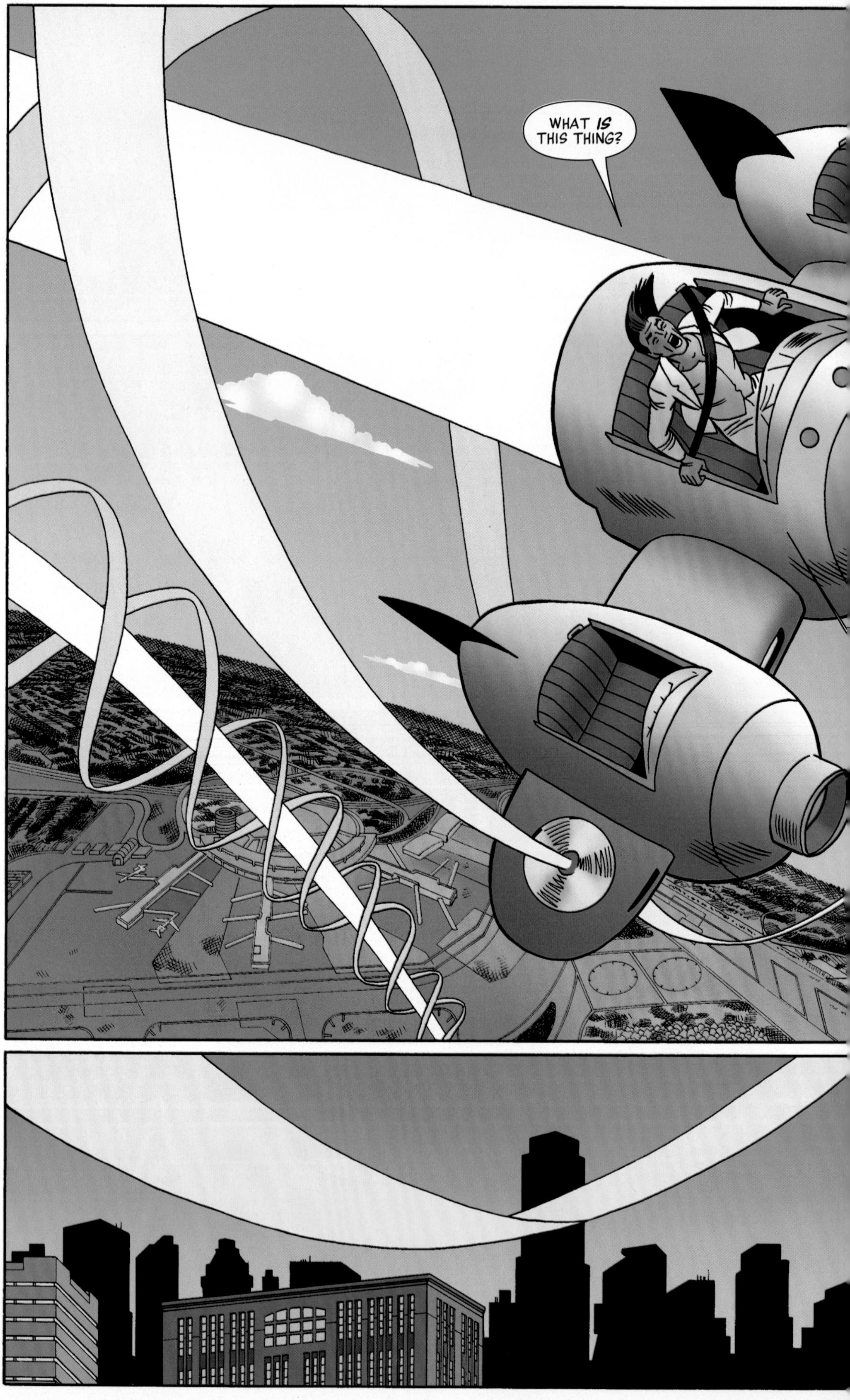
WHAT IS THIS THING?

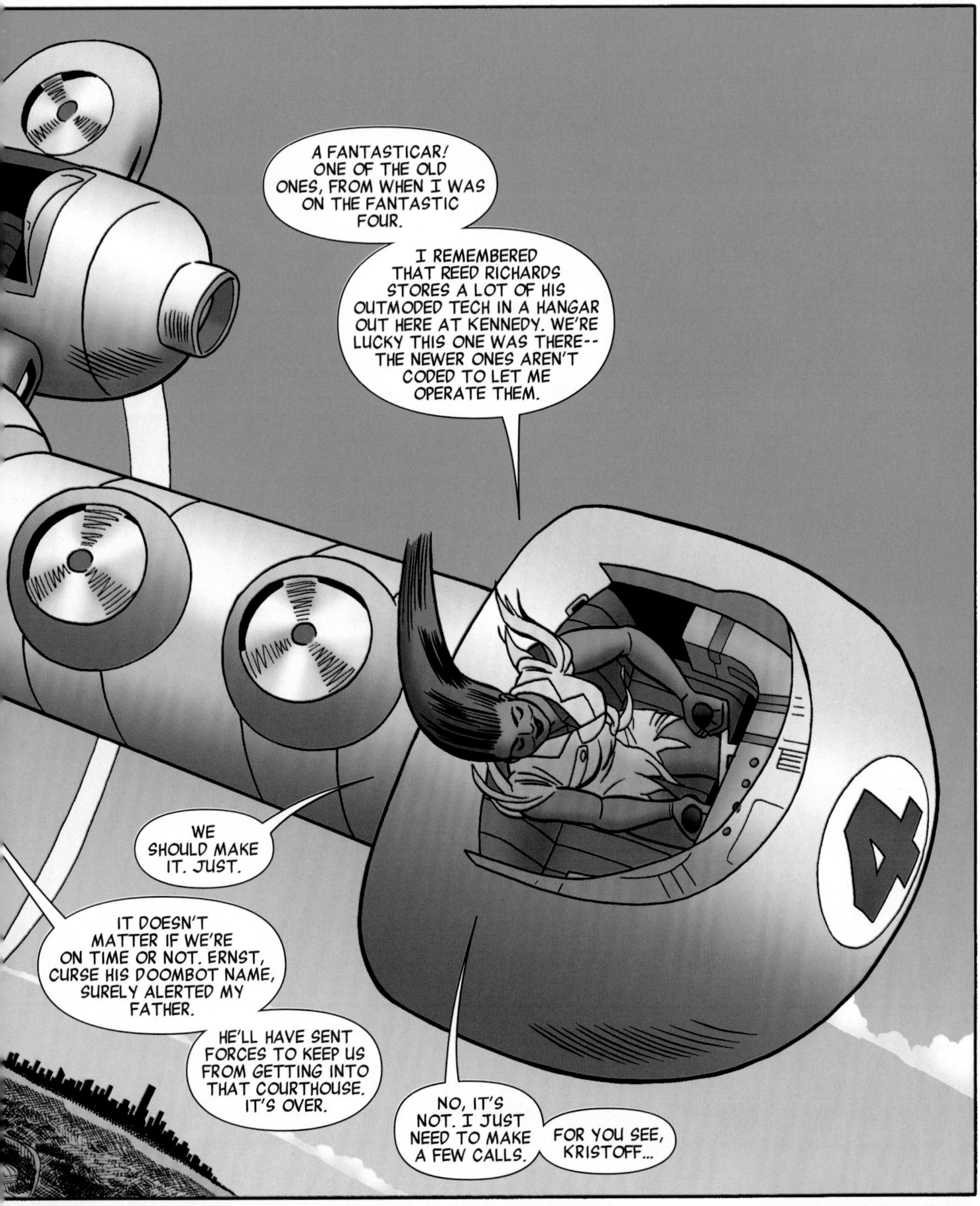
A FANTASTICAR! ONE OF THE OLD ONES, FROM WHEN I WAS ON THE FANTASTIC FOUR.
I REMEMBERED THAT REED RICHARDS STORES A LOT OF HIS OUTMODED TECH IN A HANGAR OUT HERE AT KENNEDY. WE'RE LUCKY THIS ONE WAS THERE-- THE NEWER ONES AREN'T CODED TO LET ME OPERATE THEM.
WE SHOULD MAKE IT. JUST.
IT DOESN'T MATTER IF WE'RE ON TIME OR NOT. ERNST, CURSE HIS DOOMBOT NAME, SURELY ALERTED MY FATHER.
HE'LL HAVE SENT FORCES TO KEEP US FROM GETTING INTO THAT COURTHOUSE. IT'S OVER.
NO, IT'S NOT. I JUST NEED TO MAKE A FEW CALLS.
FOR YOU SEE, KRISTOFF...

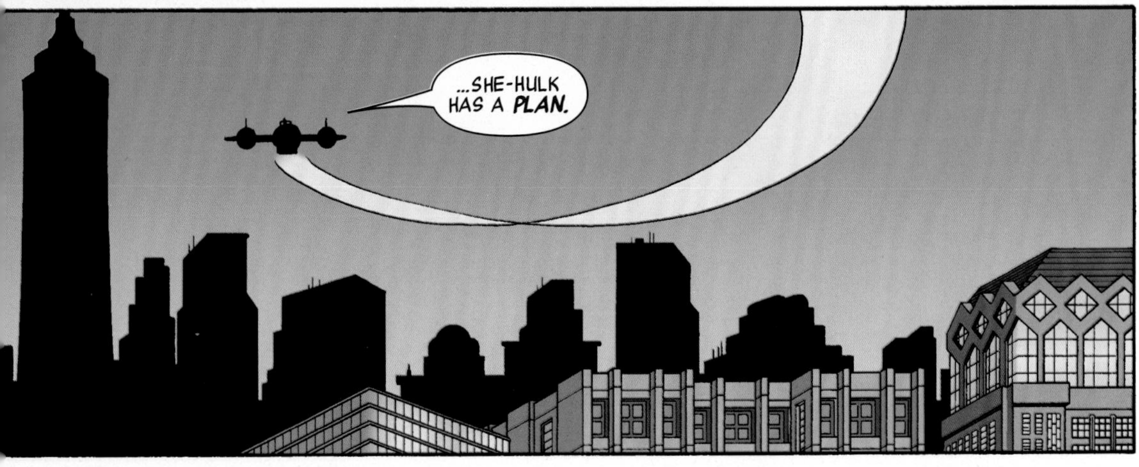
...SHE-HULK HAS A PLAN.

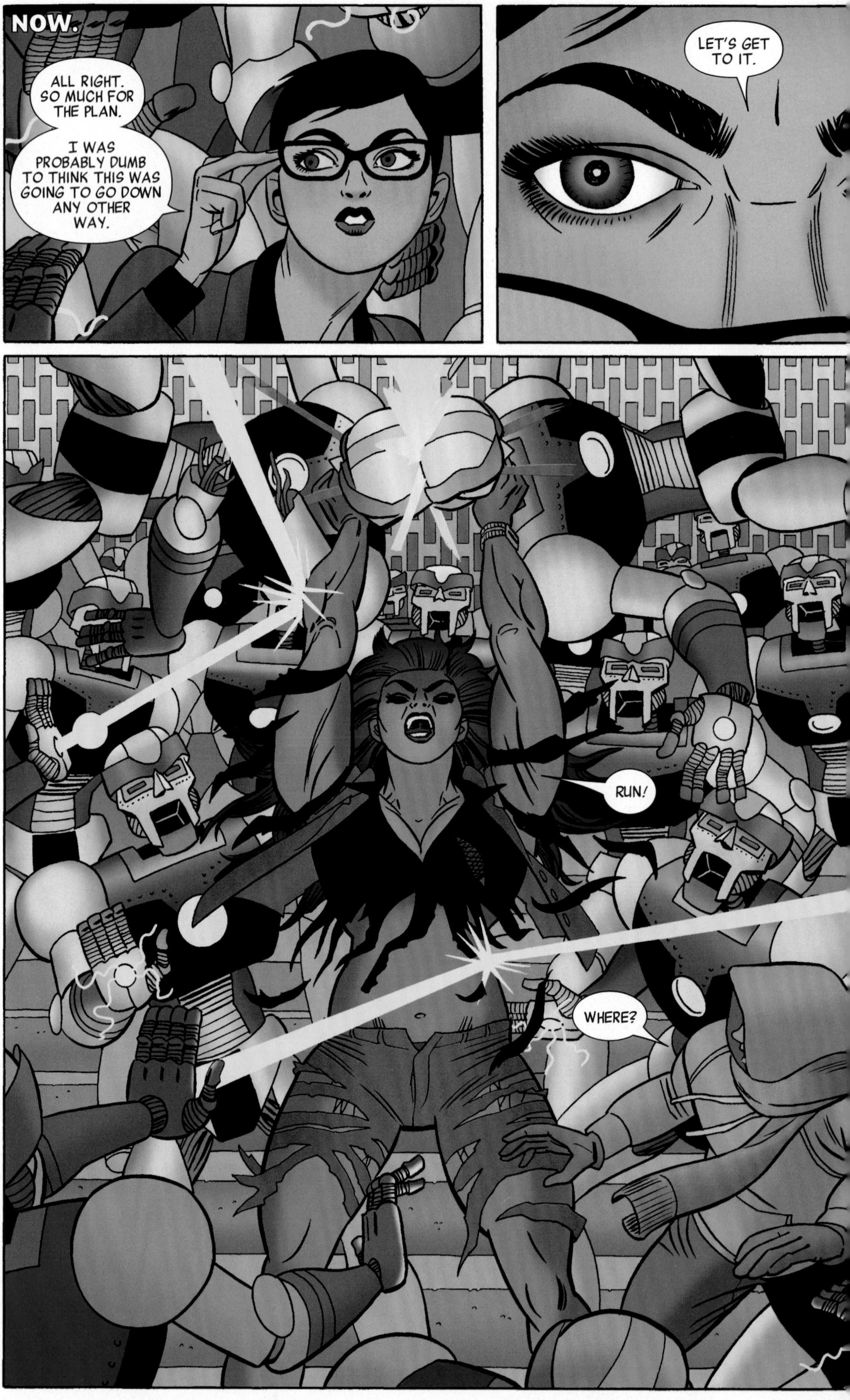
NOW.
ALL RIGHT. SO MUCH FOR THE PLAN.
I WAS PROBABLY DUMB TO THINK THIS WAS GOING TO GO DOWN ANY OTHER WAY.
LET'S GET TO IT.
RUN!
WHERE?

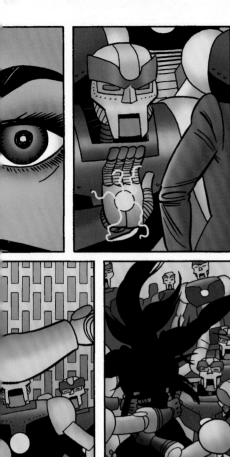

ANYWHERE!

OKAY!

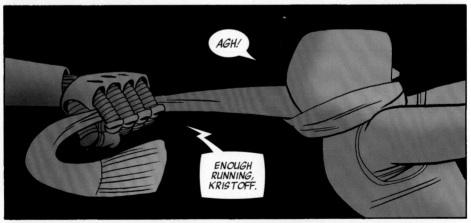

AGH!

ENOUGH RUNNING, KRISTOFF.

SHHHP

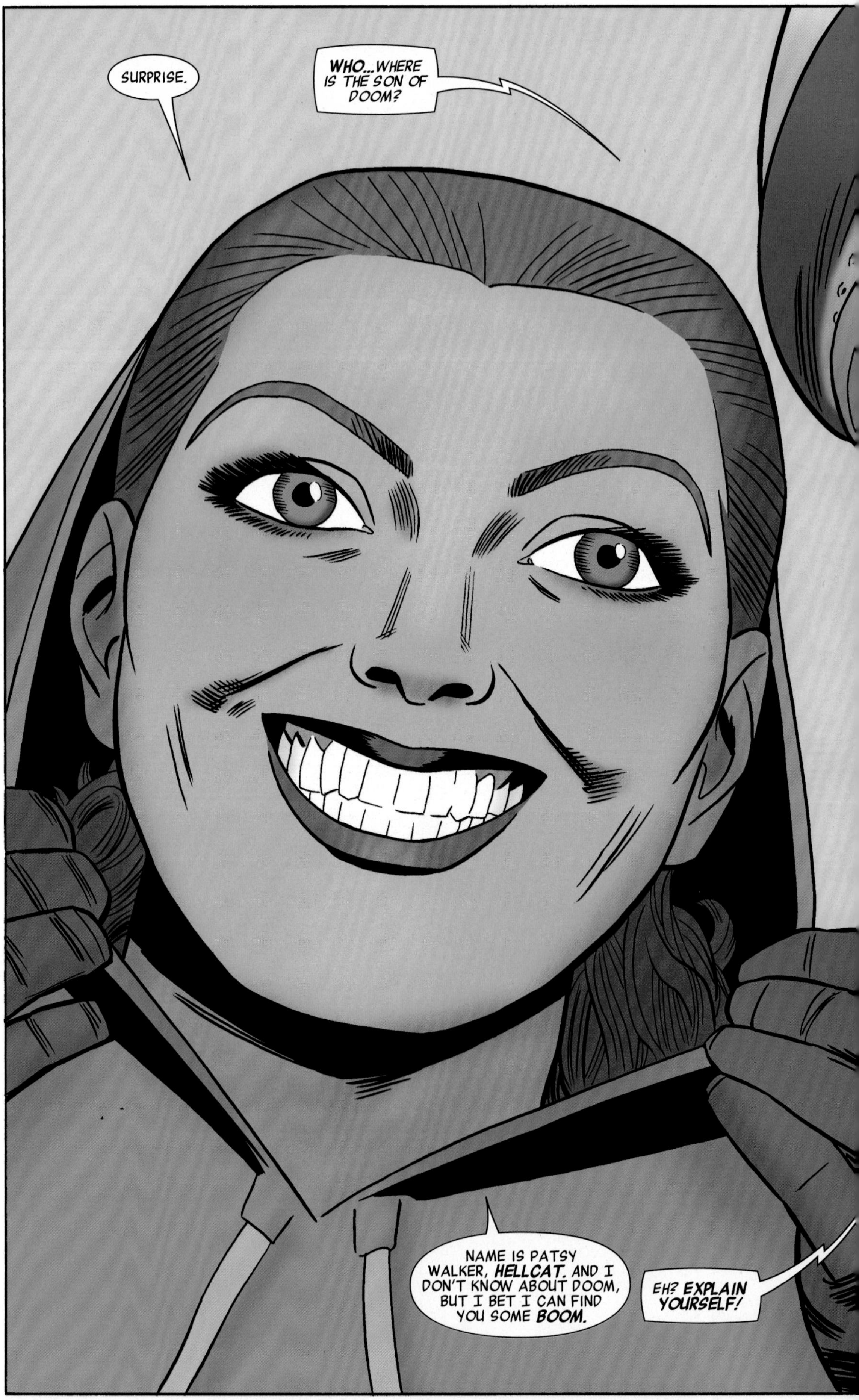
SURPRISE.
WHO... WHERE IS THE SON OF DOOM?
NAME IS PATSY WALKER, HELLCAT. AND I DON'T KNOW ABOUT DOOM, BUT I BET I CAN FIND YOU SOME BOOM.
EH? EXPLAIN YOURSELF!

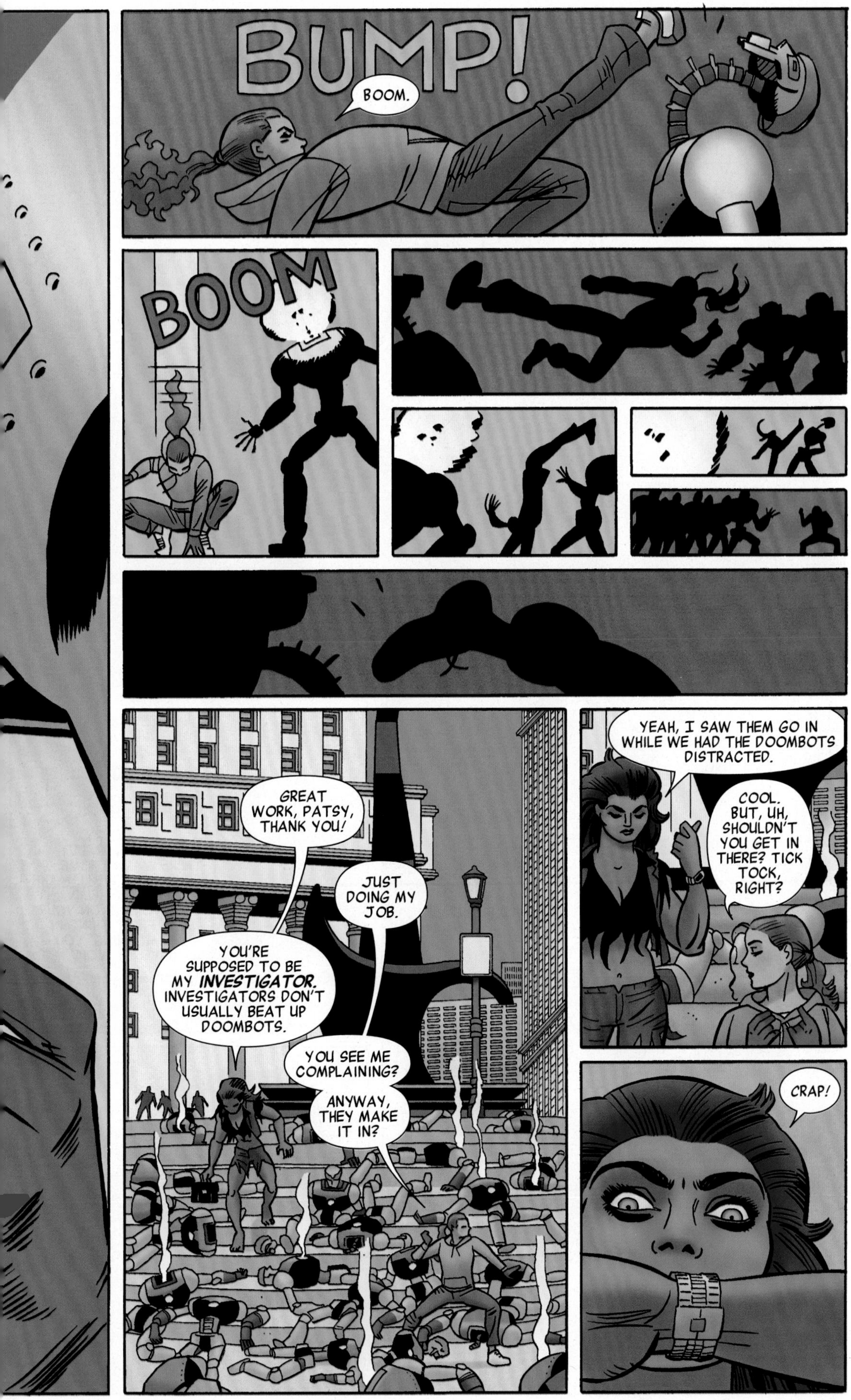
BUMP!
BOOM.
BOOM
GREAT WORK, PATSY, THANK YOU!
JUST DOING MY JOB.
YOU'RE SUPPOSED TO BE MY INVESTIGATOR. INVESTIGATORS DON'T USUALLY BEAT UP DOOMBOTS.
YOU SEE ME COMPLAINING?
ANYWAY, THEY MAKE IT IN?
YEAH, I SAW THEM GO IN WHILE WE HAD THE DOOMBOTS DISTRACTED.
COOL. BUT, UH, SHOULDN'T YOU GET IN THERE? TICK TOCK, RIGHT?
CRAP!

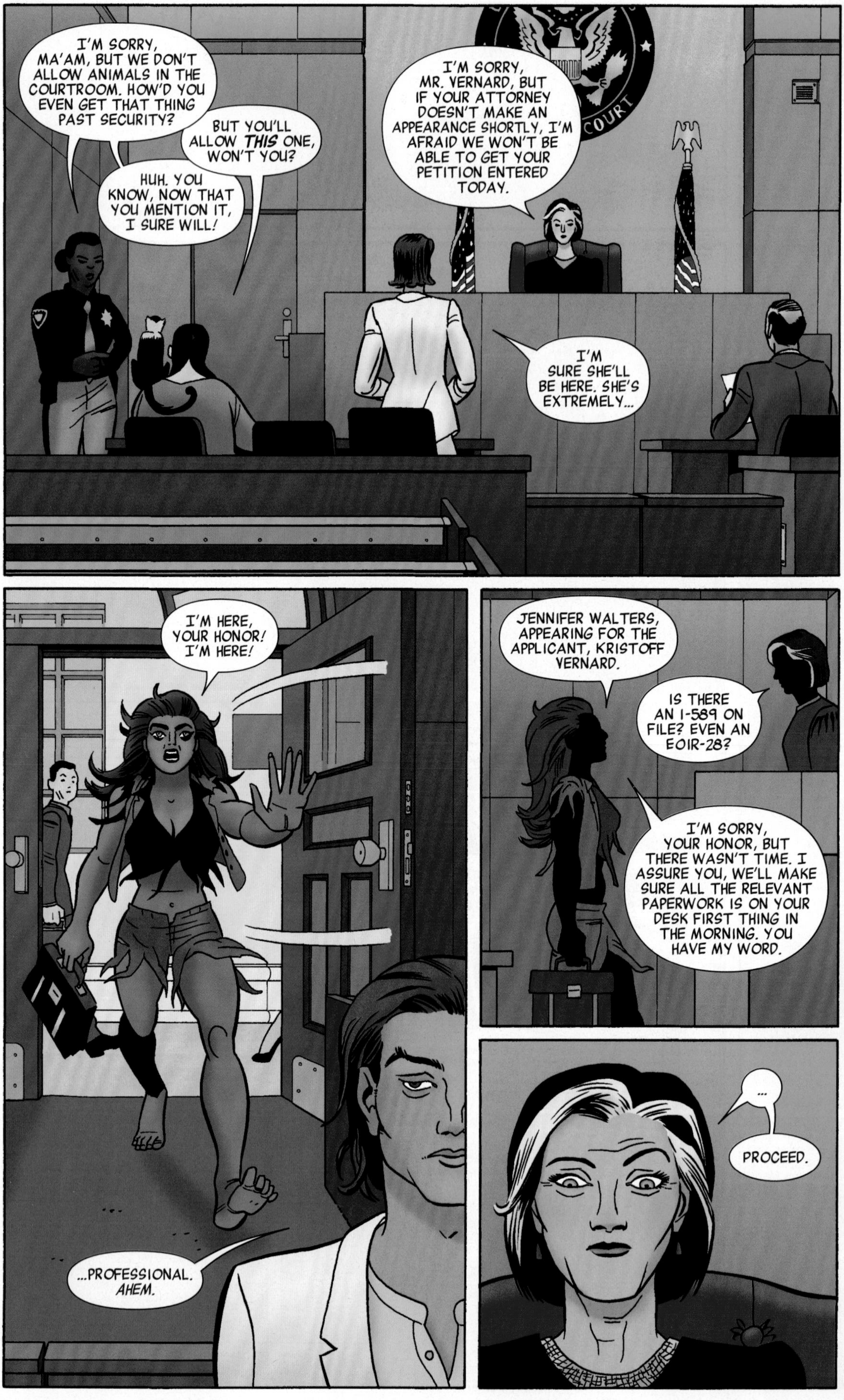
I'M SORRY, MA'AM, BUT WE DON'T ALLOW ANIMALS IN THE COURTROOM. HOW'D YOU EVEN GET THAT THING PAST SECURITY?
BUT YOU'LL ALLOW ***THIS*** ONE, WON'T YOU?
HUH. YOU KNOW, NOW THAT YOU MENTION IT, I SURE WILL!
I'M SORRY, MR. VERNARD, BUT IF YOUR ATTORNEY DOESN'T MAKE AN APPEARANCE SHORTLY, I'M AFRAID WE WON'T BE ABLE TO GET YOUR PETITION ENTERED TODAY.
I'M SURE SHE'LL BE HERE. SHE'S EXTREMELY...
I'M HERE, YOUR HONOR! I'M HERE!
...PROFESSIONAL. *AHEM.*
JENNIFER WALTERS, APPEARING FOR THE APPLICANT, KRISTOFF VERNARD.
IS THERE AN I-589 ON FILE? EVEN AN EOIR-28?
I'M SORRY, YOUR HONOR, BUT THERE WASN'T TIME. I ASSURE YOU, WE'LL MAKE SURE ALL THE RELEVANT PAPERWORK IS ON YOUR DESK FIRST THING IN THE MORNING. YOU HAVE MY WORD.
...
PROCEED.

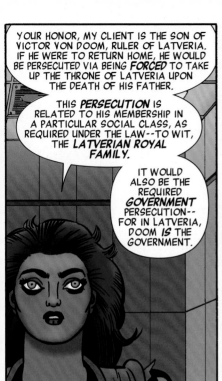

YOUR HONOR, MY CLIENT IS THE SON OF VICTOR VON DOOM, RULER OF LATVERIA. IF HE WERE TO RETURN HOME, HE WOULD BE PERSECUTED VIA BEING *FORCED* TO TAKE UP THE THRONE OF LATVERIA UPON THE DEATH OF HIS FATHER.

THIS *PERSECUTION* IS RELATED TO HIS MEMBERSHIP IN A PARTICULAR SOCIAL CLASS, AS REQUIRED UNDER THE LAW--TO WIT, THE *LATVERIAN ROYAL FAMILY.*

IT WOULD ALSO BE THE REQUIRED *GOVERNMENT* PERSECUTION-- FOR IN LATVERIA, DOOM *IS* THE GOVERNMENT.

I SUBMIT THAT MR. VERNARD MEETS ALL REQUIREMENTS FOR A FAVORABLE EXERCISE OF JUDICIAL DISCRETION, AND SHOULD BE GRANTED *POLITICAL ASYLUM* IN THE UNITED STATES.

I SEE. THERE IS ONE THING I DO NOT UNDERSTAND.

MR. VERNARD, HOW CAN BEING ASKED TO RULE A NATION BE CONSIDERED PERSECUTION?

WHEN YOU DO NOT WISH TO RULE, YOUR HONOR.

WHEN YOU ARE GIVEN NO CHOICE. HE MIGHT AS WELL BE CONDEMNING ME TO PRISON.

HMM.

DOES THE GOVERNMENT HAVE ANY OBJECTIONS?

HEY, THE GUY HAD TO GET PAST A PILE OF KILLER ROBOTS OUTSIDE THE COURTHOUSE--ONES *SENT BY HIS DAD*--JUST TO GET HERE TO MAKE HIS CLAIM. NO OBJECTIONS HERE. I'M GOOD.

AS AM I. ASYLUM GRANTED.

KA-THOOOM

HUH?

OH, DEAR.

ENOUGH OF THIS FARCE!

OH. HELLO, FATHER.

WE CAN FIGHT HIM! YOU DON'T HAVE TO GO--

OF COURSE I DO, JENNIFER. THERE *IS* NO KRISTOFF VERNARD. NOT REALLY. THERE IS ONLY DOOM.

BUT THANK YOU. YOU DID YOUR BEST.

HA!

YOU, CHILD, ARE A *GRAVE* DISAPPOINTMENT.

IT'S MY SUPER-POWER, FATHER.

YOU, LAWYER, SHOULD *DIE* TODAY FOR YOUR TRANSGRESSIONS AGAINST THE WILL OF DOOM.

THIS IS *WRONG.* I WON'T LET YOU-- I'LL *COME* FOR HIM--

...

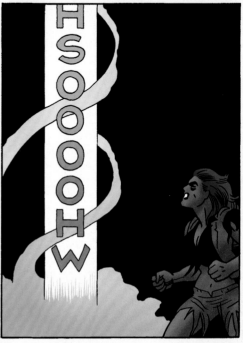

HSOOOHW

NEXT: THE ZEALOUS ADVOCATE!

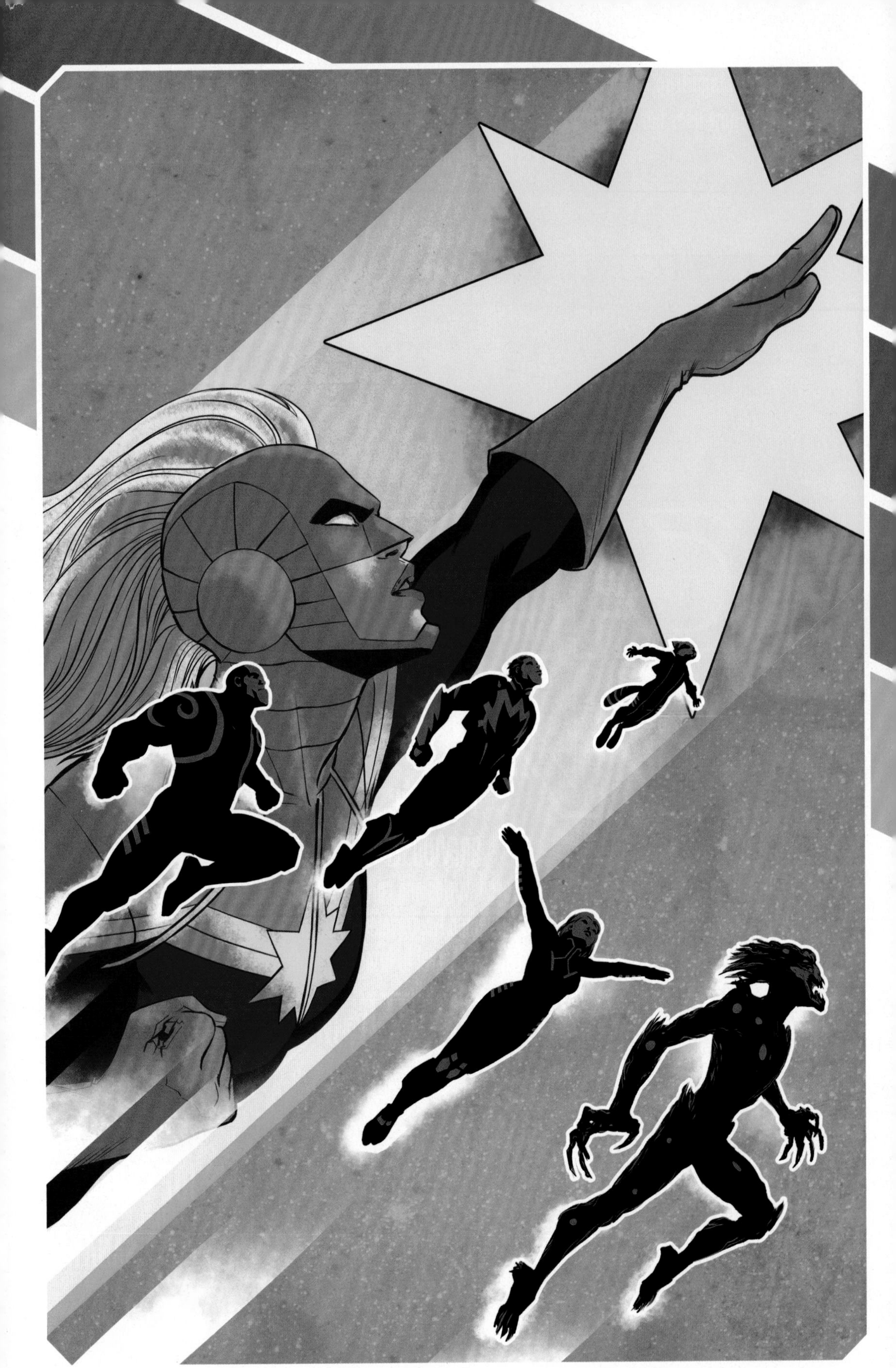

CAPTAIN MARVEL #3

When former U.S. Air Force pilot Carol Danvers was caught in the explosion of an alien device called the Psyche-Magnitron, she was transformed into one of the world's most powerful super beings. She now uses her abilities to protect her planet and fight for justice as an Avenger.
She is Earth's Mightiest Hero...she is...

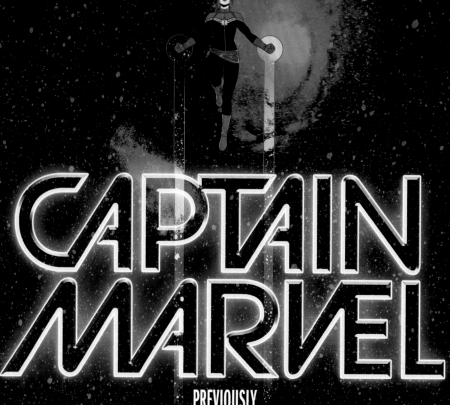

CAPTAIN MARVEL

PREVIOUSLY

When The Builders left a trail of destroyed worlds and cultures in their wake, many refugees were relocated to Torfa, a poisonous planet. One, named Tic, traveled to Earth seeking the help of the Avengers. It fell to Captain Marvel to bring her home.

HIGHER, FURTHER, FASTER, MORE. PART THREE

KELLY SUE DeCONNICK
WRITER

DAVID LOPEZ
ART

LEE LOUGHRIDGE
COLOR ART

VC'S JOE CARAMAGNA
LETTERER

DAVID LOPEZ
COVER ARTIST

ARTHUR ADAMS & PETER STEIGERWALD
VARIANT COVER ARTISTS

DEVIN LEWIS
ASSISTANT EDITOR

SANA AMANA
EDITOR

NICK LOWE
SENIOR EDITOR

AXEL ALONSO
EDITOR IN CHIEF

JOE QUESADA
CHIEF CREATIVE OFFICER

DAN BUCKLEY
PUBLISHER

ALAN FINE
EXEC. PRODUCER

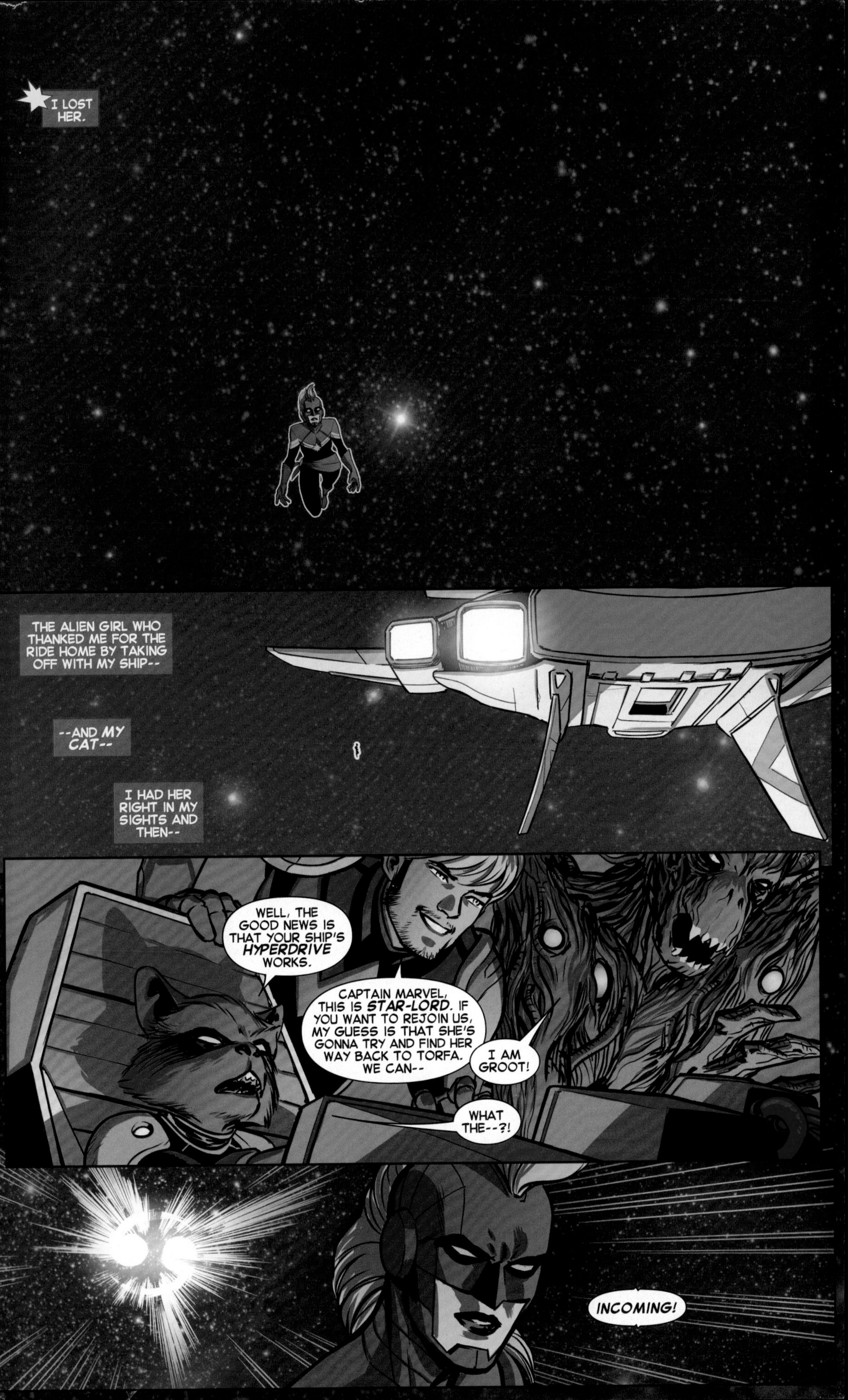

I LOST HER.
THE ALIEN GIRL WHO THANKED ME FOR THE RIDE HOME BY TAKING OFF WITH MY SHIP--
--AND MY CAT--
I HAD HER RIGHT IN MY SIGHTS AND THEN--
WELL, THE GOOD NEWS IS THAT YOUR SHIP'S HYPERDRIVE WORKS.
CAPTAIN MARVEL, THIS IS STAR-LORD. IF YOU WANT TO REJOIN US, MY GUESS IS THAT SHE'S GONNA TRY AND FIND HER WAY BACK TO TORFA. WE CAN--
I AM GROOT!
WHAT THE--?!
INCOMING!

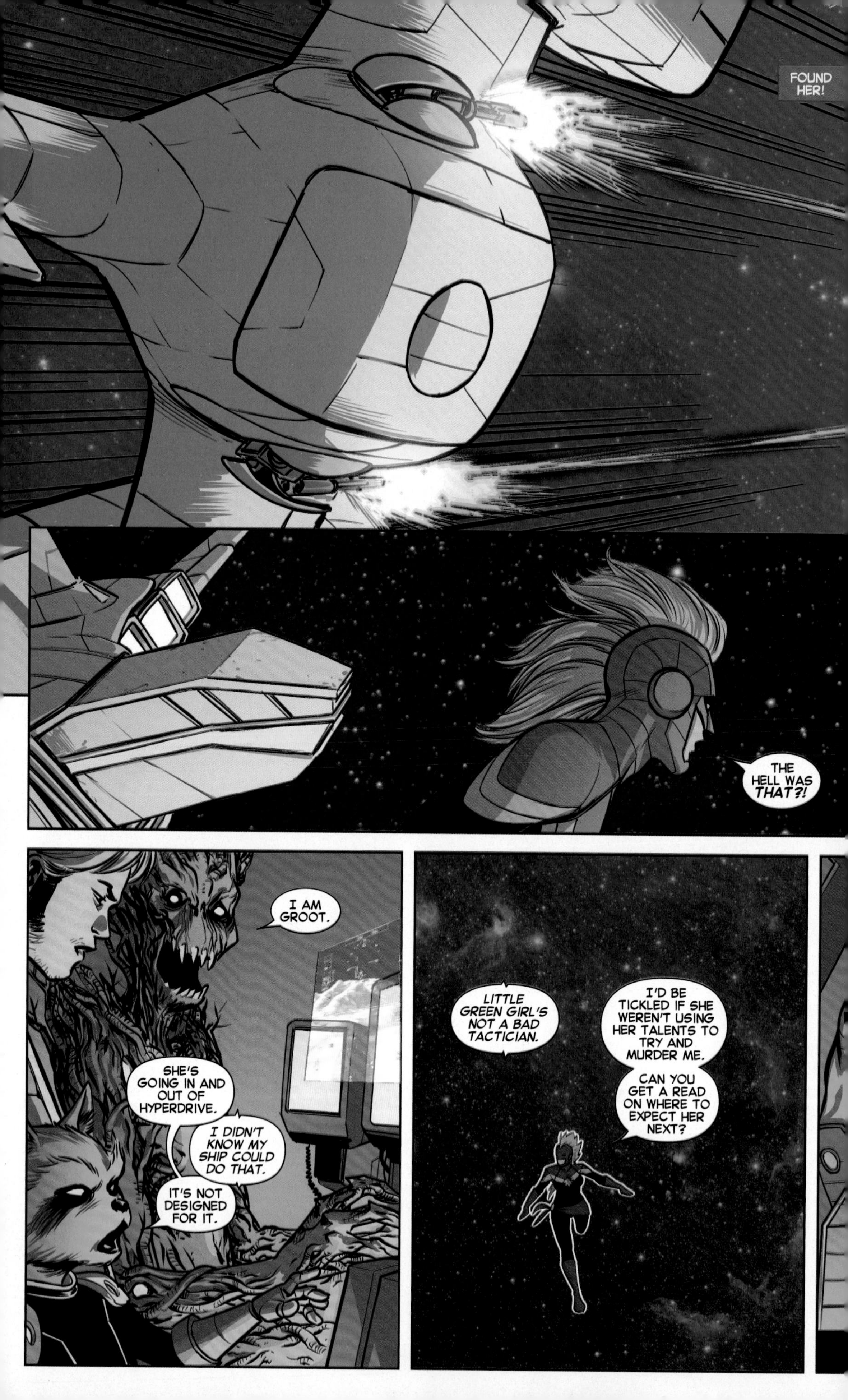
FOUND HER!
THE HELL WAS THAT?!
I AM GROOT.
SHE'S GOING IN AND OUT OF HYPERDRIVE.
I DIDN'T KNOW MY SHIP COULD DO THAT.
IT'S NOT DESIGNED FOR IT.
LITTLE GREEN GIRL'S NOT A BAD TACTICIAN.
I'D BE TICKLED IF SHE WEREN'T USING HER TALENTS TO TRY AND MURDER ME.
CAN YOU GET A READ ON WHERE TO EXPECT HER NEXT?

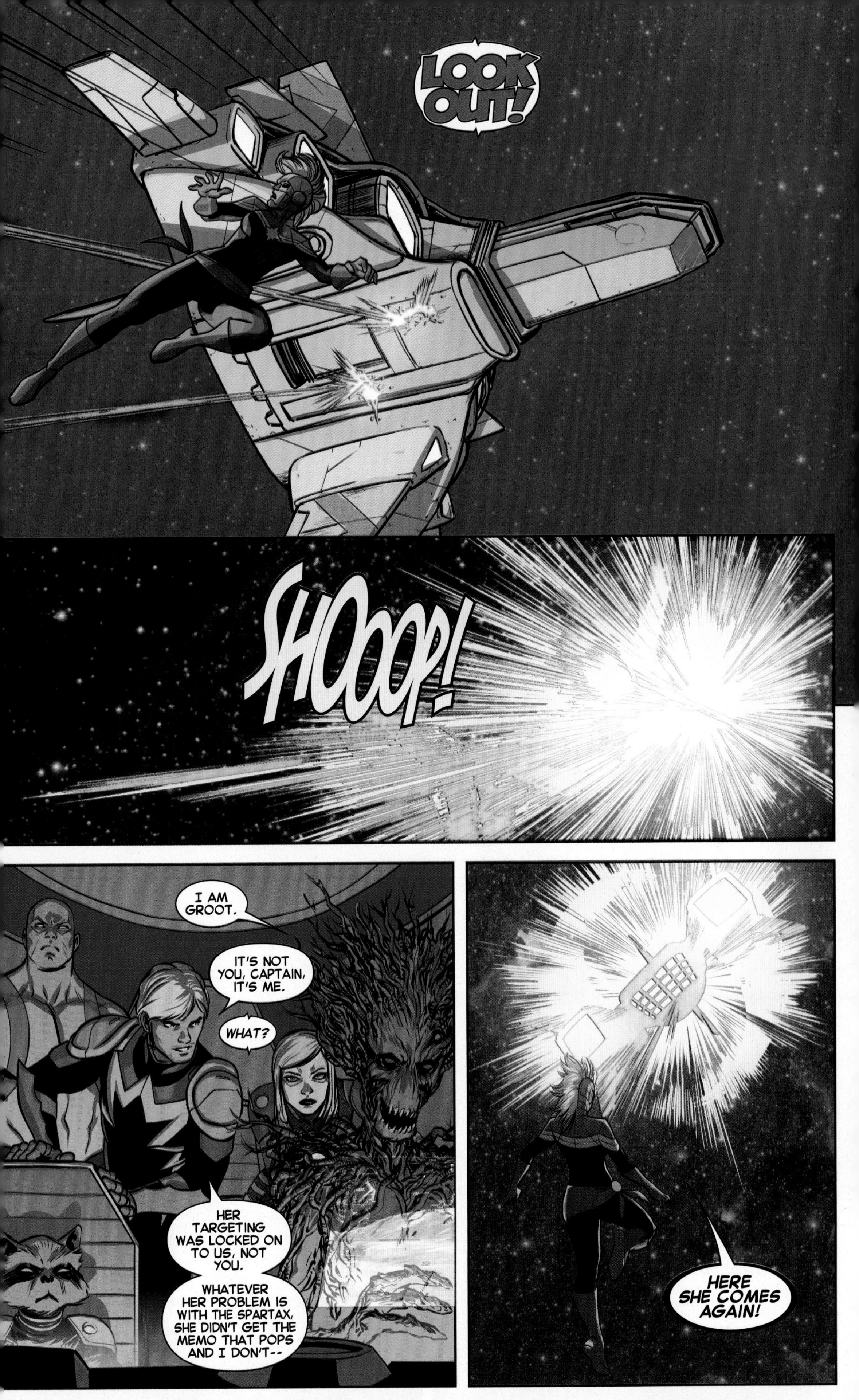
LOOK OUT!
SHOOOP!
I AM GROOT.
IT'S NOT YOU, CAPTAIN, IT'S ME.
WHAT?
HER TARGETING WAS LOCKED ON TO US, NOT YOU.
WHATEVER HER PROBLEM IS WITH THE SPARTAX, SHE DIDN'T GET THE MEMO THAT POPS AND I DON'T--
HERE SHE COMES AGAIN!

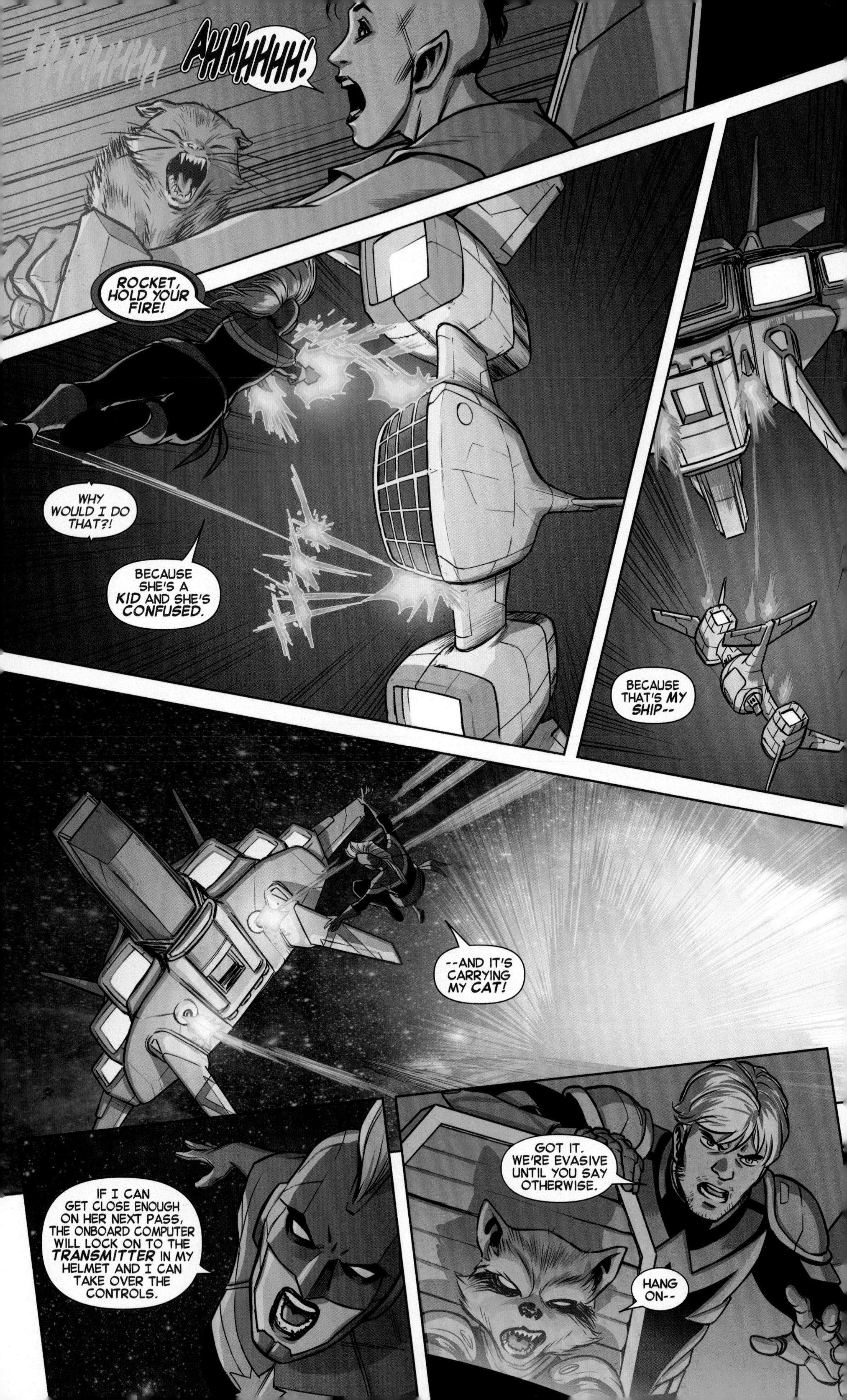
AHHHHHHH
AHHHHHHH!
ROCKET, HOLD YOUR FIRE!
WHY WOULD I DO THAT?!
BECAUSE SHE'S A KID AND SHE'S CONFUSED.
BECAUSE THAT'S MY SHIP--
--AND IT'S CARRYING MY CAT!
IF I CAN GET CLOSE ENOUGH ON HER NEXT PASS, THE ONBOARD COMPUTER WILL LOCK ON TO THE TRANSMITTER IN MY HELMET AND I CAN TAKE OVER THE CONTROLS.
GOT IT. WE'RE EVASIVE UNTIL YOU SAY OTHERWISE.
HANG ON--

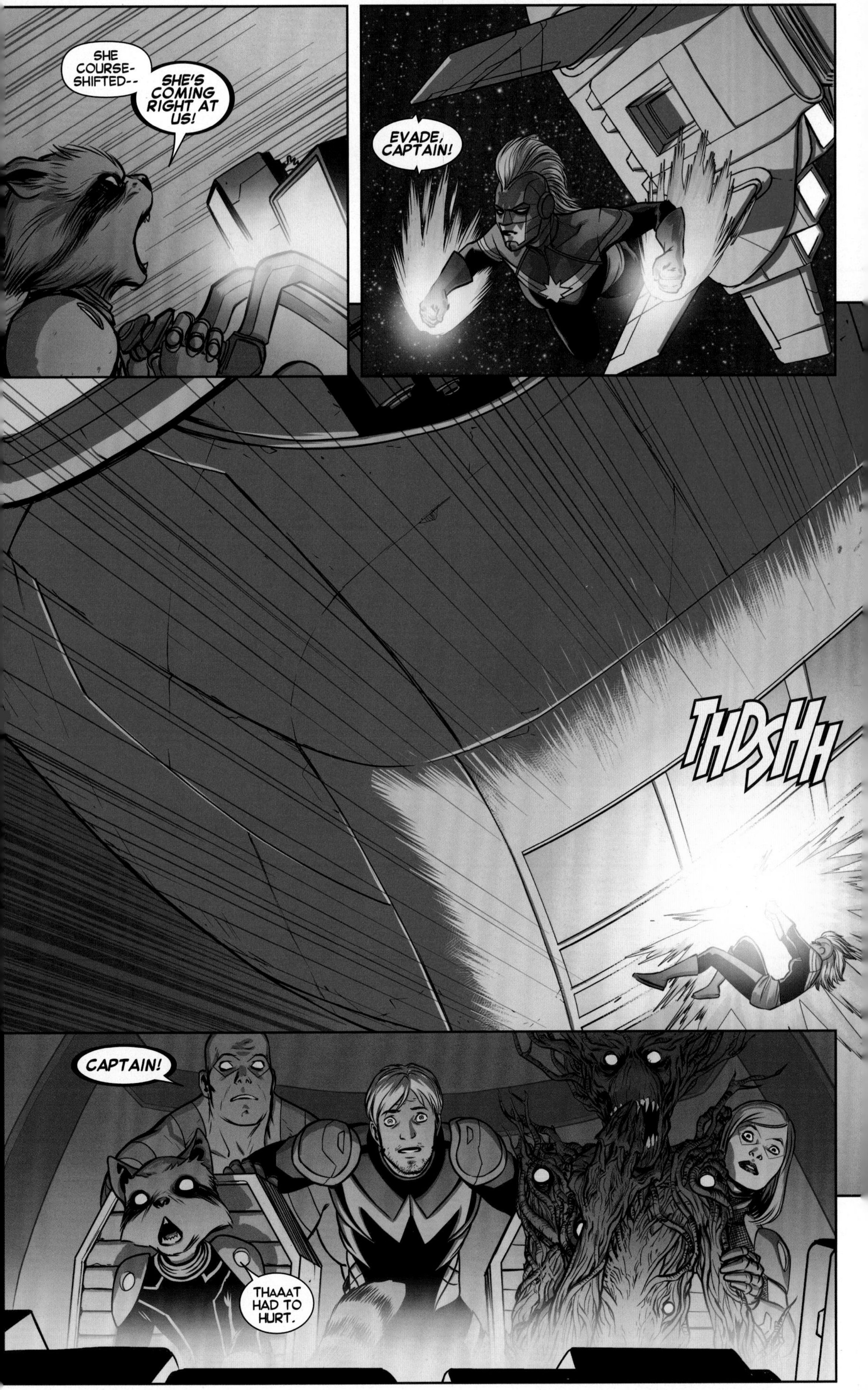
SHE COURSE-SHIFTED--
SHE'S COMING RIGHT AT US!
EVADE, CAPTAIN!
THDSHH
CAPTAIN!
THAAAT HAD TO HURT.

WHERE'D SHE GO? I LOST HER TRAJECTORY AFTER THE HIT...!
CAPTAIN, WHERE ARE YOU? DO YOU COPY?
NO, NO, NO, I DIDN'T MEAN TO--
WHERE IS SHE?!
PLEASE DON'T BE VAPORIZED...
PLEASE DON'T BE--
--WRITE DOWN THE DAY AND TIME YOU SAID THAT.

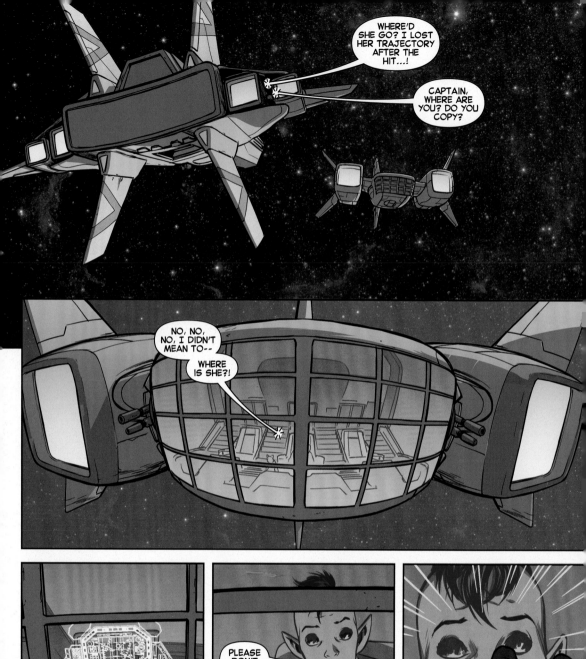

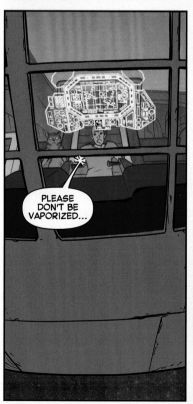

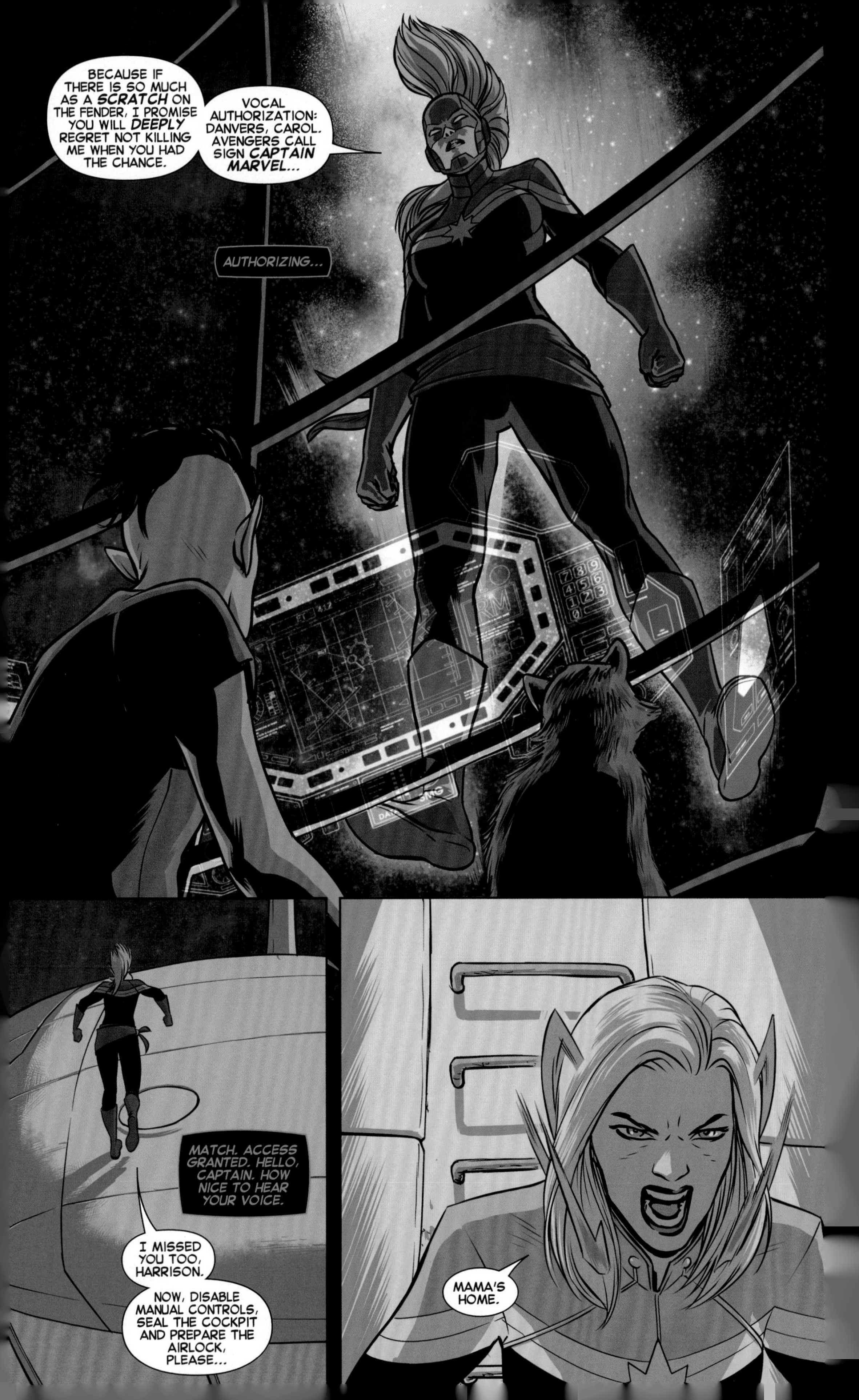
BECAUSE IF THERE IS SO MUCH AS A SCRATCH ON THE FENDER, I PROMISE YOU WILL DEEPLY REGRET NOT KILLING ME WHEN YOU HAD THE CHANCE.
VOCAL AUTHORIZATION: DANVERS, CAROL. AVENGERS CALL SIGN CAPTAIN MARVEL...
AUTHORIZING...
MATCH. ACCESS GRANTED. HELLO, CAPTAIN. HOW NICE TO HEAR YOUR VOICE.
I MISSED YOU TOO, HARRISON.
NOW, DISABLE MANUAL CONTROLS, SEAL THE COCKPIT AND PREPARE THE AIRLOCK, PLEASE...
MAMA'S HOME.

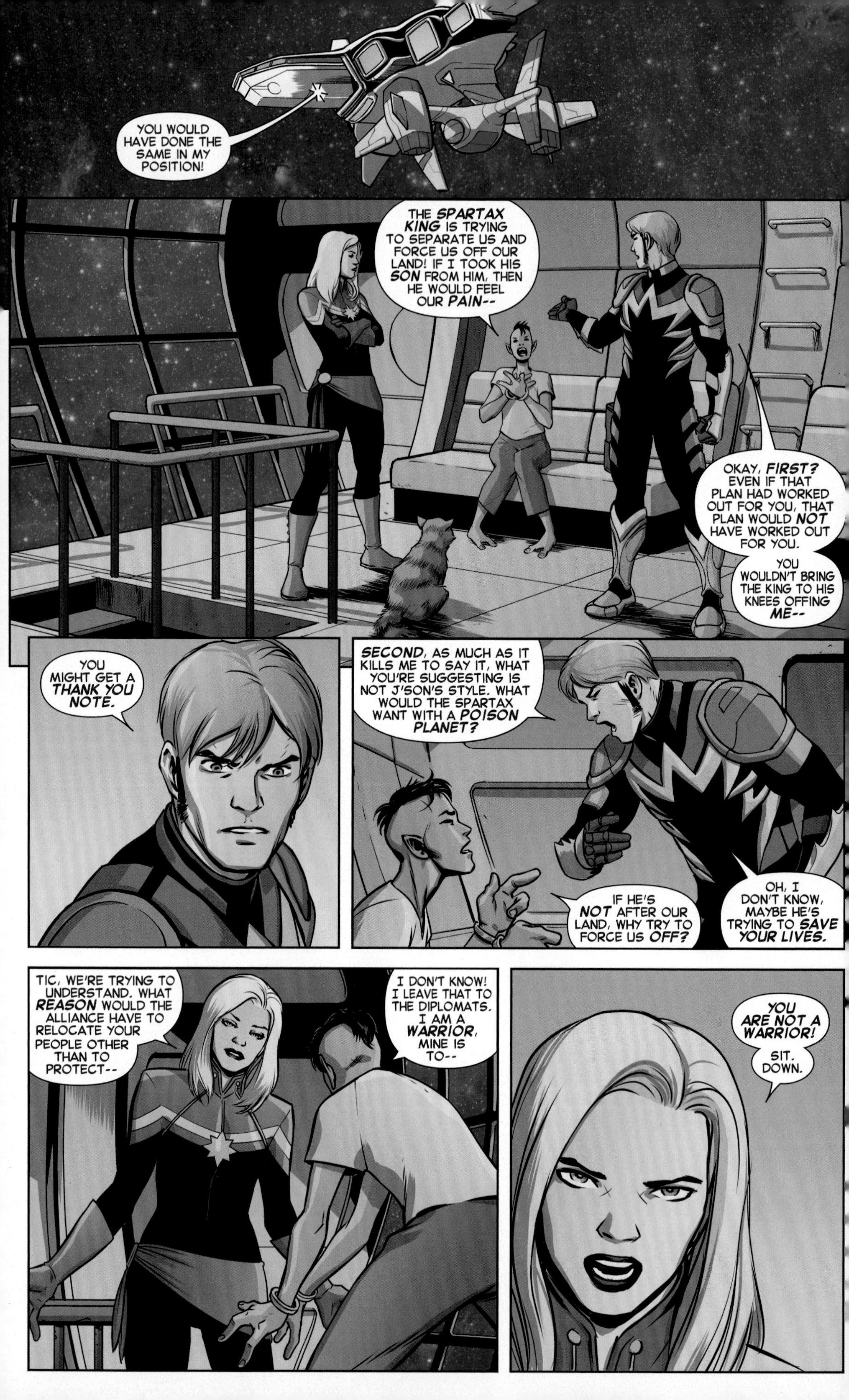
YOU WOULD HAVE DONE THE SAME IN MY POSITION!
THE SPARTAX KING IS TRYING TO SEPARATE US AND FORCE US OFF OUR LAND! IF I TOOK HIS SON FROM HIM, THEN HE WOULD FEEL OUR PAIN--
OKAY, FIRST? EVEN IF THAT PLAN HAD WORKED OUT FOR YOU, THAT PLAN WOULD NOT HAVE WORKED OUT FOR YOU.
YOU WOULDN'T BRING THE KING TO HIS KNEES OFFING ME--
YOU MIGHT GET A THANK YOU NOTE.
SECOND, AS MUCH AS IT KILLS ME TO SAY IT, WHAT YOU'RE SUGGESTING IS NOT J'SON'S STYLE. WHAT WOULD THE SPARTAX WANT WITH A POISON PLANET?
IF HE'S NOT AFTER OUR LAND, WHY TRY TO FORCE US OFF?
OH, I DON'T KNOW, MAYBE HE'S TRYING TO SAVE YOUR LIVES.
TIC, WE'RE TRYING TO UNDERSTAND. WHAT REASON WOULD THE ALLIANCE HAVE TO RELOCATE YOUR PEOPLE OTHER THAN TO PROTECT--
I DON'T KNOW! I LEAVE THAT TO THE DIPLOMATS. I AM A WARRIOR, MINE IS TO--
YOU ARE NOT A WARRIOR!
SIT. DOWN.

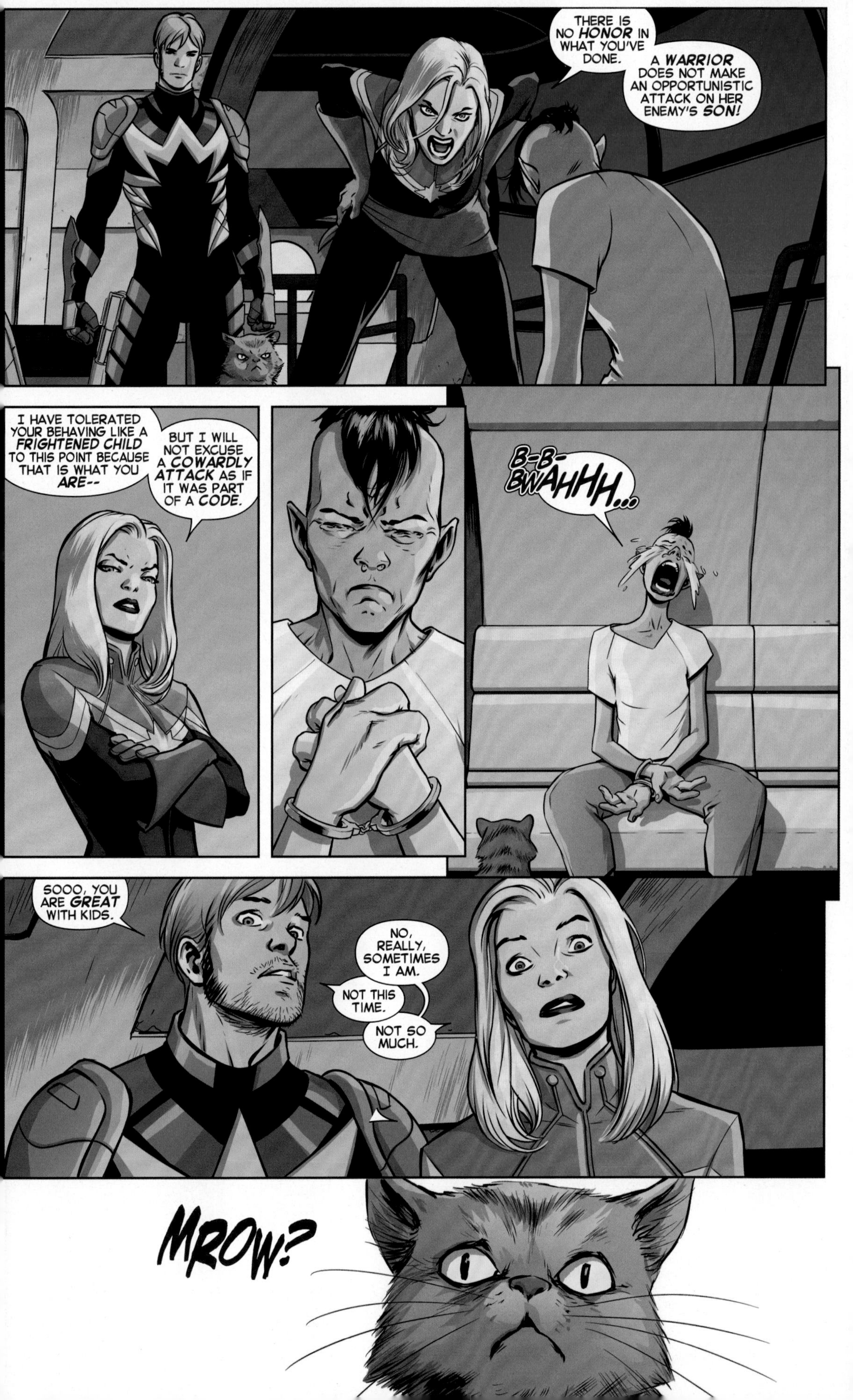
THERE IS NO HONOR IN WHAT YOU'VE DONE.
A WARRIOR DOES NOT MAKE AN OPPORTUNISTIC ATTACK ON HER ENEMY'S SON!
I HAVE TOLERATED YOUR BEHAVING LIKE A FRIGHTENED CHILD TO THIS POINT BECAUSE THAT IS WHAT YOU ARE--
BUT I WILL NOT EXCUSE A COWARDLY ATTACK AS IF IT WAS PART OF A CODE.
B-B-BWAHHH...
SOOO, YOU ARE GREAT WITH KIDS.
NO, REALLY, SOMETIMES I AM.
NOT THIS TIME.
NOT SO MUCH.
MROW?

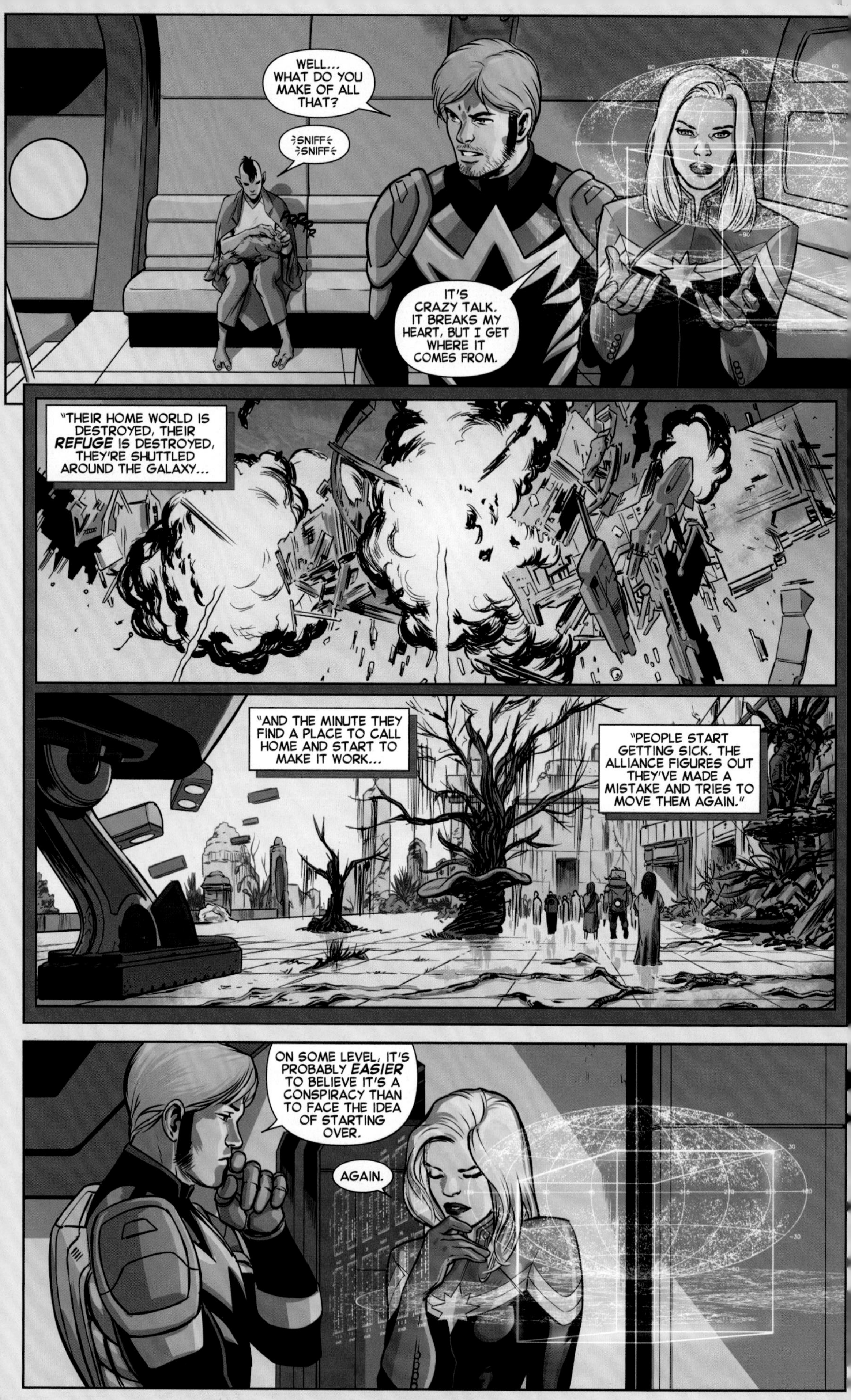
WELL... WHAT DO YOU MAKE OF ALL THAT?
SNIFF SNIFF
IT'S CRAZY TALK. IT BREAKS MY HEART, BUT I GET WHERE IT COMES FROM.
"THEIR HOME WORLD IS DESTROYED, THEIR REFUGE IS DESTROYED, THEY'RE SHUTTLED AROUND THE GALAXY...
"AND THE MINUTE THEY FIND A PLACE TO CALL HOME AND START TO MAKE IT WORK...
"PEOPLE START GETTING SICK. THE ALLIANCE FIGURES OUT THEY'VE MADE A MISTAKE AND TRIES TO MOVE THEM AGAIN."
ON SOME LEVEL, IT'S PROBABLY EASIER TO BELIEVE IT'S A CONSPIRACY THAN TO FACE THE IDEA OF STARTING OVER.
AGAIN.

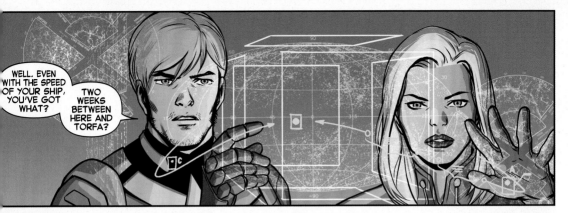

WELL. EVEN WITH THE SPEED OF YOUR SHIP, YOU'VE GOT WHAT?

TWO WEEKS BETWEEN HERE AND TORFA?

WEEK AND A HALF.

YOU OUGHT TO BE ABLE TO GAIN HER TRUST IN THAT TIME. MAYBE YOU CAN TALK SOME SENSE INTO HER.

IF *NOT*, I'M SURE I CAN MAKE SOME HEADWAY WITH THE SETTLERS' LEADERSHIP ONCE WE ARRIVE.

I'D OFFER TO HELP BUT...

NO, IF THEY THINK THE SPARTAX ARE UP TO SOMETHING, YOUR BEING THERE WOULD DO MORE HARM THAN GOOD.

FOR THE BEST, ANYWAY. I'M NOT MUCH OF A DIPLOMAT. HOW ABOUT YOU?

I'VE GOT SOME MOVES.

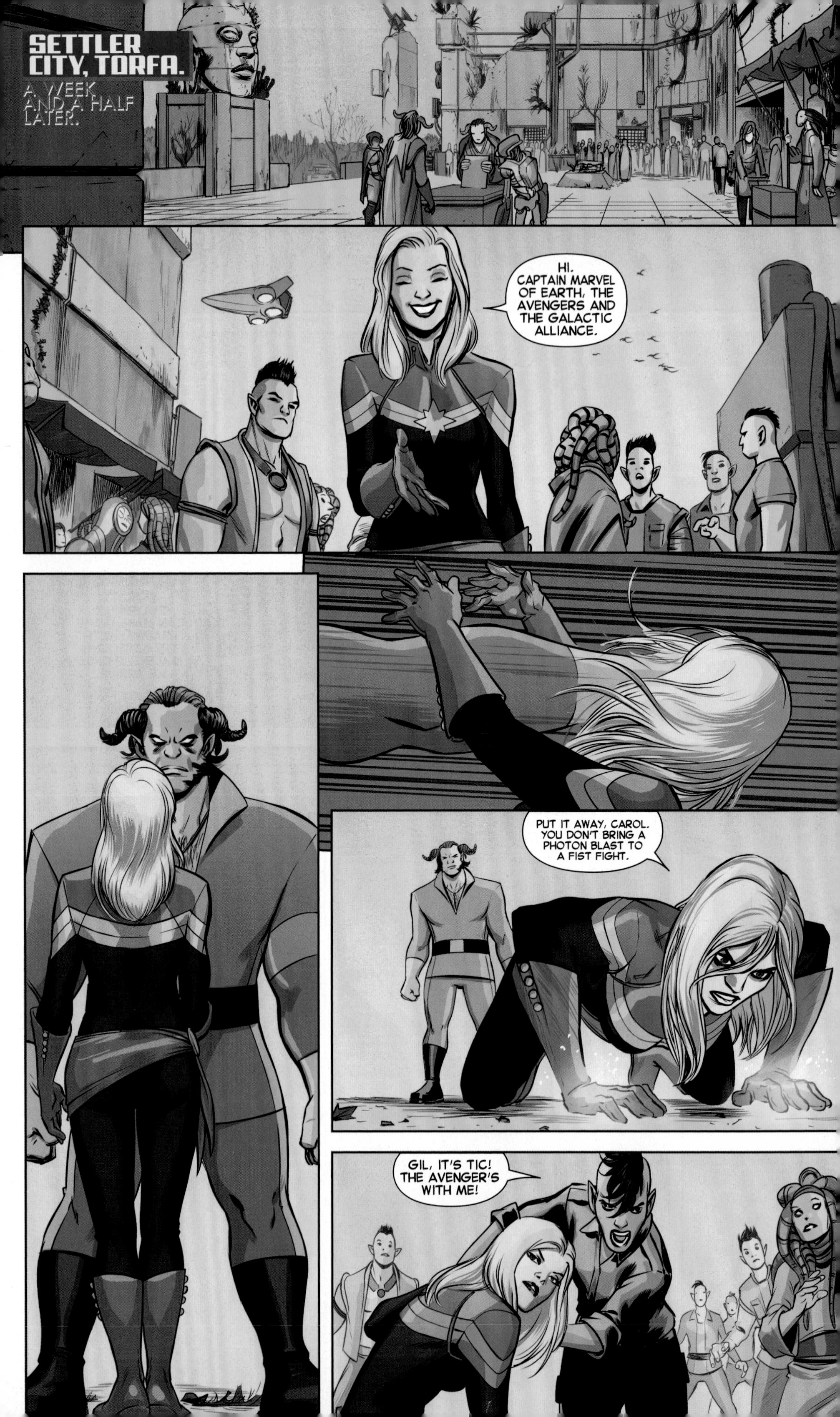
SETTLER CITY, TORFA.
A WEEK AND A HALF LATER.
HI. CAPTAIN MARVEL OF EARTH, THE AVENGERS AND THE GALACTIC ALLIANCE.
PUT IT AWAY, CAROL. YOU DON'T BRING A PHOTON BLAST TO A FIST FIGHT.
GIL, IT'S TIC! THE AVENGER'S WITH ME!

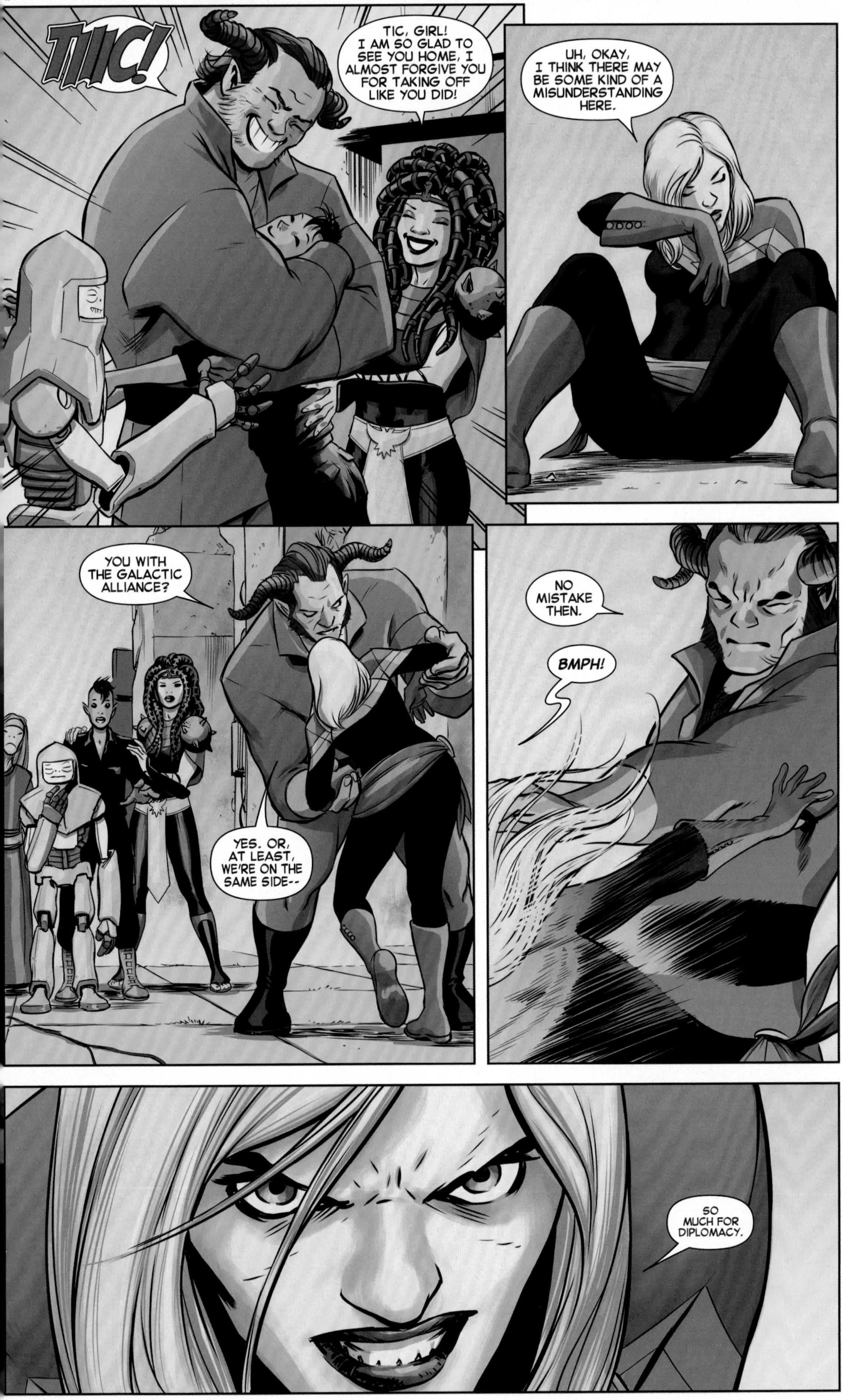
TIIIC!
TIC, GIRL! I AM SO GLAD TO SEE YOU HOME, I ALMOST FORGIVE YOU FOR TAKING OFF LIKE YOU DID!
UH, OKAY, I THINK THERE MAY BE SOME KIND OF A MISUNDERSTANDING HERE.
YOU WITH THE GALACTIC ALLIANCE?
YES. OR, AT LEAST, WE'RE ON THE SAME SIDE--
NO MISTAKE THEN.
BMPH!
SO MUCH FOR DIPLOMACY.

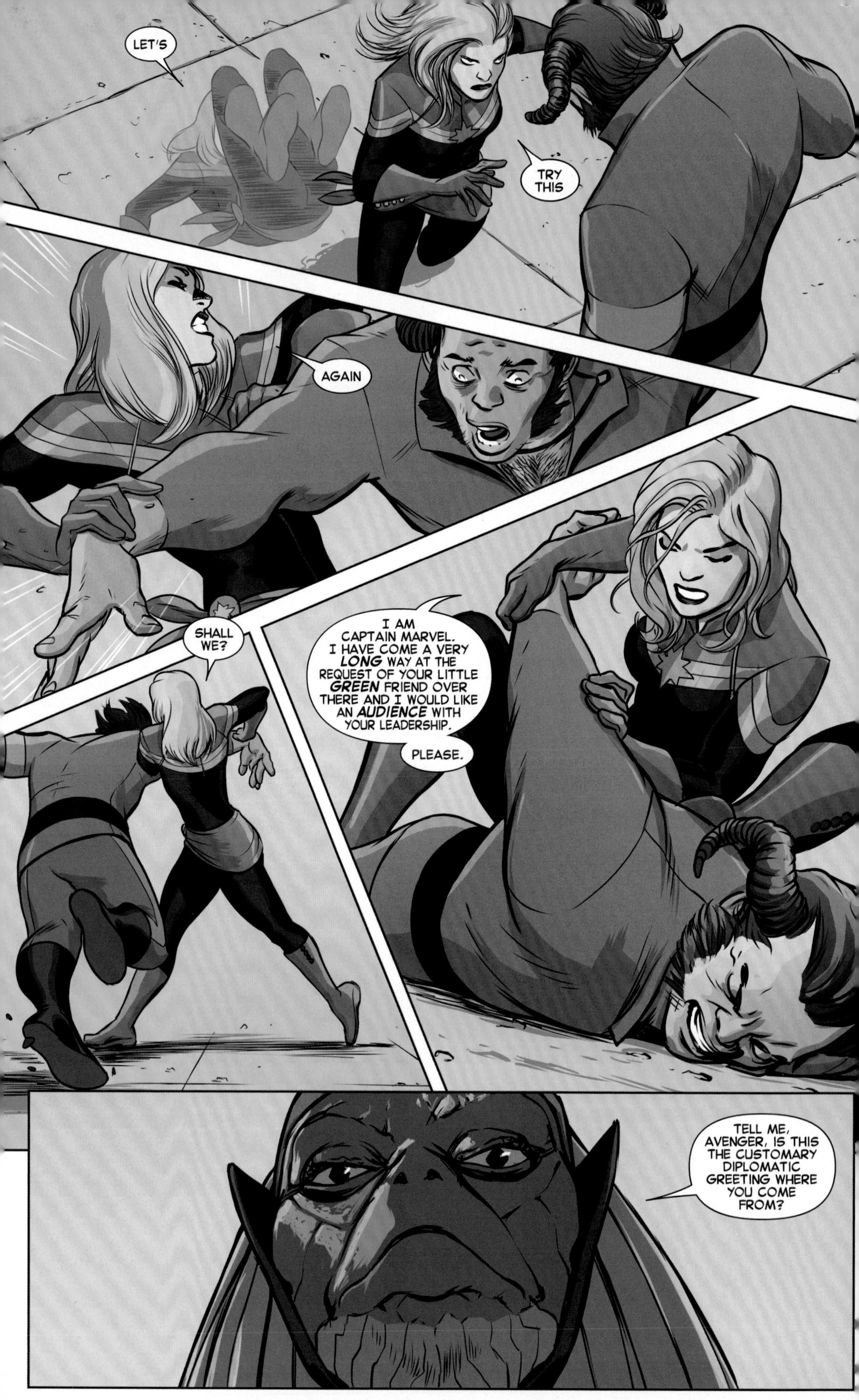
LET'S
TRY THIS
AGAIN
SHALL WE?
I AM CAPTAIN MARVEL. I HAVE COME A VERY LONG WAY AT THE REQUEST OF YOUR LITTLE GREEN FRIEND OVER THERE AND I WOULD LIKE AN AUDIENCE WITH YOUR LEADERSHIP.
PLEASE.
TELL ME, AVENGER, IS THIS THE CUSTOMARY DIPLOMATIC GREETING WHERE YOU COME FROM?

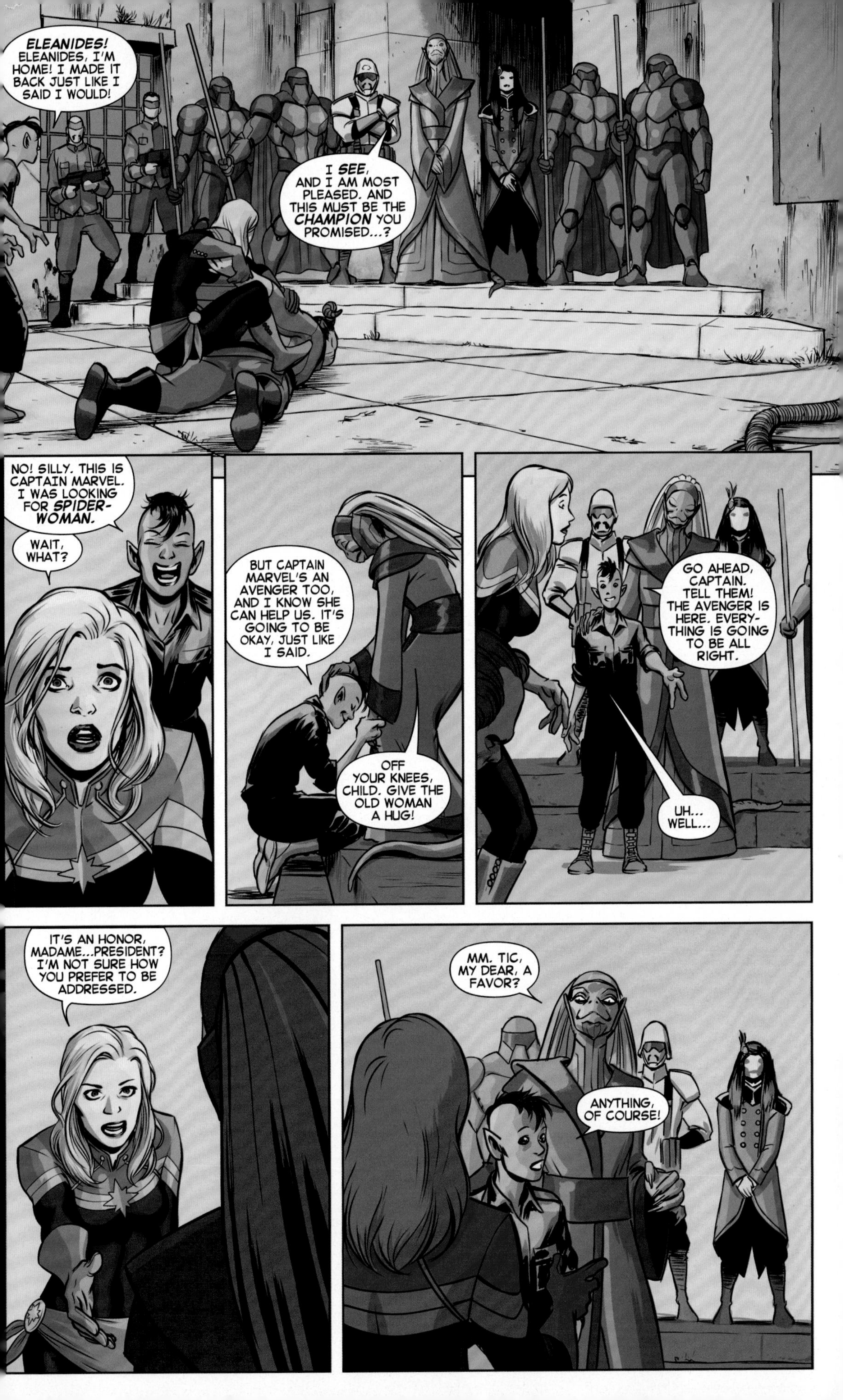
ELEANIDES! ELEANIDES, I'M HOME! I MADE IT BACK JUST LIKE I SAID I WOULD!
I SEE, AND I AM MOST PLEASED. AND THIS MUST BE THE CHAMPION YOU PROMISED...?
NO! SILLY. THIS IS CAPTAIN MARVEL. I WAS LOOKING FOR SPIDER-WOMAN.
WAIT, WHAT?
BUT CAPTAIN MARVEL'S AN AVENGER TOO, AND I KNOW SHE CAN HELP US. IT'S GOING TO BE OKAY, JUST LIKE I SAID.
OFF YOUR KNEES, CHILD. GIVE THE OLD WOMAN A HUG!
GO AHEAD, CAPTAIN. TELL THEM! THE AVENGER IS HERE. EVERYTHING IS GOING TO BE ALL RIGHT.
UH... WELL...
IT'S AN HONOR, MADAME...PRESIDENT? I'M NOT SURE HOW YOU PREFER TO BE ADDRESSED.
MM. TIC, MY DEAR, A FAVOR?
ANYTHING, OF COURSE!

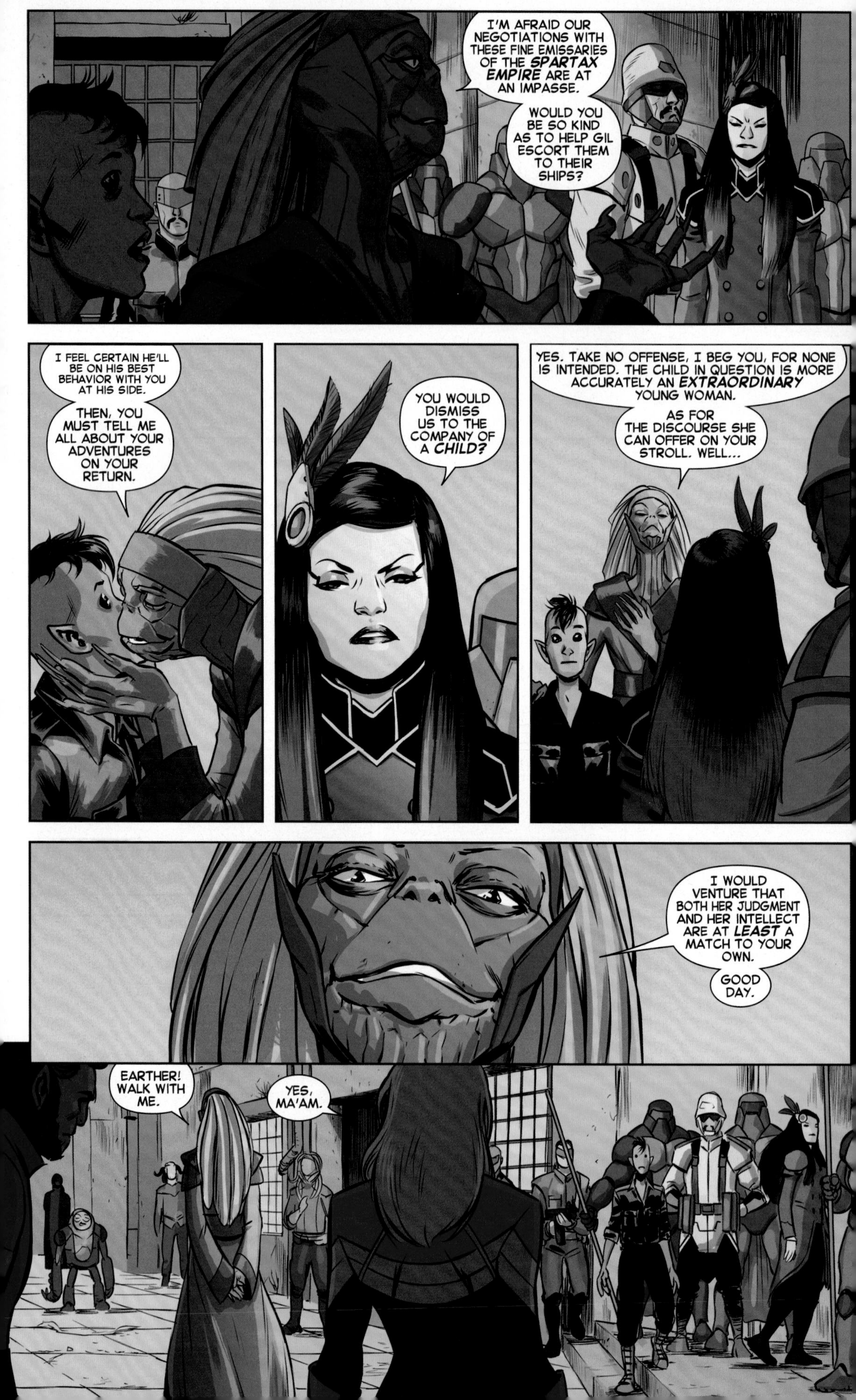
I'M AFRAID OUR NEGOTIATIONS WITH THESE FINE EMISSARIES OF THE SPARTAX EMPIRE ARE AT AN IMPASSE.
WOULD YOU BE SO KIND AS TO HELP GIL ESCORT THEM TO THEIR SHIPS?
I FEEL CERTAIN HE'LL BE ON HIS BEST BEHAVIOR WITH YOU AT HIS SIDE.
THEN, YOU MUST TELL ME ALL ABOUT YOUR ADVENTURES ON YOUR RETURN.
YOU WOULD DISMISS US TO THE COMPANY OF A CHILD?
YES. TAKE NO OFFENSE, I BEG YOU, FOR NONE IS INTENDED. THE CHILD IN QUESTION IS MORE ACCURATELY AN EXTRAORDINARY YOUNG WOMAN.
AS FOR THE DISCOURSE SHE CAN OFFER ON YOUR STROLL. WELL...
I WOULD VENTURE THAT BOTH HER JUDGMENT AND HER INTELLECT ARE AT LEAST A MATCH TO YOUR OWN.
GOOD DAY.
EARTHER! WALK WITH ME.
YES, MA'AM.

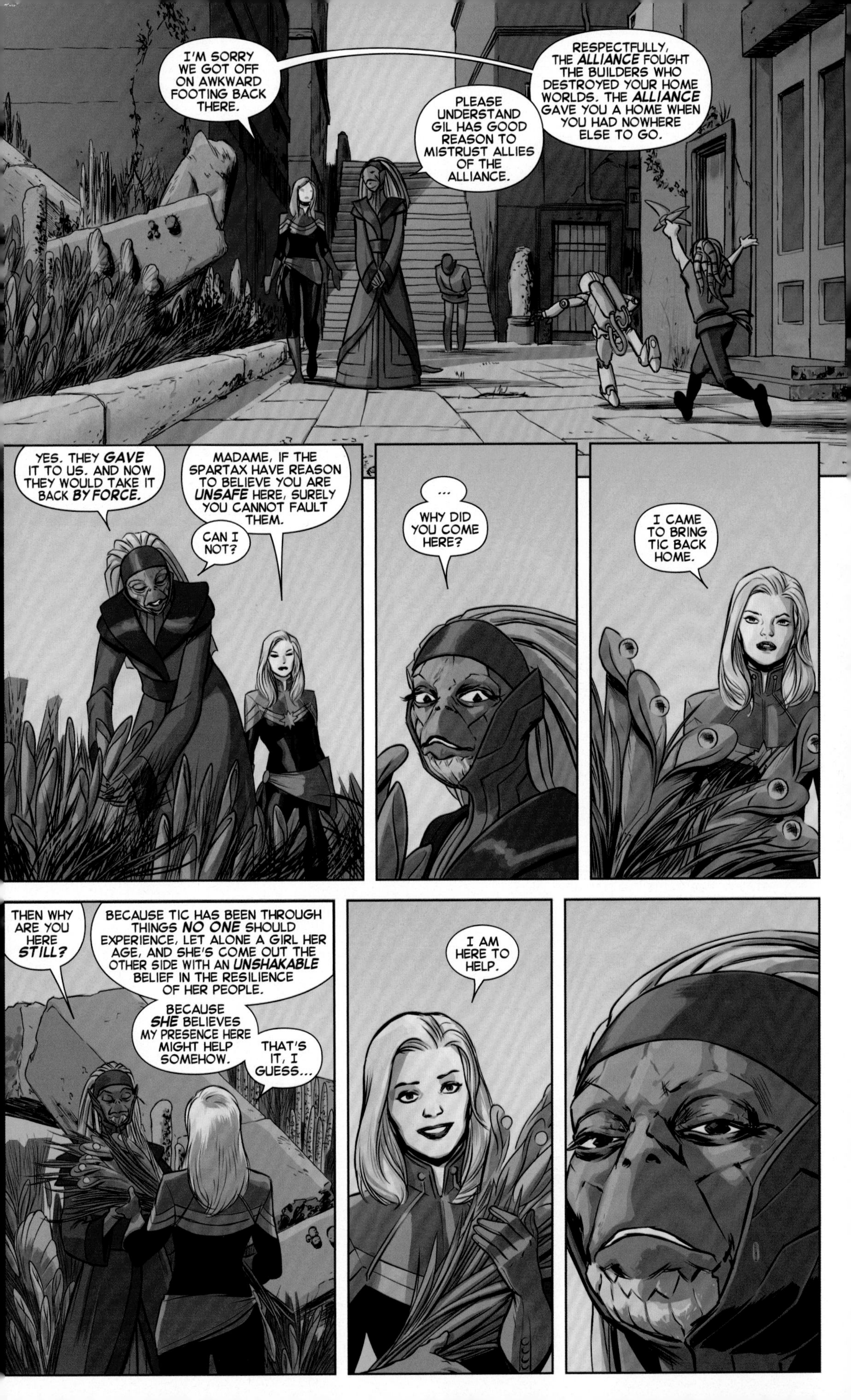
I'M SORRY WE GOT OFF ON AWKWARD FOOTING BACK THERE.
PLEASE UNDERSTAND GIL HAS GOOD REASON TO MISTRUST ALLIES OF THE ALLIANCE.
RESPECTFULLY, THE ALLIANCE FOUGHT THE BUILDERS WHO DESTROYED YOUR HOME WORLDS. THE ALLIANCE GAVE YOU A HOME WHEN YOU HAD NOWHERE ELSE TO GO.
YES. THEY GAVE IT TO US. AND NOW THEY WOULD TAKE IT BACK BY FORCE.
MADAME, IF THE SPARTAX HAVE REASON TO BELIEVE YOU ARE UNSAFE HERE, SURELY YOU CANNOT FAULT THEM.
CAN I NOT?
...
WHY DID YOU COME HERE?
I CAME TO BRING TIC BACK HOME.
THEN WHY ARE YOU HERE STILL?
BECAUSE TIC HAS BEEN THROUGH THINGS NO ONE SHOULD EXPERIENCE, LET ALONE A GIRL HER AGE, AND SHE'S COME OUT THE OTHER SIDE WITH AN UNSHAKABLE BELIEF IN THE RESILIENCE OF HER PEOPLE.
BECAUSE SHE BELIEVES MY PRESENCE HERE MIGHT HELP SOMEHOW.
THAT'S IT, I GUESS...
I AM HERE TO HELP.

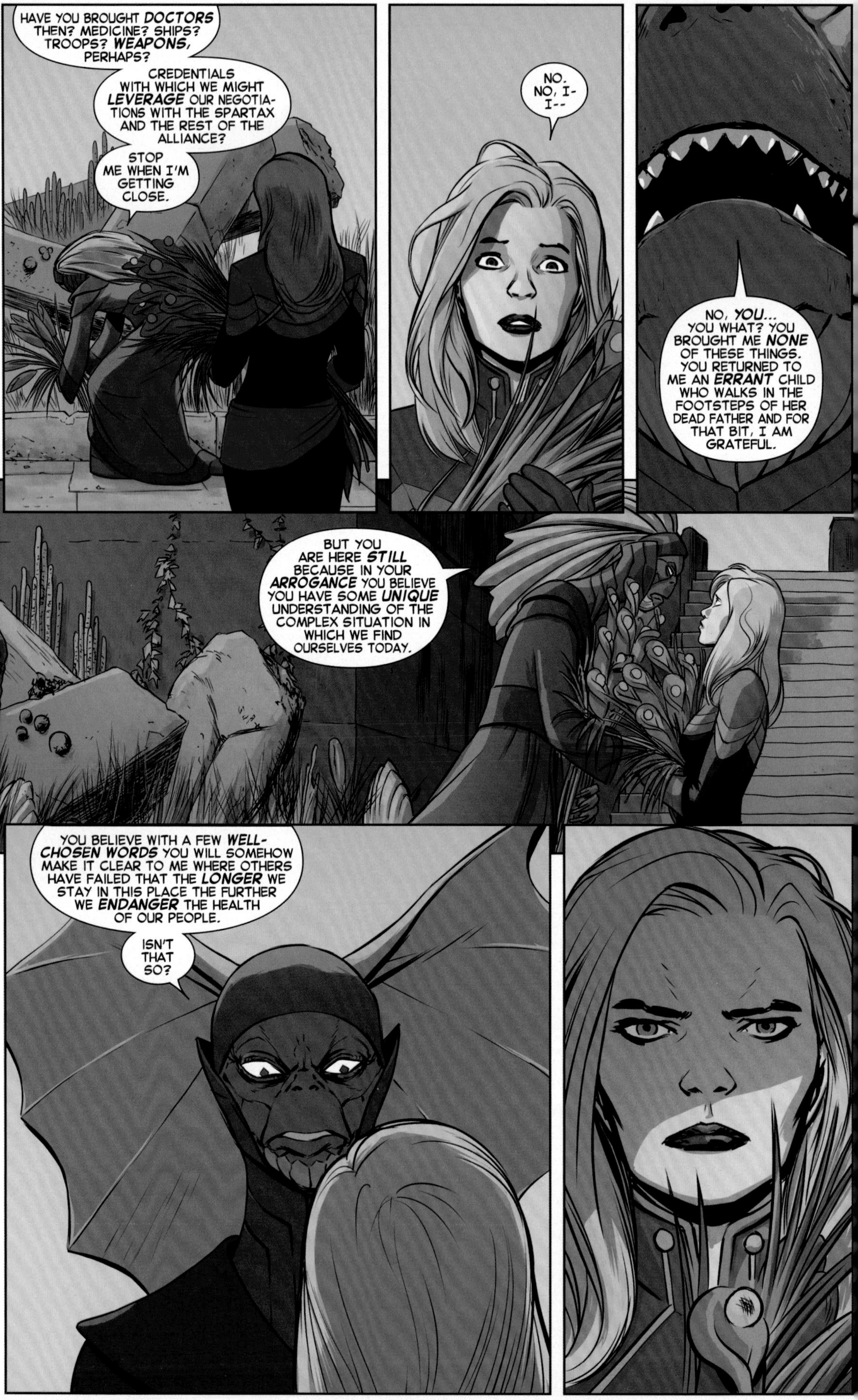
HAVE YOU BROUGHT DOCTORS THEN? MEDICINE? SHIPS? TROOPS? WEAPONS, PERHAPS?
CREDENTIALS WITH WHICH WE MIGHT LEVERAGE OUR NEGOTIATIONS WITH THE SPARTAX AND THE REST OF THE ALLIANCE?
STOP ME WHEN I'M GETTING CLOSE.
NO. NO, I-I--
NO, YOU... YOU WHAT? YOU BROUGHT ME NONE OF THESE THINGS. YOU RETURNED TO ME AN ERRANT CHILD WHO WALKS IN THE FOOTSTEPS OF HER DEAD FATHER AND FOR THAT BIT, I AM GRATEFUL.
BUT YOU ARE HERE STILL BECAUSE IN YOUR ARROGANCE YOU BELIEVE YOU HAVE SOME UNIQUE UNDERSTANDING OF THE COMPLEX SITUATION IN WHICH WE FIND OURSELVES TODAY.
YOU BELIEVE WITH A FEW WELL-CHOSEN WORDS YOU WILL SOMEHOW MAKE IT CLEAR TO ME WHERE OTHERS HAVE FAILED THAT THE LONGER WE STAY IN THIS PLACE THE FURTHER WE ENDANGER THE HEALTH OF OUR PEOPLE.
ISN'T THAT SO?

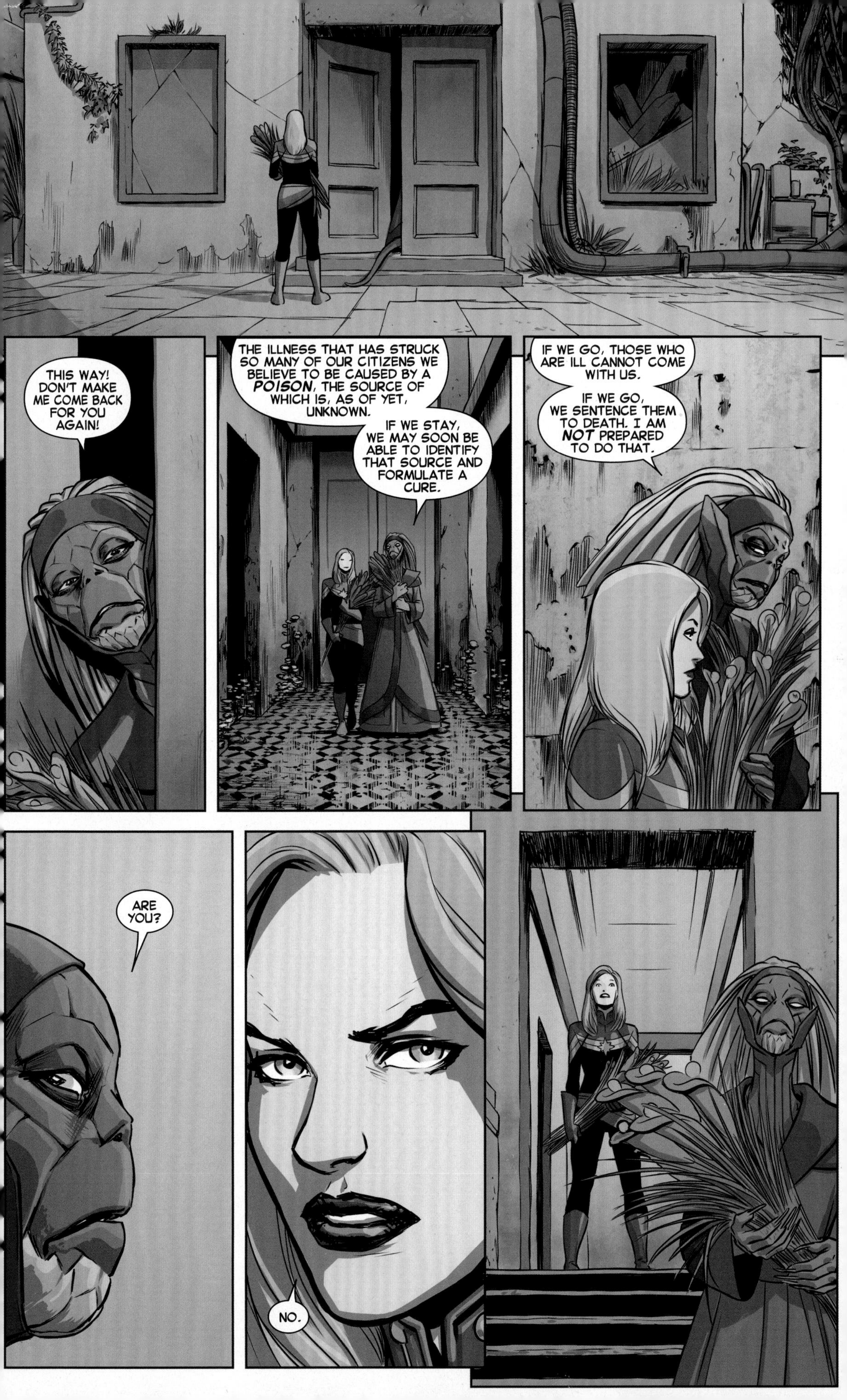
THIS WAY! DON'T MAKE ME COME BACK FOR YOU AGAIN!
THE ILLNESS THAT HAS STRUCK SO MANY OF OUR CITIZENS WE BELIEVE TO BE CAUSED BY A POISON, THE SOURCE OF WHICH IS, AS OF YET, UNKNOWN.
IF WE STAY, WE MAY SOON BE ABLE TO IDENTIFY THAT SOURCE AND FORMULATE A CURE.
IF WE GO, THOSE WHO ARE ILL CANNOT COME WITH US.
IF WE GO, WE SENTENCE THEM TO DEATH. I AM NOT PREPARED TO DO THAT.
ARE YOU?
NO.

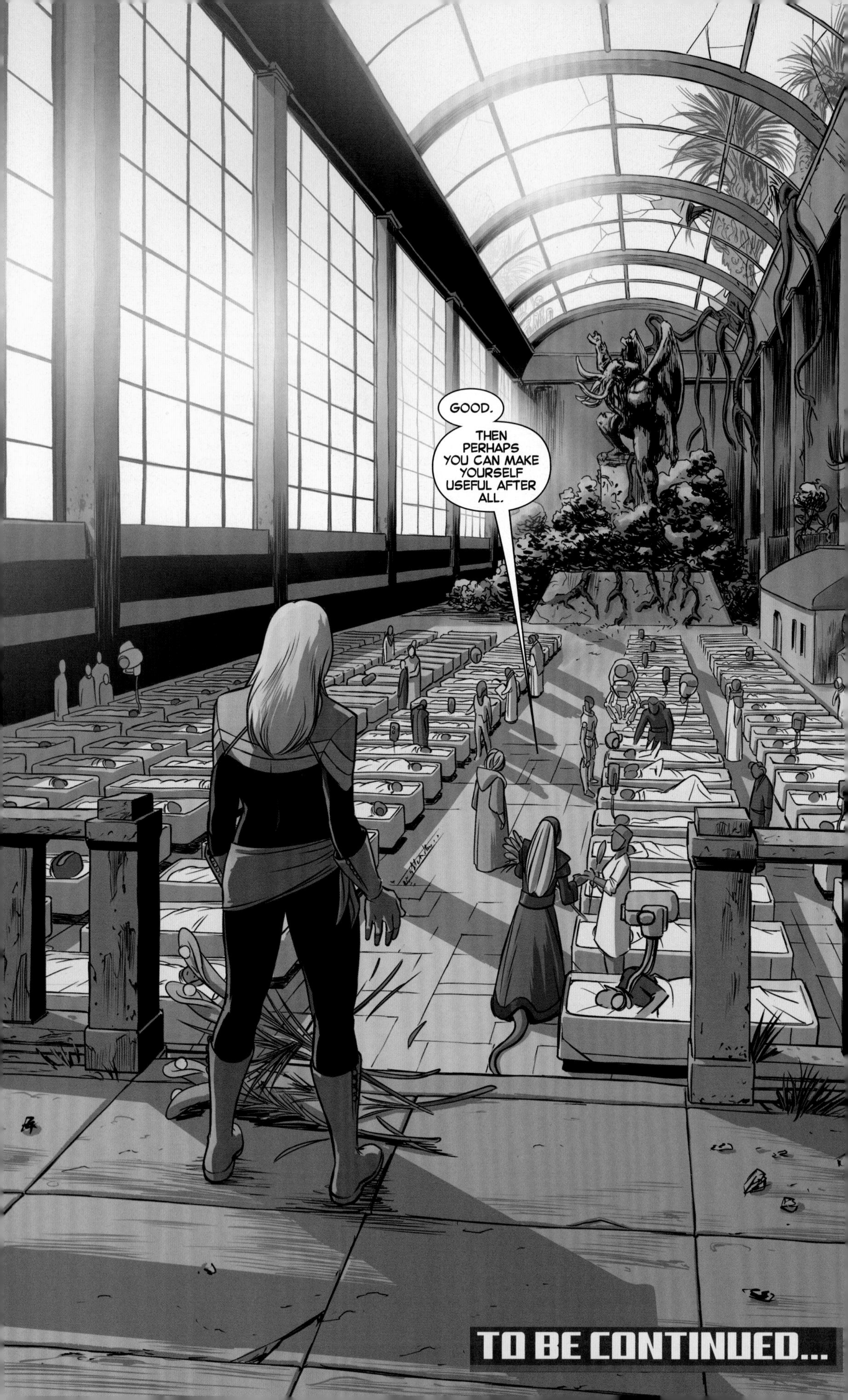
GOOD.
THEN PERHAPS YOU CAN MAKE YOURSELF USEFUL AFTER ALL.
TO BE CONTINUED...

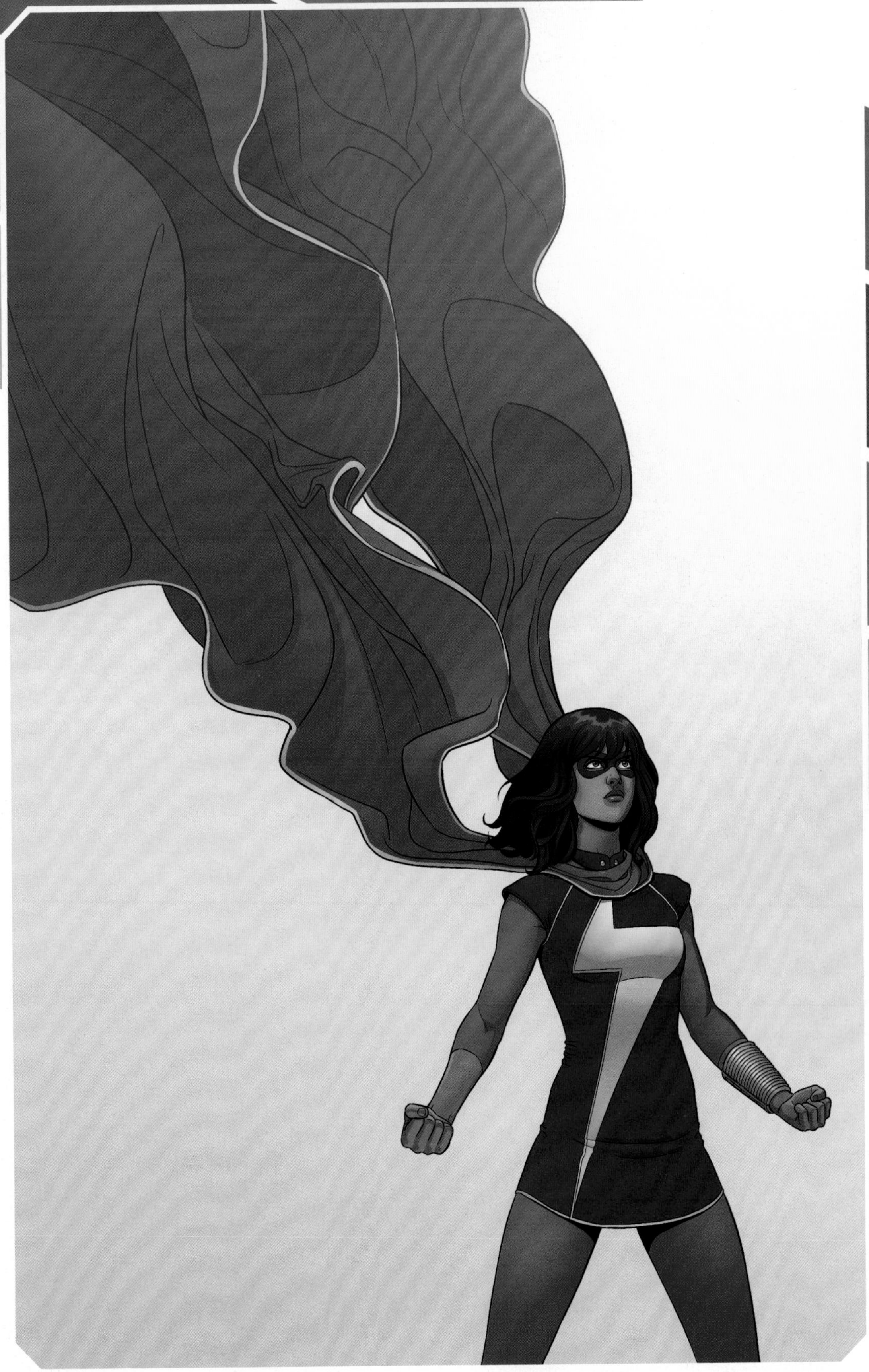

MS. MARVEL #3

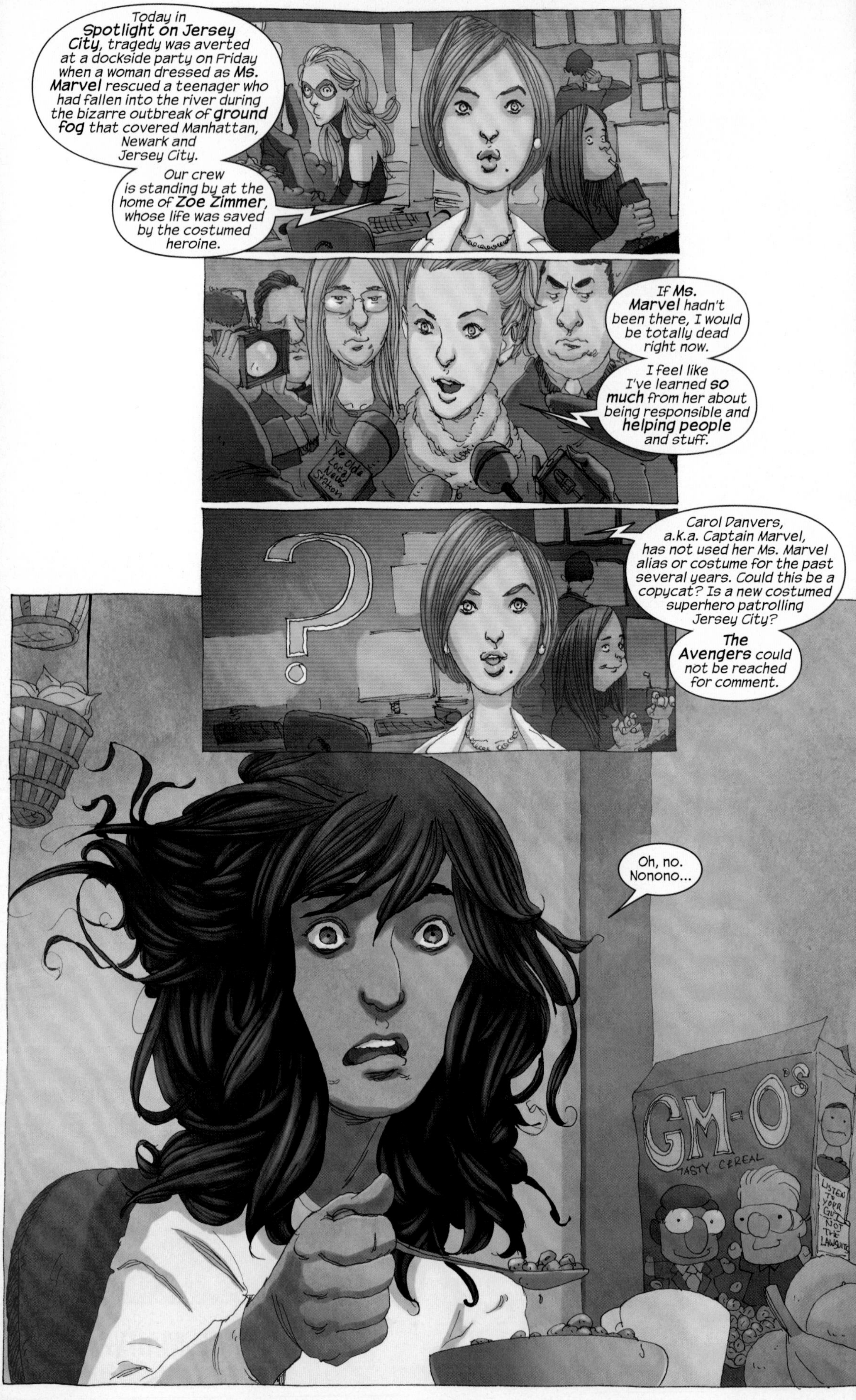
Today in Spotlight on Jersey City, tragedy was averted at a dockside party on Friday when a woman dressed as Ms. Marvel rescued a teenager who had fallen into the river during the bizarre outbreak of ground fog that covered Manhattan, Newark and Jersey City.
Our crew is standing by at the home of Zoe Zimmer, whose life was saved by the costumed heroine.
If Ms. Marvel hadn't been there, I would be totally dead right now.
I feel like I've learned so much from her about being responsible and helping people and stuff.
Ye Olde Local News Station
Carol Danvers, a.k.a. Captain Marvel, has not used her Ms. Marvel alias or costume for the past several years. Could this be a copycat? Is a new costumed superhero patrolling Jersey City?
The Avengers could not be reached for comment.
Oh, no. Nonono...
GM-O's
TASTY CEREAL
LISTEN TO YOUR GUT NOT THE LAWSUITS

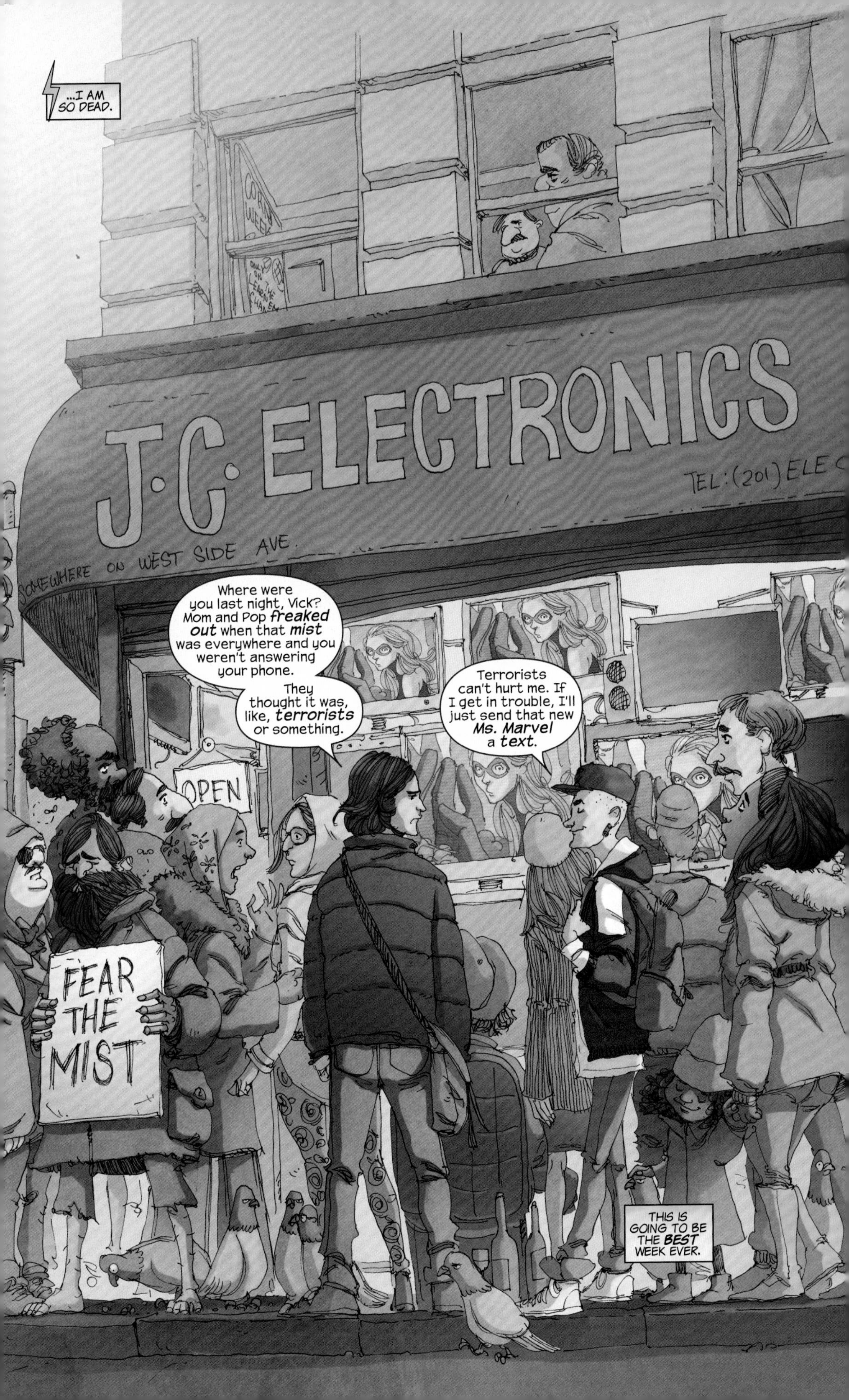

...I AM SO DEAD.
J·C· ELECTRONICS
TEL: (201) ELE
SOMEWHERE ON WEST SIDE AVE.
Where were you last night, Vick? Mom and Pop freaked out when that mist was everywhere and you weren't answering your phone.
They thought it was, like, terrorists or something.
Terrorists can't hurt me. If I get in trouble, I'll just send that new Ms. Marvel a text.
OPEN
FEAR THE MIST
THIS IS GOING TO BE THE BEST WEEK EVER.

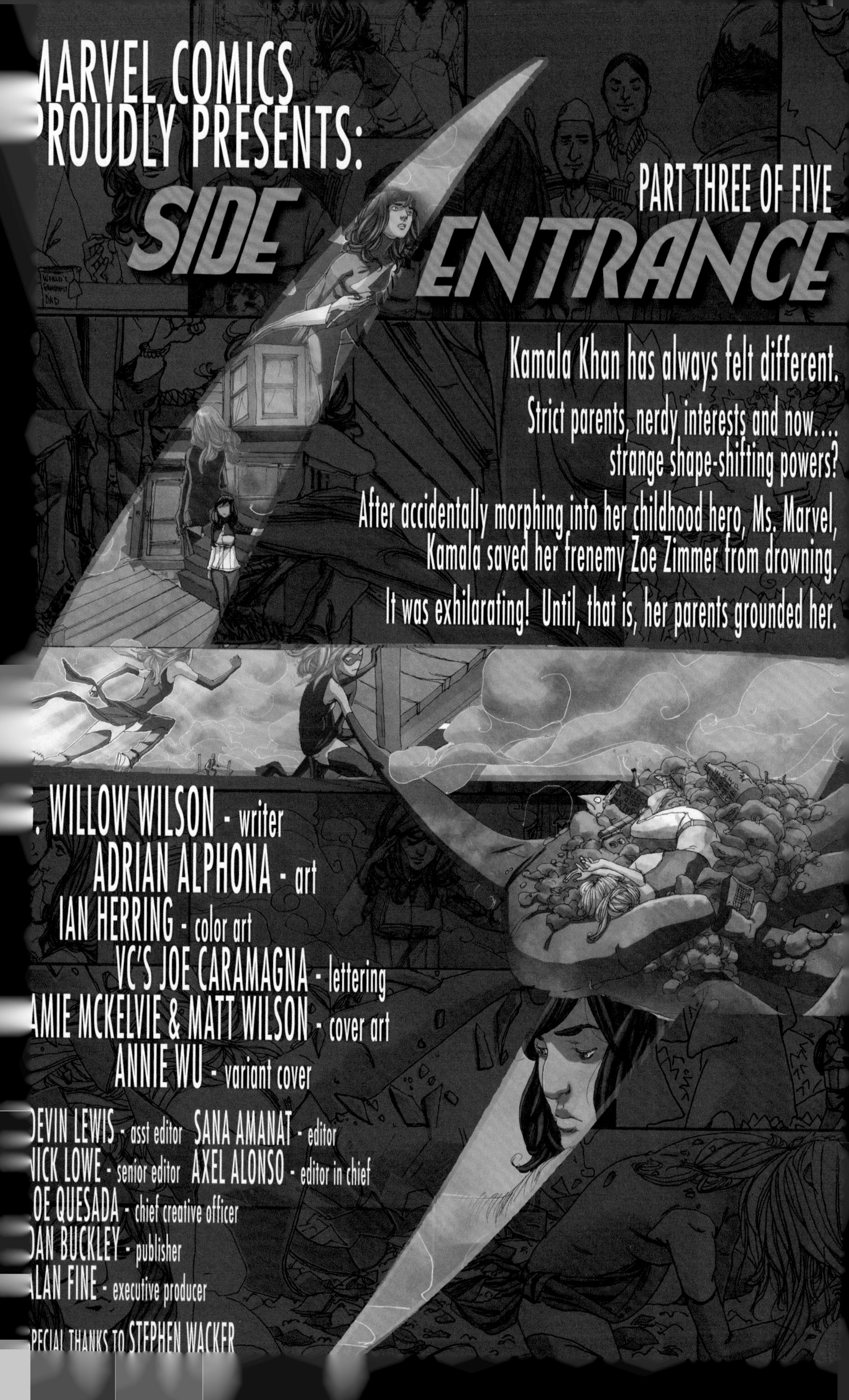

MARVEL COMICS PROUDLY PRESENTS:

PART THREE OF FIVE

SIDE ENTRANCE

Kamala Khan has always felt different.

Strict parents, nerdy interests and now.... strange shape-shifting powers?

After accidentally morphing into her childhood hero, Ms. Marvel, Kamala saved her frenemy Zoe Zimmer from drowning.

It was exhilarating! Until, that is, her parents grounded her.

. WILLOW WILSON - writer
ADRIAN ALPHONA - art
IAN HERRING - color art
VC'S JOE CARAMAGNA - lettering
AMIE MCKELVIE & MATT WILSON - cover art
ANNIE WU - variant cover

DEVIN LEWIS - asst editor SANA AMANAT - editor
NICK LOWE - senior editor AXEL ALONSO - editor in chief
OE QUESADA - chief creative officer
DAN BUCKLEY - publisher
ALAN FINE - executive producer

PECIAL THANKS TO STEPHEN WACKER

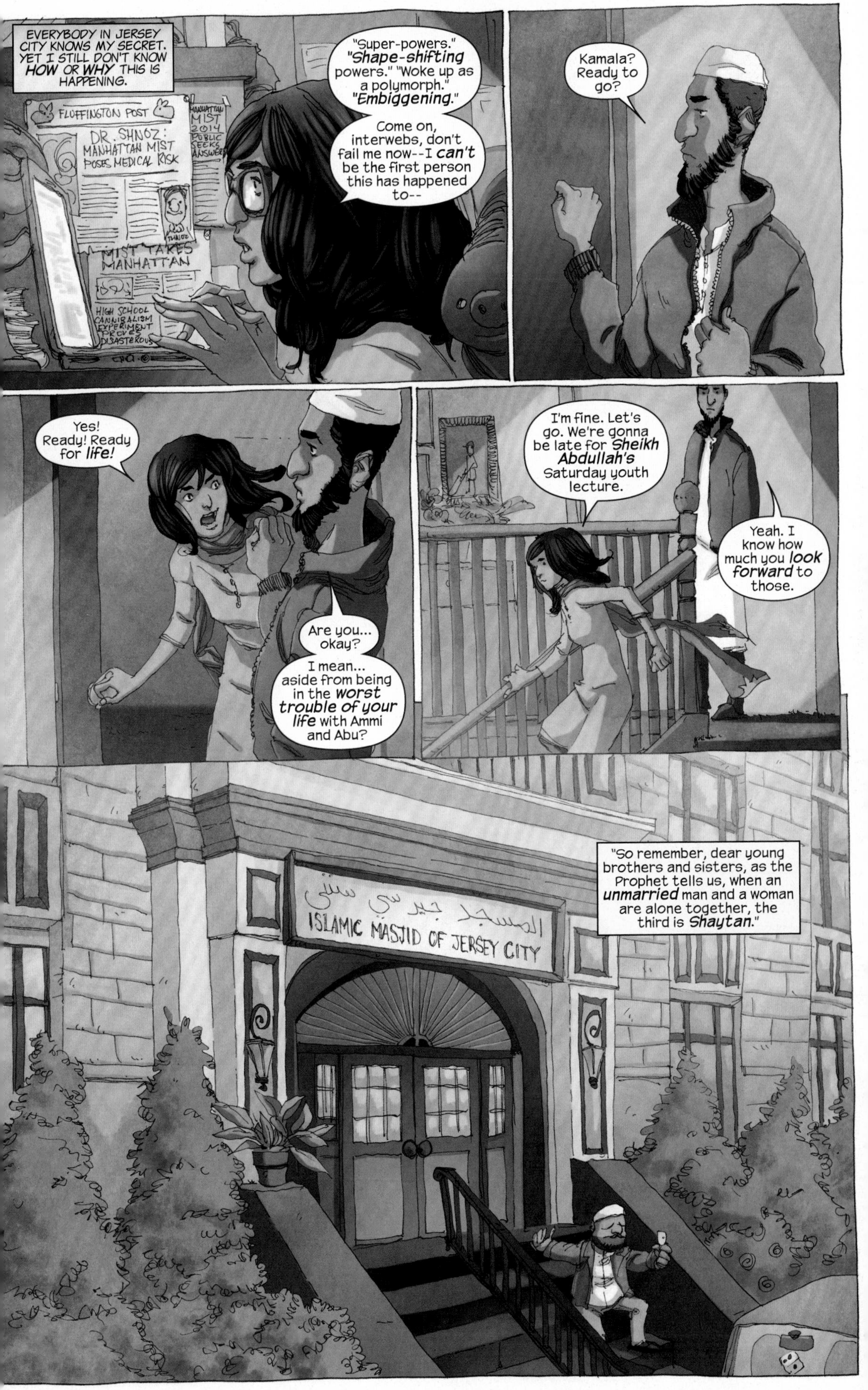
EVERYBODY IN JERSEY CITY KNOWS MY SECRET. YET I STILL DON'T KNOW HOW OR WHY THIS IS HAPPENING.
FLUFFINGTON POST
DR. SHNOZ: MANHATTAN MIST POSES MEDICAL RISK
MIST TAKES MANHATTAN
HIGH SCHOOL CANNIBALISM EXPERIMENT PROVES DISASTEROUS
MANHATTAN MIST 2014 PUBLIC SEEKS ANSWERS
"Super-powers." "Shape-shifting powers." "Woke up as a polymorph." "Embiggening."
Come on, interwebs, don't fail me now--I can't be the first person this has happened to--
Kamala? Ready to go?
Yes! Ready! Ready for life!
Are you... okay?
I mean... aside from being in the worst trouble of your life with Ammi and Abu?
I'm fine. Let's go. We're gonna be late for Sheikh Abdullah's Saturday youth lecture.
Yeah. I know how much you look forward to those.
ISLAMIC MASJID OF JERSEY CITY
"So remember, dear young brothers and sisters, as the Prophet tells us, when an unmarried man and a woman are alone together, the third is Shaytan."

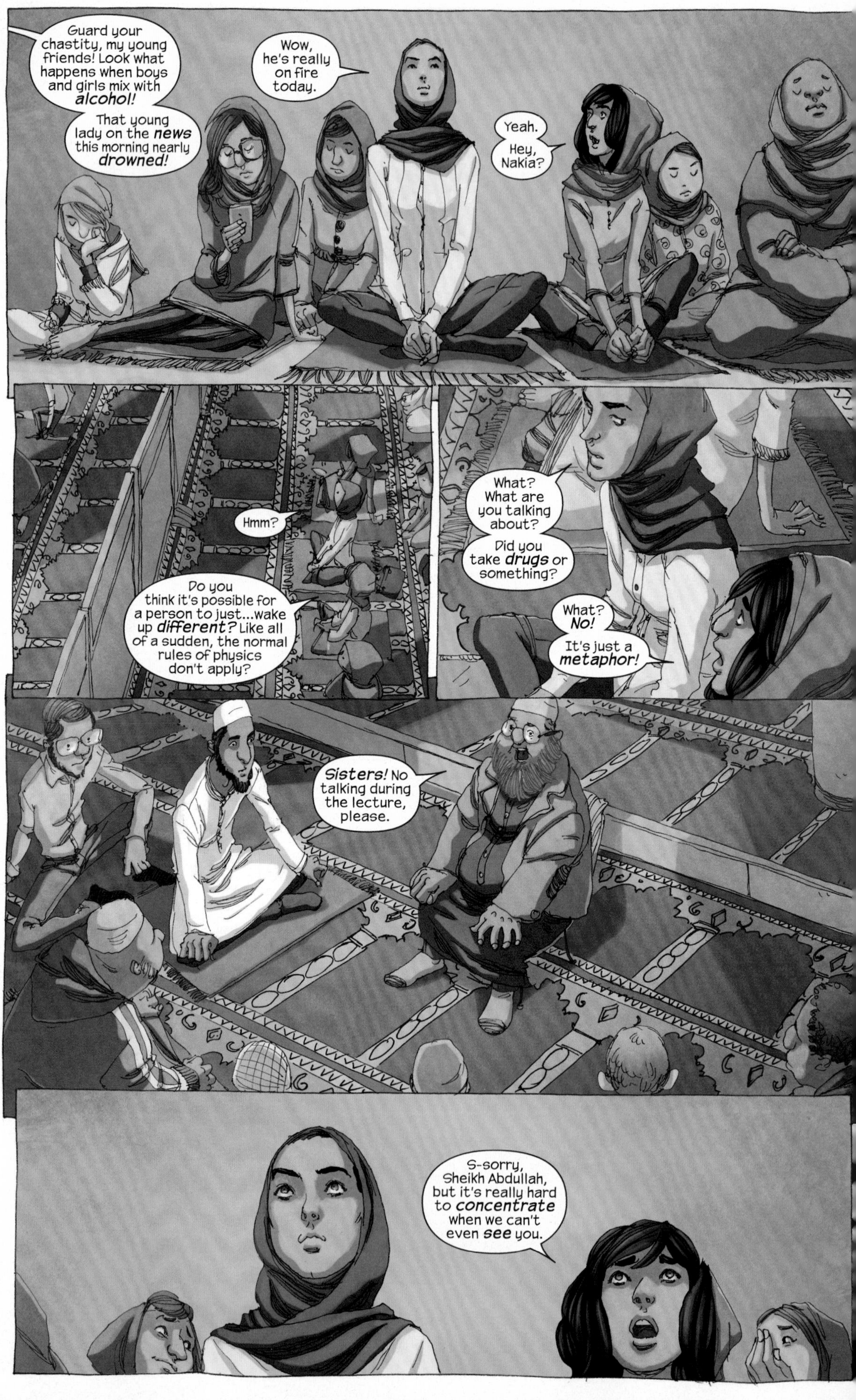
Guard your chastity, my young friends! Look what happens when boys and girls mix with alcohol!
That young lady on the news this morning nearly drowned!
Wow, he's really on fire today.
Yeah.
Hey, Nakia?
Hmm?
Do you think it's possible for a person to just...wake up different? Like all of a sudden, the normal rules of physics don't apply?
What? What are you talking about?
Did you take drugs or something?
What? No!
It's just a metaphor!
Sisters! No talking during the lecture, please.
S-sorry, Sheikh Abdullah, but it's really hard to concentrate when we can't even see you.

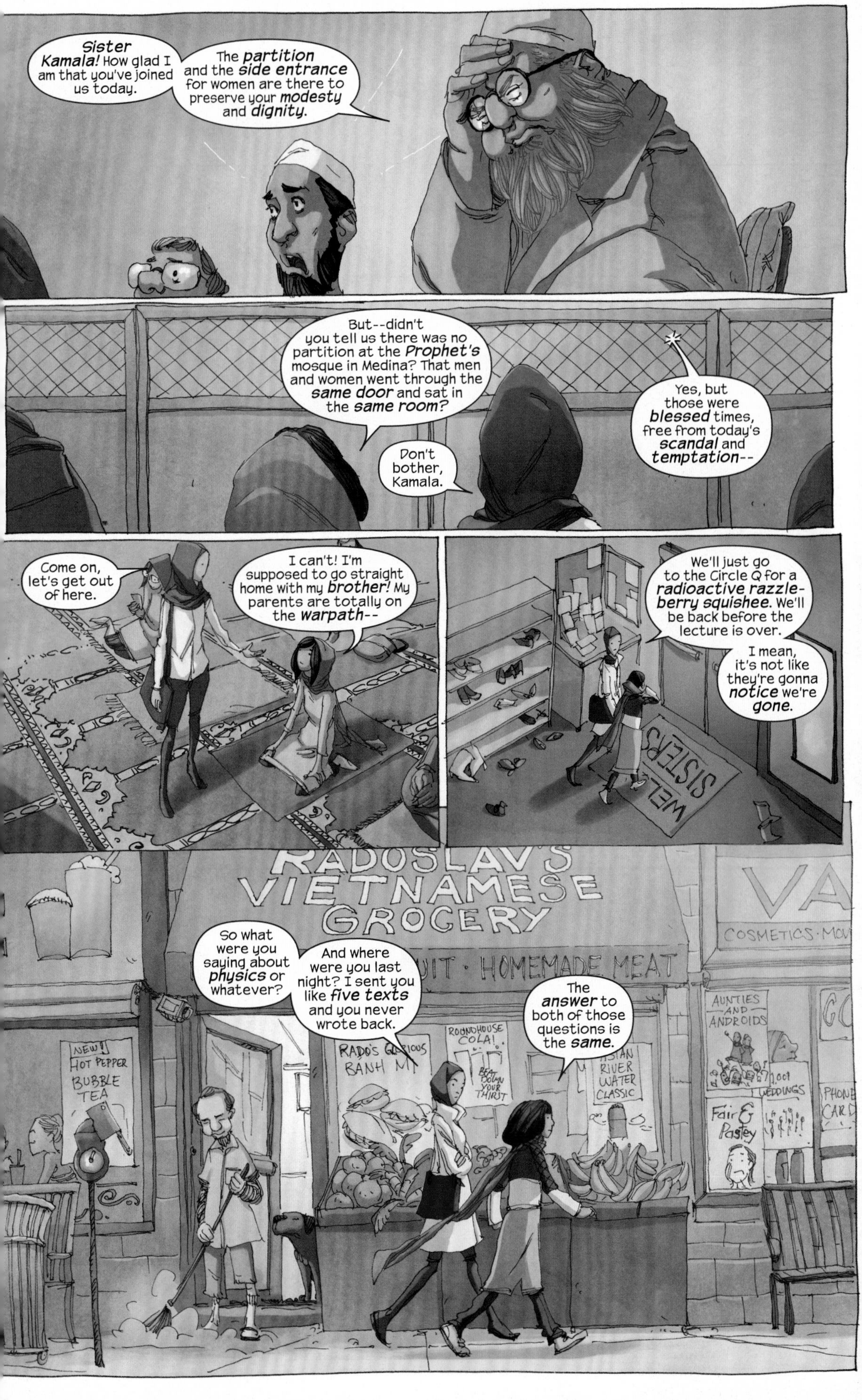

Sister Kamala! How glad I am that you've joined us today.
The partition and the side entrance for women are there to preserve your modesty and dignity.
But--didn't you tell us there was no partition at the Prophet's mosque in Medina? That men and women went through the same door and sat in the same room?
Yes, but those were blessed times, free from today's scandal and temptation--
Don't bother, Kamala.
Come on, let's get out of here.
I can't! I'm supposed to go straight home with my brother! My parents are totally on the warpath--
We'll just go to the Circle Q for a radioactive razzle-berry squishee. We'll be back before the lecture is over.
I mean, it's not like they're gonna notice we're gone.
SISTERS
RADOSLAV'S VIETNAMESE GROCERY
HOMEMADE MEAT
COSMETICS
So what were you saying about physics or whatever?
And where were you last night? I sent you like five texts and you never wrote back.
The answer to both of those questions is the same.
NEW! HOT PEPPER BUBBLE TEA
RADO'S BANH MI
ROUNDHOUSE COLA! BEAT DOWN YOUR THIRST
ASIAN RIVER WATER CLASSIC
AUNTIES AND ANDROIDS
1,001 WEDDINGS
Fair & Pastey
PHONE CARD

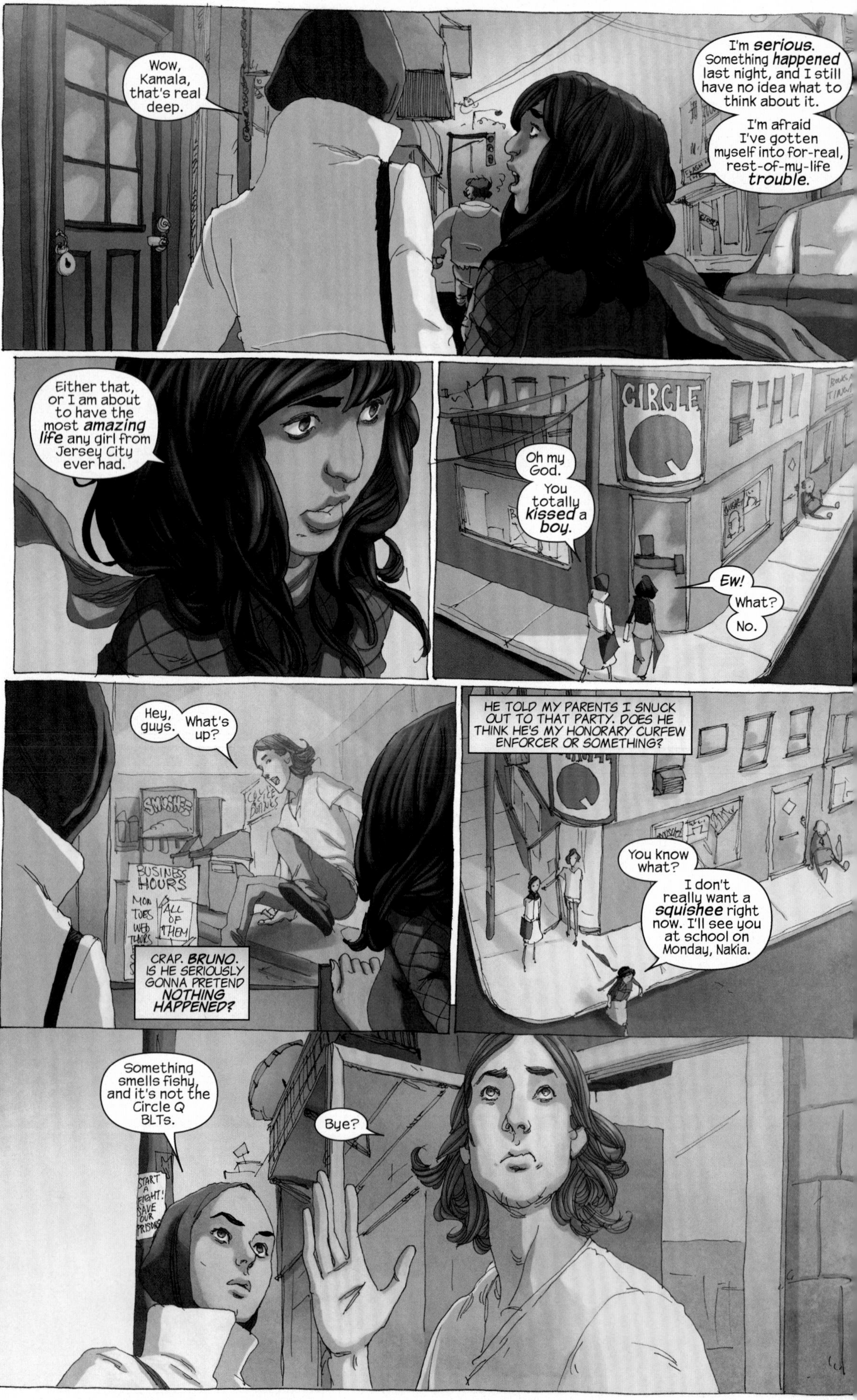
Wow, Kamala, that's real deep.
I'm serious. Something happened last night, and I still have no idea what to think about it.
I'm afraid I've gotten myself into for-real, rest-of-my-life trouble.
Either that, or I am about to have the most amazing life any girl from Jersey City ever had.
CIRCLE Q
Oh my God.
You totally kissed a boy.
Ew!
What?
No.
Hey, guys.
What's up?
BUSINESS HOURS
CRAP. BRUNO. IS HE SERIOUSLY GONNA PRETEND NOTHING HAPPENED?
HE TOLD MY PARENTS I SNUCK OUT TO THAT PARTY. DOES HE THINK HE'S MY HONORARY CURFEW ENFORCER OR SOMETHING?
You know what?
I don't really want a squishee right now. I'll see you at school on Monday, Nakia.
Something smells fishy, and it's not the Circle Q BLTs.
Bye?

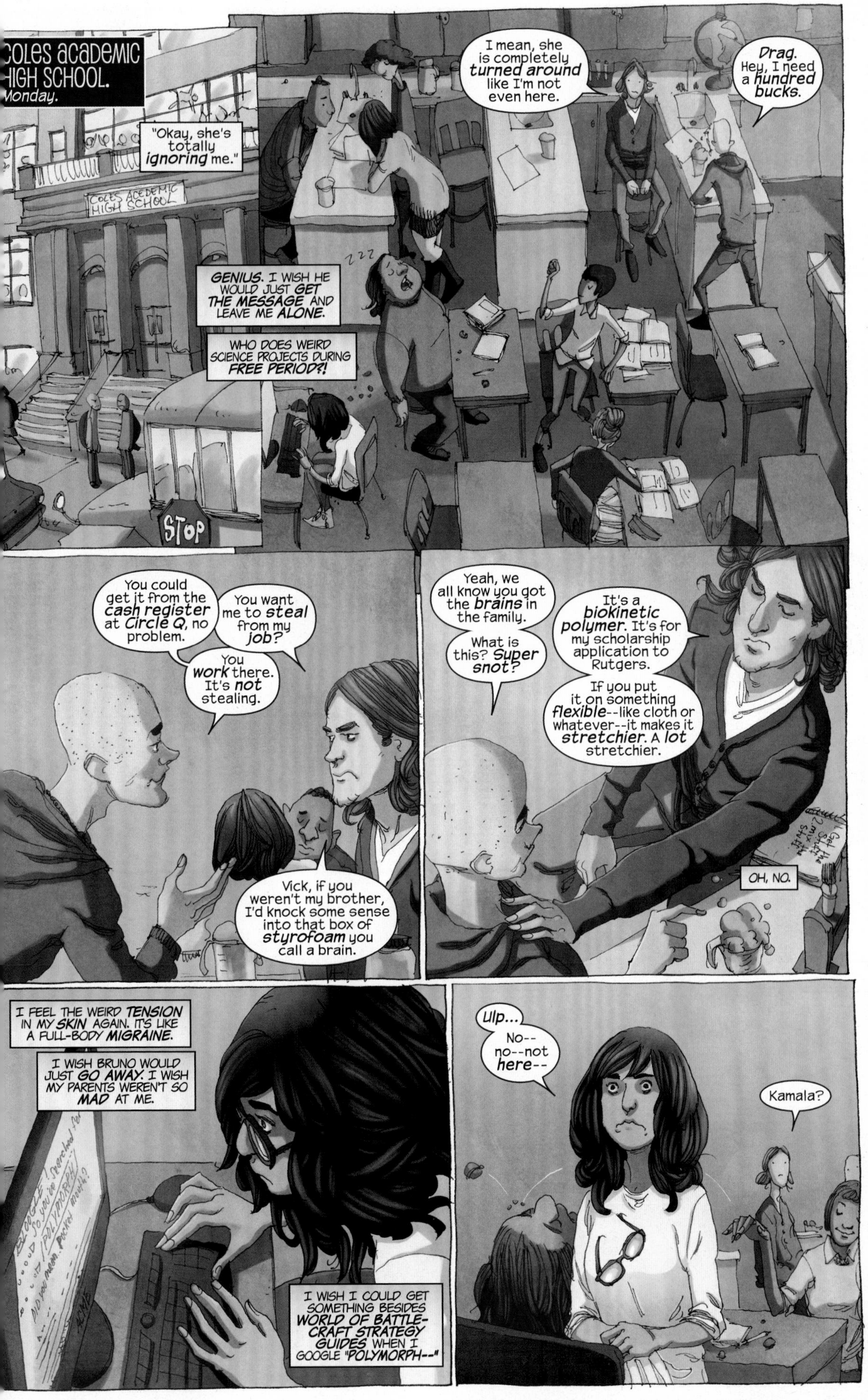
COLES ACADEMIC HIGH SCHOOL. Monday.
"Okay, she's totally ignoring me."
COLES ACADEMIC HIGH SCHOOL
I mean, she is completely turned around like I'm not even here.
Drag. Hey, I need a hundred bucks.
GENIUS. I WISH HE WOULD JUST GET THE MESSAGE AND LEAVE ME ALONE.
WHO DOES WEIRD SCIENCE PROJECTS DURING FREE PERIOD?!
STOP
You could get it from the cash register at Circle Q, no problem.
You want me to steal from my job?
You work there. It's not stealing.
Vick, if you weren't my brother, I'd knock some sense into that box of styrofoam you call a brain.
Yeah, we all know you got the brains in the family.
What is this? Super snot?
It's a biokinetic polymer. It's for my scholarship application to Rutgers.
If you put it on something flexible--like cloth or whatever--it makes it stretchier. A lot stretchier.
OH, NO.
I FEEL THE WEIRD TENSION IN MY SKIN AGAIN. IT'S LIKE A FULL-BODY MIGRAINE.
I WISH BRUNO WOULD JUST GO AWAY. I WISH MY PARENTS WEREN'T SO MAD AT ME.
I WISH I COULD GET SOMETHING BESIDES WORLD OF BATTLECRAFT STRATEGY GUIDES WHEN I GOOGLE "POLYMORPH--"
Ulp...
No-- no--not here--
Kamala?

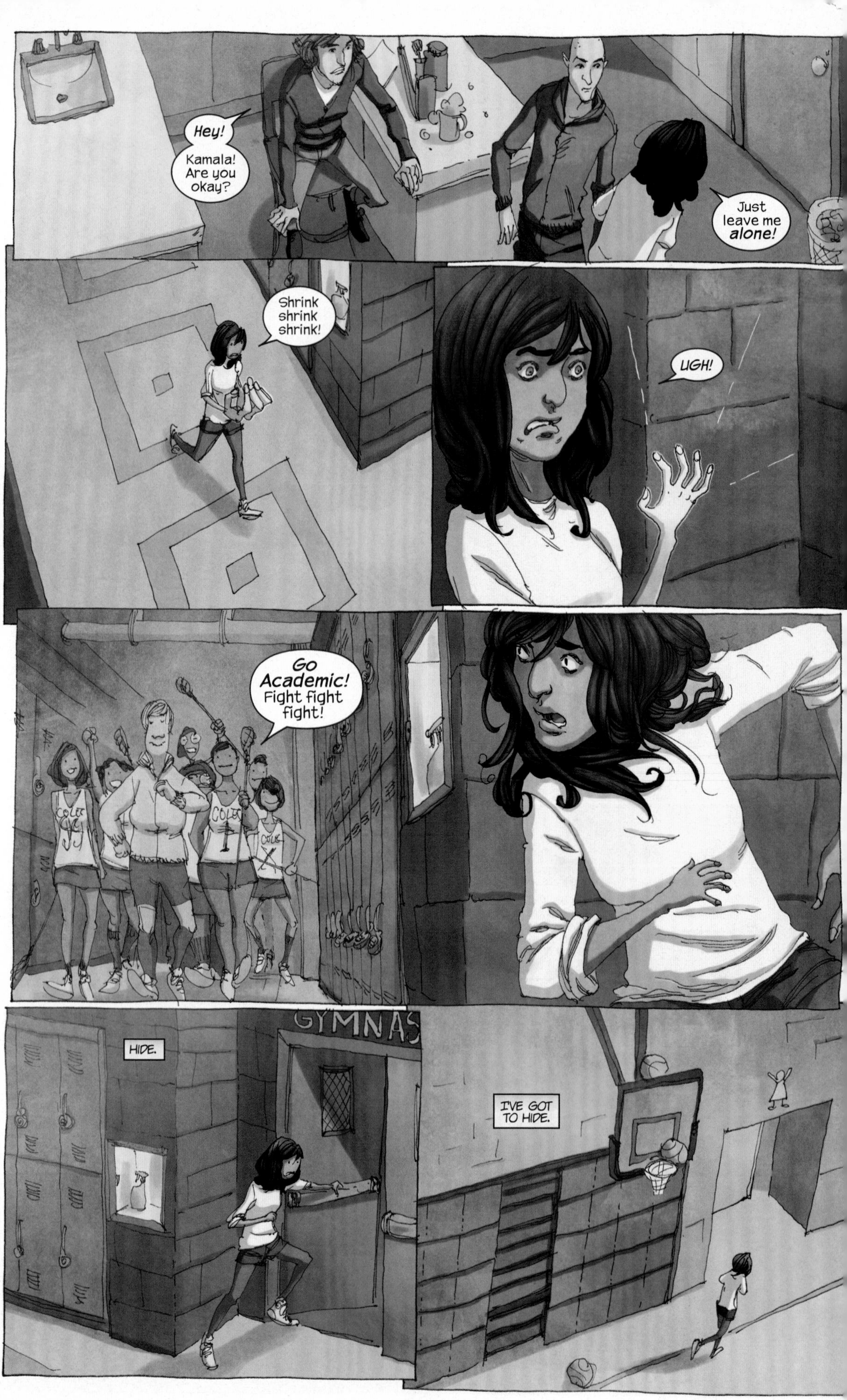
Hey!
Kamala! Are you okay?
Just leave me alone!
Shrink shrink shrink!
UGH!
Go Academic! Fight fight fight!
HIDE.
GYMNAS
I'VE GOT TO HIDE.

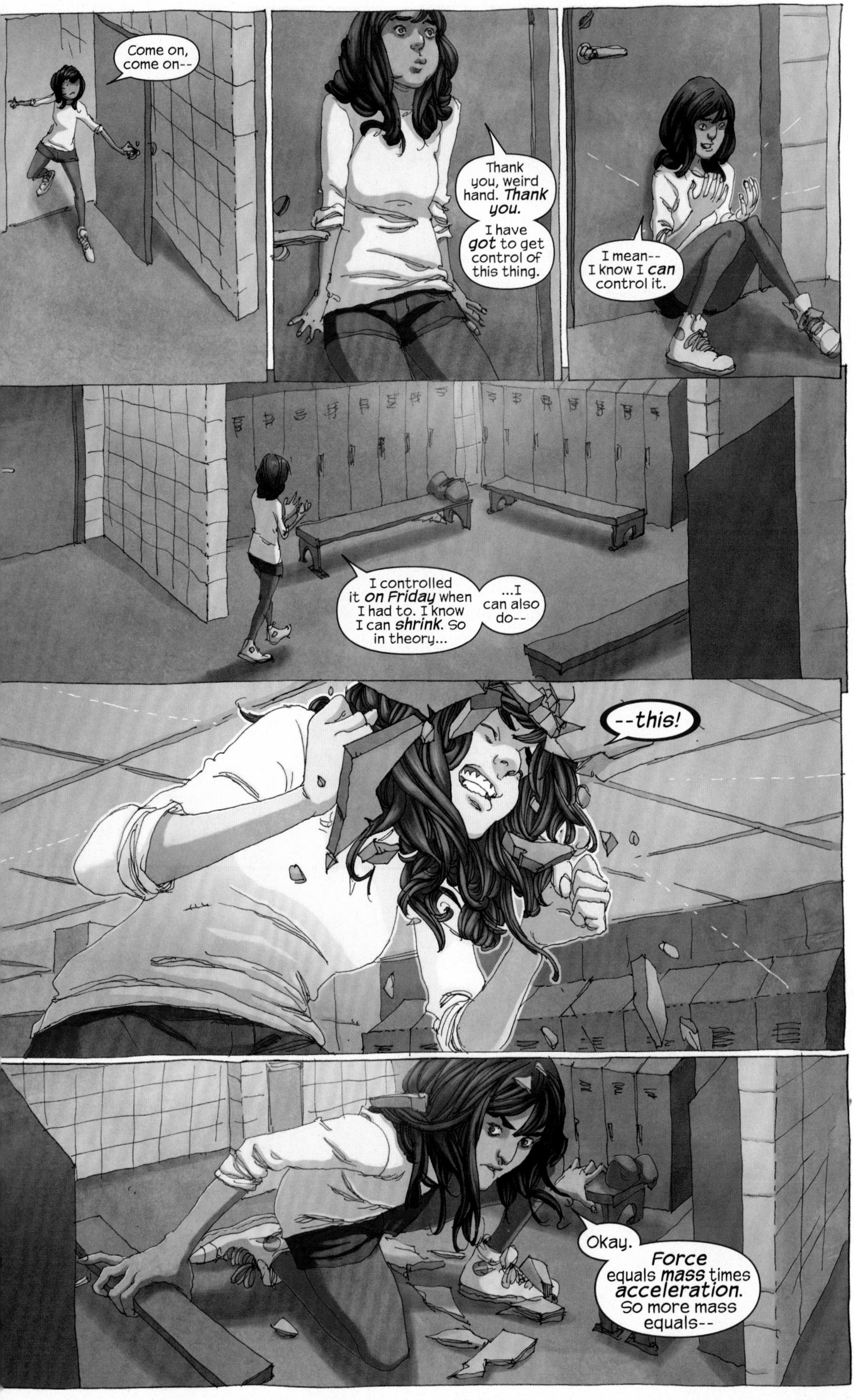
Come on, come on--
Thank you, weird hand. Thank you.
I have got to get control of this thing.
I mean-- I know I can control it.
I controlled it on Friday when I had to. I know I can shrink. So in theory...
...I can also do--
--this!
Okay.
Force equals mass times acceleration. So more mass equals--

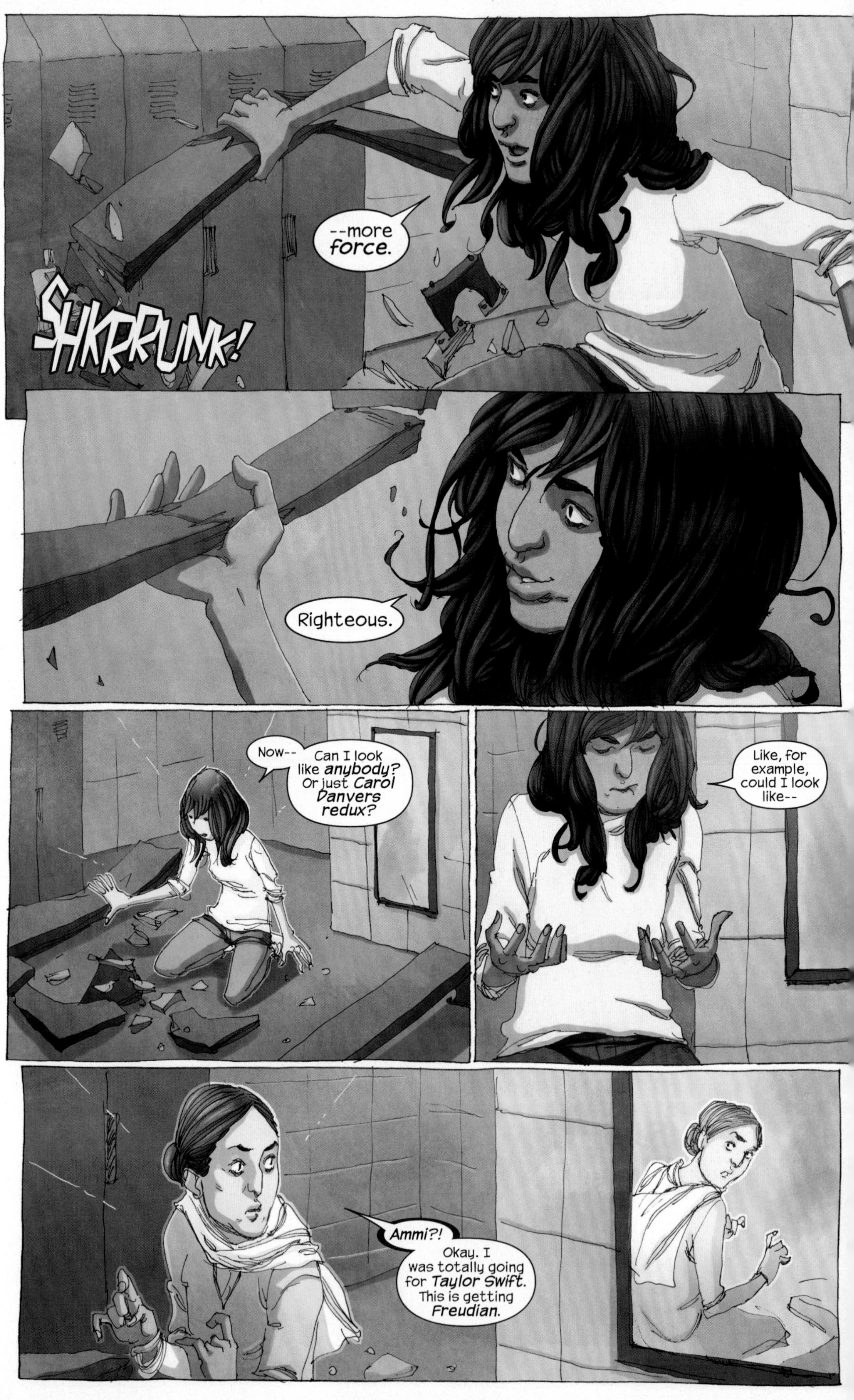
--more force.
SHKRRUNK!
Righteous.
Now--
Can I look like anybody? Or just Carol Danvers redux?
Like, for example, could I look like--
Ammi?!
Okay. I was totally going for Taylor Swift. This is getting Freudian.

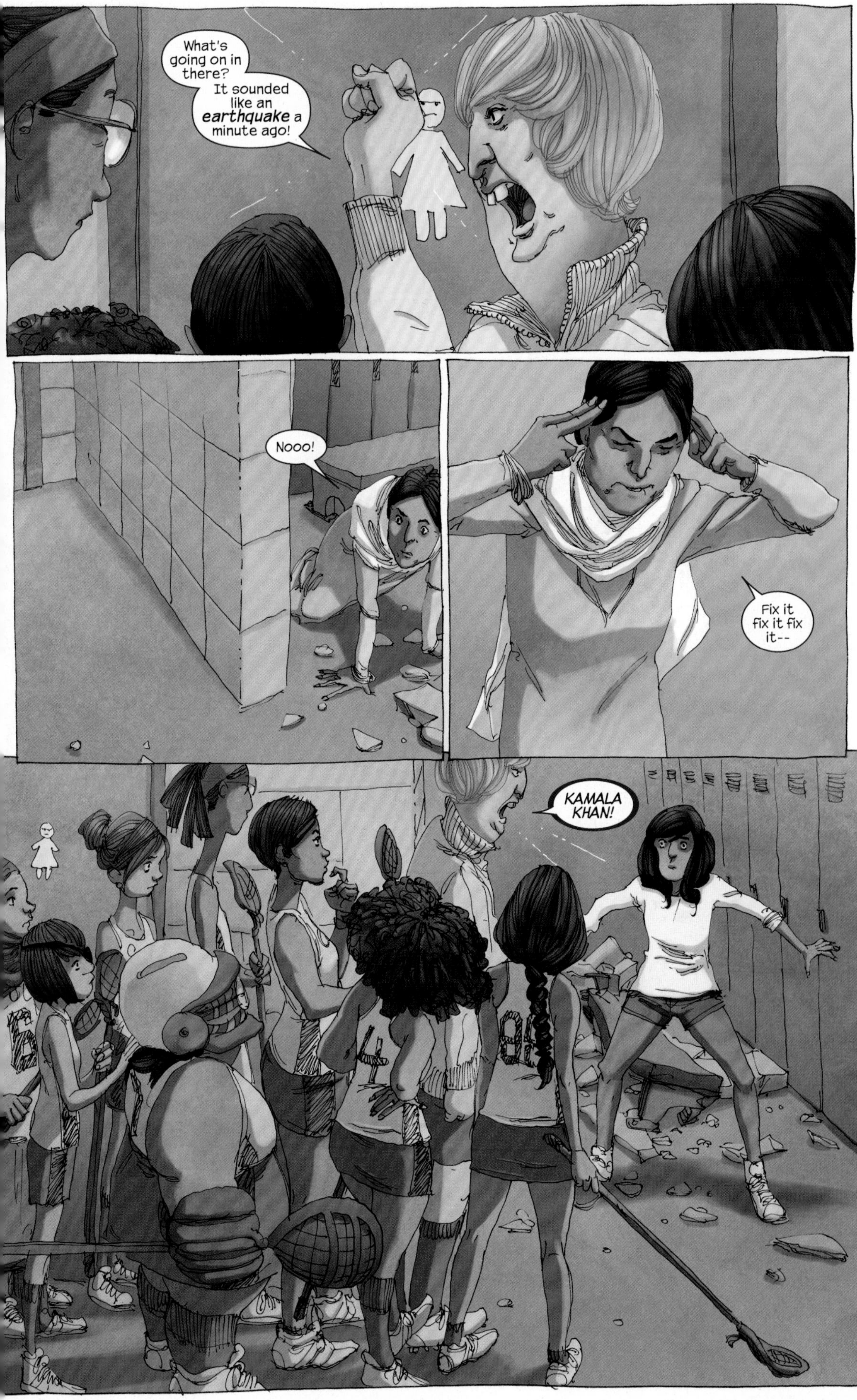
What's going on in there?
It sounded like an *earthquake* a minute ago!
Nooo!
Fix it fix it fix it--
KAMALA KHAN!

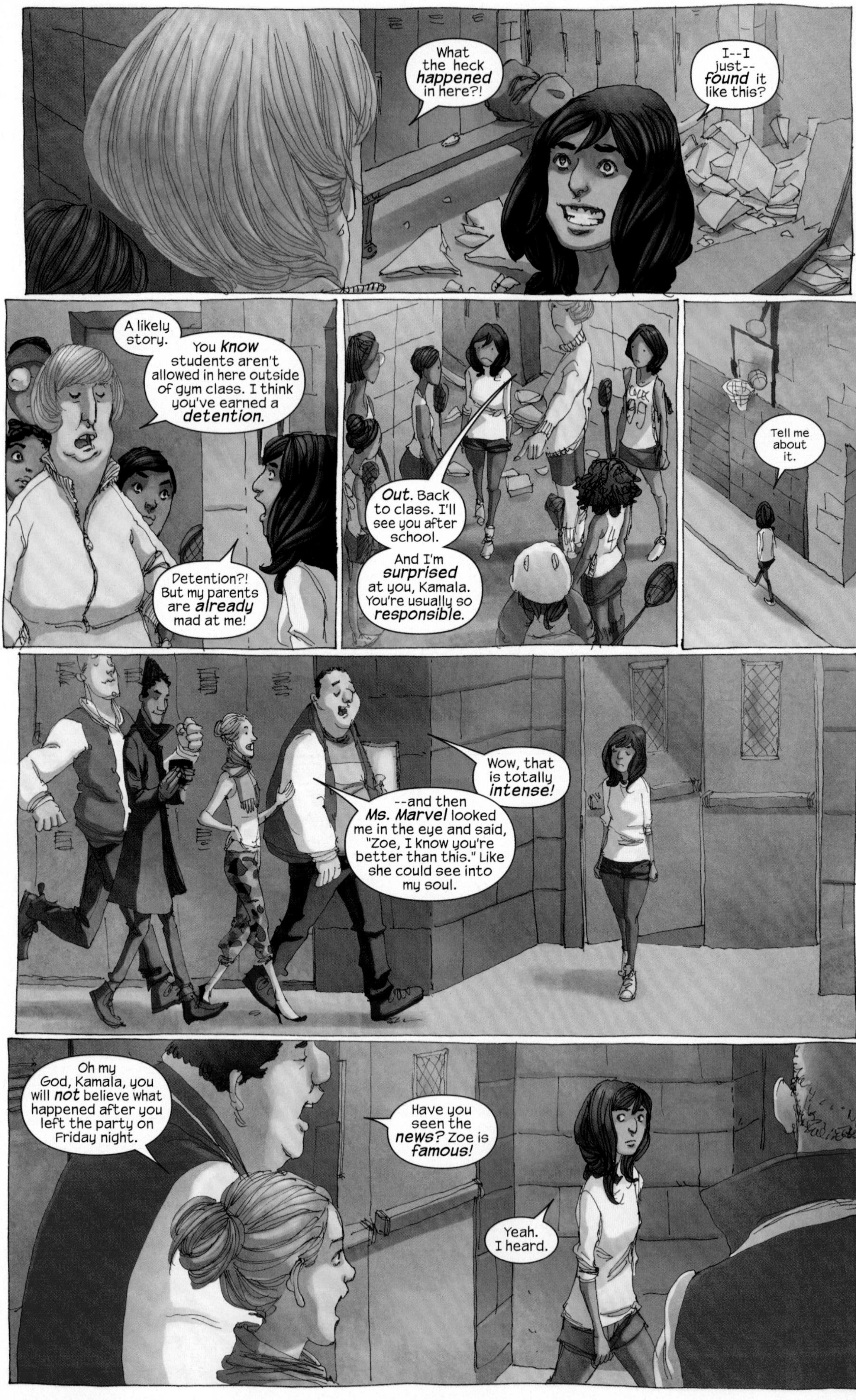
What the heck happened in here?!
I--I just-- found it like this?
A likely story.
You know students aren't allowed in here outside of gym class. I think you've earned a detention.
Detention?! But my parents are already mad at me!
Out. Back to class. I'll see you after school.
And I'm surprised at you, Kamala. You're usually so responsible.
Tell me about it.
--and then Ms. Marvel looked me in the eye and said, "Zoe, I know you're better than this." Like she could see into my soul.
Wow, that is totally intense!
Oh my God, Kamala, you will not believe what happened after you left the party on Friday night.
Have you seen the news? Zoe is famous!
Yeah. I heard.

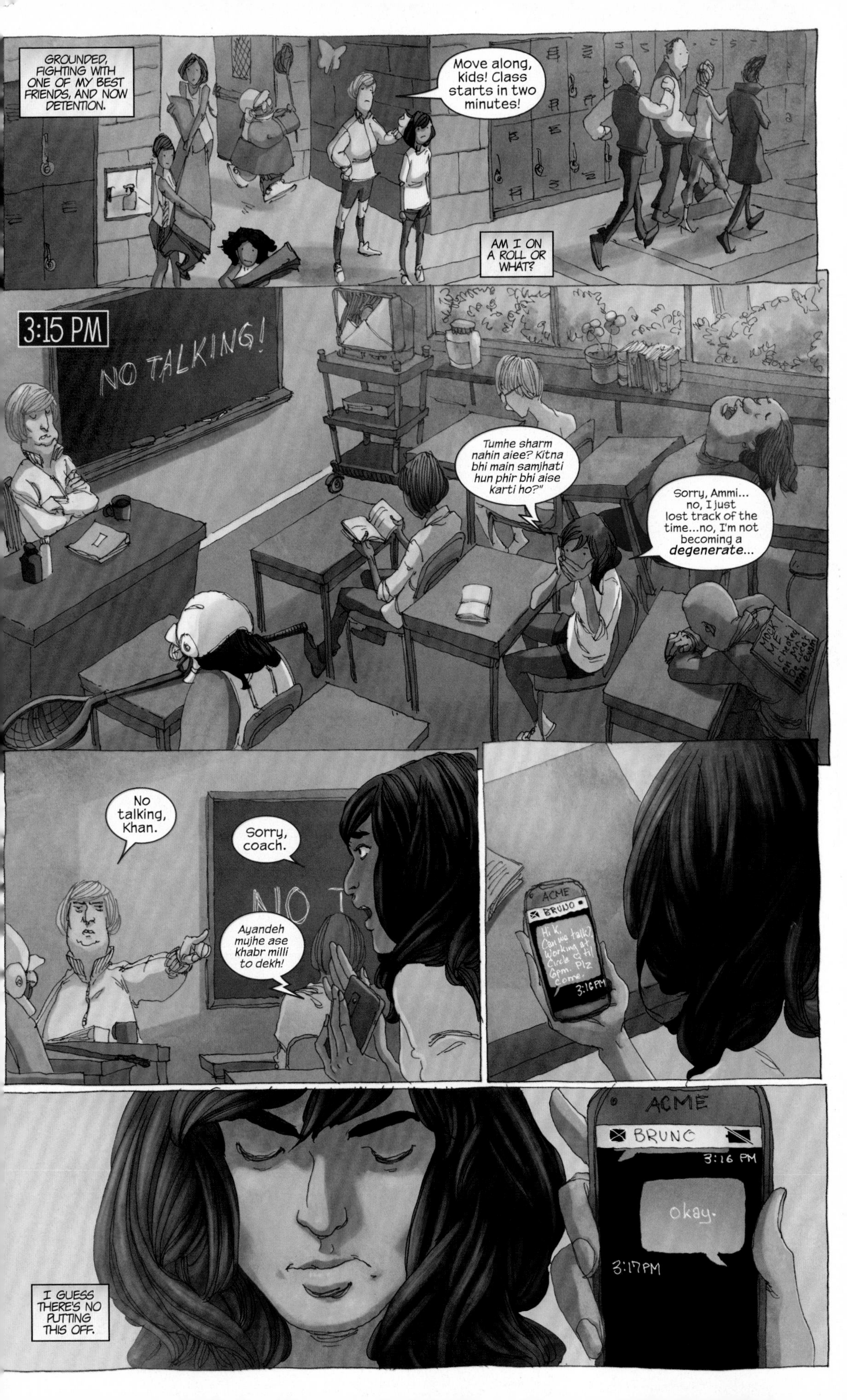
GROUNDED, FIGHTING WITH ONE OF MY BEST FRIENDS, AND NOW DETENTION.
Move along, kids! Class starts in two minutes!
AM I ON A ROLL OR WHAT?
3:15 PM
NO TALKING!
Tumhe sharm nahin aiee? Kitna bhi main samjhati hun phir bhi aise karti ho?"
Sorry, Ammi... no, I just lost track of the time...no, I'm not becoming a *degenerate*...
No talking, Khan.
Sorry, coach.
Ayandeh mujhe ase khabr milli to dekh!
ACME
BRUNO
Hi K, Can we talk? Working at Circle Q til 6pm. Plz come.
3:16PM
ACME
BRUNO
3:16 PM
okay.
3:17PM
I GUESS THERE'S NO PUTTING THIS OFF.

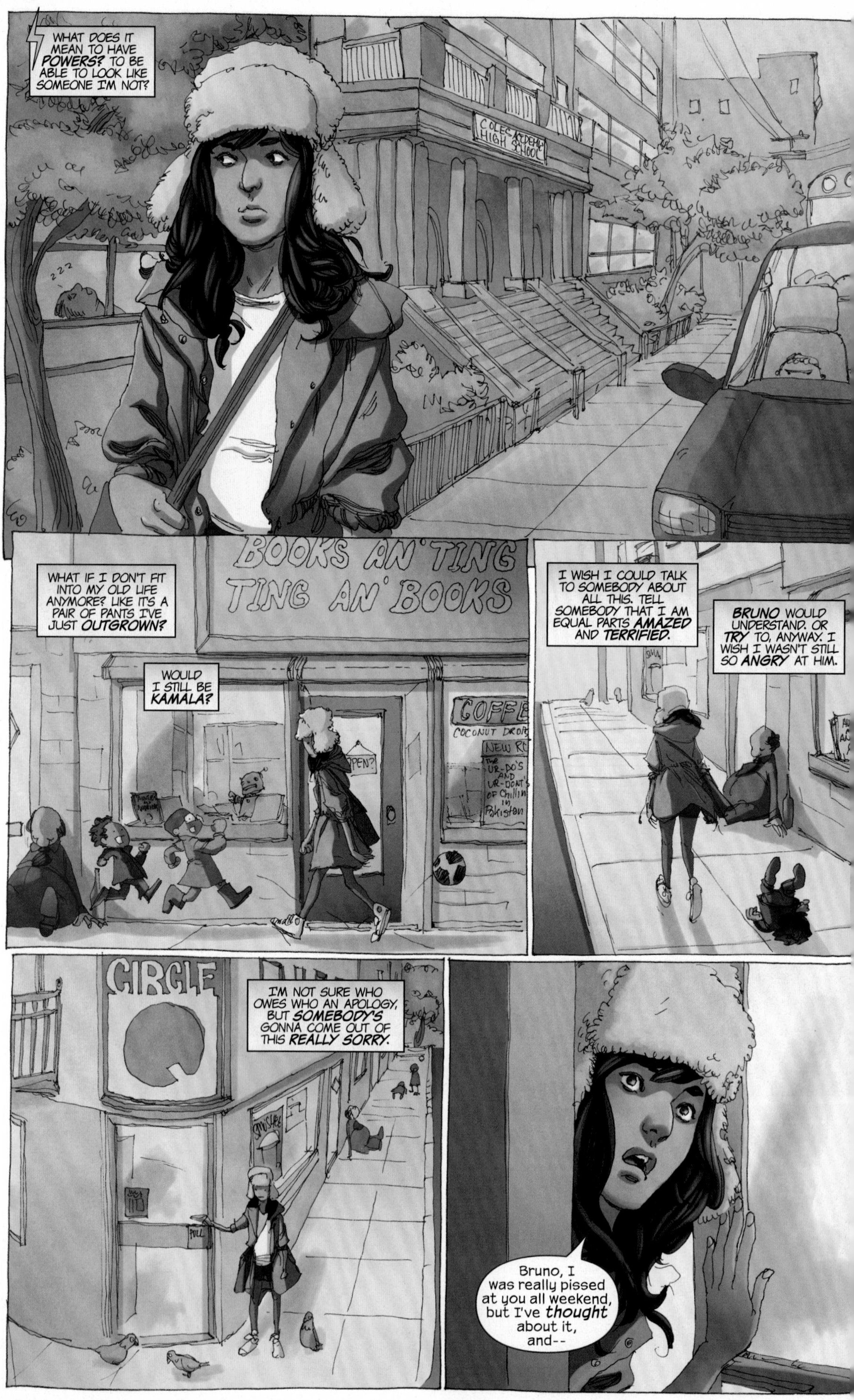
WHAT DOES IT MEAN TO HAVE POWERS? TO BE ABLE TO LOOK LIKE SOMEONE I'M NOT?
COLES ACADEMIC HIGH SCHOOL
BOOKS AN' TING TING AN' BOOKS
WHAT IF I DON'T FIT INTO MY OLD LIFE ANYMORE? LIKE IT'S A PAIR OF PANTS I'VE JUST OUTGROWN?
WOULD I STILL BE KAMALA?
COFFEE
COCONUT DROPS
OPEN?
THE UR-DO'S AND UR-DONT'S OF CHILLIN IN PAKISTAN
I WISH I COULD TALK TO SOMEBODY ABOUT ALL THIS. TELL SOMEBODY THAT I AM EQUAL PARTS AMAZED AND TERRIFIED.
BRUNO WOULD UNDERSTAND. OR TRY TO, ANYWAY. I WISH I WASN'T STILL SO ANGRY AT HIM.
CIRCLE
I'M NOT SURE WHO OWES WHO AN APOLOGY, BUT SOMEBODY'S GONNA COME OUT OF THIS REALLY SORRY.
PULL
Bruno, I was really pissed at you all weekend, but I've thought about it, and--

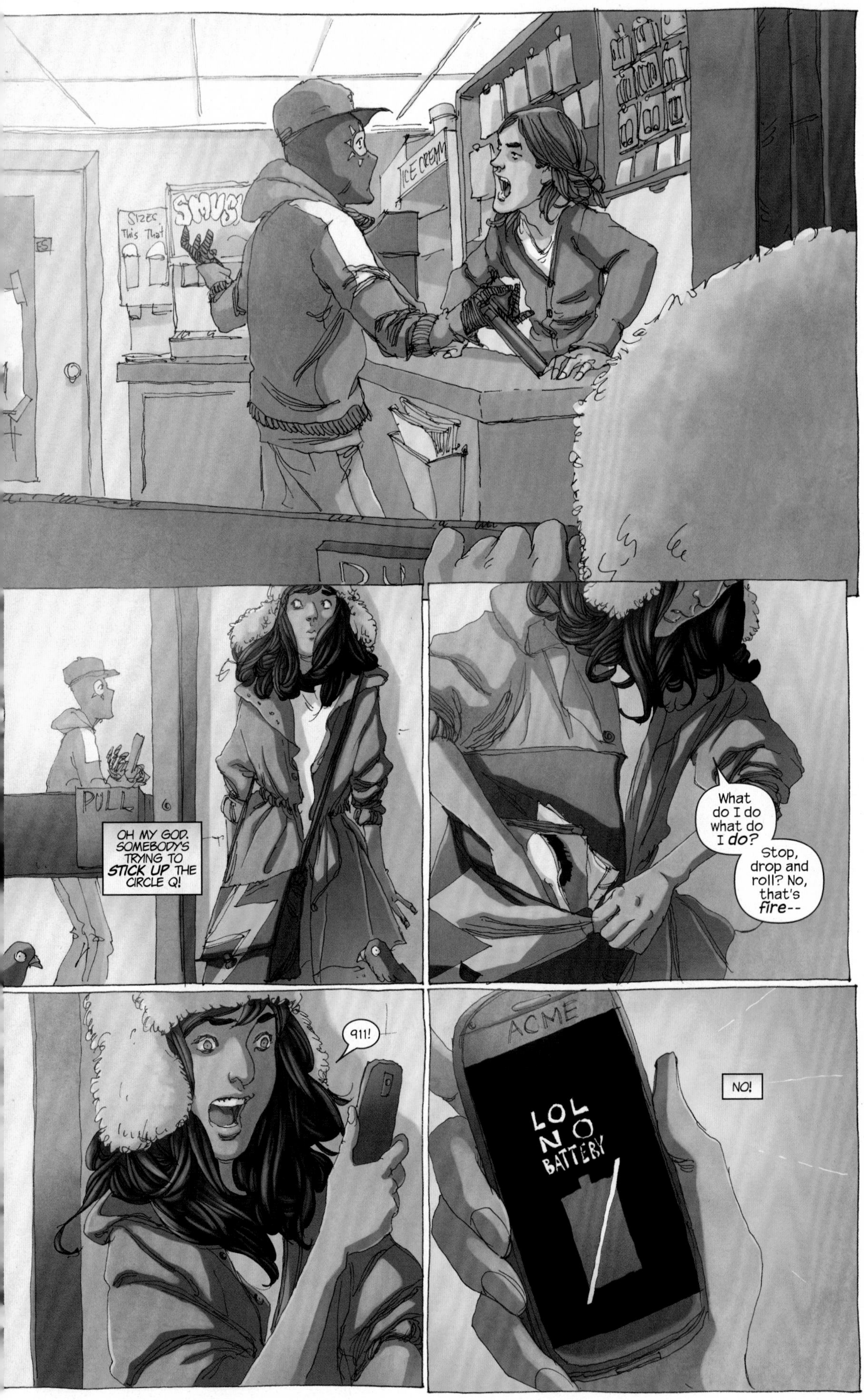
ICE CREAM
Sizes This That
PULL
OH MY GOD. SOMEBODY'S TRYING TO STICK UP THE CIRCLE Q!
What do I do what do I do?
Stop, drop and roll? No, that's fire--
911!
ACME
LOL NO BATTERY
NO!

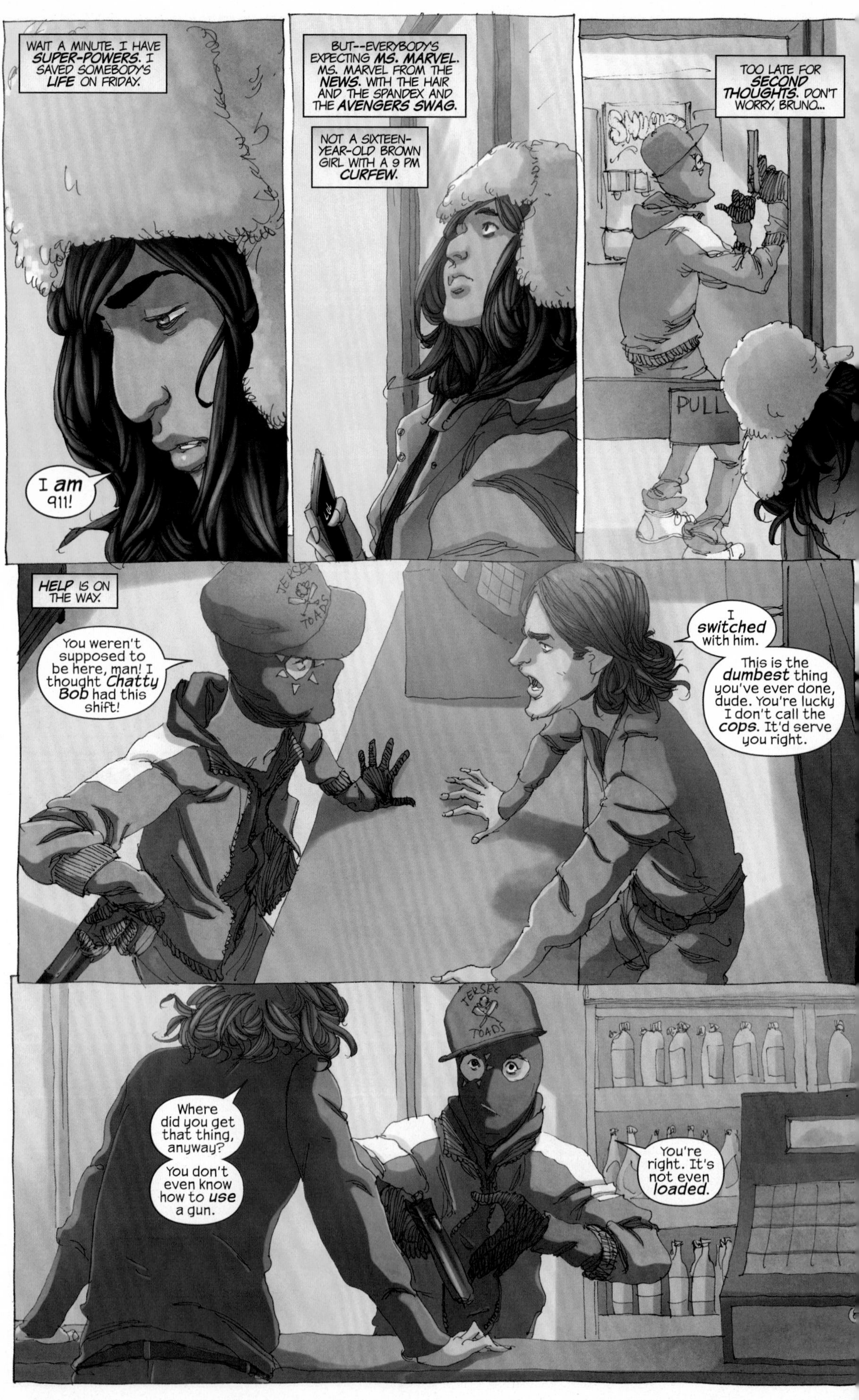
WAIT A MINUTE. I HAVE SUPER-POWERS. I SAVED SOMEBODY'S LIFE ON FRIDAY.
I am 911!
BUT--EVERYBODY'S EXPECTING MS. MARVEL. MS. MARVEL FROM THE NEWS. WITH THE HAIR AND THE SPANDEX AND THE AVENGERS SWAG.
NOT A SIXTEEN-YEAR-OLD BROWN GIRL WITH A 9 PM CURFEW.
TOO LATE FOR SECOND THOUGHTS. DON'T WORRY, BRUNO...
PULL
HELP IS ON THE WAY.
JERSEY TOADS
You weren't supposed to be here, man! I thought Chatty Bob had this shift!
I switched with him.
This is the dumbest thing you've ever done, dude. You're lucky I don't call the cops. It'd serve you right.
JERSEY TOADS
Where did you get that thing, anyway?
You don't even know how to use a gun.
You're right. It's not even loaded.

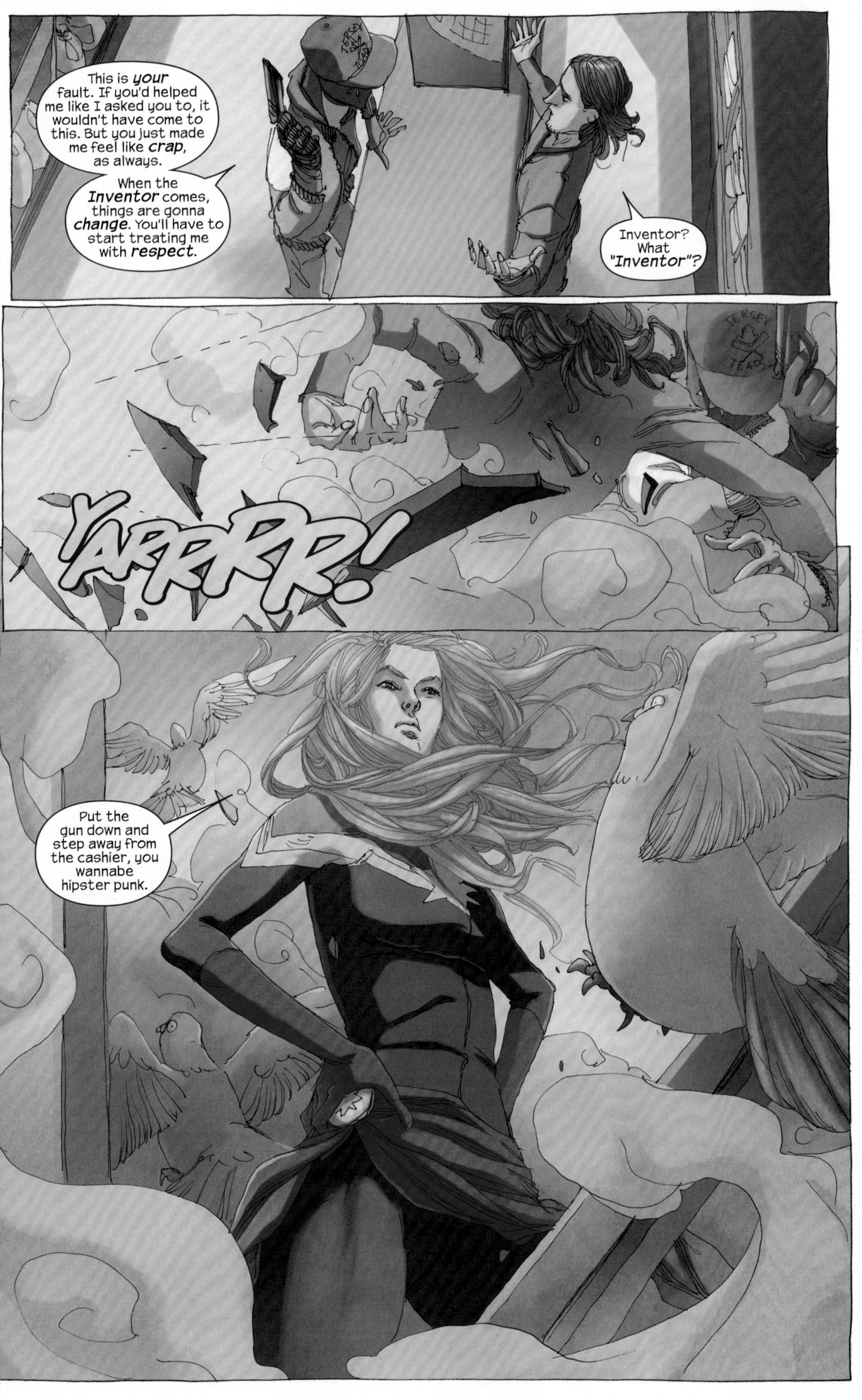
This is your fault. If you'd helped me like I asked you to, it wouldn't have come to this. But you just made me feel like crap, as always.
When the Inventor comes, things are gonna change. You'll have to start treating me with respect.
Inventor? What "Inventor"?
YARRRR!
Put the gun down and step away from the cashier, you wannabe hipster punk.

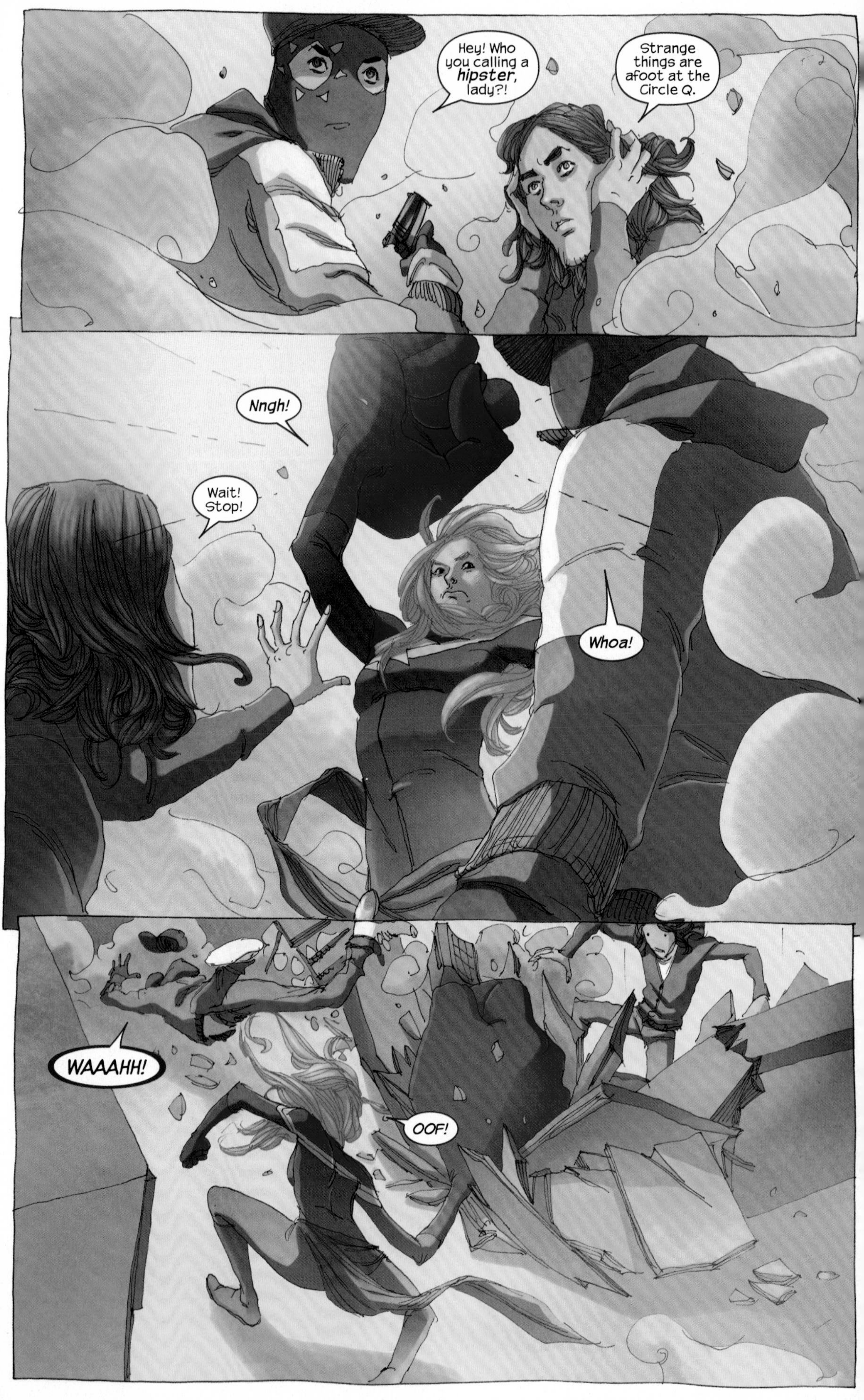
Hey! Who you calling a **hipster**, lady?!
Strange things are afoot at the Circle Q.
Nngh!
Wait! Stop!
Whoa!
WAAAHH!
OOF!

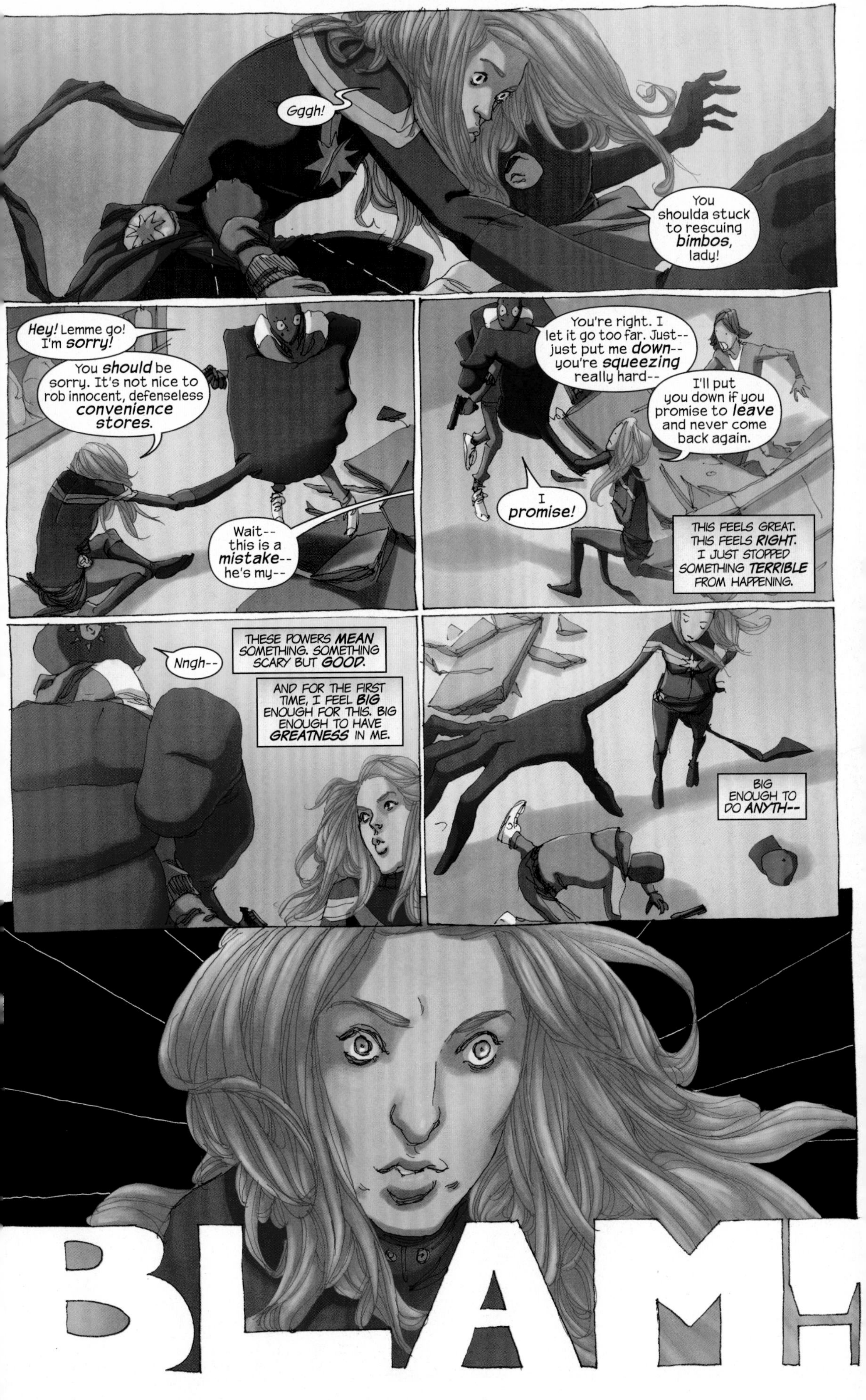
Gggh!
You shoulda stuck to rescuing bimbos, lady!
Hey! Lemme go! I'm sorry!
You should be sorry. It's not nice to rob innocent, defenseless convenience stores.
Wait-- this is a mistake-- he's my--
You're right. I let it go too far. Just-- just put me down-- you're squeezing really hard--
I'll put you down if you promise to leave and never come back again.
I promise!
THIS FEELS GREAT. THIS FEELS RIGHT. I JUST STOPPED SOMETHING TERRIBLE FROM HAPPENING.
Nngh--
THESE POWERS MEAN SOMETHING. SOMETHING SCARY BUT GOOD.
AND FOR THE FIRST TIME, I FEEL BIG ENOUGH FOR THIS. BIG ENOUGH TO HAVE GREATNESS IN ME.
BIG ENOUGH TO DO ANYTH--
BLAMH

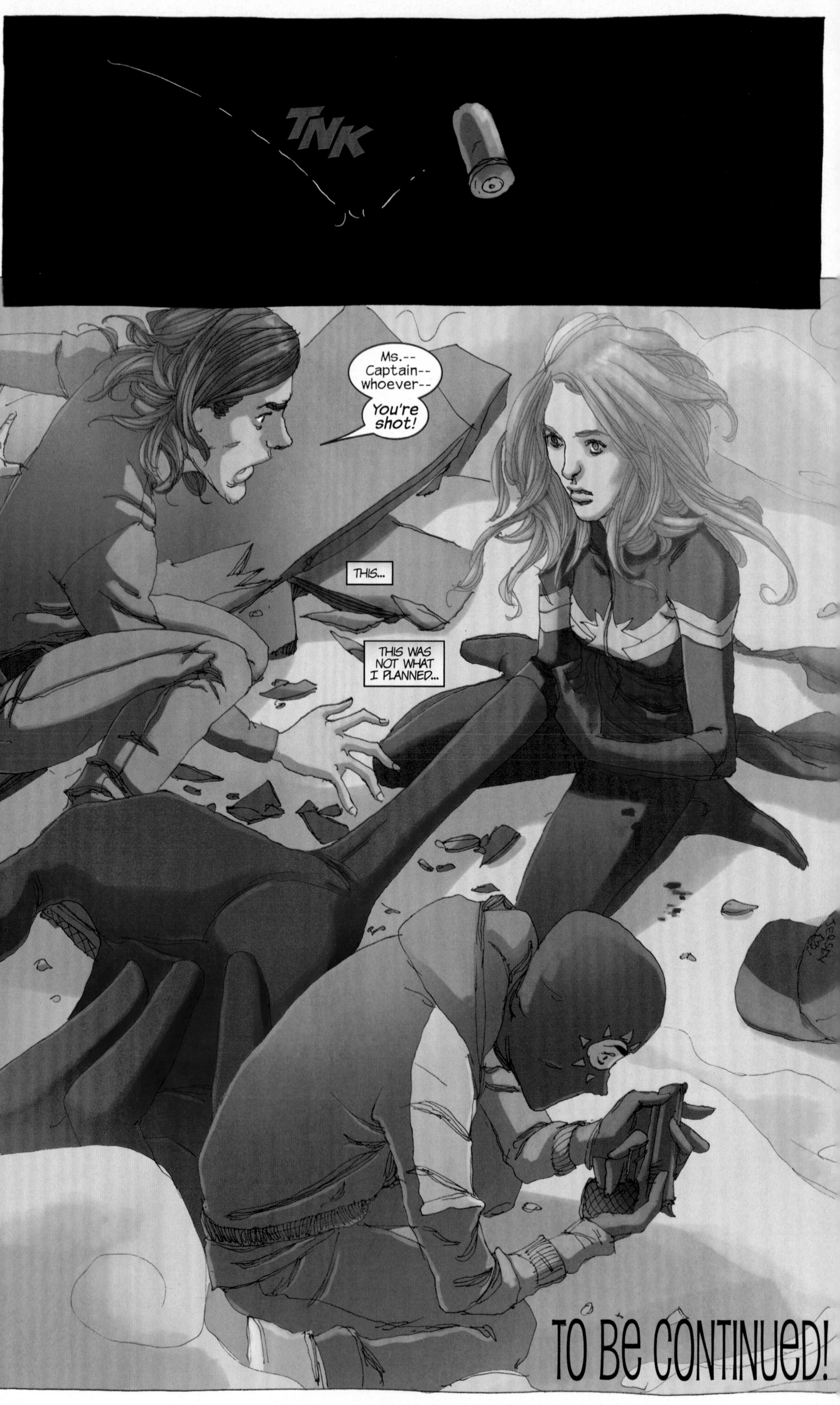
TNK
Ms.-- Captain-- whoever-- You're shot!
THIS...
THIS WAS NOT WHAT I PLANNED...
TO BE CONTINUED!

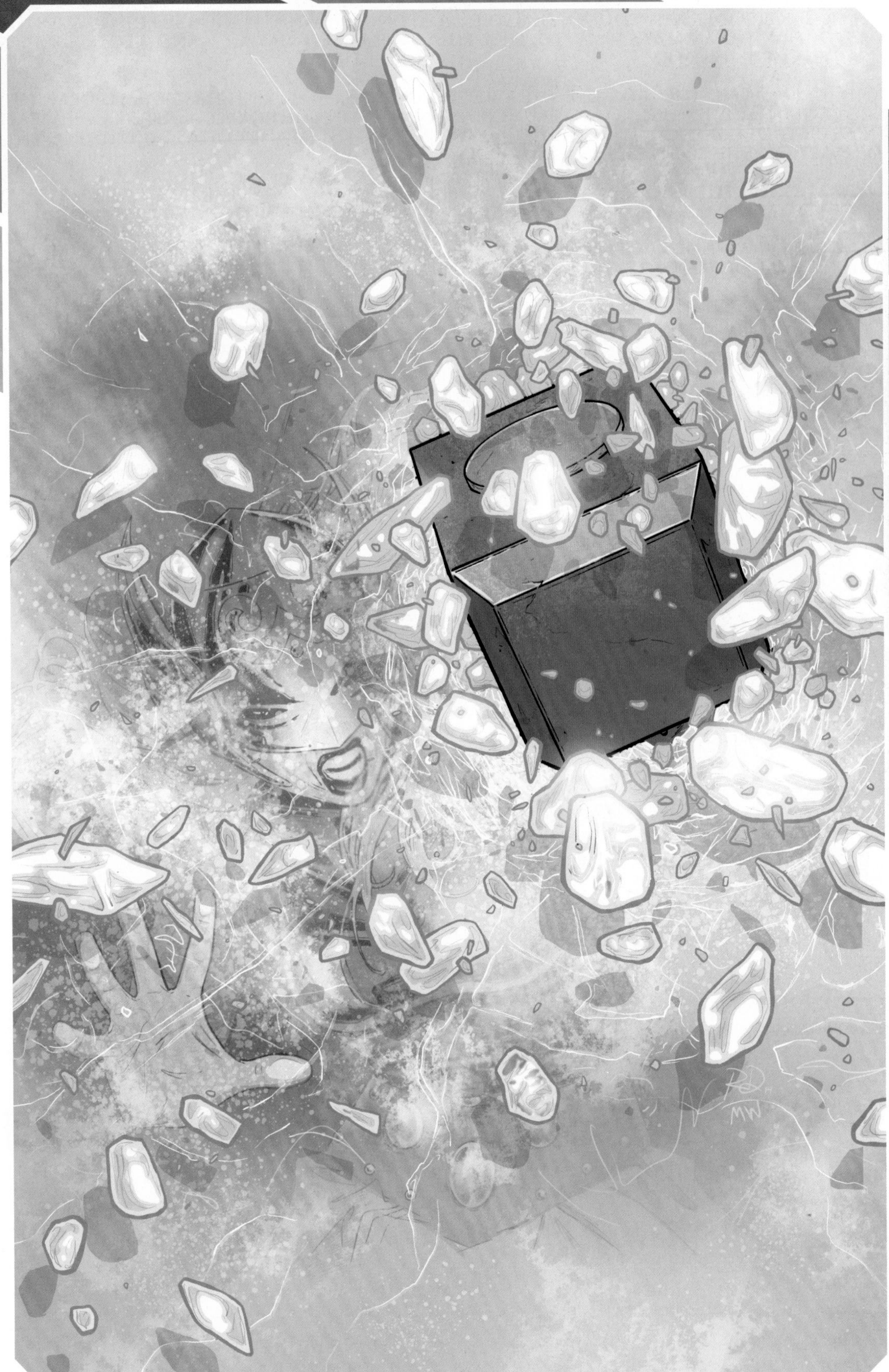

THOR #3

A NEW THOR HAS RISEN.

AFTER THOR ODINSON FOUND HIMSELF NO LONGER WORTHY OF WIELDING MJOLNIR, A MYSTERIOUS WOMAN WAS ABLE TO LIFT THE ENCHANTED HAMMER AND BECAME THE NEW GODDESS OF THUNDER.

AND JUST IN TIME, TOO. BECAUSE THE EVIL ELF SORCERER MALEKITH HAS TEAMED UP WITH THE FROST GIANTS OF JOTUNHEIM TO LAUNCH AN ASSAULT ON THE ROXXON ENERGY CORPORATION IN SEARCH OF AN ANCIENT ARTIFACT, TAKING DOWN THE ARMIES OF ASGARD AND EVEN THE AVENGERS IN THE PROCESS.

DARIO AGGER, THE CEO OF ROXXON, HAS FLED INTO THE IMPENETRABLE VAULT WHERE THE ARTIFACT IS KEPT, MANAGING TO TRAP MJOLNIR IN THE VAULT WITH HIM.

NOW THE NEW THOR MUST PROVE HERSELF THE GODDESS OF THUNDER TO STOP MALEKITH AND SAVE ALL OF MIDGARD. IF ONLY SHE COULD GET THAT HAMMER BACK...

WHEN THE ICE LORDS MAKE WAR

JASON AARON
WRITER

RUSSELL DAUTERMAN
ARTIST

MATTHEW WILSON
COLOR ARTIST

VC's JOE SABINO
LETTERER & PRODUCTION

RUSSELL DAUTERMAN & MATTHEW WILSON
COVER ARTISTS

JAMES HARREN
VARIANT COVER ARTIST

JON MOISAN
ASSISTANT EDITOR

WIL MOSS
EDITOR

AXEL ALONSO
EDITOR IN CHIEF

JOE QUESADA
CHIEF CREATIVE OFFICER

DAN BUCKLEY
PUBLISHER

ALAN FINE
EXECUTIVE PRODUCER

THOR CREATED BY STAN LEE, LARRY LIEBER & JACK KIRBY

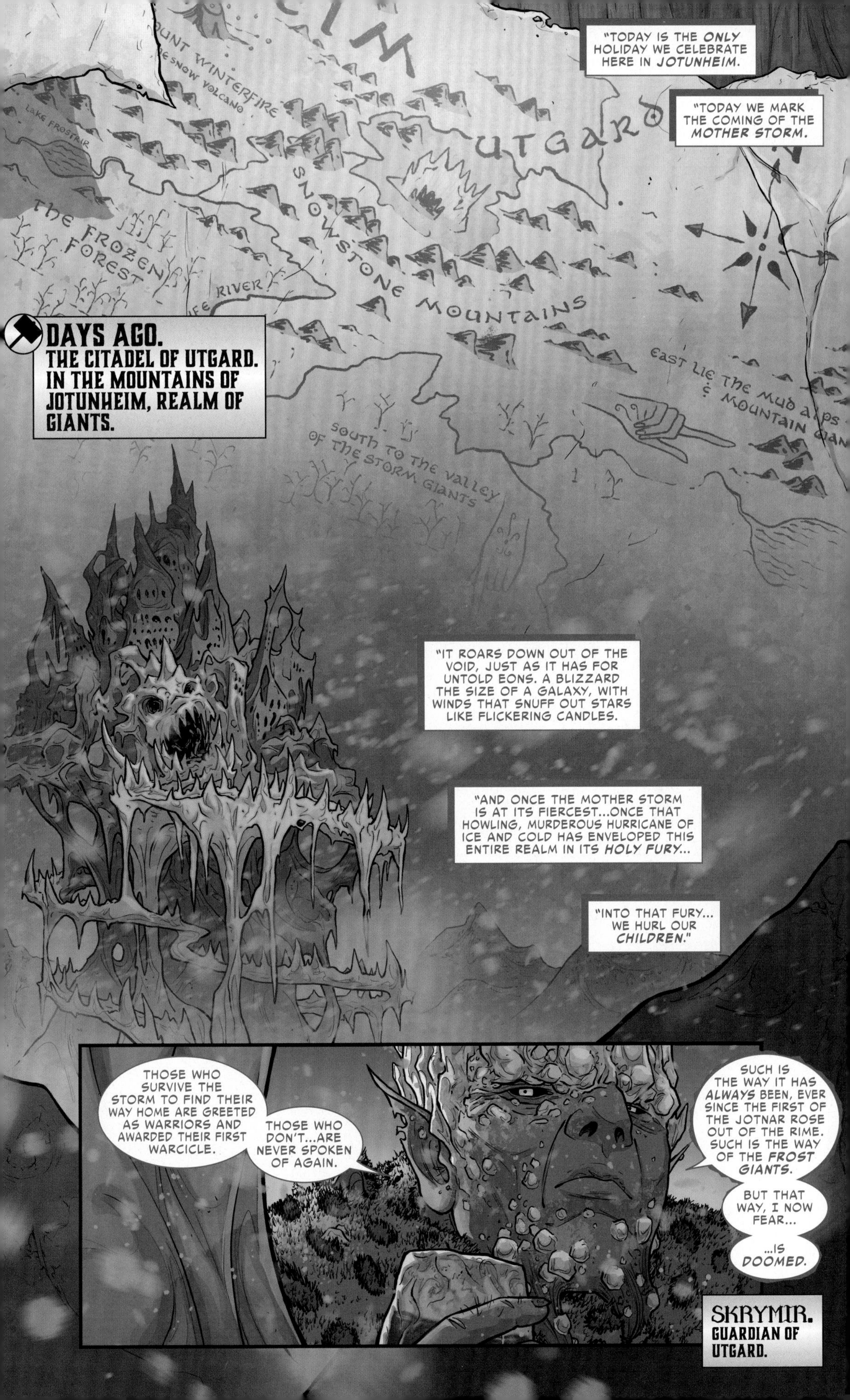

"TODAY IS THE *ONLY* HOLIDAY WE CELEBRATE HERE IN *JOTUNHEIM*.
"TODAY WE MARK THE COMING OF THE *MOTHER STORM*.
UTGARD
LAKE FROSTRIR
SNOWSTONE MOUNTAINS
THE FROZEN FOREST
RIVER
EAST LIE THE MUD ALPS
SOUTH TO THE VALLEY OF THE STORM GIANTS
DAYS AGO.
THE CITADEL OF UTGARD. IN THE MOUNTAINS OF JOTUNHEIM, REALM OF GIANTS.
"IT ROARS DOWN OUT OF THE VOID, JUST AS IT HAS FOR UNTOLD EONS. A BLIZZARD THE SIZE OF A GALAXY, WITH WINDS THAT SNUFF OUT STARS LIKE FLICKERING CANDLES.
"AND ONCE THE MOTHER STORM IS AT ITS FIERCEST...ONCE THAT HOWLING, MURDEROUS HURRICANE OF ICE AND COLD HAS ENVELOPED THIS ENTIRE REALM IN ITS *HOLY FURY*...
"INTO THAT FURY... WE HURL OUR *CHILDREN*."
THOSE WHO SURVIVE THE STORM TO FIND THEIR WAY HOME ARE GREETED AS WARRIORS AND AWARDED THEIR FIRST WARCICLE.
THOSE WHO DON'T...ARE NEVER SPOKEN OF AGAIN.
SUCH IS THE WAY IT HAS *ALWAYS* BEEN, EVER SINCE THE FIRST OF THE JOTNAR ROSE OUT OF THE RIME. SUCH IS THE WAY OF THE *FROST GIANTS*.
BUT THAT WAY, I NOW FEAR...
...IS *DOOMED*.
SKRYMIR. GUARDIAN OF UTGARD.

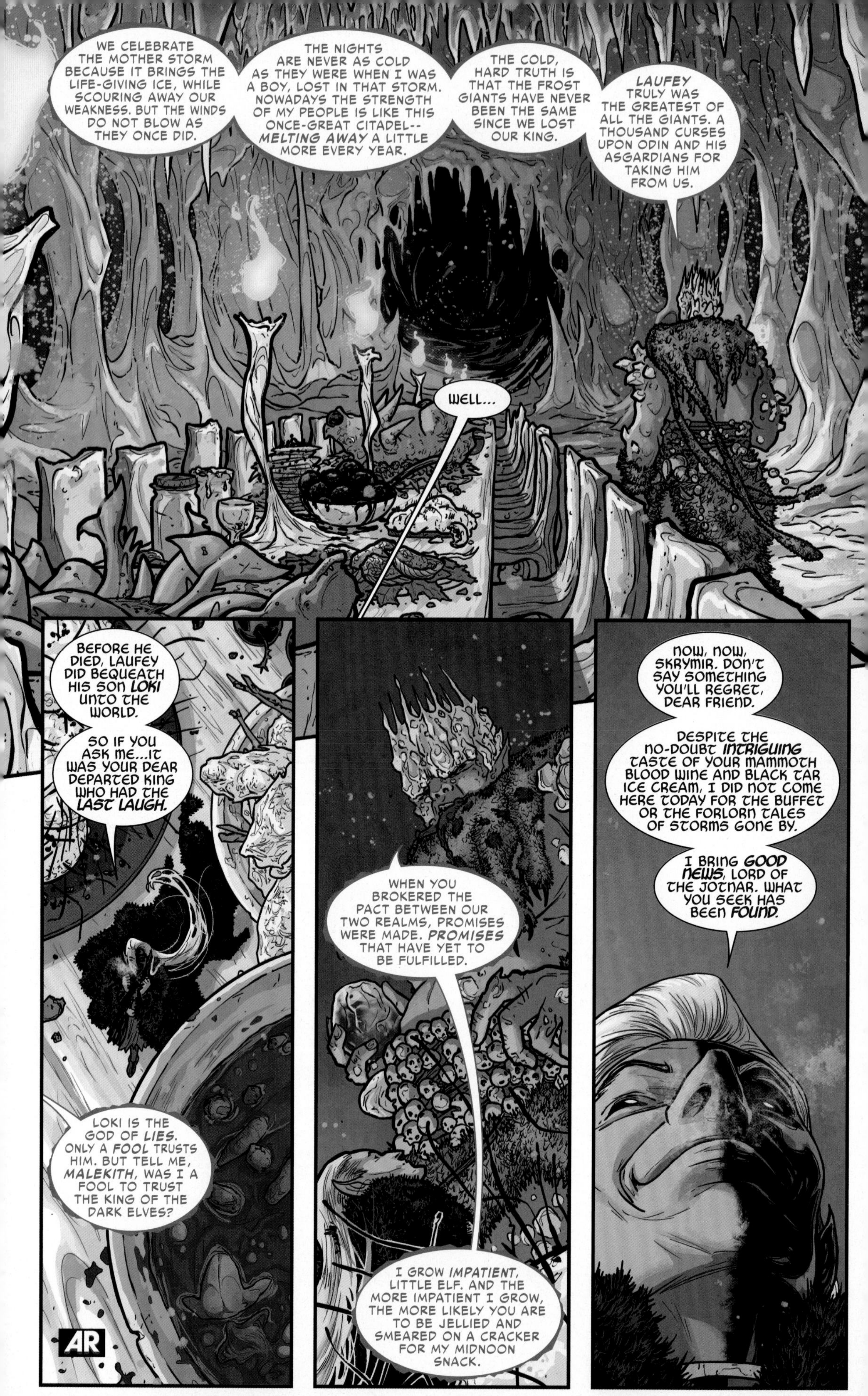
WE CELEBRATE THE MOTHER STORM BECAUSE IT BRINGS THE LIFE-GIVING ICE, WHILE SCOURING AWAY OUR WEAKNESS. BUT THE WINDS DO NOT BLOW AS THEY ONCE DID.
THE NIGHTS ARE NEVER AS COLD AS THEY WERE WHEN I WAS A BOY, LOST IN THAT STORM. NOWADAYS THE STRENGTH OF MY PEOPLE IS LIKE THIS ONCE-GREAT CITADEL-- MELTING AWAY A LITTLE MORE EVERY YEAR.
THE COLD, HARD TRUTH IS THAT THE FROST GIANTS HAVE NEVER BEEN THE SAME SINCE WE LOST OUR KING.
LAUFEY TRULY WAS THE GREATEST OF ALL THE GIANTS. A THOUSAND CURSES UPON ODIN AND HIS ASGARDIANS FOR TAKING HIM FROM US.
WELL...
BEFORE HE DIED, LAUFEY DID BEQUEATH HIS SON LOKI UNTO THE WORLD.
SO IF YOU ASK ME...IT WAS YOUR DEAR DEPARTED KING WHO HAD THE LAST LAUGH.
LOKI IS THE GOD OF LIES. ONLY A FOOL TRUSTS HIM. BUT TELL ME, MALEKITH, WAS I A FOOL TO TRUST THE KING OF THE DARK ELVES?
WHEN YOU BROKERED THE PACT BETWEEN OUR TWO REALMS, PROMISES WERE MADE. PROMISES THAT HAVE YET TO BE FULFILLED.
I GROW IMPATIENT, LITTLE ELF. AND THE MORE IMPATIENT I GROW, THE MORE LIKELY YOU ARE TO BE JELLIED AND SMEARED ON A CRACKER FOR MY MIDNOON SNACK.
NOW, NOW, SKRYMIR. DON'T SAY SOMETHING YOU'LL REGRET, DEAR FRIEND.
DESPITE THE NO-DOUBT INTRIGUING TASTE OF YOUR MAMMOTH BLOOD WINE AND BLACK TAR ICE CREAM, I DID NOT COME HERE TODAY FOR THE BUFFET OR THE FORLORN TALES OF STORMS GONE BY.
I BRING GOOD NEWS, LORD OF THE JOTNAR. WHAT YOU SEEK HAS BEEN FOUND.
AR

YOU *HAVE* IT? THE LOST *SKULL* OF KING LAUFEY?

AH, I SAID IT HAD BEEN *FOUND.* I DID NOT SAY BY ME. THE AUGURIES TELL ME IT WAS RECENTLY UNEARTHED BY SOMETHING CALLED *ROXXON.* APPARENTLY A GUILD OF MINERS AND TRADESMEN.

LIKE DWARVES?

YES, BUT WORSE. *HUMANS.*

DAMN YOUR *EYES,* ELF! LAUFEY'S BONES ARE STILL ON *MIDGARD,* WHERE THEY WERE LOST CENTURIES AGO?!

IT WAS YOUR JOB TO *PROCURE* THAT SKULL, NOT JUST LOCATE IT!

WHAT WOULD YOU HAVE ME DO, *INVADE* MIDGARD?

WELL, NOW THAT YOU MENTION IT...

INVADING MIDGARD MEANS GOING TO *WAR* WITH ASGARD. WITH *THOR.* WE ARE NOT READY FOR SUCH A WAR. NOT WITHOUT THE SKULL. NOT WITHOUT OUR KING.

I WILL NOT SEE US FALL YET AGAIN TO THAT DAMNED ODINSON AND HIS WRETCHED HAMMER!

YOU MAY JUST CHANGE YOUR MIND ONCE YOU'VE HEARD WHAT MY *SPIES* IN ASGARDIA HAVE BEEN SO EXCITEDLY WHISPERING.

TELL ME, SKRYMIR...WHAT IS THOR *WITHOUT* HIS MJOLNIR?

WITHOUT THE HAMMER...?

NOTHING.

NOTHING BUT A GOD.

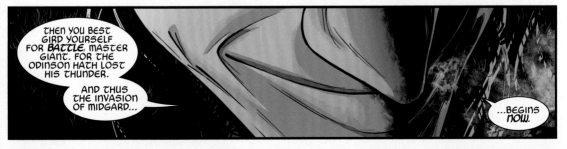

THEN YOU BEST GIRD YOURSELF FOR *BATTLE,* MASTER GIANT. FOR THE ODINSON HATH LOST HIS THUNDER.

AND THUS THE INVASION OF MIDGARD...

...BEGINS *NOW.*

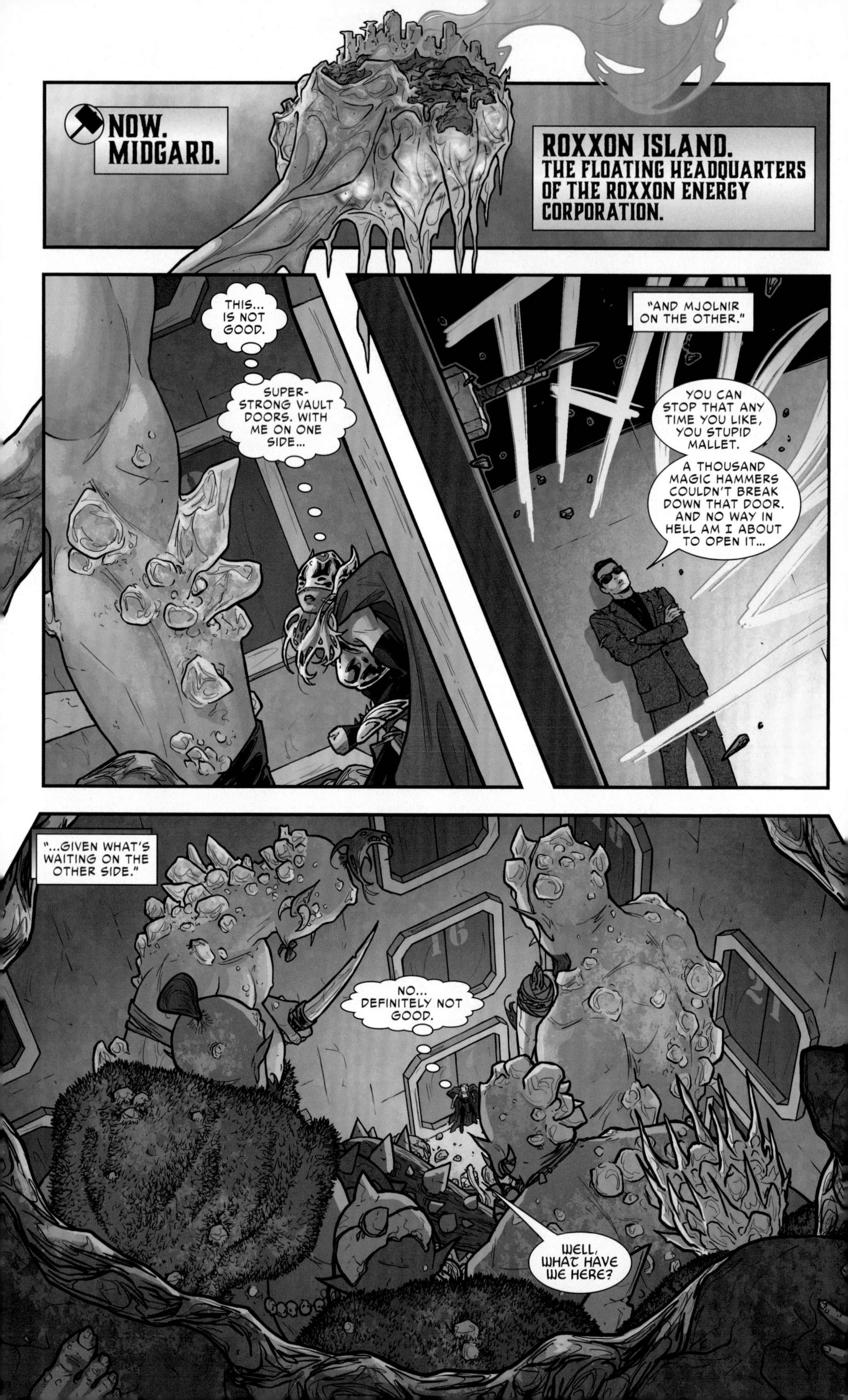
NOW. MIDGARD.
ROXXON ISLAND.
THE FLOATING HEADQUARTERS OF THE ROXXON ENERGY CORPORATION.
THIS... IS NOT GOOD.
SUPER-STRONG VAULT DOORS. WITH ME ON ONE SIDE...
"AND MJOLNIR ON THE OTHER."
YOU CAN STOP THAT ANY TIME YOU LIKE, YOU STUPID MALLET.
A THOUSAND MAGIC HAMMERS COULDN'T BREAK DOWN THAT DOOR. AND NO WAY IN HELL AM I ABOUT TO OPEN IT...
"...GIVEN WHAT'S WAITING ON THE OTHER SIDE."
NO... DEFINITELY NOT GOOD.
WELL, WHAT HAVE WE HERE?

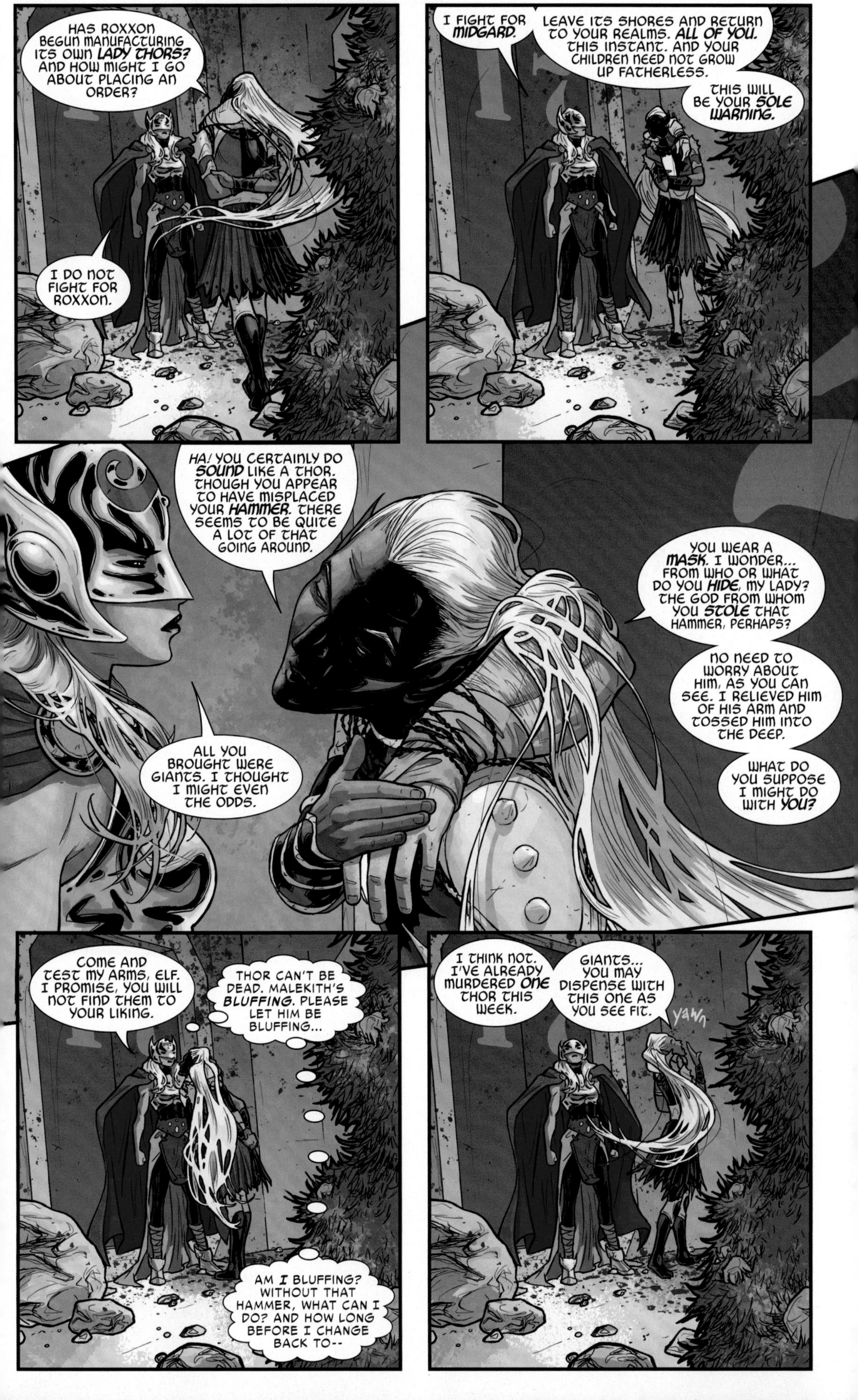
HAS ROXXON BEGUN MANUFACTURING ITS OWN LADY THORS? AND HOW MIGHT I GO ABOUT PLACING AN ORDER?
I DO NOT FIGHT FOR ROXXON.
I FIGHT FOR MIDGARD.
LEAVE ITS SHORES AND RETURN TO YOUR REALMS. ALL OF YOU. THIS INSTANT. AND YOUR CHILDREN NEED NOT GROW UP FATHERLESS.
THIS WILL BE YOUR SOLE WARNING.
HA! YOU CERTAINLY DO SOUND LIKE A THOR. THOUGH YOU APPEAR TO HAVE MISPLACED YOUR HAMMER. THERE SEEMS TO BE QUITE A LOT OF THAT GOING AROUND.
ALL YOU BROUGHT WERE GIANTS. I THOUGHT I MIGHT EVEN THE ODDS.
YOU WEAR A MASK. I WONDER... FROM WHO OR WHAT DO YOU HIDE, MY LADY? THE GOD FROM WHOM YOU STOLE THAT HAMMER, PERHAPS?
NO NEED TO WORRY ABOUT HIM, AS YOU CAN SEE. I RELIEVED HIM OF HIS ARM AND TOSSED HIM INTO THE DEEP.
WHAT DO YOU SUPPOSE I MIGHT DO WITH YOU?
COME AND TEST MY ARMS, ELF. I PROMISE, YOU WILL NOT FIND THEM TO YOUR LIKING.
THOR CAN'T BE DEAD. MALEKITH'S BLUFFING. PLEASE LET HIM BE BLUFFING...
AM I BLUFFING? WITHOUT THAT HAMMER, WHAT CAN I DO? AND HOW LONG BEFORE I CHANGE BACK TO--
I THINK NOT. I'VE ALREADY MURDERED ONE THOR THIS WEEK.
GIANTS... YOU MAY DISPENSE WITH THIS ONE AS YOU SEE FIT.
YAWN

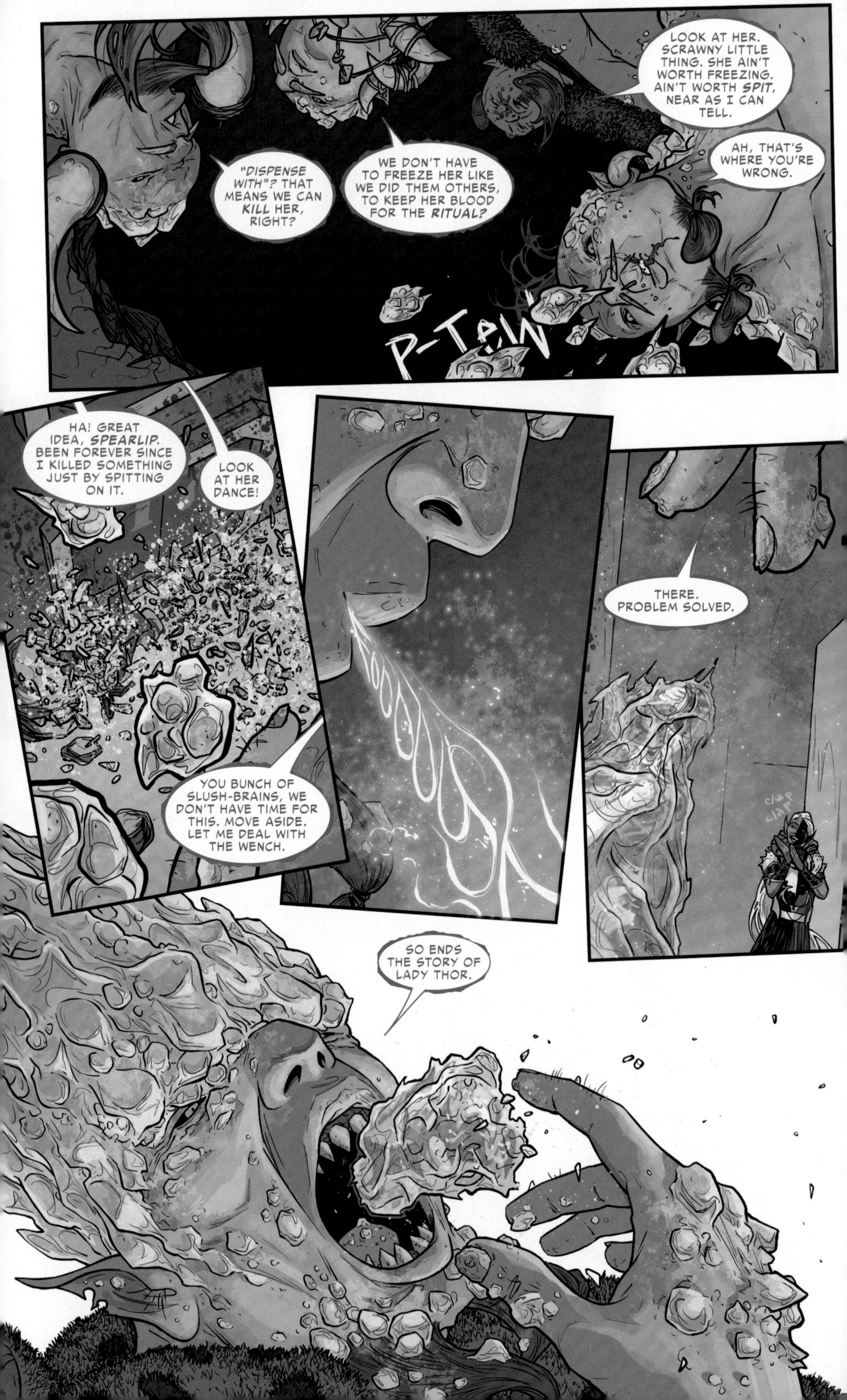
LOOK AT HER. SCRAWNY LITTLE THING. SHE AIN'T WORTH FREEZING. AIN'T WORTH SPIT, NEAR AS I CAN TELL.
"DISPENSE WITH"? THAT MEANS WE CAN KILL HER, RIGHT?
WE DON'T HAVE TO FREEZE HER LIKE WE DID THEM OTHERS, TO KEEP HER BLOOD FOR THE RITUAL?
AH, THAT'S WHERE YOU'RE WRONG.
P-TEW
HA! GREAT IDEA, SPEARLIP. BEEN FOREVER SINCE I KILLED SOMETHING JUST BY SPITTING ON IT.
LOOK AT HER DANCE!
YOU BUNCH OF SLUSH-BRAINS, WE DON'T HAVE TIME FOR THIS. MOVE ASIDE. LET ME DEAL WITH THE WENCH.
THERE. PROBLEM SOLVED.
clap clap
SO ENDS THE STORY OF LADY THOR.

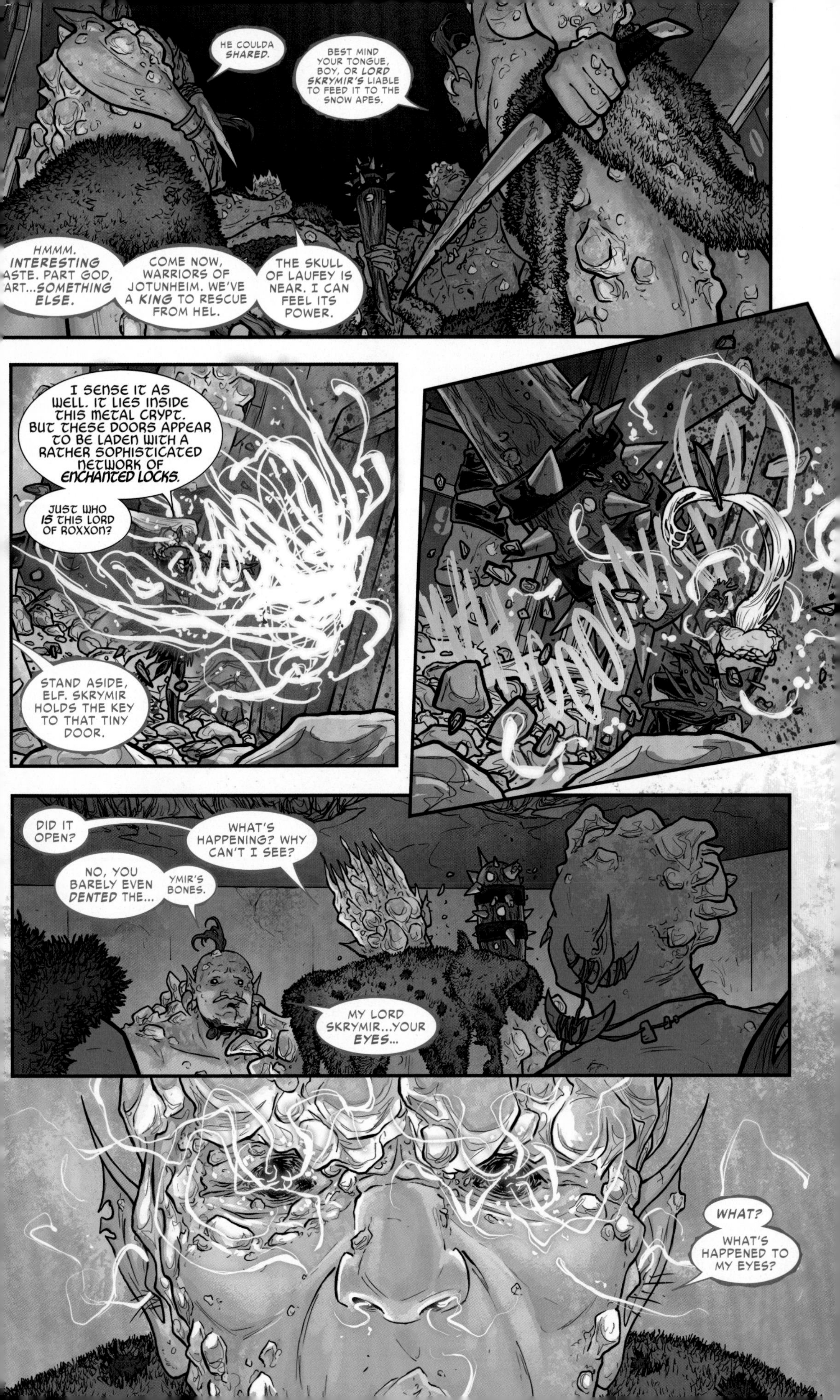
HE COULDA SHARED.
BEST MIND YOUR TONGUE, BOY, OR LORD SKRYMIR'S LIABLE TO FEED IT TO THE SNOW APES.
HMMM. INTERESTING ASTE. PART GOD, ART...SOMETHING ELSE.
COME NOW, WARRIORS OF JOTUNHEIM. WE'VE A KING TO RESCUE FROM HEL.
THE SKULL OF LAUFEY IS NEAR. I CAN FEEL ITS POWER.
I SENSE IT AS WELL. IT LIES INSIDE THIS METAL CRYPT. BUT THESE DOORS APPEAR TO BE LADEN WITH A RATHER SOPHISTICATED NETWORK OF ENCHANTED LOCKS.
JUST WHO IS THIS LORD OF ROXXON?
STAND ASIDE, ELF. SKRYMIR HOLDS THE KEY TO THAT TINY DOOR.
WHHOOOM
DID IT OPEN?
WHAT'S HAPPENING? WHY CAN'T I SEE?
NO, YOU BARELY EVEN DENTED THE...
YMIR'S BONES.
MY LORD SKRYMIR...YOUR EYES...
WHAT?
WHAT'S HAPPENED TO MY EYES?

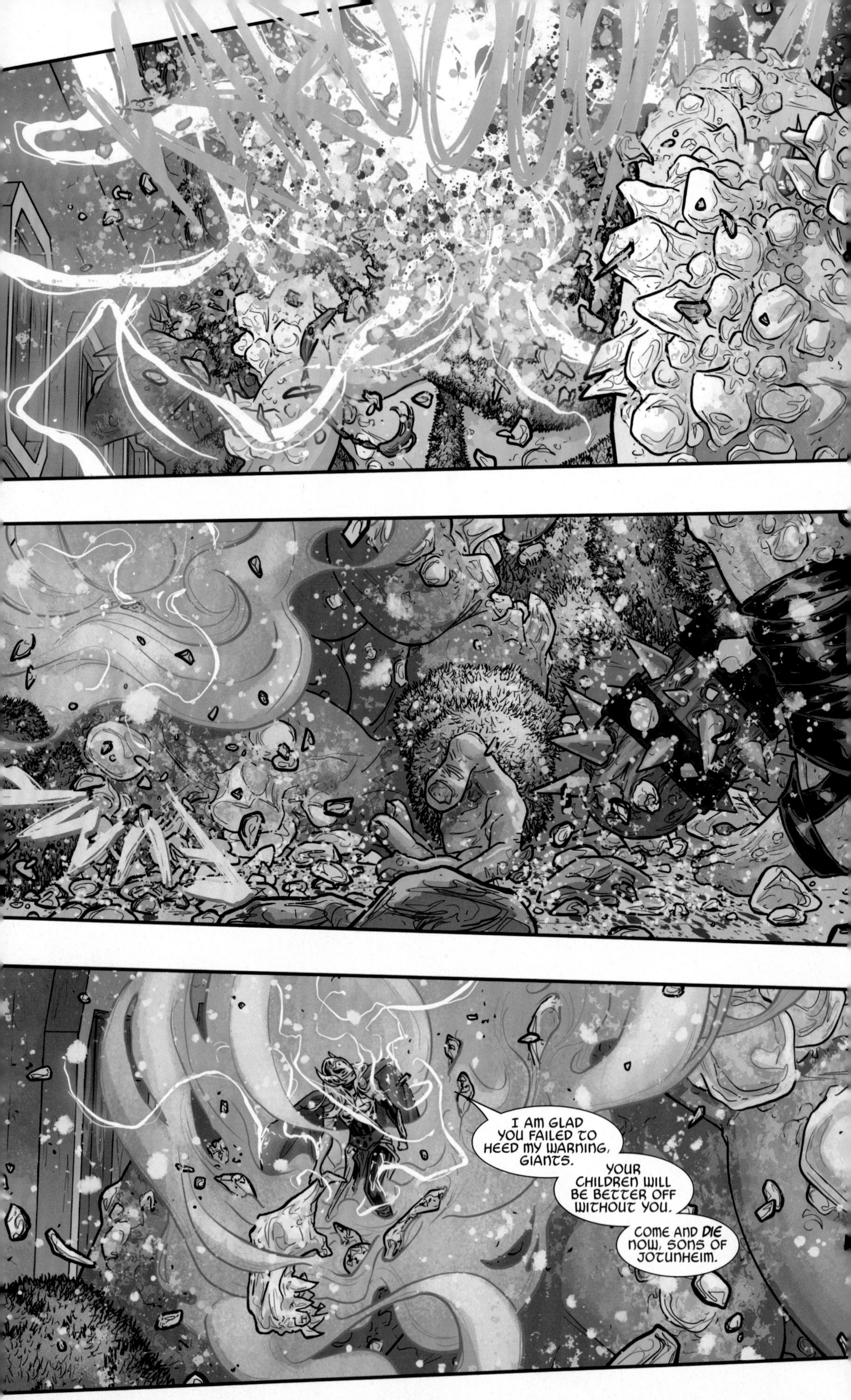
I AM GLAD YOU FAILED TO HEED MY WARNING, GIANTS.
YOUR CHILDREN WILL BE BETTER OFF WITHOUT YOU.
COME AND DIE NOW, SONS OF JOTUNHEIM.

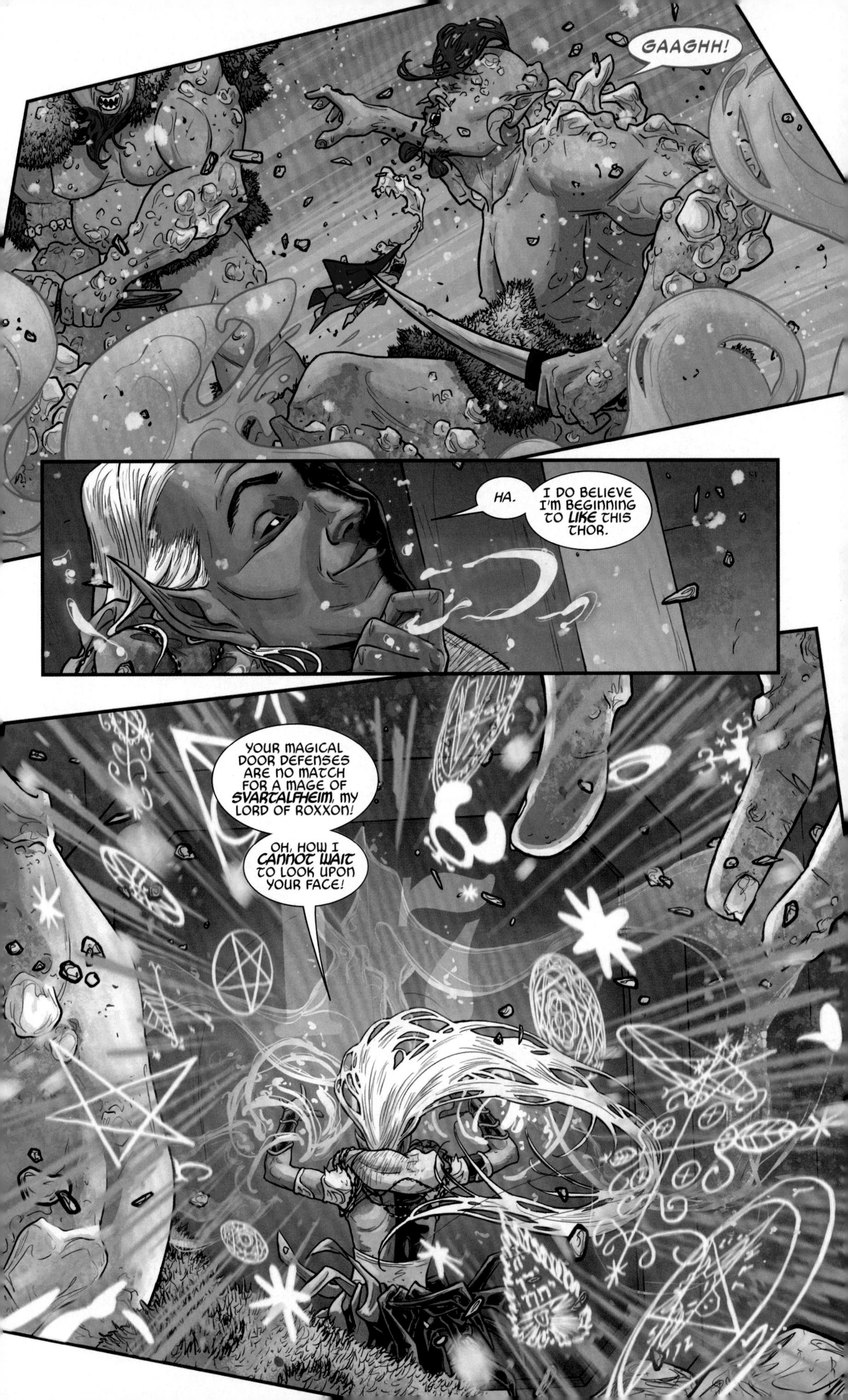
GAAGHH!
HA.
I DO BELIEVE I'M BEGINNING TO LIKE THIS THOR.
YOUR MAGICAL DOOR DEFENSES ARE NO MATCH FOR A MAGE OF SVARTALFHEIM, MY LORD OF ROXXON!
OH, HOW I CANNOT WAIT TO LOOK UPON YOUR FACE!

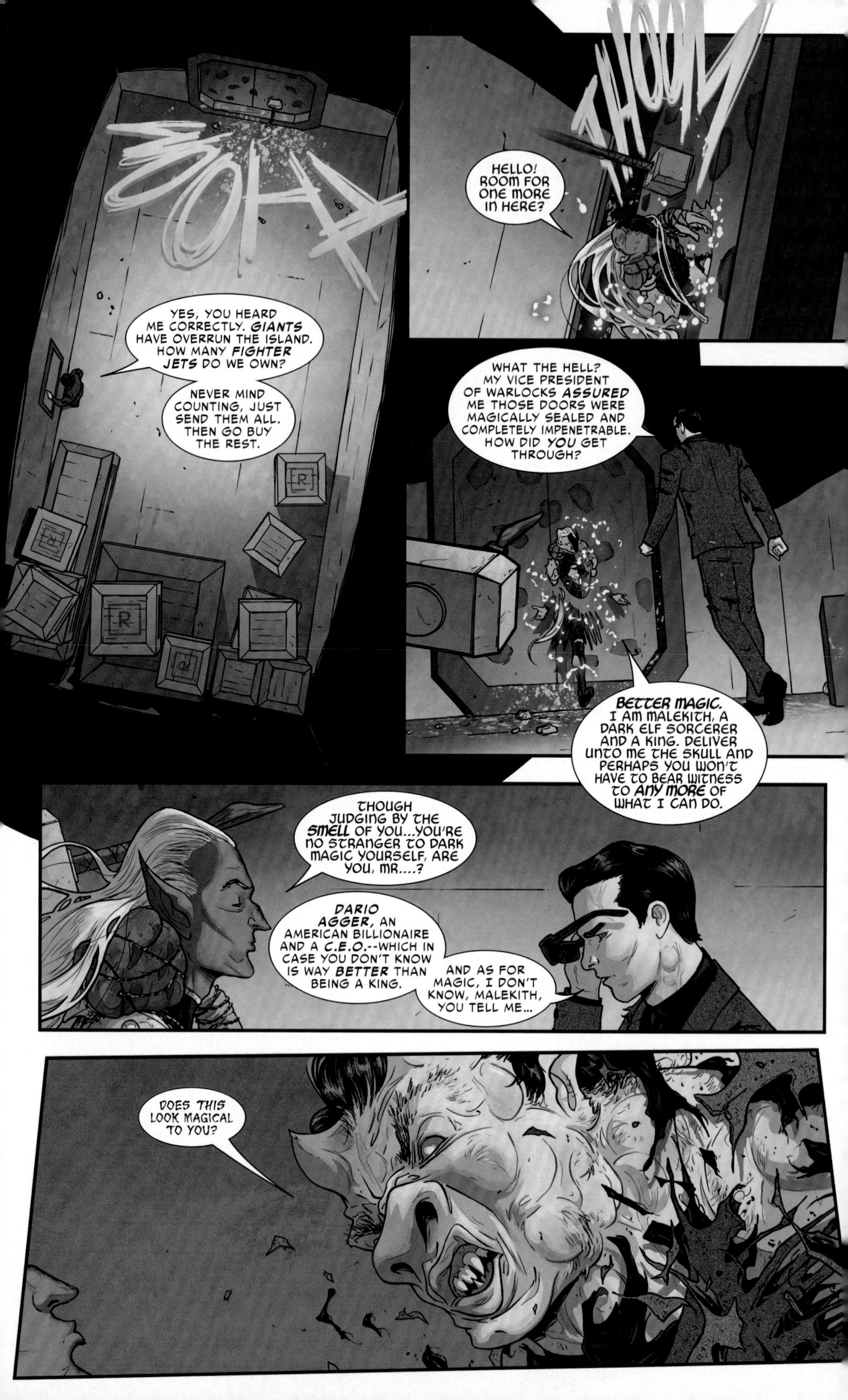
BOOM
YES, YOU HEARD ME CORRECTLY. GIANTS HAVE OVERRUN THE ISLAND. HOW MANY FIGHTER JETS DO WE OWN?
NEVER MIND COUNTING, JUST SEND THEM ALL. THEN GO BUY THE REST.
THOOM
HELLO! ROOM FOR ONE MORE IN HERE?
WHAT THE HELL? MY VICE PRESIDENT OF WARLOCKS ASSURED ME THOSE DOORS WERE MAGICALLY SEALED AND COMPLETELY IMPENETRABLE. HOW DID YOU GET THROUGH?
BETTER MAGIC. I AM MALEKITH, A DARK ELF SORCERER AND A KING. DELIVER UNTO ME THE SKULL AND PERHAPS YOU WON'T HAVE TO BEAR WITNESS TO ANY MORE OF WHAT I CAN DO.
THOUGH JUDGING BY THE SMELL OF YOU...YOU'RE NO STRANGER TO DARK MAGIC YOURSELF, ARE YOU, MR....?
DARIO AGGER, AN AMERICAN BILLIONAIRE AND A C.E.O.--WHICH IN CASE YOU DON'T KNOW IS WAY BETTER THAN BEING A KING.
AND AS FOR MAGIC, I DON'T KNOW, MALEKITH, YOU TELL ME...
DOES THIS LOOK MAGICAL TO YOU?

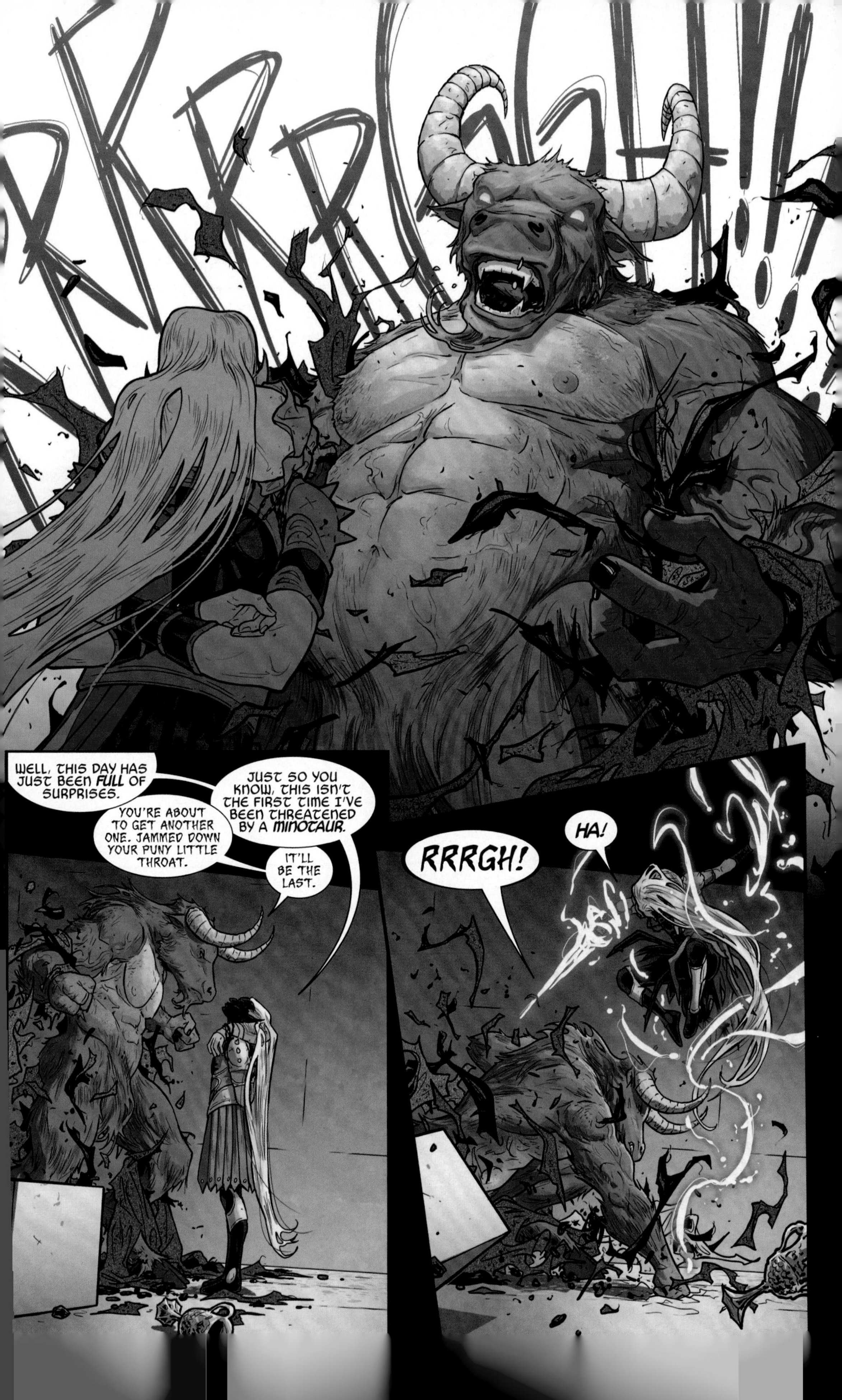
RRRRRAGGH!!!
WELL, THIS DAY HAS JUST BEEN FULL OF SURPRISES.
YOU'RE ABOUT TO GET ANOTHER ONE. JAMMED DOWN YOUR PUNY LITTLE THROAT.
JUST SO YOU KNOW, THIS ISN'T THE FIRST TIME I'VE BEEN THREATENED BY A MINOTAUR.
IT'LL BE THE LAST.
RRRGH!
HA!

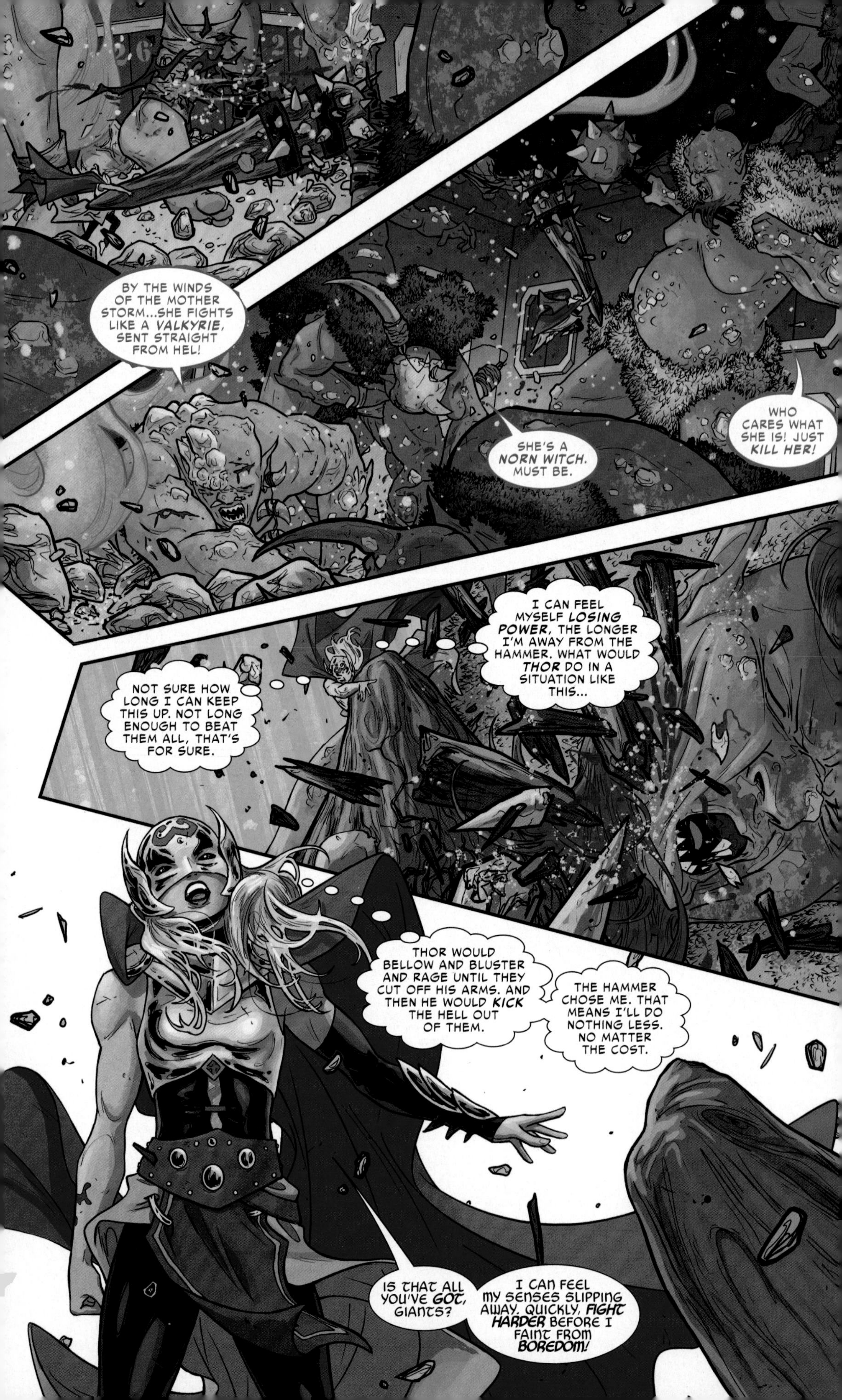

BY THE WINDS OF THE MOTHER STORM...SHE FIGHTS LIKE A VALKYRIE, SENT STRAIGHT FROM HEL!
SHE'S A NORN WITCH. MUST BE.
WHO CARES WHAT SHE IS! JUST KILL HER!
NOT SURE HOW LONG I CAN KEEP THIS UP. NOT LONG ENOUGH TO BEAT THEM ALL, THAT'S FOR SURE.
I CAN FEEL MYSELF LOSING POWER, THE LONGER I'M AWAY FROM THE HAMMER. WHAT WOULD THOR DO IN A SITUATION LIKE THIS...
THOR WOULD BELLOW AND BLUSTER AND RAGE UNTIL THEY CUT OFF HIS ARMS. AND THEN HE WOULD KICK THE HELL OUT OF THEM.
THE HAMMER CHOSE ME. THAT MEANS I'LL DO NOTHING LESS. NO MATTER THE COST.
IS THAT ALL YOU'VE GOT, GIANTS?
I CAN FEEL MY SENSES SLIPPING AWAY. QUICKLY, FIGHT HARDER BEFORE I FAINT FROM BOREDOM!

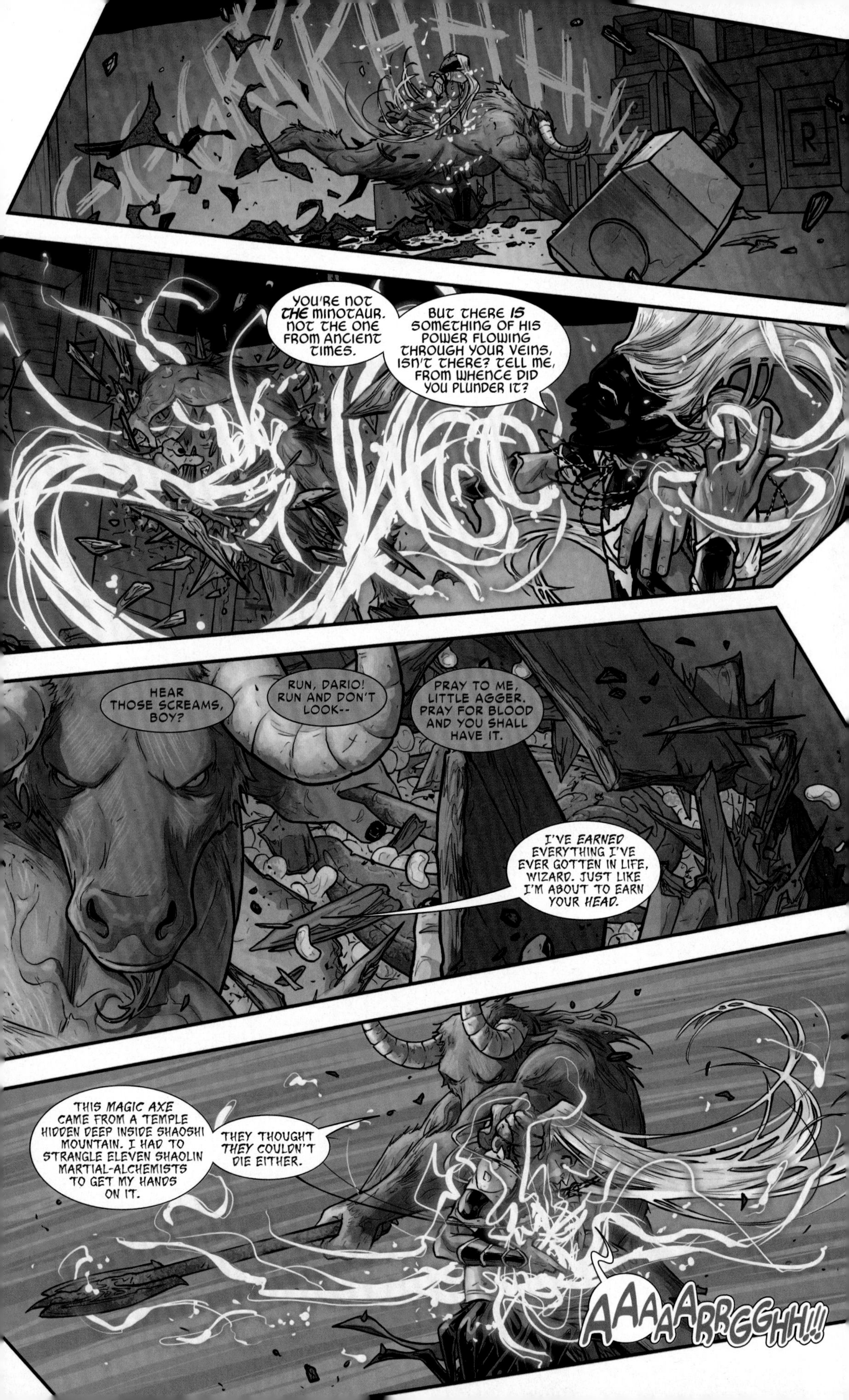
YOU'RE NOT THE MINOTAUR. NOT THE ONE FROM ANCIENT TIMES.
BUT THERE IS SOMETHING OF HIS POWER FLOWING THROUGH YOUR VEINS, ISN'T THERE? TELL ME, FROM WHENCE DID YOU PLUNDER IT?
HEAR THOSE SCREAMS, BOY?
RUN, DARIO! RUN AND DON'T LOOK--
PRAY TO ME, LITTLE AGGER. PRAY FOR BLOOD AND YOU SHALL HAVE IT.
I'VE EARNED EVERYTHING I'VE EVER GOTTEN IN LIFE, WIZARD. JUST LIKE I'M ABOUT TO EARN YOUR HEAD.
THIS MAGIC AXE CAME FROM A TEMPLE HIDDEN DEEP INSIDE SHAOSHI MOUNTAIN. I HAD TO STRANGLE ELEVEN SHAOLIN MARTIAL-ALCHEMISTS TO GET MY HANDS ON IT.
THEY THOUGHT THEY COULDN'T DIE EITHER.
AAAAARRGGHH!!!

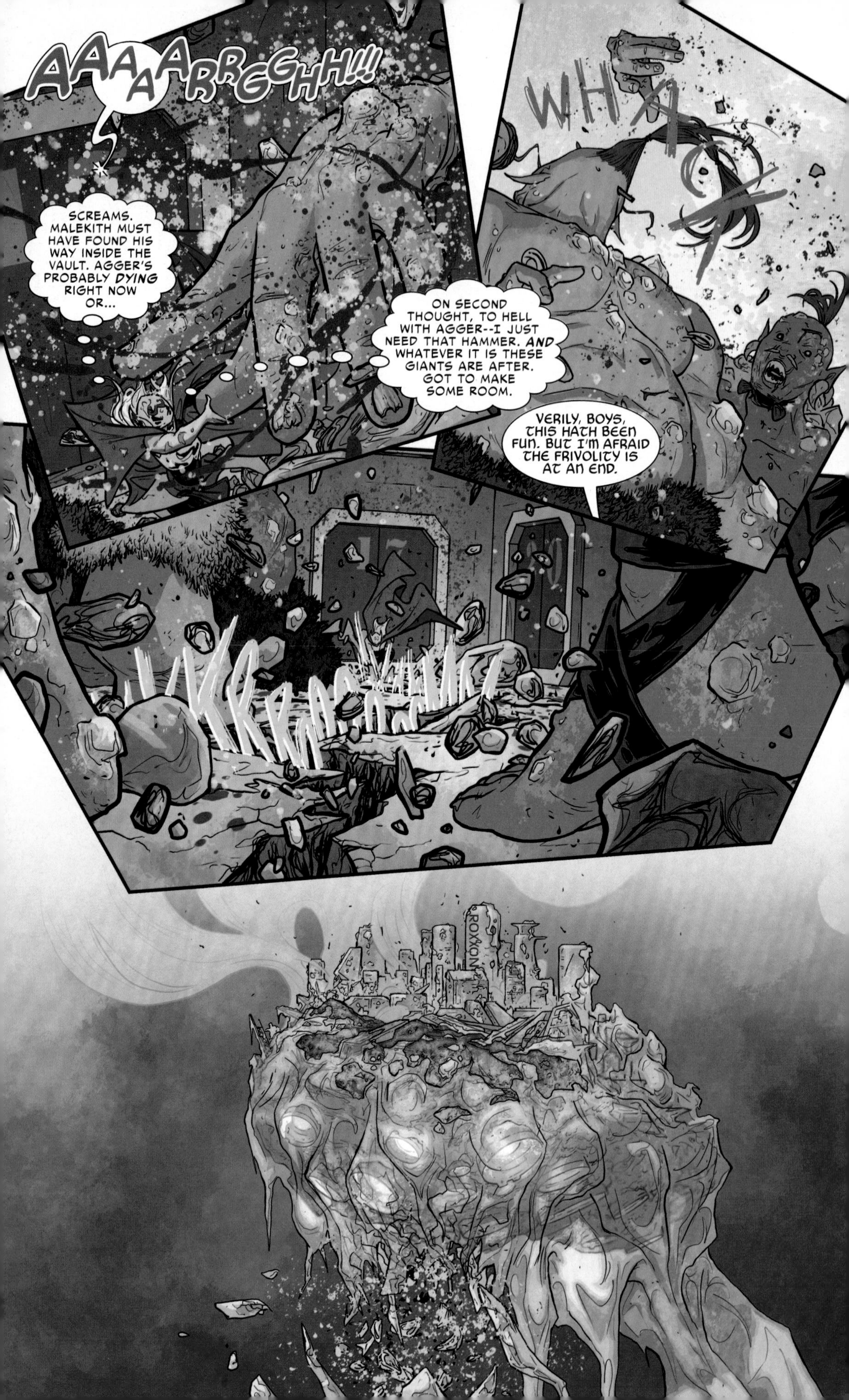
AAAAARRGHH!!!
SCREAMS. MALEKITH MUST HAVE FOUND HIS WAY INSIDE THE VAULT. AGGER'S PROBABLY DYING RIGHT NOW OR...
ON SECOND THOUGHT, TO HELL WITH AGGER--I JUST NEED THAT HAMMER. AND WHATEVER IT IS THESE GIANTS ARE AFTER. GOT TO MAKE SOME ROOM.
WHAK
VERILY, BOYS, THIS HATH BEEN FUN. BUT I'M AFRAID THE FRIVOLITY IS AT AN END.
KRAKOOM
ROXXON

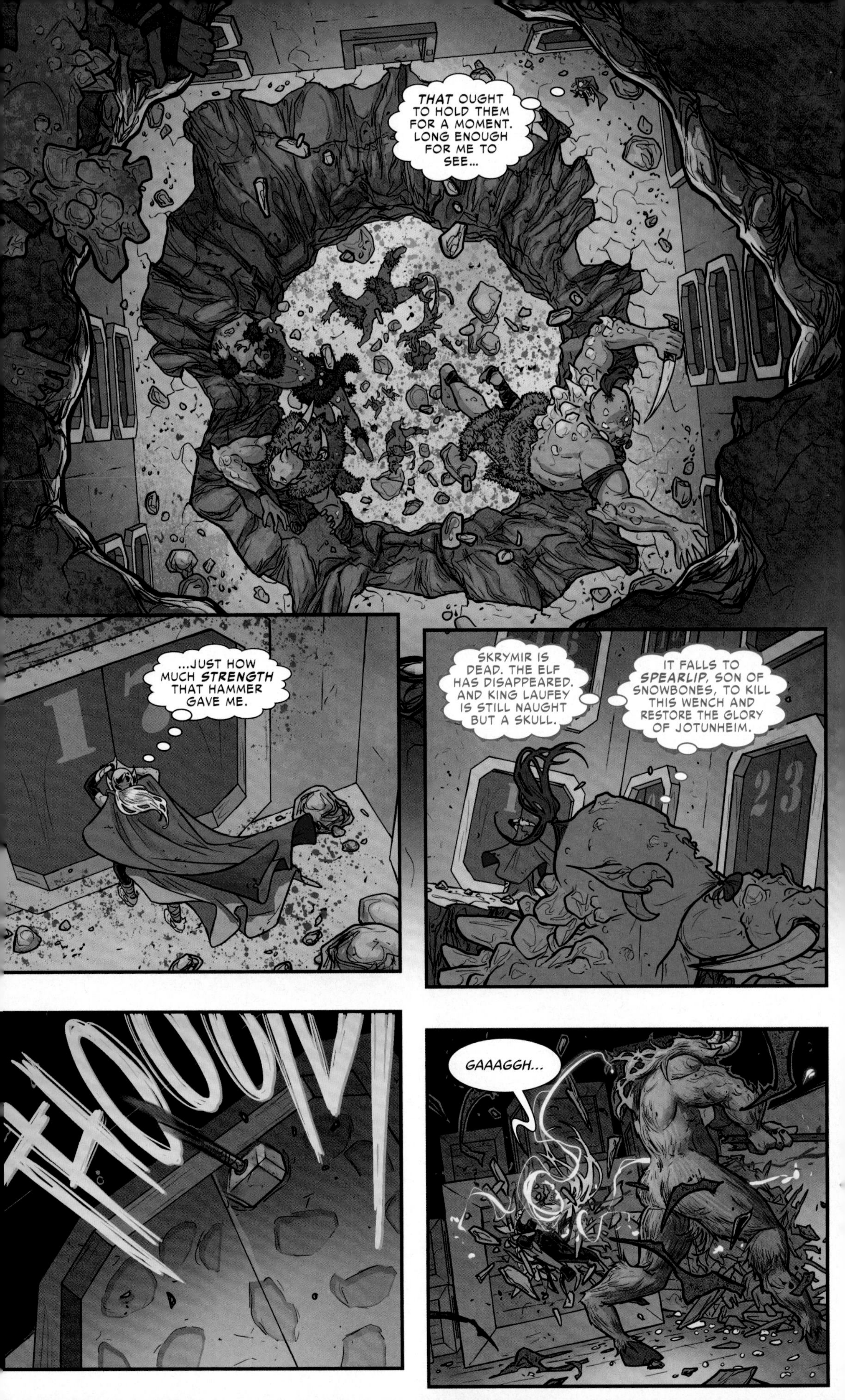
THAT OUGHT TO HOLD THEM FOR A MOMENT. LONG ENOUGH FOR ME TO SEE...
...JUST HOW MUCH STRENGTH THAT HAMMER GAVE ME.
SKRYMIR IS DEAD. THE ELF HAS DISAPPEARED. AND KING LAUFEY IS STILL NAUGHT BUT A SKULL.
IT FALLS TO SPEARLIP, SON OF SNOWBONES, TO KILL THIS WENCH AND RESTORE THE GLORY OF JOTUNHEIM.
THOOOM
GAAAGGH...

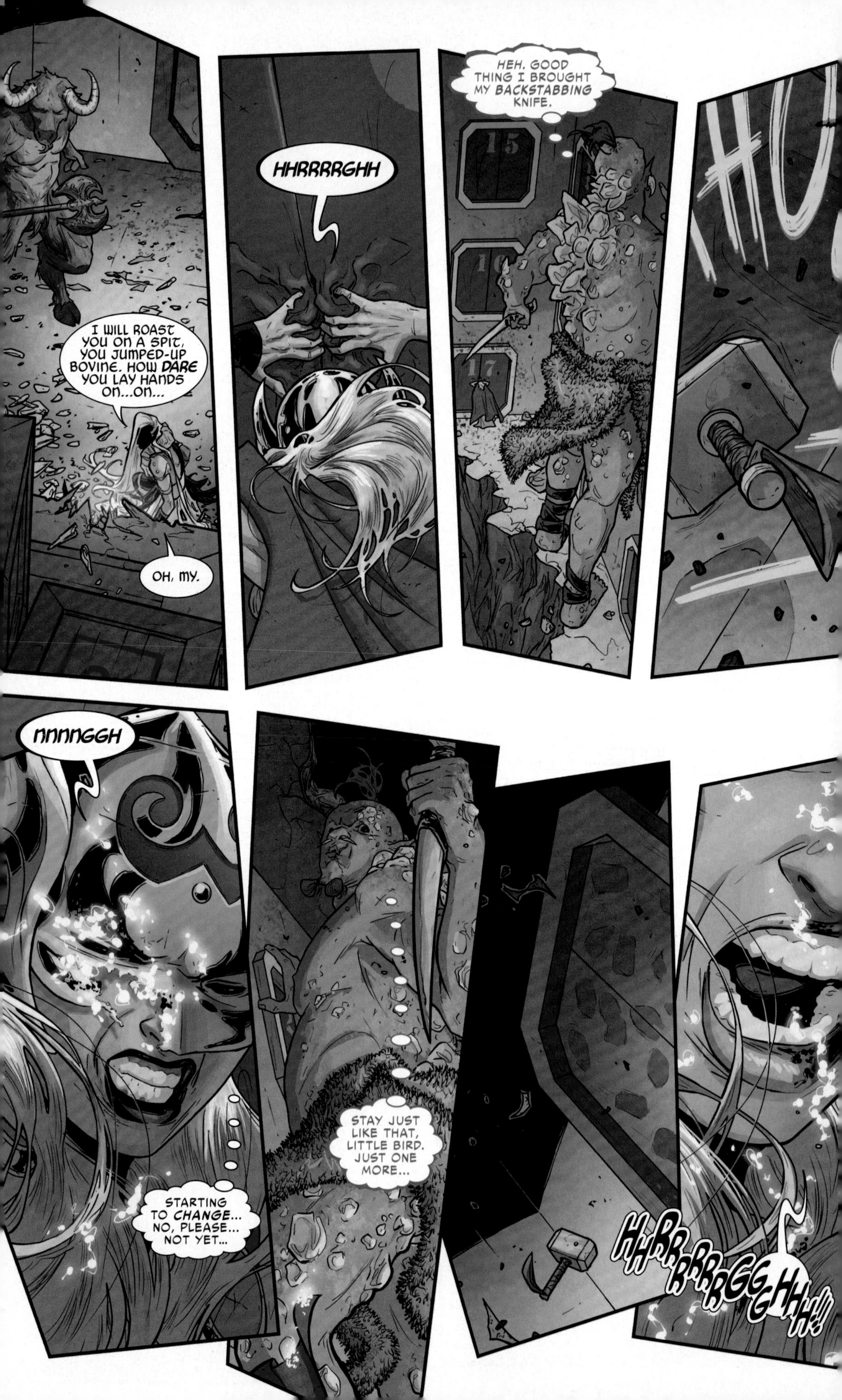

I WILL ROAST YOU ON A SPIT, YOU JUMPED-UP BOVINE. HOW DARE YOU LAY HANDS ON...ON...
OH, MY.
HHRRRRGHH
HEH. GOOD THING I BROUGHT MY BACKSTABBING KNIFE.
15
16
17
NNNNGGH
STARTING TO CHANGE... NO, PLEASE... NOT YET...
STAY JUST LIKE THAT, LITTLE BIRD. JUST ONE MORE...
HHRRRRRRGGGHHH!!

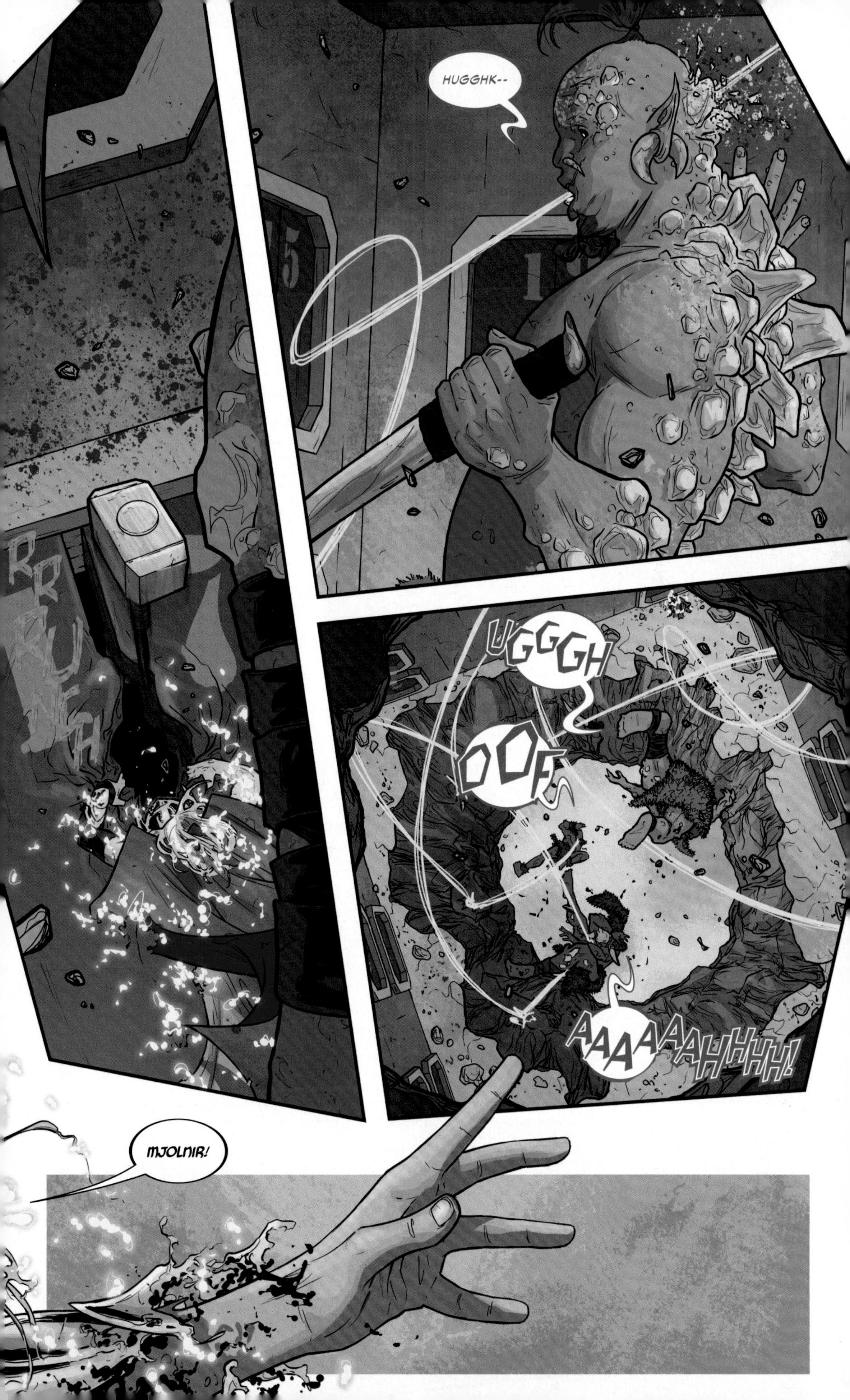
HUGGHK--
RRRUNCH
UGGGH
OOF
AAAAAAHHHHH!
MJOLNIR!

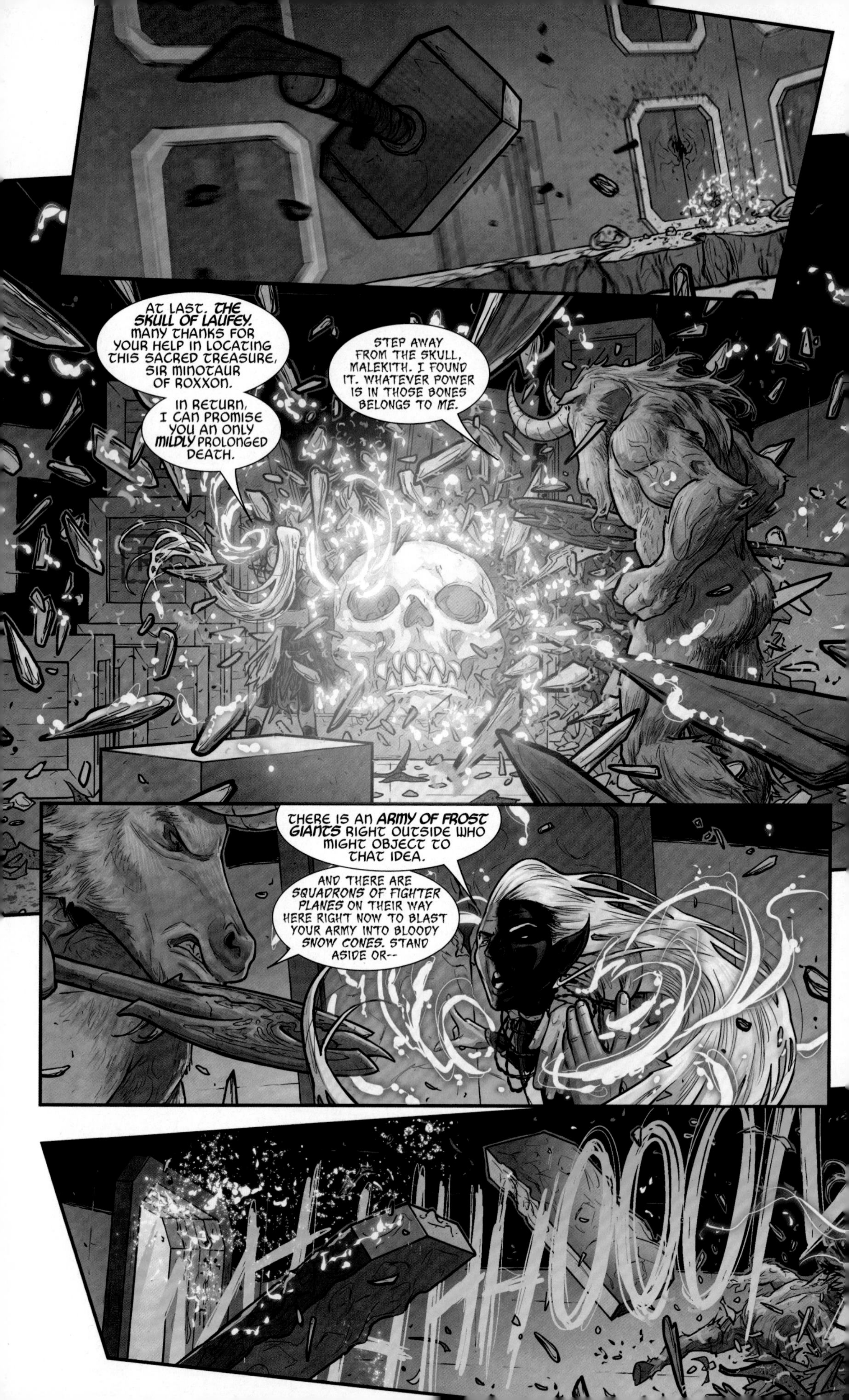
AT LAST. THE SKULL OF LAUFEY. MANY THANKS FOR YOUR HELP IN LOCATING THIS SACRED TREASURE, SIR MINOTAUR OF ROXXON.
IN RETURN, I CAN PROMISE YOU AN ONLY MILDLY PROLONGED DEATH.
STEP AWAY FROM THE SKULL, MALEKITH. I FOUND IT. WHATEVER POWER IS IN THOSE BONES BELONGS TO ME.
THERE IS AN ARMY OF FROST GIANTS RIGHT OUTSIDE WHO MIGHT OBJECT TO THAT IDEA.
AND THERE ARE SQUADRONS OF FIGHTER PLANES ON THEIR WAY HERE RIGHT NOW TO BLAST YOUR ARMY INTO BLOODY SNOW CONES. STAND ASIDE OR--
WHHOOOM

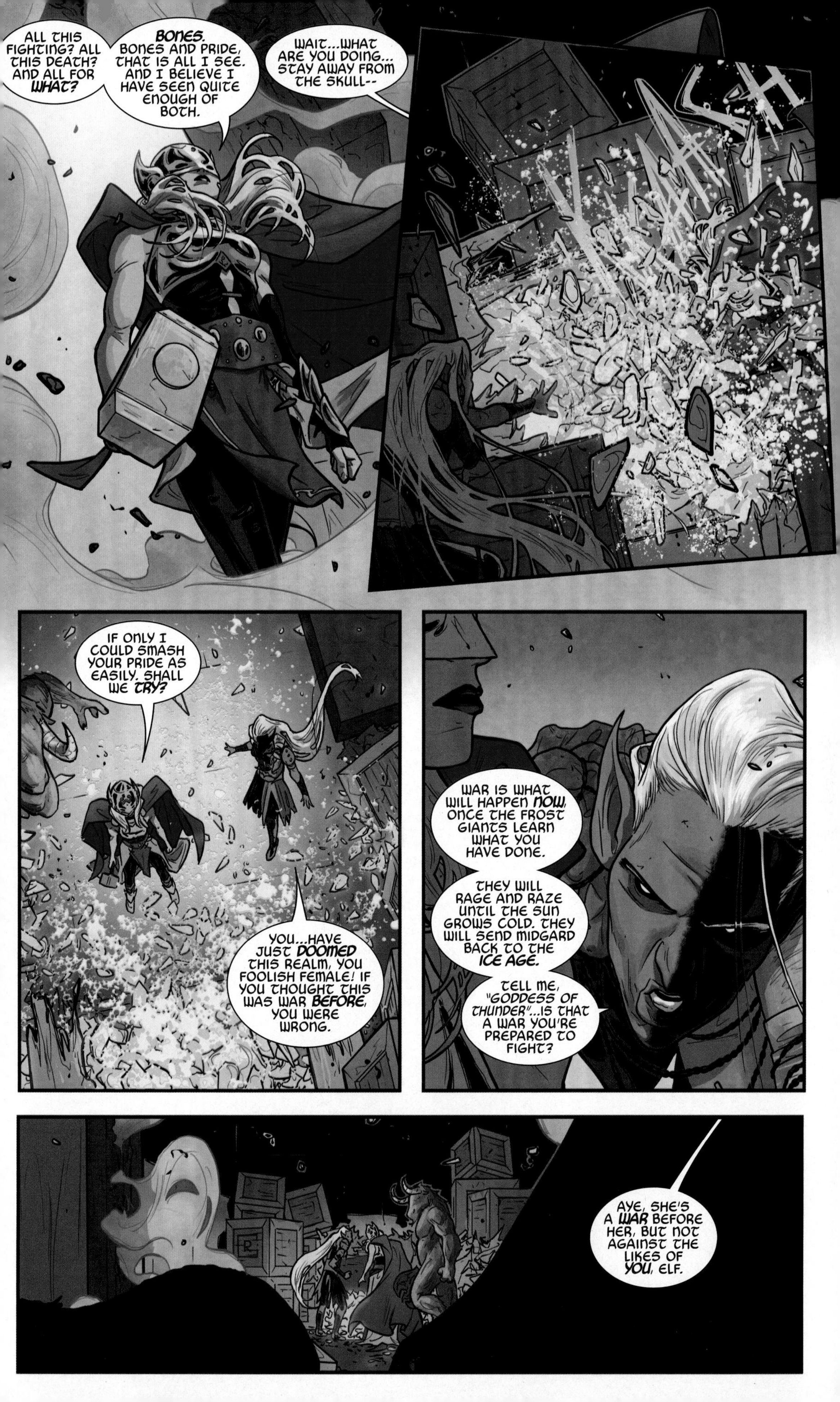

ALL THIS FIGHTING? ALL THIS DEATH? AND ALL FOR WHAT?
BONES. BONES AND PRIDE, THAT IS ALL I SEE. AND I BELIEVE I HAVE SEEN QUITE ENOUGH OF BOTH.
WAIT...WHAT ARE YOU DOING... STAY AWAY FROM THE SKULL--
IF ONLY I COULD SMASH YOUR PRIDE AS EASILY. SHALL WE TRY?
YOU...HAVE JUST DOOMED THIS REALM, YOU FOOLISH FEMALE! IF YOU THOUGHT THIS WAS WAR BEFORE, YOU WERE WRONG.
WAR IS WHAT WILL HAPPEN NOW, ONCE THE FROST GIANTS LEARN WHAT YOU HAVE DONE.
THEY WILL RAGE AND RAZE UNTIL THE SUN GROWS COLD. THEY WILL SEND MIDGARD BACK TO THE ICE AGE.
TELL ME, "GODDESS OF THUNDER"...IS THAT A WAR YOU'RE PREPARED TO FIGHT?
AYE, SHE'S A WAR BEFORE HER, BUT NOT AGAINST THE LIKES OF YOU, ELF.

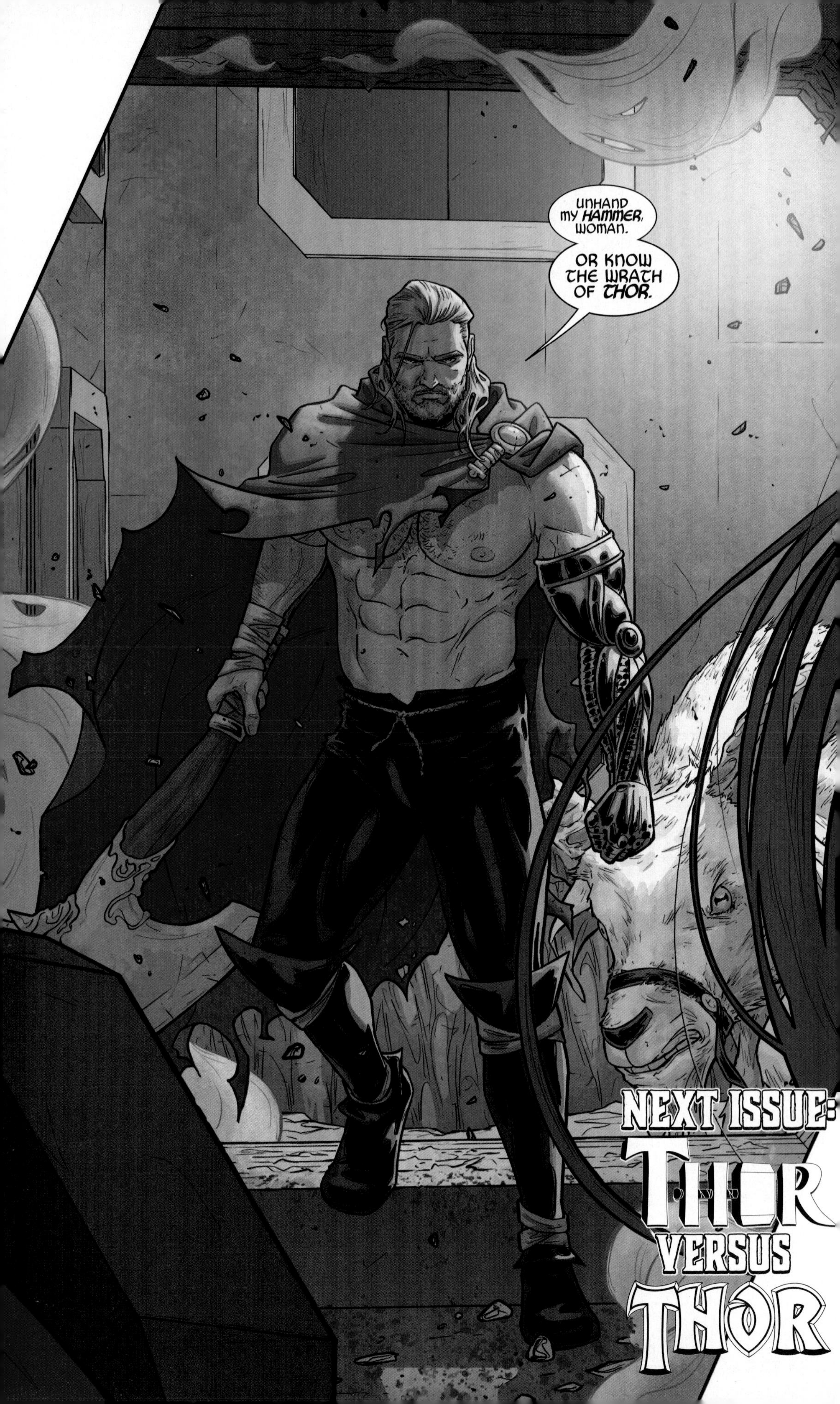
UNHAND my HAMMER, WOMAN.
OR KNOW THE WRATH OF THOR.
NEXT ISSUE:
THOR VERSUS THOR

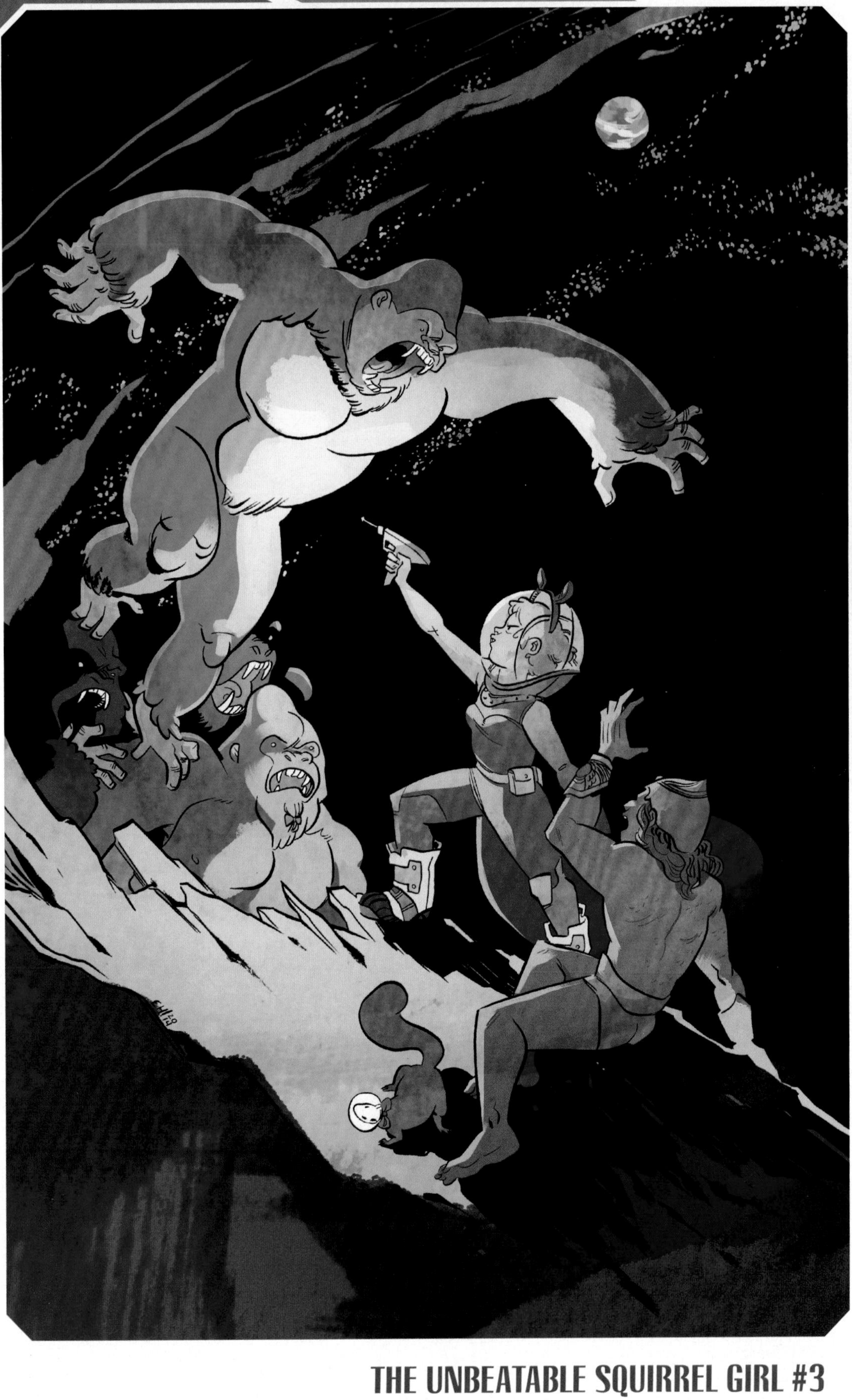

THE UNBEATABLE SQUIRREL GIRL #3

Doreen Green isn't just a first-year computer science student: she secretly also has all the powers of both squirrel and girl.
She uses her amazing abilities to fight crime **and** be as awesome as possible. You know her as...**The Unbeatable Squirrel Girl!**
Let's catch up with what she's been up to until now, with....

Squirrel Girl *in a nutshell*

search! 🔍

#OWNED

#everythingisnormalinspace

Welcome to

#USG

Number Three

Hope you like falafel jokes

Squirrel Girl! @unbeatablesg
Did you guys see how I took care of Kraven the other day?

xKravenTheHunterx @unshavenkraven
NOBODY LISTEN TO @unbeatablesg, SHE DIDN'T TAKE CARE OF ME, I MERELY DECIDED TO STOP FIGHTING HER

Squirrel Girl! @unbeatablesg
@unshavenkraven hey dude did you kill any gigantos underwater like I suggested?

xKravenTheHunterx @unshavenkraven
@unbeatablesg listen

xKravenTheHunterx @unshavenkraven
@unbeatablesg these things take time

Squirrel Girl! @unbeatablesg
Apparently I'm the only one that can see that GALACTUS IS COMING TO EARTH!!

Tippy-Toe @yoitstippytoe
CHIT CHUKKA CHITTY

Squirrel Girl! @unbeatablesg
Apparently me and @yoitstippytoe are the only ones that can see GALACTUS IS COMING TO EARTH!!

Squirrel Girl! @unbeatablesg
Oh well

Squirrel Girl! @unbeatablesg
guess we'll just have to stop him ourselves then

Squirrel Girl! @unbeatablesg
ON THE FRIGGIN' MOON

Tony Stark @starkmantony ✓
Whoever "borrowed" Iron Man armor parts from my NYC offices, please return them. Looking at you, @unbeatablesg.

Squirrel Girl! @unbeatablesg
@starkmantony Tony it's REALLY IMPORTANT. Like COSMIC important.

Squirrel Girl! @unbeatablesg
@starkmantony I don't know why I'm being coy. It's for Galactus.

Squirrel Girl! @unbeatablesg
@starkmantony I'm gonna beat up @xGALACTUSx, Tony!! ON THE MOON

Tony Stark @starkmantony ✓
@unbeatablesg You break it, you bought it.

Whiplash @realwhiplash22
I JUST WHIPPED @STARKMANTONY OUT OF THE SKY WITH MY ENERGY WHIPS YES YES #OWNED

Tony Stark @starkmantony ✓
Wasn't me. I'm in San Francisco, @realwhiplash22.

Whiplash @realwhiplash22
@starkmantony SORRY I CANNOT HEAR YOU OVER HOW BADLY YOU GOT #OWNED

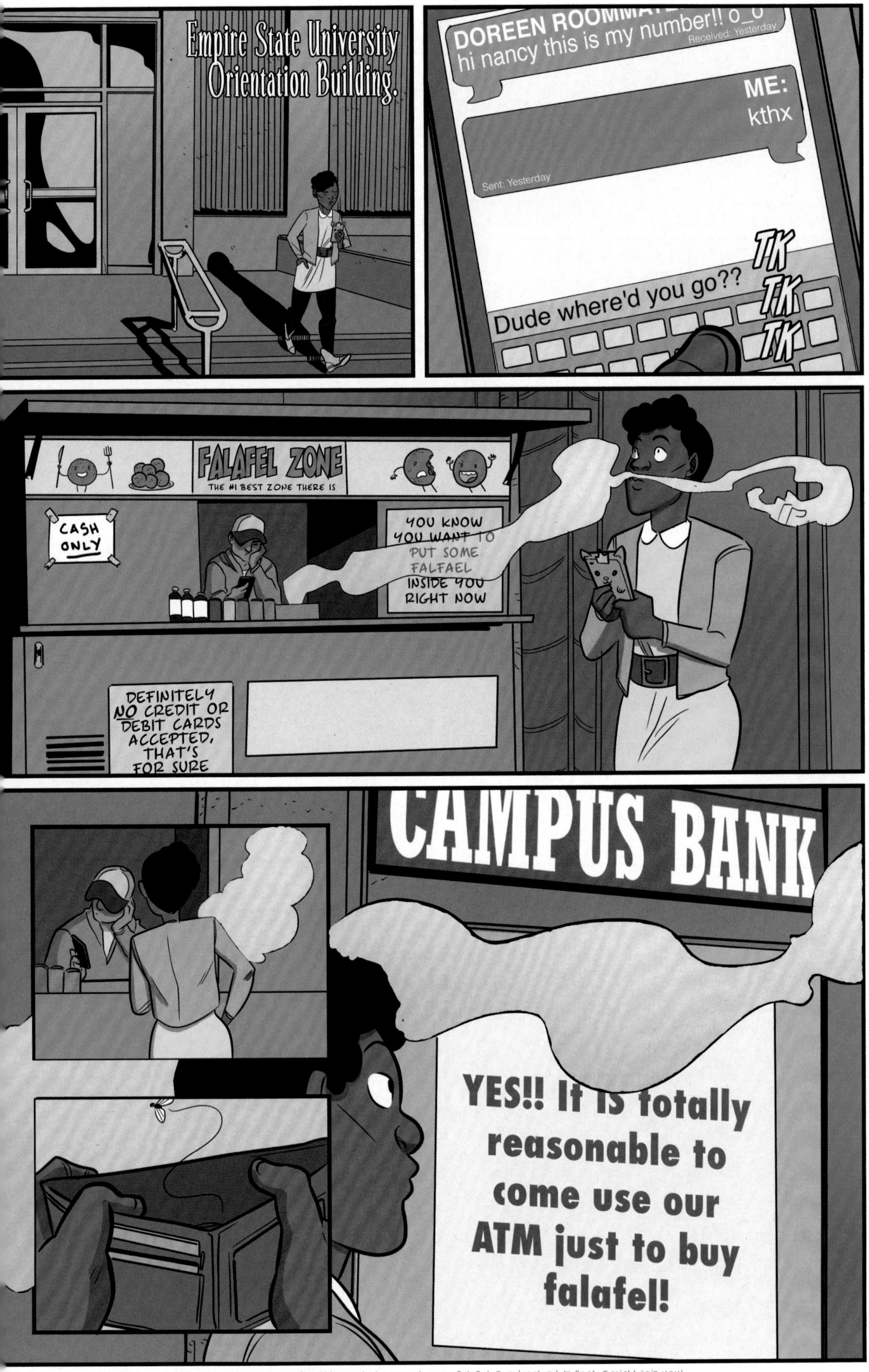
Empire State University Orientation Building.
DOREEN ROOMM
hi nancy this is my number!!
Received: Yesterday
ME:
kthx
Sent: Yesterday
Dude where'd you go??
TK
TK
TK
FALAFEL ZONE
THE #1 BEST ZONE THERE IS
CASH ONLY
YOU KNOW YOU WANT TO PUT SOME FALFAEL INSIDE YOU RIGHT NOW
DEFINITELY NO CREDIT OR DEBIT CARDS ACCEPTED, THAT'S FOR SURE
CAMPUS BANK
YES!! It is totally reasonable to come use our ATM just to buy falafel!

If you want to stop reading this comic to go get some falafel, I understand. In fact, I might join you!

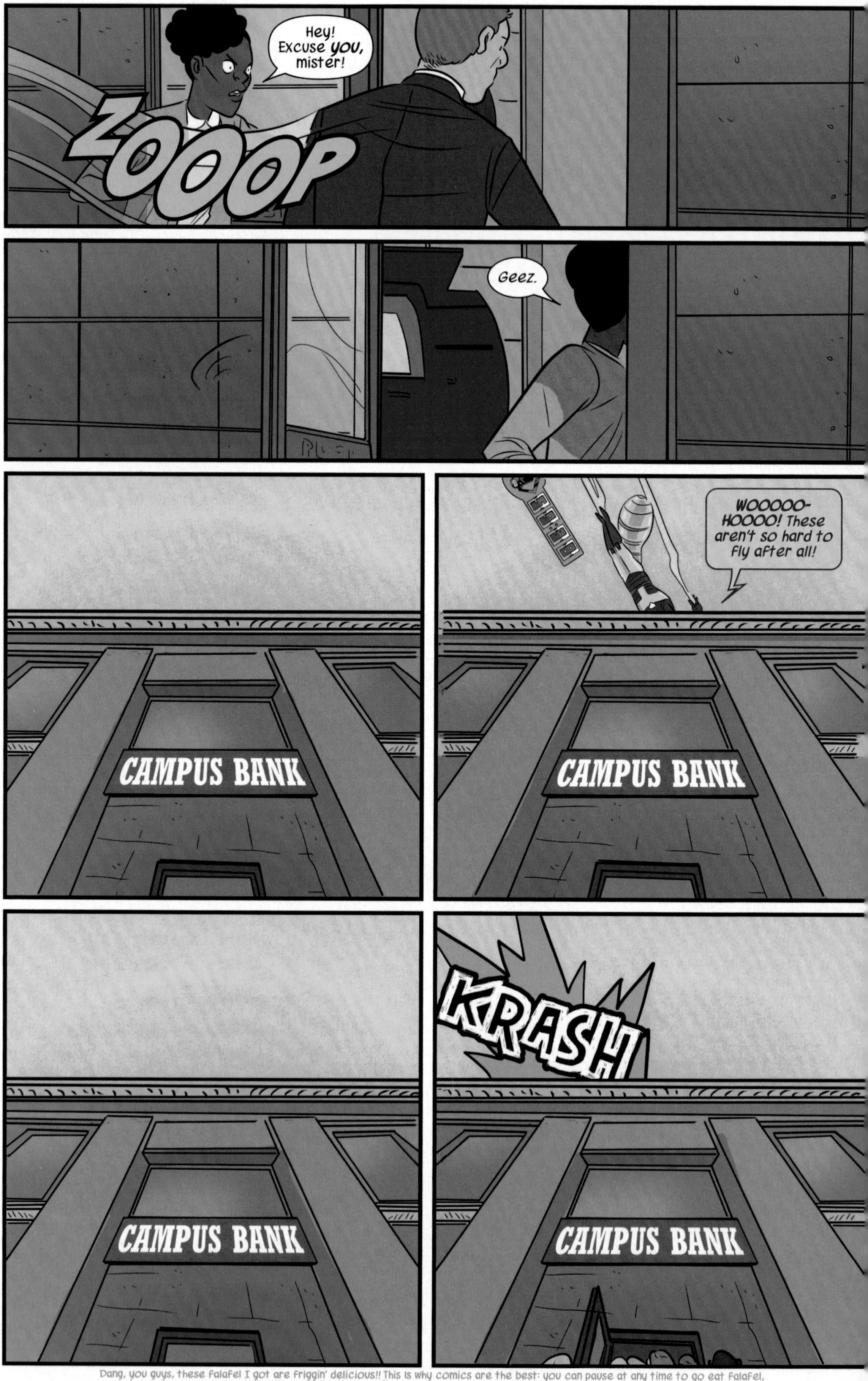
Hey! Excuse YOU, mister!
ZOOOP
Geez.
CAMPUS BANK
WOOOOO-HOOOO! These aren't so hard to fly after all!
CAMPUS BANK
CAMPUS BANK
KRASH
CAMPUS BANK

Dang, you guys, these falafel I got are friggin' delicious!! This is why comics are the best: you can pause at any time to go eat falafel, so check and mate, ***all other media.*** Except books, I guess. ***Fine,*** books are good, too.

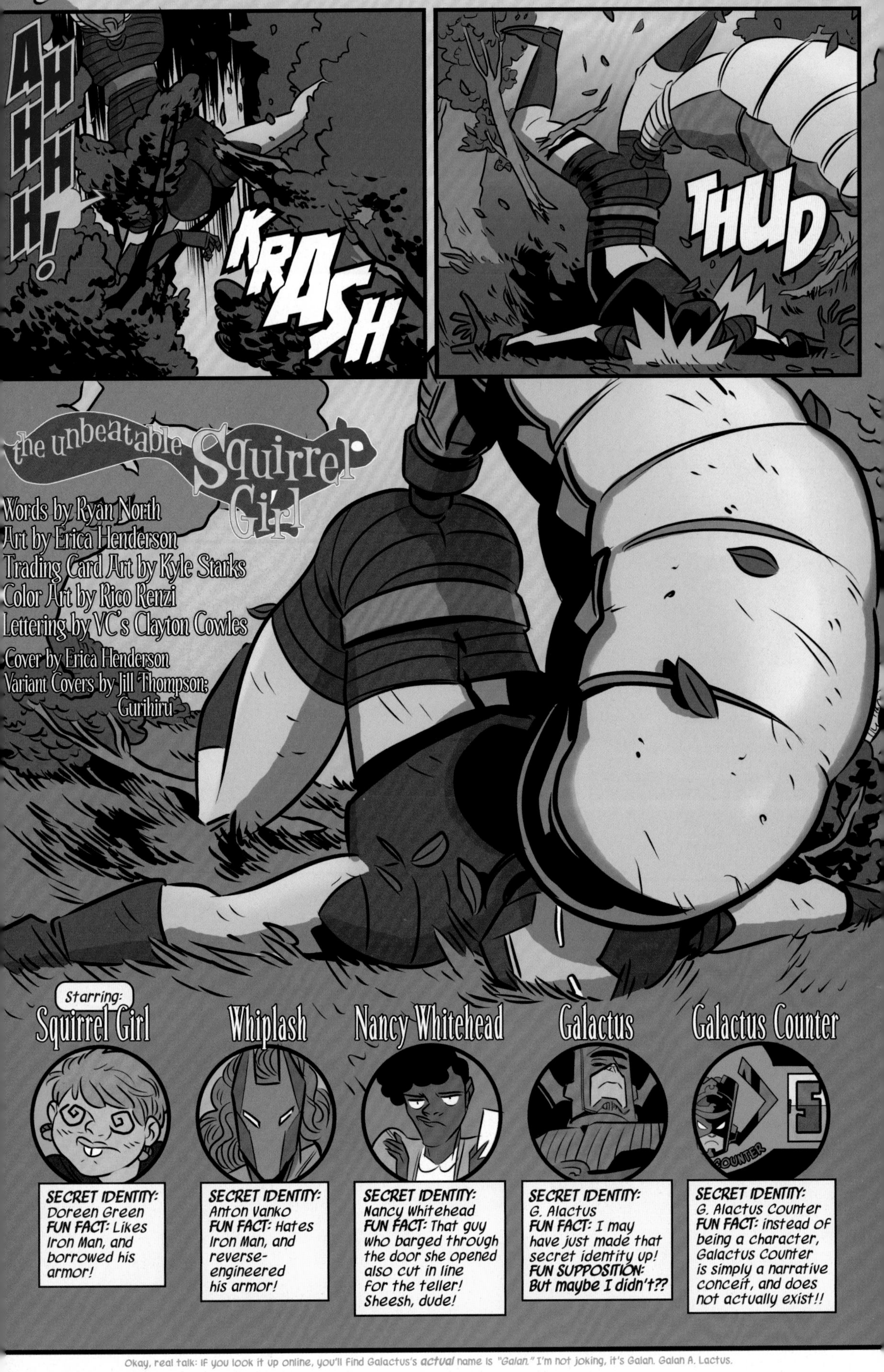
AHHHH!
KRASH
THUD
the unbeatable Squirrel Girl
Words by Ryan North
Art by Erica Henderson
Trading Card Art by Kyle Starks
Color Art by Rico Renzi
Lettering by VC's Clayton Cowles
Cover by Erica Henderson
Variant Covers by Jill Thompson; Gurihiru
Starring:
Squirrel Girl
Whiplash
Nancy Whitehead
Galactus
Galactus Counter
COUNTER
SECRET IDENTITY: Doreen Green FUN FACT: Likes Iron Man, and borrowed his armor!
SECRET IDENTITY: Anton Vanko FUN FACT: Hates Iron Man, and reverse-engineered his armor!
SECRET IDENTITY: Nancy Whitehead FUN FACT: That guy who barged through the door she opened also cut in line for the teller! Sheesh, dude!
SECRET IDENTITY: G. Alactus FUN FACT: I may have just made that secret identity up! FUN SUPPOSITION: But maybe I didn't??
SECRET IDENTITY: G. Alactus Counter FUN FACT: instead of being a character, Galactus Counter is simply a narrative conceit, and does not actually exist!!

Okay, real talk: If you look it up online, you'll find Galactus's *actual* name is *"Galan."* I'm not joking, it's Galan. Galan A. Lactus.

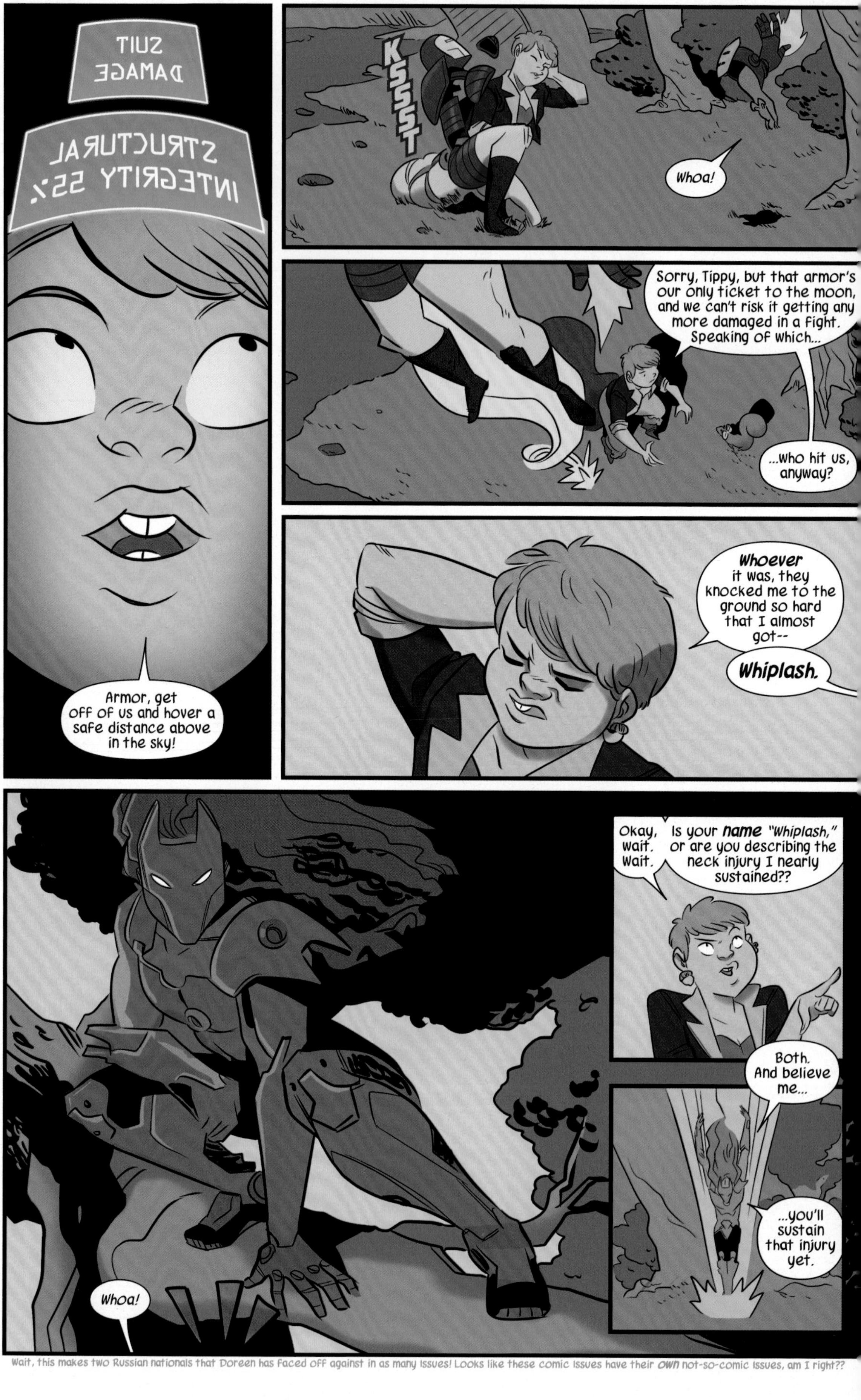
SUIT DAMAGE
STRUCTURAL INTEGRITY 55%
Armor, get off of us and hover a safe distance above in the sky!
KSSST
Whoa!
Sorry, Tippy, but that armor's our only ticket to the moon, and we can't risk it getting any more damaged in a fight. Speaking of which...
...who hit us, anyway?
Whoever it was, they knocked me to the ground so hard that I almost got--
Whiplash.
Whoa!
Okay, wait. Wait.
Is your name "Whiplash," or are you describing the neck injury I nearly sustained??
Both. And believe me...
...you'll sustain that injury yet.

Wait, this makes two Russian nationals that Doreen has faced off against in as many issues! Looks like these comic issues have their *own* not-so-comic issues, am I right??

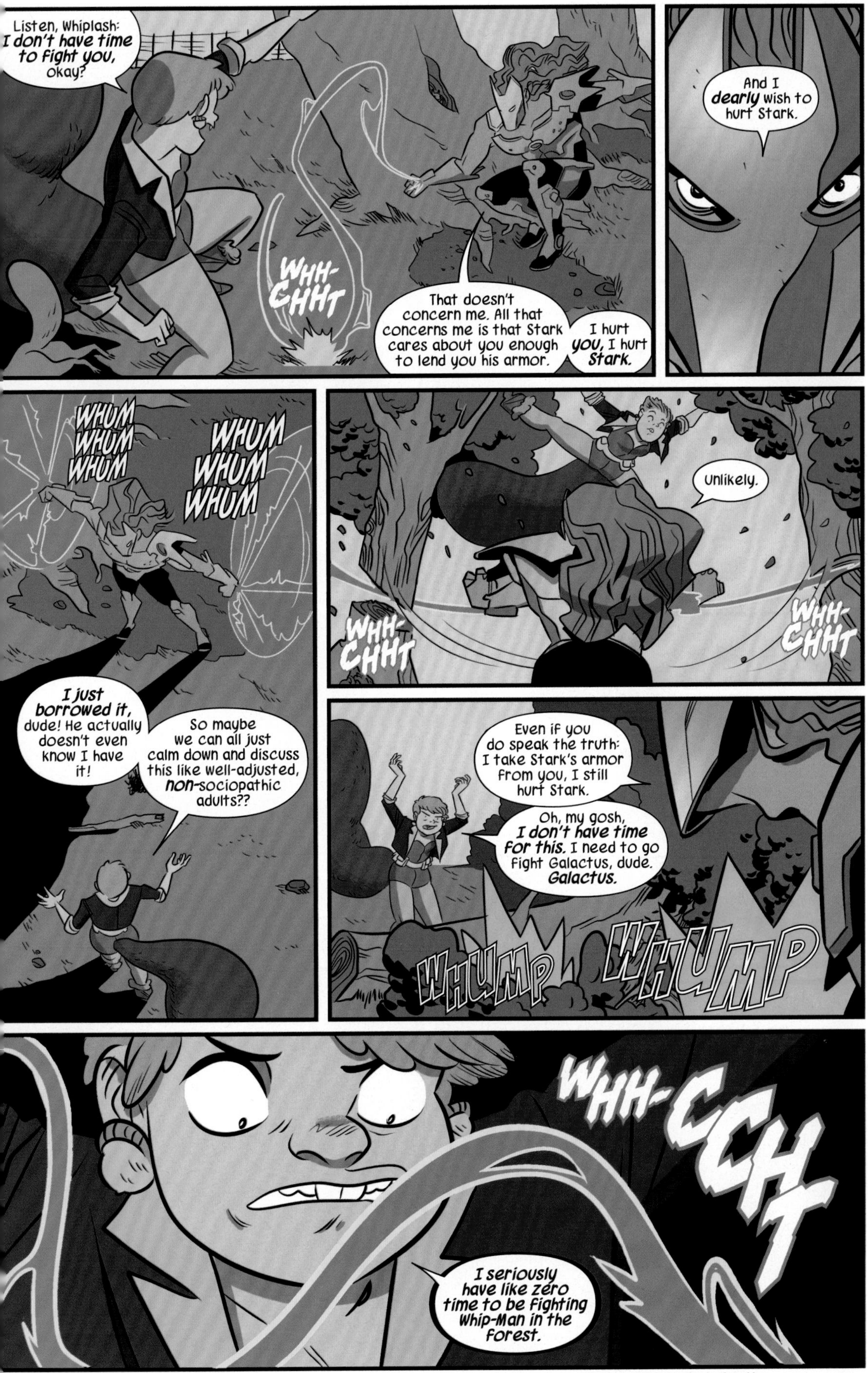
Listen, Whiplash: I don't have time to fight you, okay?
WHH-CHHT
That doesn't concern me. All that concerns me is that Stark cares about you enough to lend you his armor.
I hurt you, I hurt Stark.
And I dearly wish to hurt Stark.
WHUM WHUM WHUM
WHUM WHUM WHUM
I just borrowed it, dude! He actually doesn't even know I have it!
So maybe we can all just calm down and discuss this like well-adjusted, non-sociopathic adults??
Unlikely.
WHH-CHHT
WHH-CHHT
Even if you do speak the truth: I take Stark's armor from you, I still hurt Stark.
Oh, my gosh, I don't have time for this. I need to go fight Galactus, dude. Galactus.
WHUMP
WHUMP
WHH-CCHT
I seriously have like zero time to be fighting Whip-Man in the forest.

Excuse me, but I'm "Whiplash." "Whip-Man" is just an annoying friend of mine with some cheap knock-off of my very expensive technowhips.

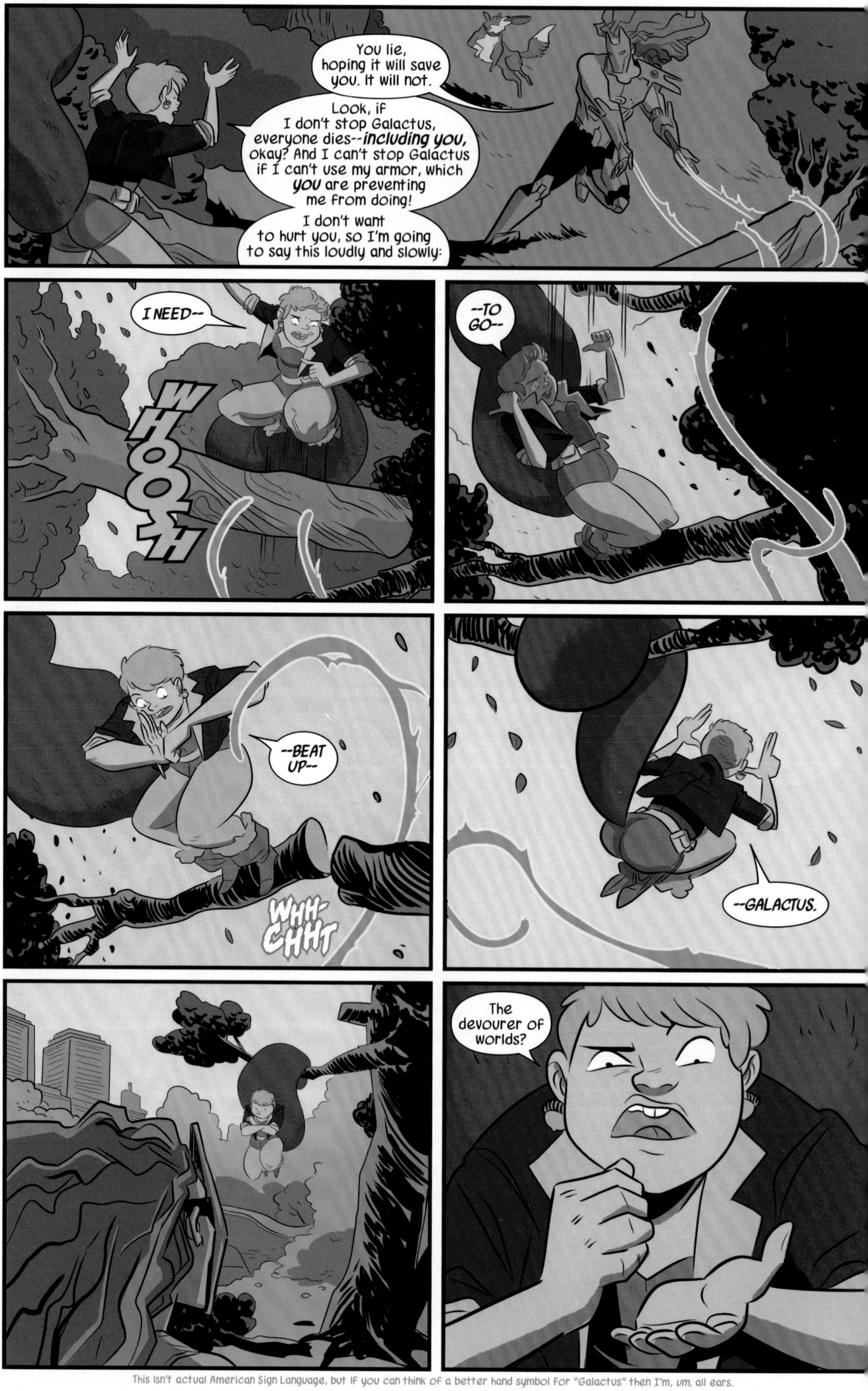
You lie, hoping it will save you. It will not.
Look, if I don't stop Galactus, everyone dies--*including you,* okay? And I can't stop Galactus if I can't use my armor, which *you* are preventing me from doing!
I don't want to hurt you, so I'm going to say this loudly and slowly:
I NEED--
WHOOSH
--TO GO--
--BEAT UP--
WHH-CHHT
--GALACTUS.
The devourer of worlds?

This isn't actual American Sign Language, but if you can think of a better hand symbol for "Galactus" then I'm, *um,* all ears.

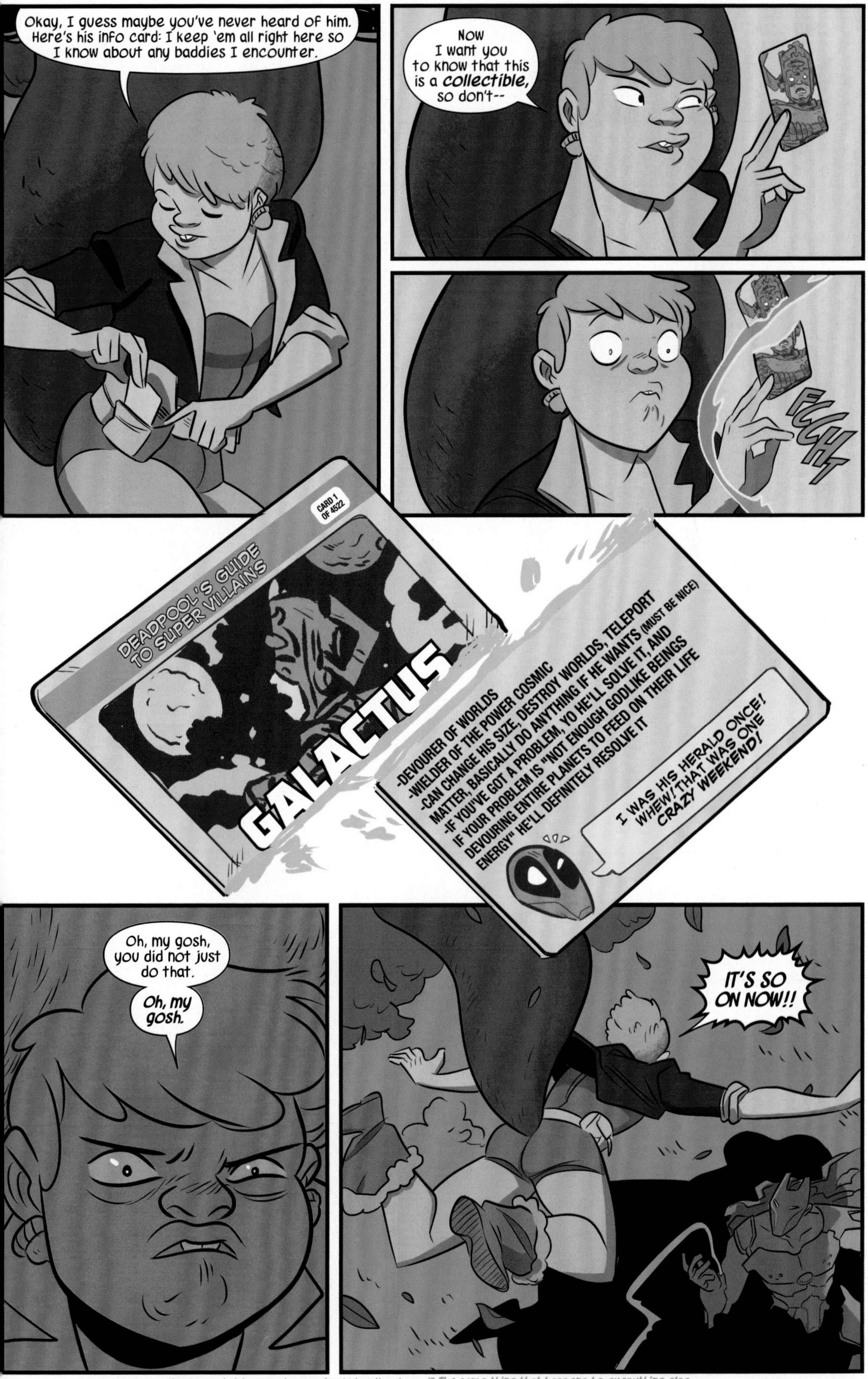
Okay, I guess maybe you've never heard of him. Here's his info card: I keep 'em all right here so I know about any baddies I encounter.
Now I want you to know that this is a ***collectible,*** so don't--
FCCHT
CARD 1 OF 4522
DEADPOOL'S GUIDE TO SUPER VILLAINS
GALACTUS
-DEVOURER OF WORLDS
-WIELDER OF THE POWER COSMIC
-CAN CHANGE HIS SIZE, DESTROY WORLDS, TELEPORT MATTER, BASICALLY DO ANYTHING IF HE WANTS (MUST BE NICE)
-IF YOU'VE GOT A PROBLEM, YO HE'LL SOLVE IT, AND IF YOUR PROBLEM IS "NOT ENOUGH GODLIKE BEINGS DEVOURING ENTIRE PLANETS TO FEED ON THEIR LIFE ENERGY" HE'LL DEFINITELY RESOLVE IT
I WAS HIS HERALD ONCE! WHEW! THAT WAS ONE ***CRAZY WEEKEND!***
Oh, my gosh, you did not just do that.
Oh, my gosh.
IT'S SO ON NOW!!

You know what happens to a squirrel when it gets mad? ***The same thing that happens to everything else.***
Which is to say, increased heart rate, elevated adrenaline and norepinephrine production, a lessened capacity for self-monitoring, etc., etc.

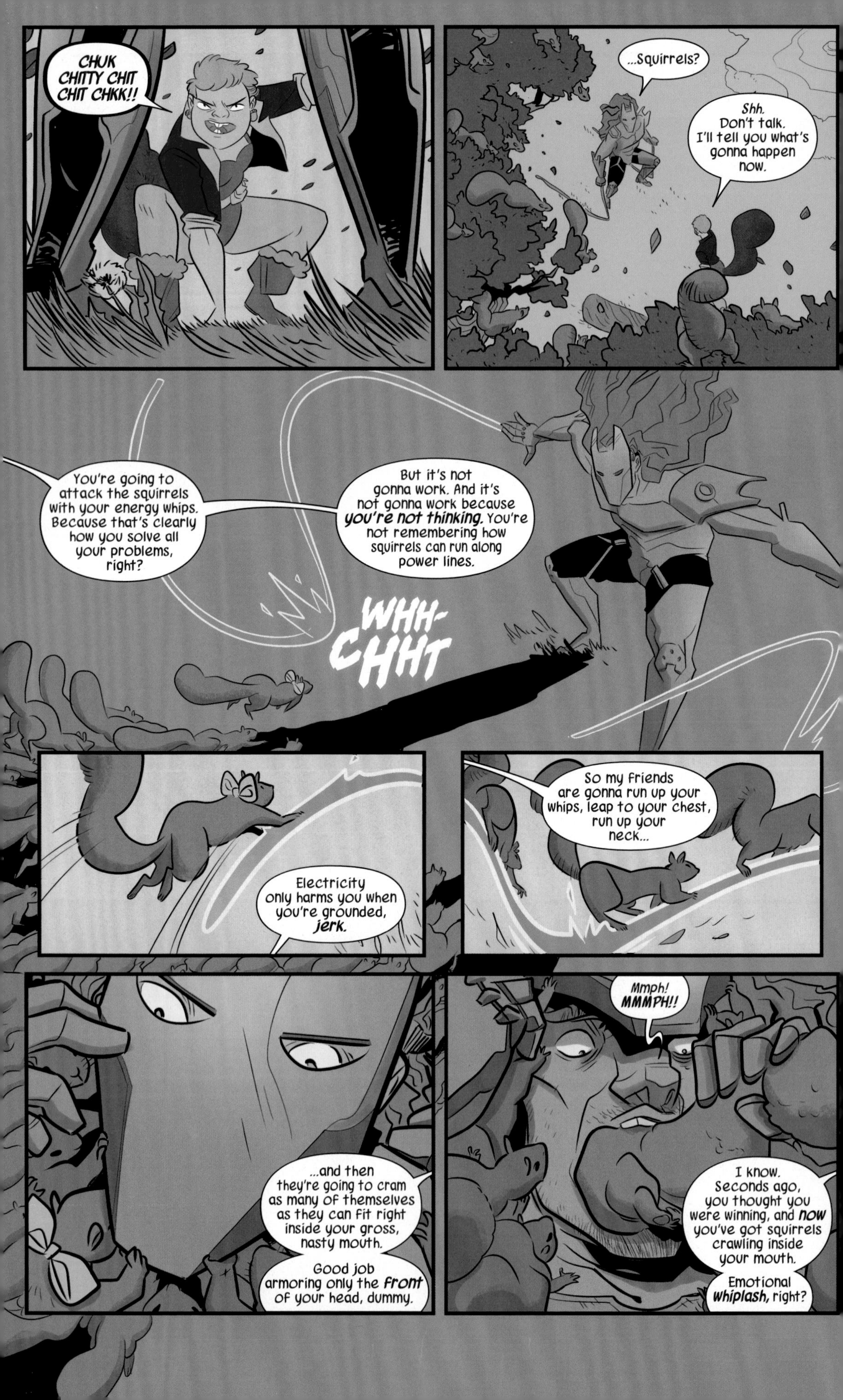

CHUK CHITTY CHIT CHIT CHKK!!
...Squirrels?
Shh. Don't talk. I'll tell you what's gonna happen now.
You're going to attack the squirrels with your energy whips. Because that's clearly how you solve all your problems, right?
But it's not gonna work. And it's not gonna work because *you're not thinking.* You're not remembering how squirrels can run along power lines.
WHH-CHHT
Electricity only harms you when you're grounded, *jerk.*
So my friends are gonna run up your whips, leap to your chest, run up your neck...
...and then they're going to cram as many of themselves as they can fit right inside your gross, nasty mouth.
Good job armoring only the *front* of your head, dummy.
Mmph! MMMPH!!
I know. Seconds ago, you thought you were winning, and *now* you've got squirrels crawling inside your mouth.
Emotional *whiplash,* right?

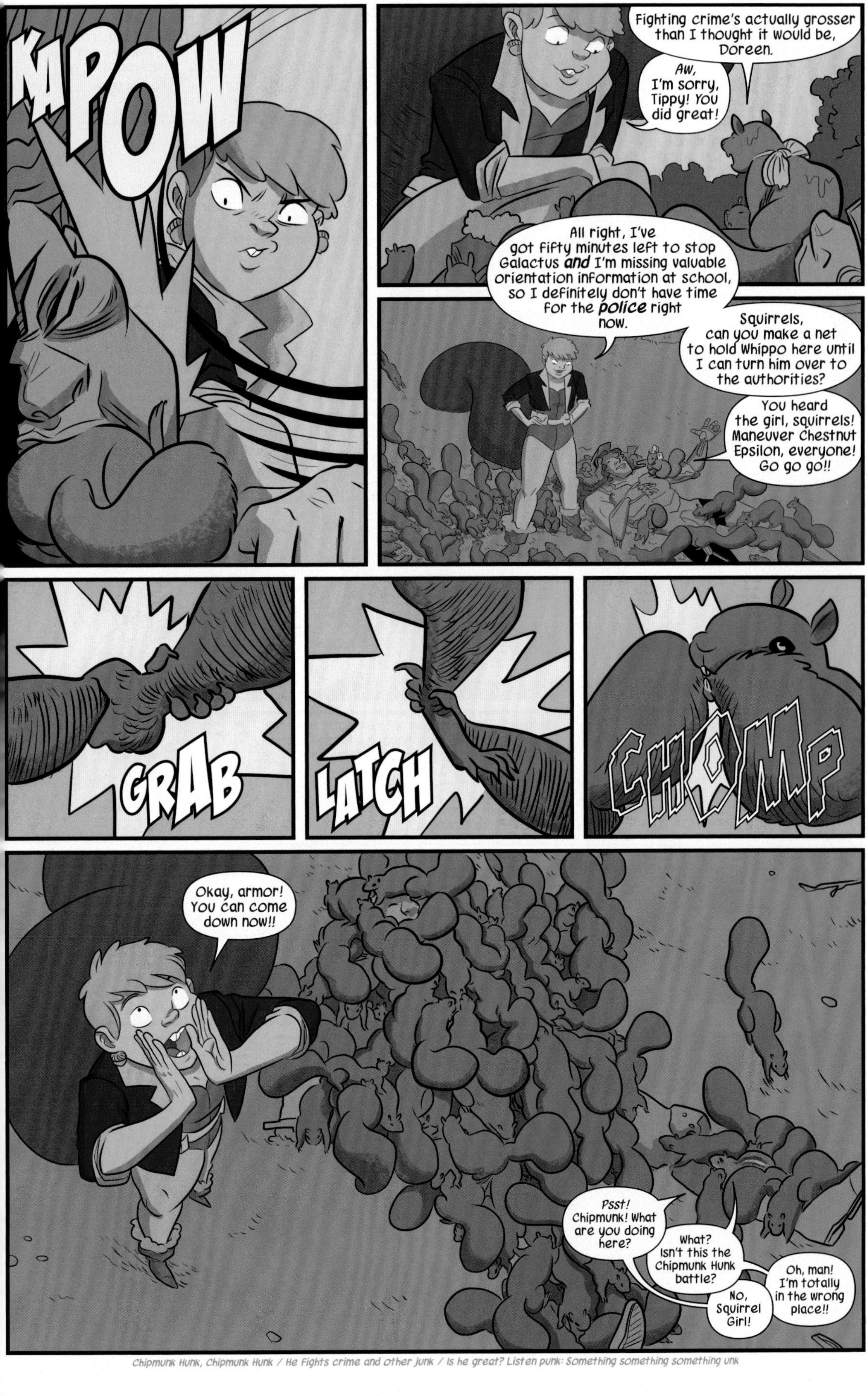
KAPOW
Fighting crime's actually grosser than I thought it would be, Doreen.
Aw, I'm sorry, Tippy! You did great!
All right, I've got fifty minutes left to stop Galactus *and* I'm missing valuable orientation information at school, so I definitely don't have time for the *police* right now.
Squirrels, can you make a net to hold Whippo here until I can turn him over to the authorities?
You heard the girl, squirrels! Maneuver Chestnut Epsilon, everyone! Go go go!!
GRAB
LATCH
CHOMP
Okay, armor! You can come down now!!
Psst! Chipmunk! What are you doing here?
What? Isn't this the Chipmunk Hunk battle?
No, Squirrel Girl!
Oh, man! I'm totally in the wrong place!!

Chipmunk Hunk, Chipmunk Hunk / He fights crime and other junk / Is he great? Listen punk: Something something something unk

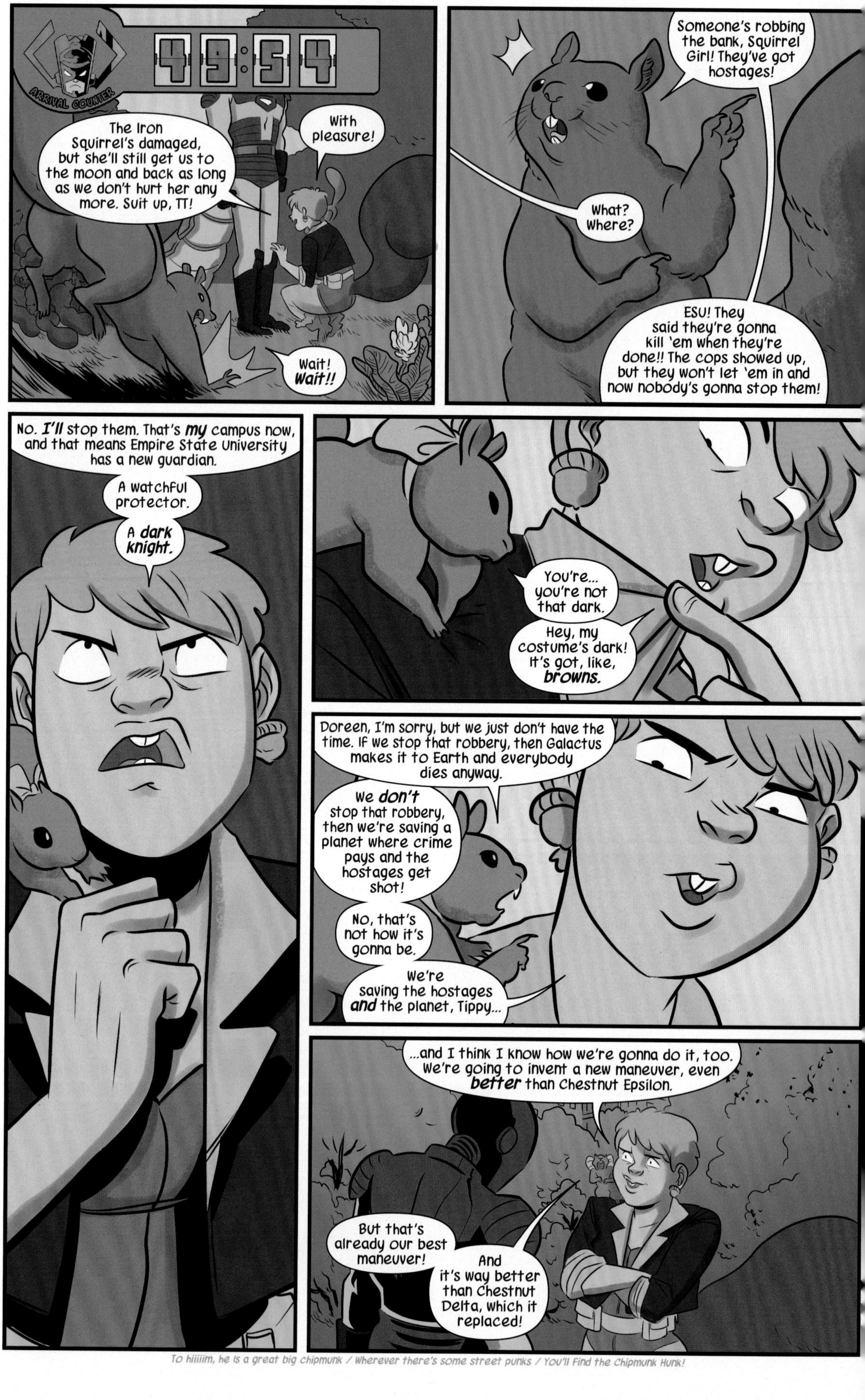
ARRIVAL COUNTER
49:54
The Iron Squirrel's damaged, but she'll still get us to the moon and back as long as we don't hurt her any more. Suit up, TT!
With pleasure!
Wait! Wait!!
Someone's robbing the bank, Squirrel Girl! They've got hostages!
What? Where?
ESU! They said they're gonna kill 'em when they're done!! The cops showed up, but they won't let 'em in and now nobody's gonna stop them!
No. I'll stop them. That's my campus now, and that means Empire State University has a new guardian.
A watchful protector.
A dark knight.
You're... you're not that dark.
Hey, my costume's dark! It's got, like, browns.
Doreen, I'm sorry, but we just don't have the time. If we stop that robbery, then Galactus makes it to Earth and everybody dies anyway.
We don't stop that robbery, then we're saving a planet where crime pays and the hostages get shot!
No, that's not how it's gonna be.
We're saving the hostages and the planet, Tippy...
...and I think I know how we're gonna do it, too. We're going to invent a new maneuver, even better than Chestnut Epsilon.
But that's already our best maneuver!
And it's way better than Chestnut Delta, which it replaced!

To hiiiiim, he is a great big chipmunk / Wherever there's some street punks / You'll find the Chipmunk Hunk!

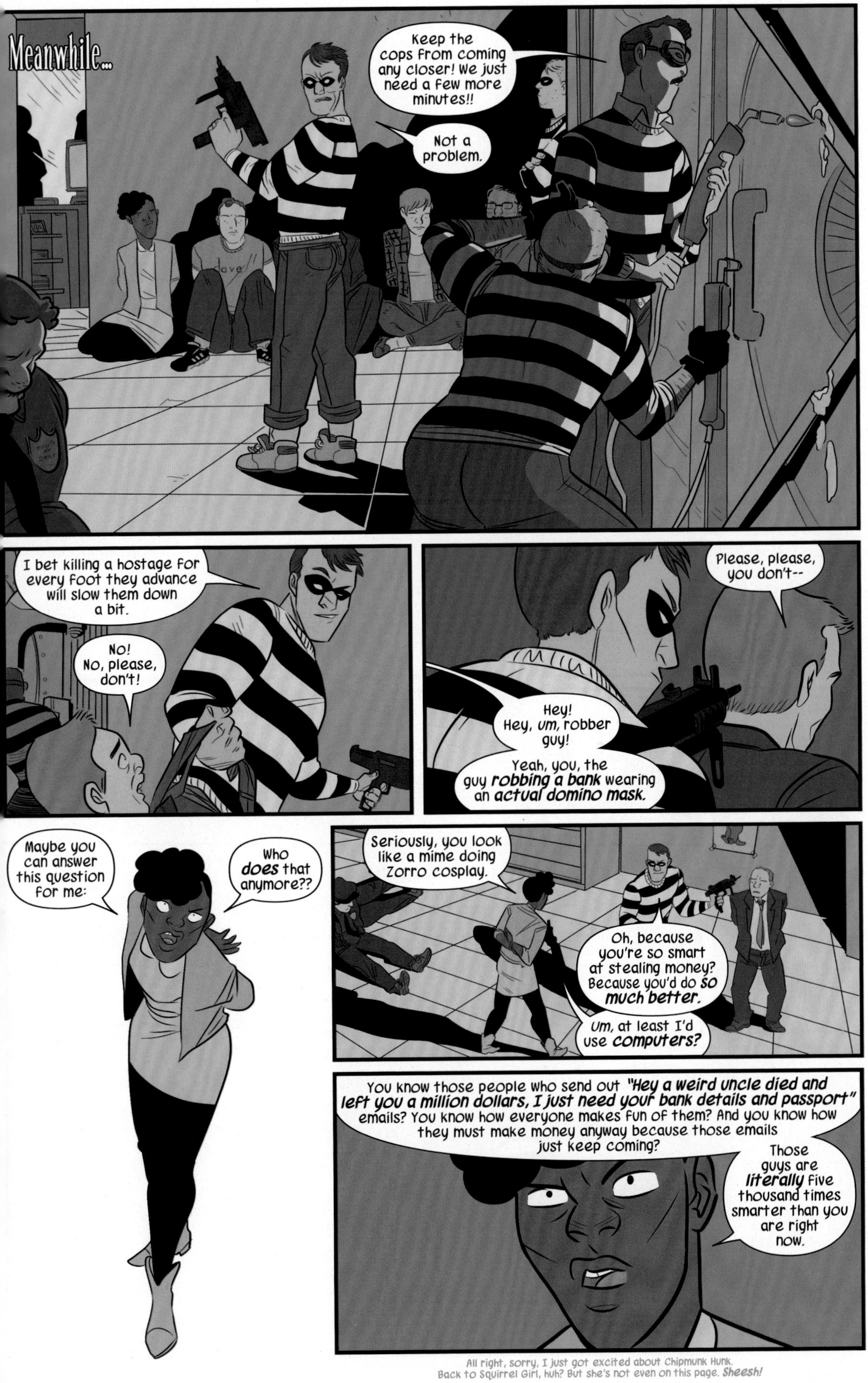
Meanwhile...
Keep the cops from coming any closer! We just need a few more minutes!!
Not a problem.
I bet killing a hostage for every foot they advance will slow them down a bit.
No! No, please, don't!
Please, please, you don't--
Hey! Hey, um, robber guy!
Yeah, you, the guy robbing a bank wearing an actual domino mask.
Maybe you can answer this question for me:
Who does that anymore??
Seriously, you look like a mime doing Zorro cosplay.
Oh, because you're so smart at stealing money? Because you'd do so much better.
Um, at least I'd use computers?
You know those people who send out "Hey a weird uncle died and left you a million dollars, I just need your bank details and passport" emails? You know how everyone makes fun of them? And you know how they must make money anyway because those emails just keep coming?
Those guys are literally five thousand times smarter than you are right now.

All right, sorry, I just got excited about Chipmunk Hunk.
Back to Squirrel Girl, huh? But she's not even on this page. *Sheesh!*

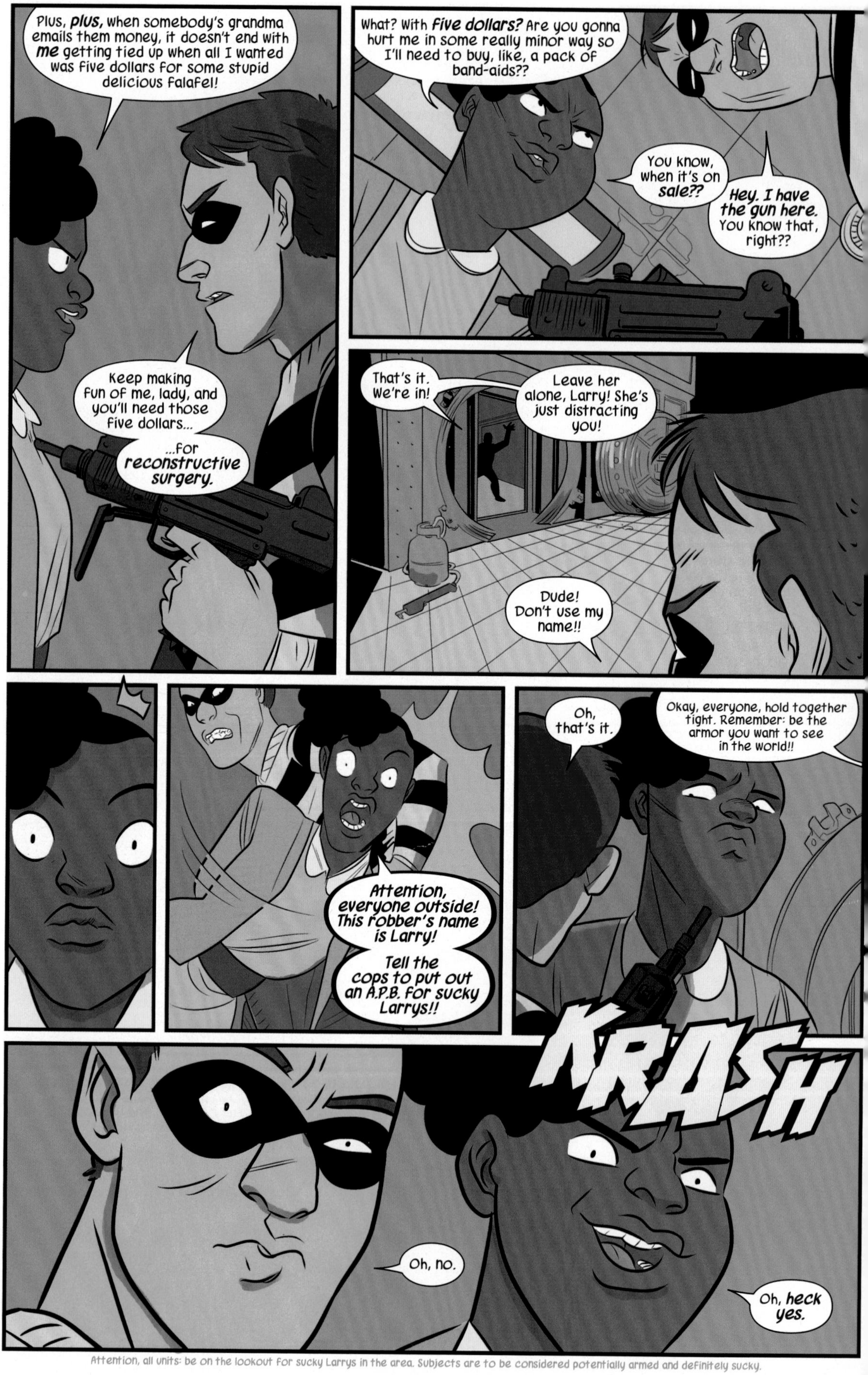
Plus, plus, when somebody's grandma emails them money, it doesn't end with me getting tied up when all I wanted was five dollars for some stupid delicious falafel!
Keep making fun of me, lady, and you'll need those five dollars...
...for reconstructive surgery.
What? With five dollars? Are you gonna hurt me in some really minor way so I'll need to buy, like, a pack of band-aids??
You know, when it's on sale??
Hey. I have the gun here. You know that, right??
That's it. We're in!
Leave her alone, Larry! She's just distracting you!
Dude! Don't use my name!!
Attention, everyone outside! This robber's name is Larry!
Tell the cops to put out an A.P.B. for sucky Larrys!!
Oh, that's it.
Okay, everyone, hold together tight. Remember: be the armor you want to see in the world!!
KRASH
Oh, no.
Oh, heck yes.

Attention, all units: be on the lookout for sucky Larrys in the area. Subjects are to be considered potentially armed and definitely sucky.

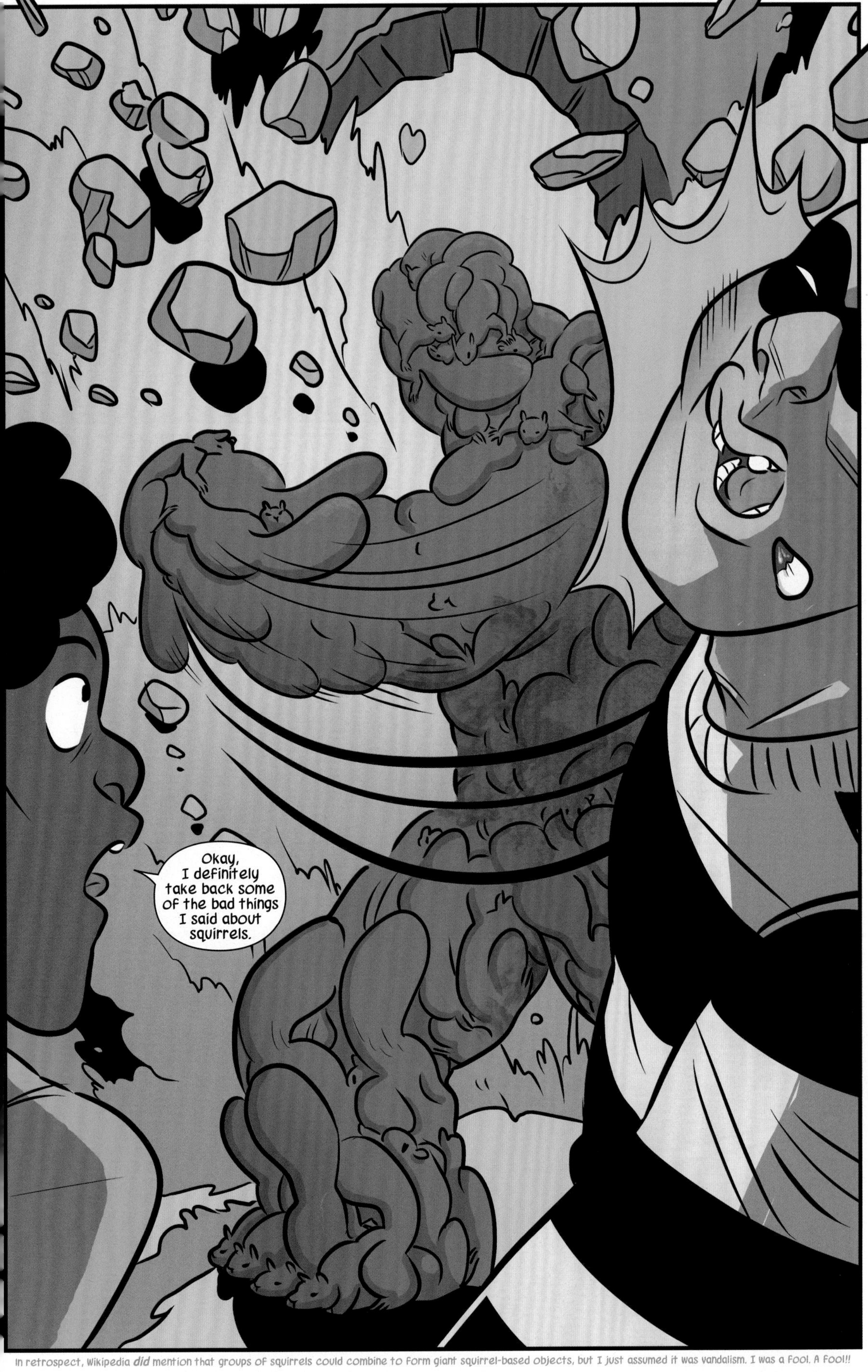
Okay, I definitely take back some of the bad things I said about squirrels.

In retrospect, Wikipedia *did* mention that groups of squirrels could combine to form giant squirrel-based objects, but I just assumed it was vandalism. I was a fool. A fool!!

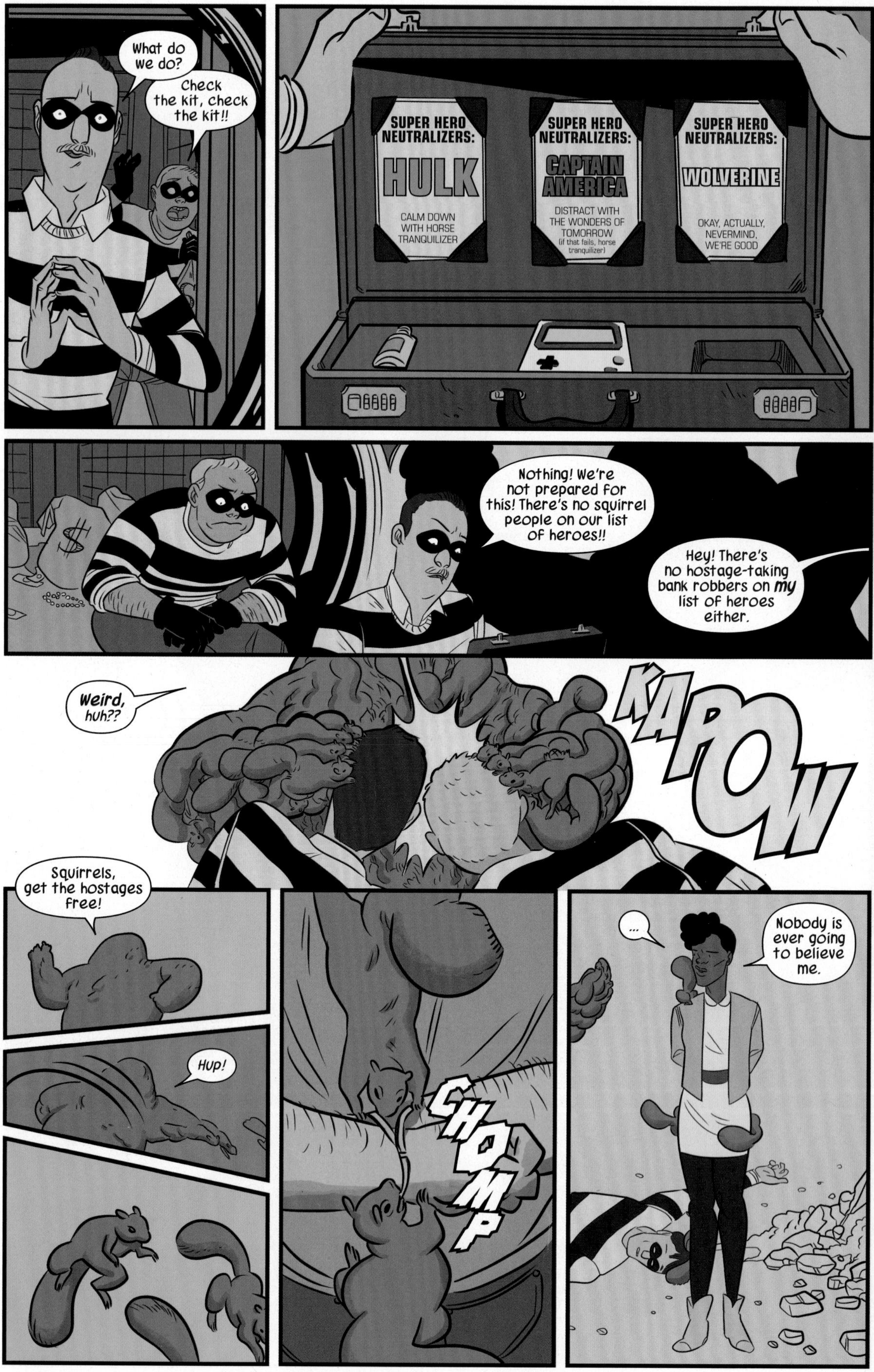
What do we do?
Check the kit, check the kit!!
SUPER HERO NEUTRALIZERS:
HULK
CALM DOWN WITH HORSE TRANQUILIZER
SUPER HERO NEUTRALIZERS:
CAPTAIN AMERICA
DISTRACT WITH THE WONDERS OF TOMORROW
(if that fails, horse tranquilizer)
SUPER HERO NEUTRALIZERS:
WOLVERINE
OKAY, ACTUALLY, NEVERMIND, WE'RE GOOD
Nothing! We're not prepared for this! There's no squirrel people on our list of heroes!!
Hey! There's no hostage-taking bank robbers on *my* list of heroes either.
Weird, huh??
KAPOW
Squirrels, get the hostages free!
Hup!
CHOMP
...
Nobody is ever going to believe me.

This is worse than the time that famous actor guy stole my fries right out of my hand!

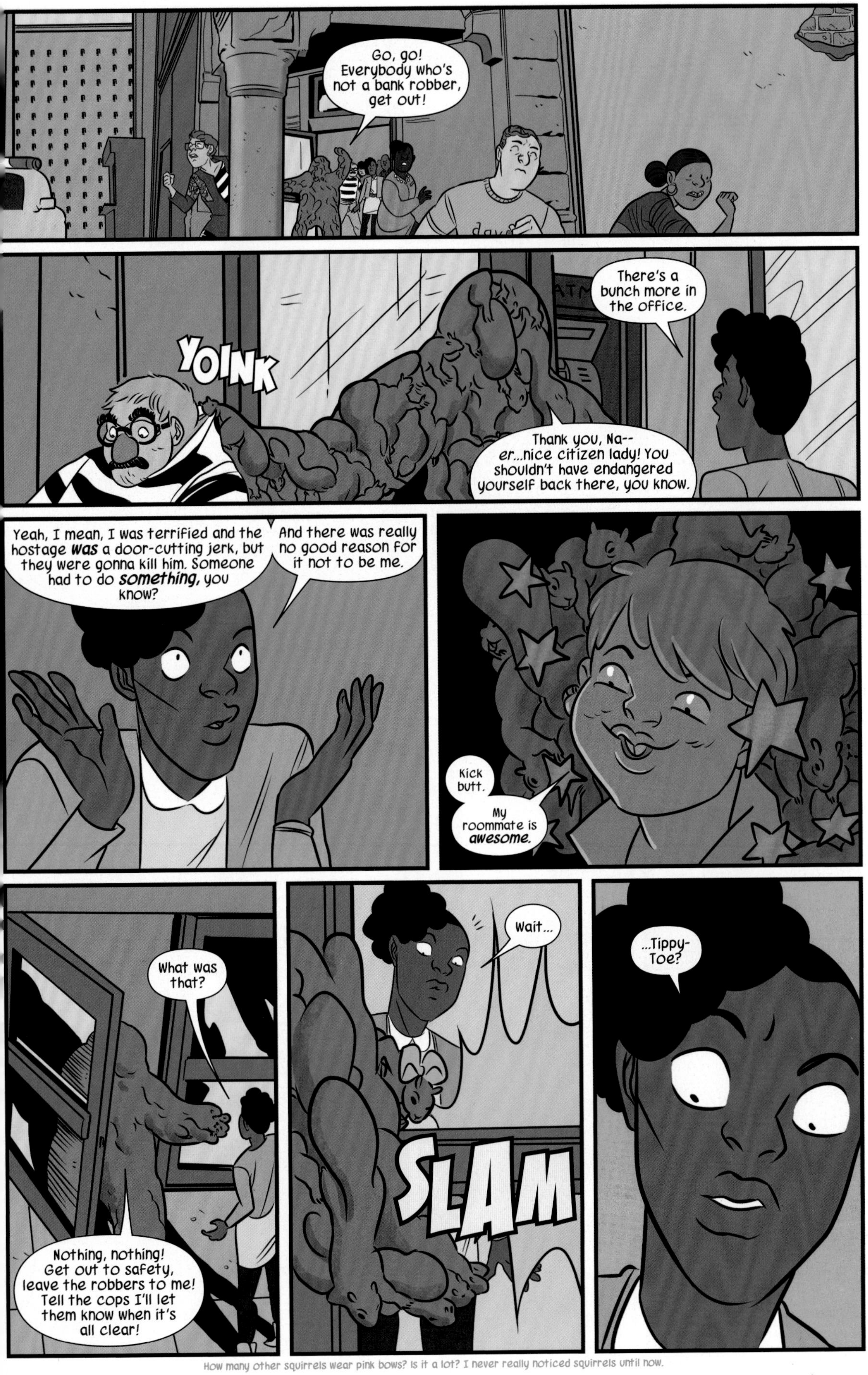
Go, go! Everybody who's not a bank robber, get out!
YOINK
There's a bunch more in the office.
Thank you, Na-- er...nice citizen lady! You shouldn't have endangered yourself back there, you know.
Yeah, I mean, I was terrified and the hostage *was* a door-cutting jerk, but they were gonna kill him. Someone had to do *something,* you know?
And there was really no good reason for it not to be me.
Kick butt.
My roommate is *awesome.*
What was that?
Nothing, nothing! Get out to safety, leave the robbers to me! Tell the cops I'll let them know when it's all clear!
Wait...
SLAM
...Tippy-Toe?

How many other squirrels wear pink bows? Is it a lot? I never really noticed squirrels until now.

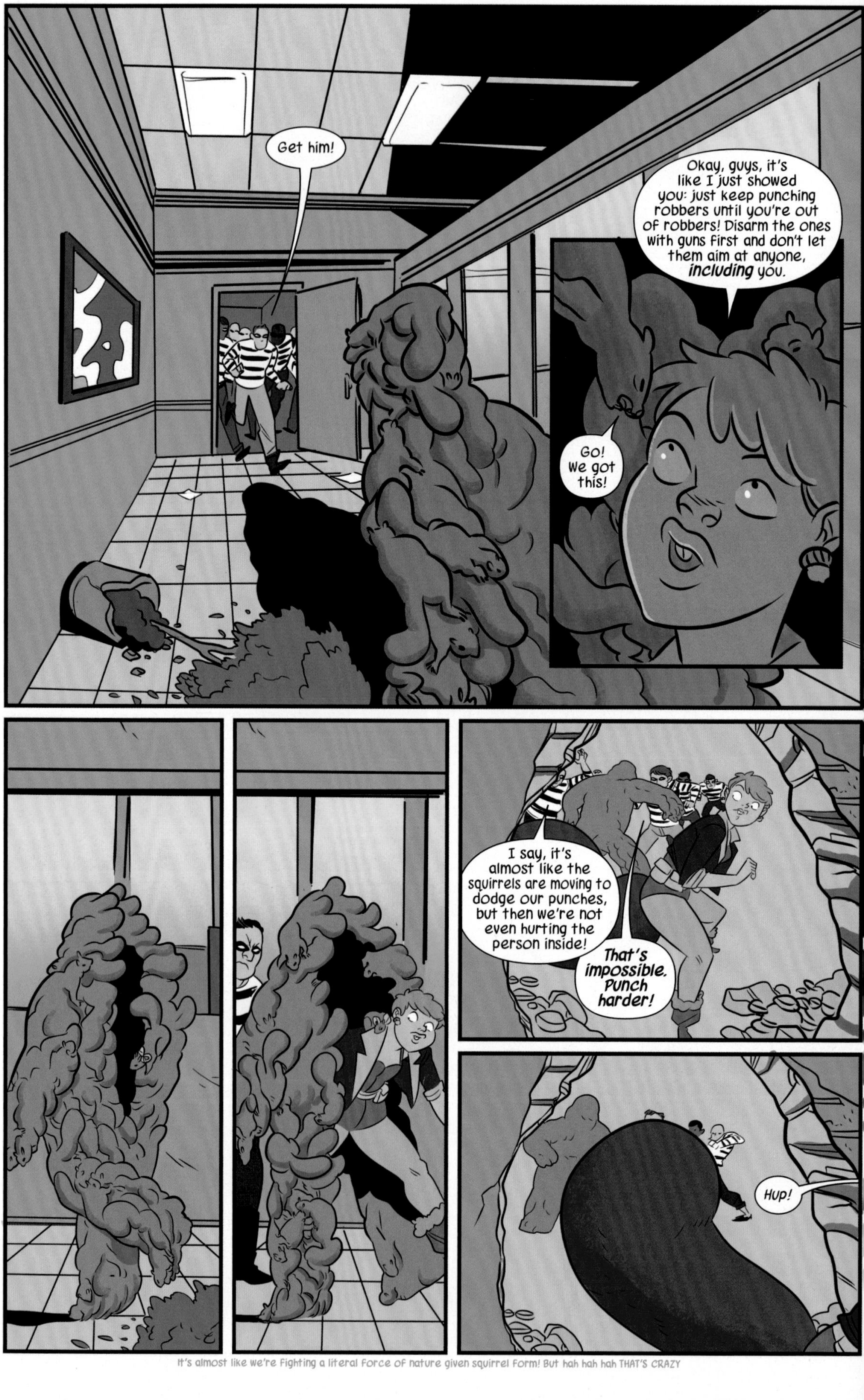
Get him!
Okay, guys, it's like I just showed you: just keep punching robbers until you're out of robbers! Disarm the ones with guns first and don't let them aim at anyone, *including* you.
Go! We got this!
I say, it's almost like the squirrels are moving to dodge our punches, but then we're not even hurting the person inside!
That's impossible. Punch harder!
Hup!

It's almost like we're fighting a literal force of nature given squirrel form! But hah hah hah THAT'S CRAZY

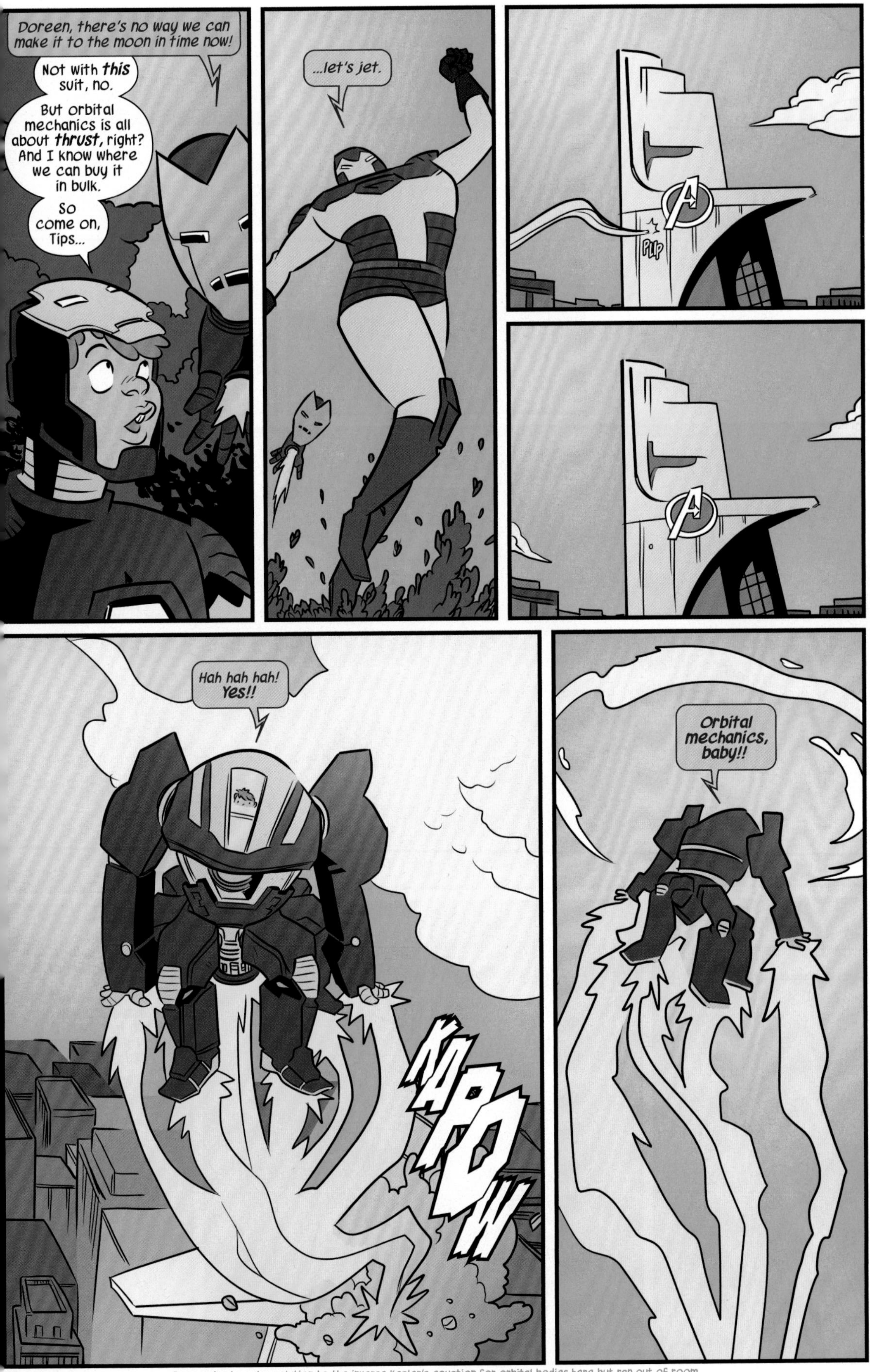
Doreen, there's no way we can make it to the moon in time now!
Not with *this* suit, no.
But orbital mechanics is all about *thrust*, right? And I know where we can buy it in bulk.
So come on, Tips...
...let's jet.
PLIP
Hah hah hah! Yes!!
KAPOW
Orbital mechanics, baby!!

I was going to put a solution to the inverse Kepler's equation for orbital bodies here but ran out of room, so you'll just have to take my word for it that the physics in my talking squirrel comic are 100% ultralegit

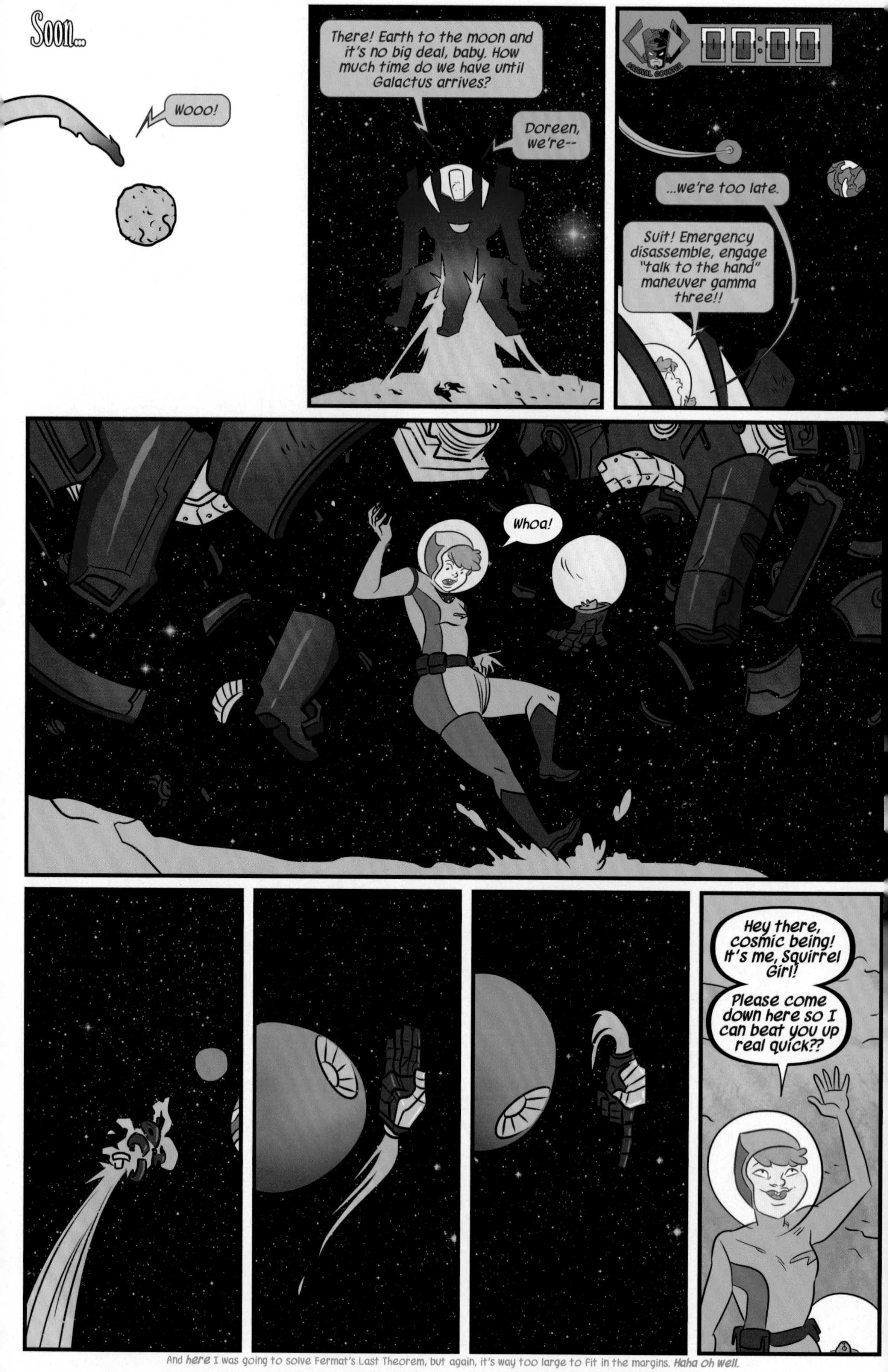
Soon...
WOOO!
There! Earth to the moon and it's no big deal, baby. How much time do we have until Galactus arrives?
Doreen, we're--
...we're too late.
Suit! Emergency disassemble, engage "talk to the hand" maneuver gamma three!!
Whoa!
Hey there, cosmic being! It's me, Squirrel Girl!
Please come down here so I can beat you up real quick??

And *here* I was going to solve Fermat's Last Theorem, but again, it's way too large to fit in the margins. *Haha oh well.*

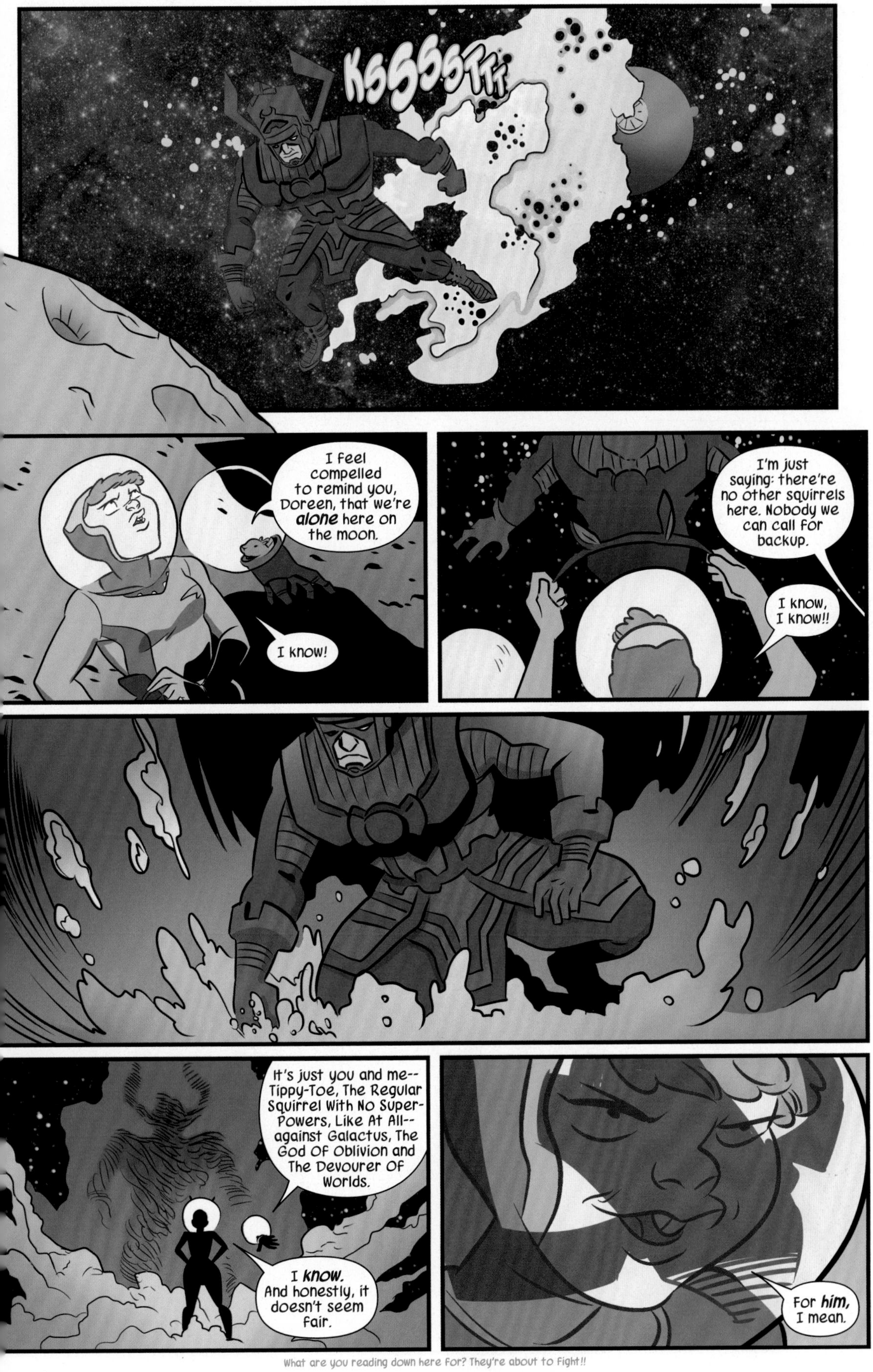
KSSSSTTT
I feel compelled to remind you, Doreen, that we're alone here on the moon.
I know!
I'm just saying: there're no other squirrels here. Nobody we can call for backup.
I know, I know!!
It's just you and me--Tippy-Toe, The Regular Squirrel With No Super-Powers, Like At All--against Galactus, The God Of Oblivion and The Devourer Of Worlds.
I know. And honestly, it doesn't seem fair.
For him, I mean.

What are you reading down here for? They're about to Fight!!

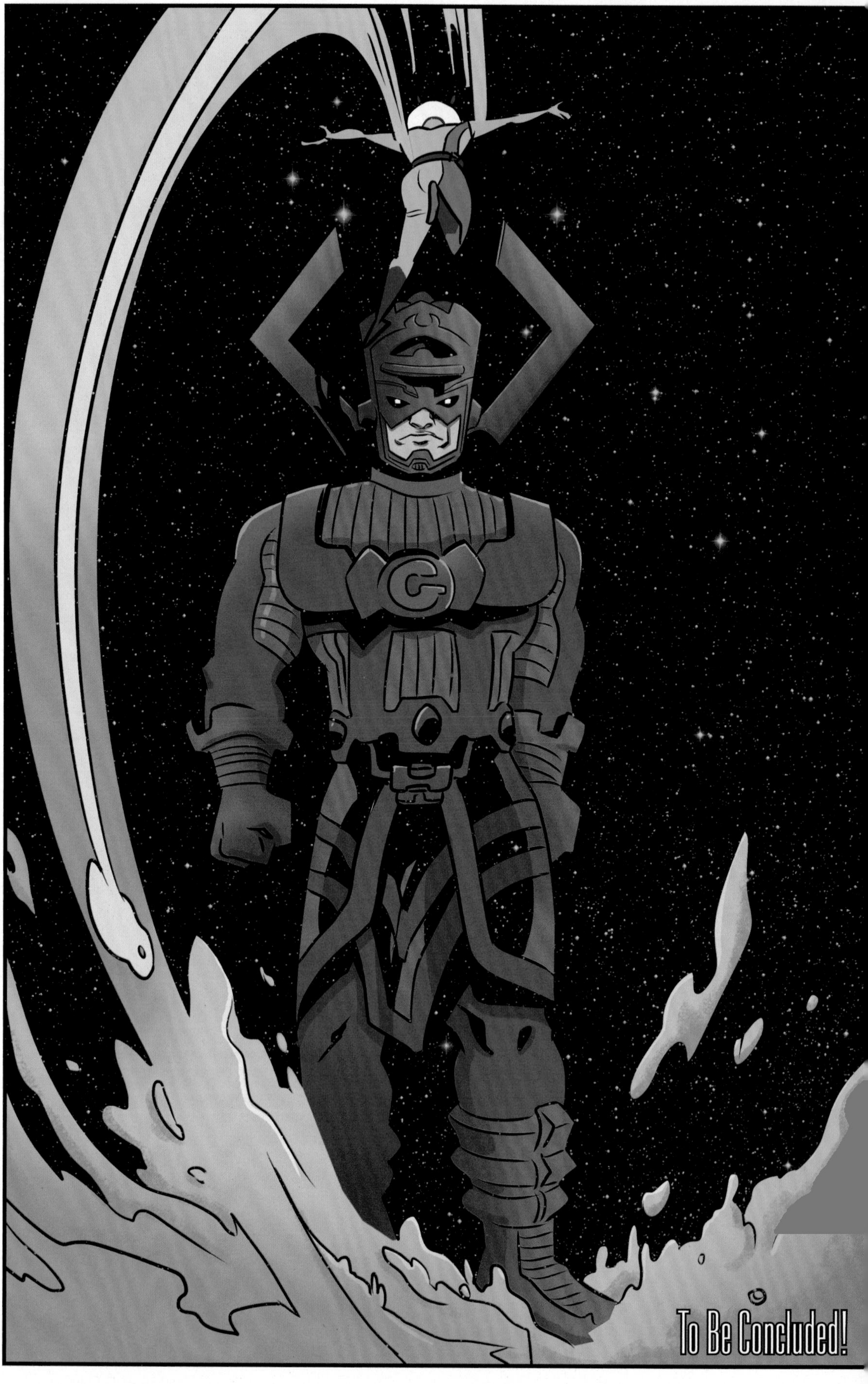
To Be Concluded!

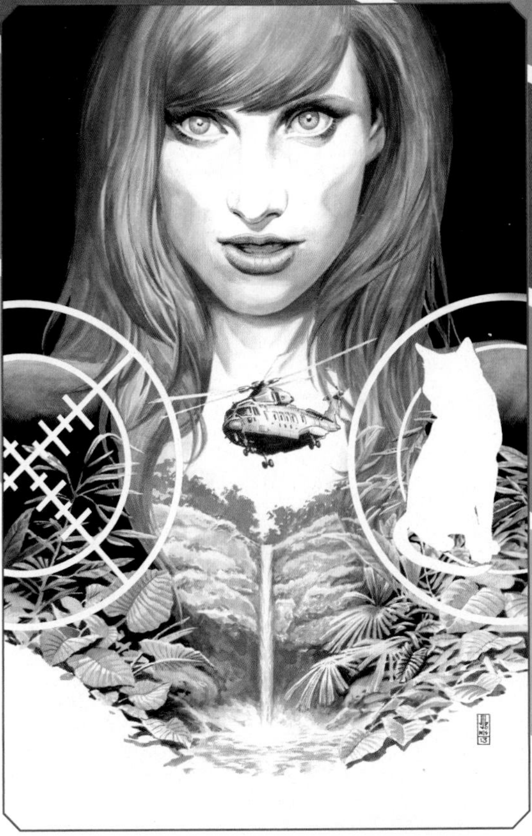

BLACK WIDOW #3
Variant by J.G. Jones

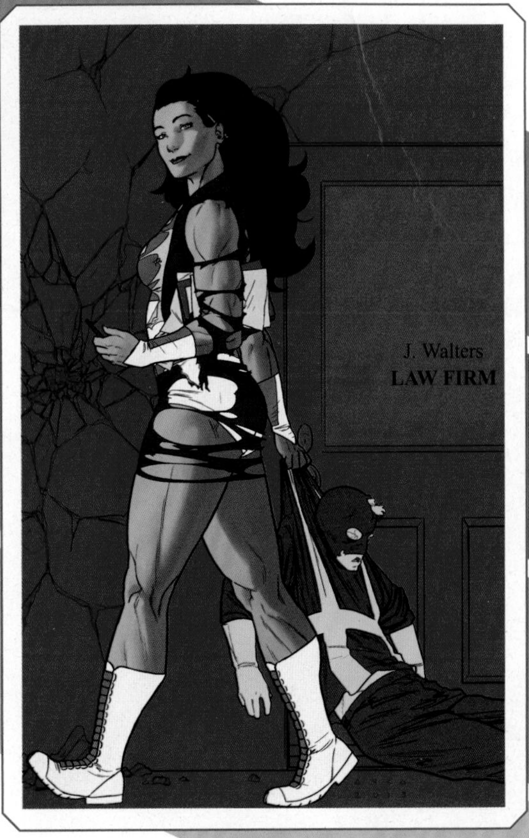
J. Walters
LAW FIRM

SHE-HULK #3
Variant by Kris Anka

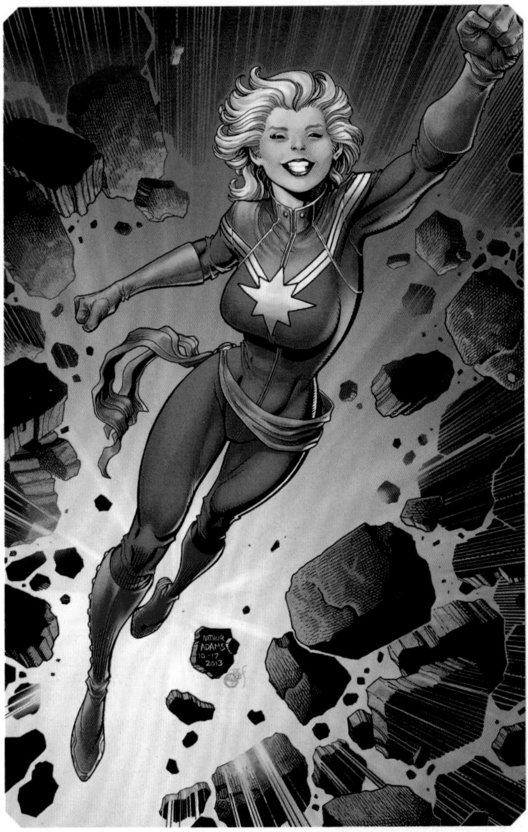

CAPTAIN MARVEL #3
Variant by Arthur Adams & Peter Steigerwald

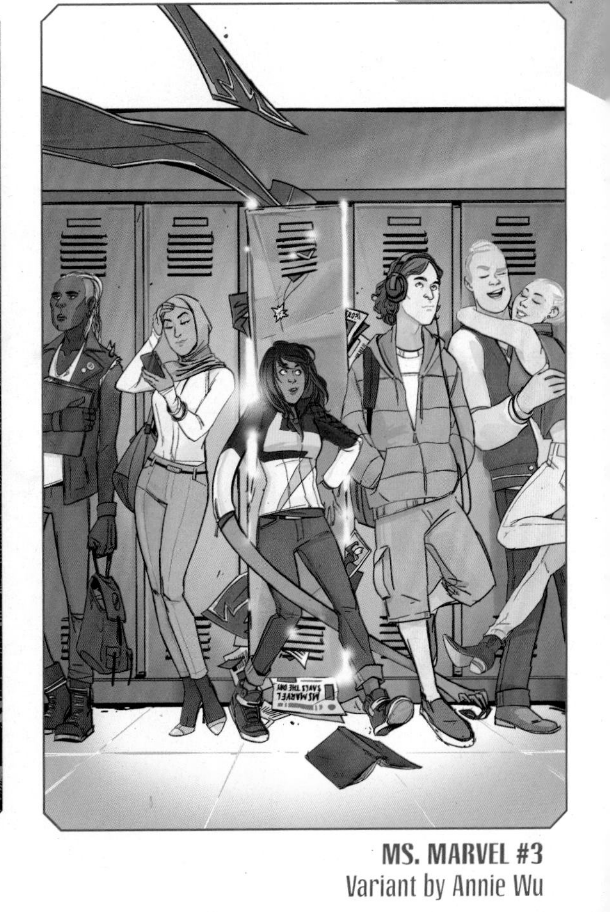

MS. MARVEL #3
Variant by Annie Wu

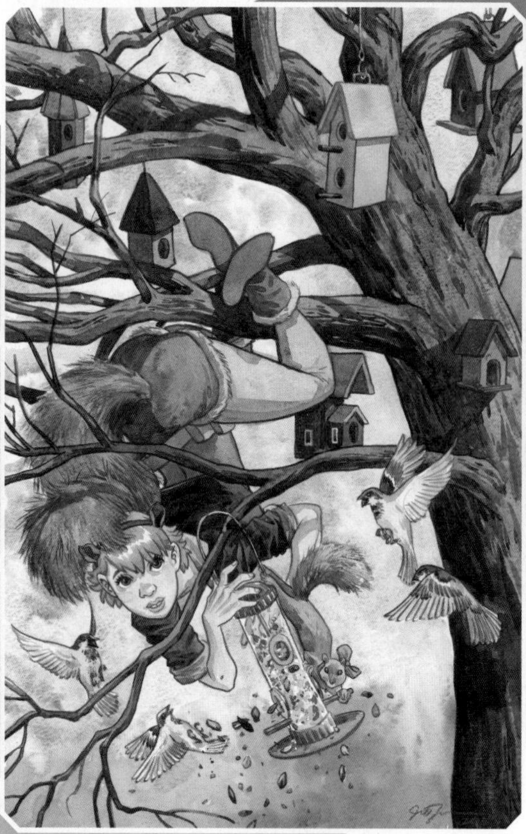

THE UNBEATABLE SQUIRREL GIRL #3
Variant by Jill Thompson

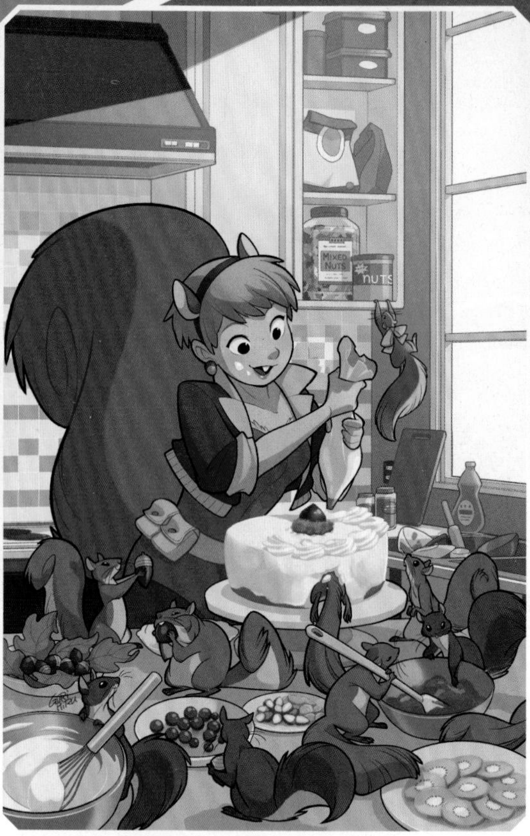
MIXED NUTS
NUTS

THE UNBEATABLE SQUIRREL GIRL #3
Variant by Gurihiru

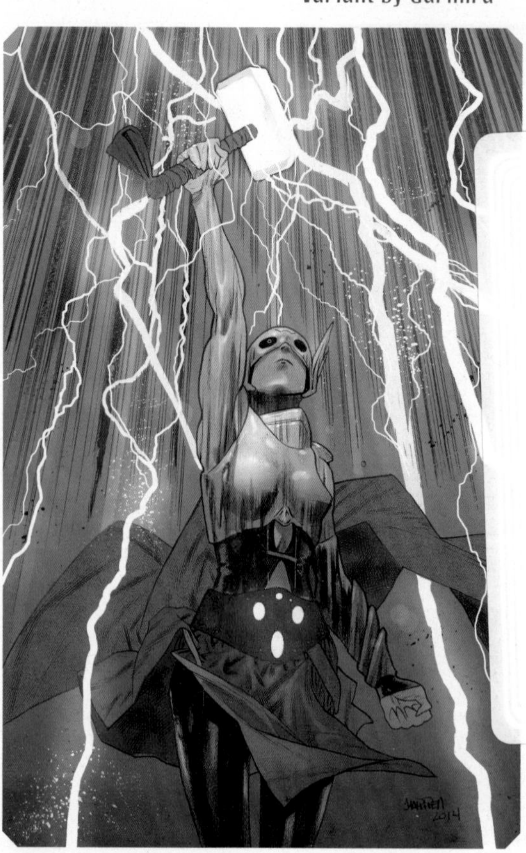

THOR #3
Variant by James Harren